ARCTIC

WARGAME

Ethan Jones

Cover photography: Fation Plaku

Cover design: Enita Meadows

First edition: May 2012

ISBN: 1468152297

ISBN-13: 978-1468152296

To the brave women and men defending our country,

whose names we will never know

Also by Ethan Jones

Carved in Memory

The Last Confession

Tripoli's Target – coming out in fall 2012

This work would have not been possible without the great support of my wife and son. I would like to thank Ty Hutchinson, Kenneth Teicher and Claude Dancourt for their helpful suggestions. I am also thankful to my great editors and proofreaders at Last Draft Editing.

"We are challenged more by operating in our own domain than in operating around the world. It is harder to sustain operations in our High Arctic than it is to sustain operations in Kandahar or Kabul because in the Arctic, it's what you bring."

General Walt Natynczyk,
Chief of the Defence Staff of the Canadian Defence Forces

PROLOGUE

Ghadames, Libya
Six months ago
October 10, 3:00 a.m.

The sand dunes sank into darkness as a curtain of clouds dimmed the glow of the crescent moon. Justin limped closer to the small barred window of his prison cell. His bruised chest pressed against the rough surface of the bloodstained wall. He squinted and tried to stand on his toes for a better look. The rusty shackles clawed against the scarred skin of his ankles, and the heavy chain rattled on the cement floor.

"Quiet. Be quiet, you bastard infidel," a guard growled in Arabic from down the shadowy prison hallway.

Justin stood still and drew in a deep breath, the cold night air of the Sahara desert filling his heaving lungs. Everything went silent again. No rapid steps rushing to his cell. No swearing bellowed by other inmates. He lifted his head, wrapped his free hands around the iron bars, and clenched his teeth, ignoring the jolts of pain from his fingers. With his eyes about an inch over the windowsill, Justin scoped the landscape, searching for the long-awaited rescue team.

Abdul, his connection within Libya's Internal Security Agency who lay in the cell next door, had confirmed their escape was to take place early that morning. Their previous attempt the night before had failed, despite the inside help of one of the terrorists. Justin hoped this time their plan would be executed with no glitches.

At first, he noticed nothing except the rugged outlines of the steep dunes and the whitewashed walls of the sleepy town. Straining his eyes, he peered again. A small shadow slithered toward the prison wall. Justin blinked to clear his vision and stared at the approaching figure.

Bent at the waist, the shadow advanced at a rapid pace. It quickly disappeared from his sight, and he wondered whether the man had encountered a guard.

Justin's heart pounded. He placed his ear to the wall and sensed a low grating noise. Someone, the shadow he hoped, was scaling the wall.

The window was at least twelve feet above the ground. He wondered how long it would take the shadow to reach it. A long minute dragged by and Justin was still alone. He breathed faster and faster and urged the man on the freedom side of the wall to make good time.

Finally, a hushed voice whispered in Arabic, "Abdul, Abdul, it's me, Bashir. You there?"

"I'm Justin," he replied softly.

"You're the Canadian agent. Where's Abdul?"

"In the other cell, around the corner, but that one has no window."

"When did they move him?"

"A few hours ago, after they gave him a good beating."

"Can he walk?"

"I think so."

Bashir went silent for a moment. Justin looked up, but could not see the man's face through the window. He asked slowly, "Bashir?"

"Shhhh."

A few seconds later, he heard a scraping sound. Bashir was offering him a large metal key through the window bars. "That's for the shackles," Bashir said under his breath, "and this is for the guard." He produced a black dagger.

Justin grabbed the handle and weighed the weapon in his weak hand. A ray of moonlight glinted off the ten-inch blade.

"Can you do this?" Bashir whispered.

"Yes."

"You have only one chance. I'll wait for you and Abdul in two black Nissans by the main gate. Then we'll drive across the border to Tunisia."

Justin frowned. "What about the hostages? The two Canadian doctors?"

"The Algerians moved them from their safe house to another location, out of the prison but still in town. My men are on their way there."

"And Carrie?"

"Yes, your partner is with them."

Justin breathed a sigh of relief. "OK. I'll make sure Abdul and I meet you by the gate."

"You'll have to be quiet. About twenty men are guarding the prison, and we can't defeat them all."

"OK."

"Abdul knows the way, but if you can't free him, walk down the stairs and go left. The hall will take you to a small courtyard on the ground floor. There will be a guard or two by the gate. You need to cross into the house next door."

"Downstairs, then left, then to the house," Justin said, finding it a bit difficult to concentrate on Bashir's words.

"Yes. Get to the roof of the house and drop down along the side facing the mosque. Follow the road leading to the main gate. Is it clear?"

"Yes, it is."

Bashir's clothes rubbed against the wall, and then silence returned to Justin's cell. He stared at the key and the dagger in his right hand. Stepping back from the window, he was careful not to jerk the chain and alert the guard beyond the solid metal door. The key fit into the shackles' padlock. He coughed loudly as he turned the key to cover the dull clunk of the lock snapping open. Now almost free, he removed the metal loops from around his ankles.

First imprisoned in Tripoli after their hostage rescue operation went wrong, Justin and Abdul were subjected to torture by the Algerian hostage takers for two days. After Justin and Abdul attempted an escape and killed a guard in the process, the Algerians––with the help of the Libyan secret police––moved them to Ghadames, an isolated and less risky place in their minds.

Justin wasted no time. He took a deep breath, gripped the dagger tightly, and called out to the guard, "Hey, open the door."

"Shut up," the guard roared back.

"I need to talk to you."

"No. Just shut up."

Justin banged twice on the heavy door.

The guard's voice grew louder as he drew nearer to the door. "What's the matter with you? You want me to break your leg?"

Justin slammed his fist against the door.

"That's it. You asked for it," the guard shouted.

Keys clattered as the guard struggled to find the right one to unlock the door. Justin stepped to the side and lifted his dagger high, waiting for the right moment. His hand shook. The weapon felt heavy, straining his muscles.

"I'm going to beat some sense into you now," the guard barked.

As the guard shoved open the door, Justin thrust his hand toward the man's throat. The blade slashed deep under the man's thick chin, severing his windpipe. The guard dropped dead into his stretched arms, blood sputtering from the man's mangled neck.

Justin used the guard's black robe and turban to wipe the blood stains from his face and his arms. He stripped the man of his keys, his side arm—an old Beretta 92 pistol—his AK-47 assault rifle and two magazines. Justin dragged the body to a corner of his cell and locked the door behind him.

He tiptoed to Abdul's cell. On the second try, he found the right key. As he opened the door, the powerful stench of sweat and urine almost twisted his stomach inside out. Abdul was lying against a wall, asleep.

"Abdul, Abdul, wake up." Justin rustled him.

"Huh? What?" Abdul mumbled with a big yawn.

"Time to go, man."

"Justin, how did you…" Abdul sat up slowly and stared into Justin's eyes.

"Bashir gave me a key and a knife."

"Bashir? When did he come?"

"Tell you later. Let's go. Can you walk?"

"Yes, yes, I can."

Justin unchained Abdul's bruised legs and helped him to his feet. Abdul leaned against the wall before taking a few unsteady steps.

"I'm good. I can do this," Abdul said.

"OK, follow me."

"First, give me that." Abdul pointed at the assault rifle.

"Bashir said we need to break out in silence. Too many fighters for us to kill them all."

Abdul held the AK-47 in his hands with difficulty and fumbled with the safety switch. Finally, he switched it to full automatic. "Just in case," he mumbled.

"Let's go."

Justin threw a glance down the hall and signaled for Abdul to follow him. They moved quickly to the end of the narrow hallway, their bare feet tapping lightly on the concrete floor, grains of sand gritting their toes.

"We go to the first floor, then left," Justin said as they came to a spiral staircase.

"Then what?"

"Left through the hall until we reach the courtyard. We have to go through the door taking us to the house next to the prison. Bashir will wait for us at the main gate."

"What? That's Bashir's plan? There's always a group of guards in the back."

"He said there should be only one, two at the most, and we have to get rid of them quietly."

"That's impossible. They'll see us as we go outside and kill us."

"Maybe they're dozing off."

"If not, we shoot first."

"No. We'll have the rest of the Algerians coming after us."

Justin winced as his left foot landed on the coarse surface of the first stair. He took two more steps and turned his head. Abdul nodded and followed behind him. Holding the dagger ready in his hand, Justin continued down the stairs. He reached the bottom. The hall forked right and left. A light flickered from the right. Justin stepped back, gesturing for Abdul to stop.

"What's that way?" Justin asked in a hushed tone, pointing toward the light.

"A kitchen and a dining area. And someone's awake.""Don't worry about it. We're slipping out the other way."

Justin glimpsed again toward the dim light, then to the opposite side and began creeping down the hall. He saw a door about twenty steps ahead and figured it was the one opening into the courtyard. Pressing on, he quickened his pace. Abdul's feet shuffled loudly behind him.

"Quiet, quiet, Abdul," he said.

"That's not me."

Justin turned his head and looked over Abdul's shoulders. He stared right into the eyes of a man standing five or six steps behind Abdul and pointing a pistol at them. The gunman was of a small, thin stature, clad in a white robe and a black headdress.

"Stop or I'll blow your head off," he said in Arabic.

The gunman's voice crackled abruptly. Its unexpected high pitch startled Justin. The pistol shook in the young man's hands.

"He's just a kid," Justin whispered to Abdul, who was preparing to turn his rifle toward the gunman.

"I will shoot you," the young man squeaked, this time louder. "You, turn around with your hands in the air," he ordered Abdul.

Abdul swung on his heels, firing a quick burst.

"No," Justin shouted.

Bullets went through the gunman. Two large purple stains appeared on his chest as he collapsed over a chair.

"No, no, no," Justin cried. "He was a kid, just a kid."

"Who was going to blow our heads off," Abdul replied.

"We could have talked to him."

Abdul shook his head. "No time for talk. Now run."

Before Justin could say anything, someone kicked open the door behind him.

"Down," Abdul shouted and pointed his AK-47 toward the door.

Justin fell to the floor, while Abdul kept his finger on the assault rifle's trigger. Bullets pierced the bodies of two guards who entered the hall. Loud cries and barking orders came from two stories above. Rapid thuds of heavy boots echoed throughout the prison. Justin pulled out the Beretta from a pocket of his tattered khakis. As soon as two men running downstairs entered his sights, he planted a couple of bullets in each man's neck.

"Go, go, go. Move, move!" he yelled at Abdul.

Abdul checked the door and fired a short burst into the courtyard. A few shrieks confirmed he hit his mark, and he dove outside. More gunfire followed. The reports of assault rifles echoed in the night. Heavy machine guns hammering in the distance pounded the urgency of their escape into the Canadian agent. After trading his Beretta for a high-powered AK-47 next to the body of a dead guard, Justin joined Abdul in the courtyard.

"This way, quick," Abdul called.

Justin followed the Libyan beyond the arched gate, now wide open. The bodies of three men lay sprawled across the sandy path. As Justin dashed inside the house, a few bullets whizzed past his head, boring deep holes in the mud brick walls.

"Faster, faster, come on," Abdul shouted.

Justin noticed Abdul was panting and stopped for a closer look.

"What's wrong?" Abdul asked.

"Did they get you?"

"No. Don't stop."

The corridors of the house were pitch-black, but the moonlight trickling through barred windows guided their steps. They slid around a few stone benches set along the walls. Justin kept looking around for a way to climb to the roof, like Bashir had advised, but Abdul kept pushing them deeper into the maze of narrow halls snaking in all directions.

"We need to get to the roof," Justin said.

"No, they'll make us out. Up there we have no cover."

"So how are we getting to the main gate?"

"I know a shortcut."

Abdul went through a couple of doors straight ahead then turned left. The maze of covered streets in Ghadames stretched for miles. The town, at the edge of the Sahara Desert and just seven miles from the border with Algeria and Tunisia, was built over the ground but with a roof on top, to keep out destructive sandstorms and sweltering heat waves. Skylight openings and arched windows drew in the faint glow of the moon.

Whiz, whiz.

Two bullets struck the wall only inches away from Justin's head. Their airwaves swept over his face and dust flew out of the ricochet holes.

"Stay away from the windows," Justin shouted at Abdul.

"OK. We're almost there."

Abdul slowed down after a dozen steps and waited for Justin to catch up to him. Standing by a small doorway, he pointed outside. "You can see the town's gate, right over there."

Justin followed Abdul's hand. The tall archway stood about two hundred yards away.

"We're not gonna make it." Justin pointed at a white Toyota truck parked about ninety feet to their left. Four men wielding assault rifles and rocket-propelled grenades were positioned behind the car, barricading the fugitives' only escape route.

"Cover me." Abdul slammed a fresh magazine into his rifle.

Justin pointed his weapon toward the truck and sprayed a barrage of bullets. One man plopped to the ground. Another started twitching and pulling at his left leg. The last two crawled to the rear without returning fire.

Abdul bolted toward the Toyota, as fast as he could push his weak frame. Justin ran after and kept firing until he heard the hollow click of the gun's hammer striking the empty chamber. He ducked for cover behind a small wall to his left then inserted a full magazine into his weapon. Gunfire erupted from the barricade. Bullets scraped the wall and the ground around him. Moments later, there was a brief moment of relative calm, and Justin took a quick peek.

"They're all dead." Abdul climbed inside the Toyota.

Justin ran toward him, glancing only once at the row of houses behind them. "You're wounded." He pointed at Abdul's right side.

A bullet had pierced Abdul's body a couple of inches underneath his ribcage.

"Flesh wound. Nothing serious," Abdul replied. "Get in."

Justin jumped into the passenger's seat. Abdul stepped on the gas pedal. He raised a storm of dust as the Toyota bounced over bumps and ruts, swerving toward the main gate. A second later, a torrent of bullets thudded against the truck's tailgate and the cabin's doors. A group of men were firing at their truck from the houses' rooftops. Justin shot back. One of the men fell over the wall. The rest withdrew beyond his sight.

"There's a car behind us," Abdul said.

Out of the corner of his eye, Justin took in a Jeep gaining on them. "I'm empty."

"So am I."

Justin looked at the back seats, but there were no weapons or ammunition. His eyes moved to the end of the truck, where he saw a RPG launcher and a wooden box loaded with grenades.

"Got it," he said.

He crawled to the back seat and squeezed through the small window, landing against the rails. He snatched a grenade from the box and checked the RPG launcher before attaching the grenade to the front of the weapon. He shouldered it with a swing, struggling for balance on one knee, and then he pulled the trigger, just as the Toyota veered to the left.

The projectile screamed out of the weapon. A plume of gray smoke billowing from the weapon's blast cone engulfed the truck. Justin coughed and heaved. As the smoke cleared, he saw the grenade exploding into the dome of the town's mosques, tearing it to shreds. The six-story-high minaret went tumbling to the ground like a sandcastle swept by a strong wave.

"The Jeep," Abdul shouted. "That's the target."

"Thank you. What was I thinking?"

The Jeep was now about eighty yards behind them. Before Justin could reach for another grenade, sparks flared up from the bullets thumping against the truck. Rifle muzzles flashed from two assailants firing from both sides of the Jeep. A bullet ricocheted off the wooden box and grazed his left leg.

With a loud shout, Justin screwed another warhead to the launcher. He readied the RPG for the next round of fire. Abdul steered the truck around a corner, the last one inside the town. They raced through a narrow tunnel, the main gate of Ghadames. Two black Nissans were parked about one hundred yards outside the town walls. Three silhouettes stood by the vehicles. One of them, slimmer than the others, sported a long ponytail.

"Bashir's cars," Abdul said.

"So those should be the freed hostages."

Abdul peered for a long second before answering, "Yes, they are."

"And I see Carrie too," Justin said, his joy clear in his voice after seeing his partner was safe. "Now stop the car."

"Why?"

"So I can aim the RPG."

Abdul stopped. Justin aimed at the mouth of the tunnel and pressed the launcher firmly against his right shoulder. As soon as the Jeep appeared halfway through the gate, he fired the RPG. The grenade barreled toward the target with a swishing screech. The warhead slammed into the Jeep. Swallowed up in flames, the vehicle burst into a massive, fiery explosion. The entire tunnel caved in over the burning hulk.

"We're home free now." Justin dropped the launcher by his feet and collapsed against the cabin.

"Yes, brother, we are," Abdul said.

He waited until Justin was back in his passenger's seat before saying, "My boss won't be pleased with you blowing up the mosque and destroying the gate."

"He might change his mind once he learns the terrorists are crushed and the hostages are free."

The truck growled while its tires spun over loose sand. Abdul eased off the gas pedal, allowing the tires to regain traction. They covered the short distance to Bashir's cars, and Justin jumped out of the truck, right into Carrie's arms.

"Are you OK?" she asked.

"Yes. So happy to see you." Justin enjoyed the safety and the comfort of her embrace. "And you guys." He nodded at the two doctors.

The former hostages' faces were pale, but they gave Justin bright smiles.

"Sorry it took the cavalry some time to get here," Carrie said.

"It's all good. Let's go." Justin headed toward one of the Nissans.

CHAPTER ONE

Canadian Intelligence Service Headquarters, Ottawa, Canada
April 10, 7:50 a.m.
Present day

"Good morning, Justin." Carrie smiled as she entered his sparsely furnished office, bearing a tray holding coffee cups and a brown paper bag. A foot-high pile of bank transaction printouts took up half the space on his desk, with very little room for Justin's laptop. He was sitting behind it. Carrie took one of the seats.

"Hi, Carrie. How are you?" He took one of the coffee cups from the tray. "Thanks for this," he said before taking a small sip. "What do you have in there?" He pointed at a brown paper bag she placed precariously over the bank records.

"Breakfast. I bet you haven't eaten anything yet."

"No time. Couldn't wait to come to the office and pore over these financial statements. As a child, this is what I always dreamed of doing. Bookkeeping."

He rubbed his dimpled chin, then ran his fingers through his hair. Justin had a Mediterranean complexion—dark olive skin, raven wavy hair, big black eyes and a large thick nose—inherited from his Italian mother.

"Have a blueberry muffin. It will cheer you up. Fresh baked."

"Thanks."

Justin chewed on a small piece. "Hmmm, these are really good," he said when finished. "But not as good as the ones you used to make for us."

Carrie said nothing for a couple of seconds, then shook her head. Her auburn shoulder-length hair, which she usually kept in a semi ponytail, flowed down her slender neck. "Yes, I *used to* make," she said quietly after a deep sigh, "but not anymore. Have you heard from the army?" she asked, eager to change the conversation.

"Yes, I did." Justin's voice rang with a tinge of despair. "They rejected my application. They consider me, how did they put it, oh, a 'liability,' regardless of my flawless service until the Libyan episode."

"I know what you mean. It took me a long time and a great amount of luck to get in. I've heard mil intel selection is even harder than regular army entrance."

Before joining the Canadian Intelligence Service, Carrie had served in two tours of duty in Afghanistan with the Joint Task Force Two, the elite counter-terrorism unit of the Special Operations Forces. Justin had always been in the CIS, operating mainly in Northern Africa. After returning from Libya, both Justin and Carrie were suspended from field missions until the completion of an internal inquiry on the deadly prison escape. The inquiry was still pending. For the meantime, they were assigned routine desk duties.

"You know," Justin said, "I got a paper cut yesterday, and I was glad it happened. It's good to know I still have some blood left in me and that this office hasn't sucked it all out."

Carrie smiled. "I think I'm going blind reading figures and names and more names and figures every single freaking day. Some first-year analyst should do this, not intelligence officers like us."

Justin sighed. Then a smile spread across his face. "Perhaps we'll get our wish. Did you see Johnson's last e-mail?"

"The one from last night?"

"No. She sent another one this morning."

"I haven't been to my office yet." She took a sip from her coffee.

"The CSE has recorded another sighting of icebreakers, this time off the coast of Cape Combermere, southeast of Ellesmere Island."

"Could they determine who they belong to?"

Justin shook his head. "No, they couldn't."

"So, what does Johnson want us to do?"

"She didn't give any specifics, but she called a briefing for this morning."

"I see. What did you tell her?"

"I suggested a recon op and pretty much volunteered for it."

Carrie put her coffee cup on his desk. "What? This is the Arctic, in the middle of winter."

"Well, office boredom is killing me. I've got to get out there in the field." Justin pointed at his office door.

"More like the ice field."

"It's not like I have a lot of options. The Libyans didn't take the destruction of their mosque and half of their world heritage town by an 'infidel' lightly. Abdul and I were running for our lives, after being tortured by their operatives working with the Algerian terrorists." Justin's voice rose up. "After coming back, it was either this crappy job or administrative leave. Now an opportunity shows up and since no one is going to hand it over to me, I'm going to seize it."

"You don't have to explain it to me; we're in the same boat. I didn't destroy much of the town, like you did, but I heard I made room for twenty new recruits at the Algerian terrorist camps. Still, you want to go to the Arctic?"

"If Johnson decides to dispatch a team up there, which I'm sure she will, I'd like to go. After all, how else can we confirm the icebreakers' identity?"

"You're right. If only those damn satellites would work." Carrie took a bite of her muffin and washed it down with a gulp from her coffee. "So, it's safe to assume I'll need to pack my bags."

"I didn't volunteer you."

"Johnson won't let you go on your own. That's if she even decides to assign you to such a task force."

Justin held her gray-blue eyes. He nodded. "You're right about that. She's bringing in a couple of other people to this briefing. Some bigwig from DND and a lawyer from our legal services."

"You know them?"

"No, and I don't understand why they're here."

"I'm sure Johnson will give us her excuse for calling them in."

"Yes, she will."

Justin glanced at his wristwatch. "Shall we head up?"

Carrie finished her muffin and her coffee and stood up. "Sure. Let's not make her wait."

* * *

The office of Claire Johnson, Director General of Intelligence for North Africa, was at the northeast corner of the sixth floor. Justin walked in fast, short steps, listening to the rhythmic thud of his shoes over the hardwood floor. He stopped once in the hall. The corner of his left eye caught a glimpse of a huge painting on the wall, depicting an impressive Arctic landscape and three determined explorers. Their weary faces were very much alive as they stoically pressed ahead with dogsleds toward the white horizon peppered with snow-capped ridges. The ice packs, the snow banks, and the heavy blizzard appeared quite real. Justin shook his head in awe before resuming his swift pace. He turned the corner and saw Carrie pacing in front of Johnson's office door.

"Justin, what took you so long?"

"The painting. And it was only a minute."

"Everyone's here."

"If they are, they're early. We're on time."

Justin knocked.

"Come in," called Johnson.

Johnson's office was neatly arranged, with an L-shaped desk and matching bookcases. Two women sat around an oval glass table that took almost half of the office space.

Johnson nodded at Justin and Carrie while still swiveling in her black leather chair and tapping the keyboard of her desktop computer. She stood up. "Welcome, welcome. Let me introduce you to Colonel Alisha Gunn, with the NDHQ. She's the chief of the Defence Intelligence Section." Johnson gestured toward the older woman.

The National Defence Headquarters in Ottawa was the heart of Canada's military defense machine, where every nut and bolt of all operational forces joined together. The colonel was in a perfect position to feel the pulse of the armed forces. She had access to every piece of information streaming into the Department of National Defence databases.

She was in her late forties, with her gray, curly hair sticking out unevenly. Almost a head shorter than Carrie, she stood at about five feet, dressed in a gray pinstripe suit. The colonel had a strong handshake. She gave Justin a nod while her small brown eyes sparked with a tiny, almost invisible, glint of mischief.

Justin said, "My pleasure."

"Nice to meet you, Agent Hall." Her voice was coarse and throaty, as if she had just recovered from a serious case of sinus infection.

"Please call me Justin."

She nodded. "That's great, Justin, and you can address me as Alisha," she said with a sincere smile before moving on to exchange pleasantries with Carrie.

"And this is Anna Worthley. She's an Operational Liaison with our Legal Services," said Johnson.

"It's a pleasure to meet you, Agent Hall, especially after hearing so much about you," the young woman said.

Justin fought the initial impulse to frown as the counsel's delicate fingers touched his large, rugged hand. Anna was in her late twenties, with short raven hair that sported an odd red highlight. She wore a black woolen sweater and black dress pants.

Justin disliked all lawyers working for the CIS's most controversial department. They complicated his life and his operations with lengthy and dimwitted arguments, motions, and inquiries. Security and intelligence meant little to these kinds of people. They were more concerned about the legal aspects of the agency's operations than their actual impact on the safety of all Canadians. But the innocence of the Anna's blue eyes—peering timidly at him from behind rimless glasses—and her soft voice—slightly insecure and with a certain amount of agitation—disarmed Justin's defenses and melted away all his objections.

"I'm very happy to meet you, Ms. Worthley," he said.

"Simply Anna." Her blue eyes glowed.

"OK, Anna." Justin nodded. "Call me Justin."

Johnson gestured for them to sit down at the glass table.

"The colonel brought over the latest CSE report," she began, handing out four copies of a briefing note to Justin. He took one and passed the others to Carrie. "It details the movements of the two icebreakers, but we're still uncertain about their identity."

Justin skimmed through the pages. The Communications Security Establishment served as the national cryptologic agency. It analyzed foreign intelligence signals and provided technical and operational assistance to the CIS. The briefing note was signed by Jacob Stryker, the Associate Director of Signals Intelligence. Stryker had a reputation as very meticulous when accomplishing his tasks. If Stryker had highlighted on the last page that "there is inconclusive evidence to determine the port of origin, the destination, or the identity of the icebreakers," one could rest assured he had not overlooked any seemingly unimportant detail.

"There's strong reason to believe," said Alisha, "the two vessels infringing on our sovereignty are part of the Russian Navy."

Justin held her gaze while folding his arms across his chest. "What makes you believe the Russians have sent these warships?"

"Wait a second." Johnson held up her hand. "Two assumptions right off the bat. First, Russians, second, warships. The CSE report confirms only that two icebreakers navigated through a steady course in international waters, then crossed over into our territorial waters by Ellesmere Island. Nothing more. Let's be careful with our assumptions, shall we?"

Alisha nodded her understanding. "The Russian generals are constantly declaring their support for the Arctic militarization. Their Murmansk Air Base is buzzing with jet fighters and nuclear subs are always lurking underneath the North Pole. Remember when they planted their flag on the seabed, proclaiming the Pole as a part of Russia? They've tried to cross into our airspace in the past many times. All tracks point to the Russian bear, if I were to make an educated guess."

Justin glanced at Johnson. "I don't want to come across as dismissive of the colonel's assertions." He chose his words very carefully. "But the Russians are just one of the major players in the Arctic. If Stryker's report offers no decisive answers, our opinions, although based on previous experiences, amount to little more than speculation."

"You don't think the Russian Navy is involved?" Alisha asked Justin. Her left eyebrow arched up slightly, and her lips puckered.

Justin realized his words, regardless of how soft he intended them to be, had still bruised the colonel's strong ego. "They're a top candidate," he conceded, spreading his palms over the table. "But until we determine the ships' identity beyond any reasonable doubt, it's not wise to jump to conclusions."

Alisha leaned back in her chair. "Right. We agree that further investigation is necessary. And, like other investigations, it pays to line up the usual suspects."

Carrie was sitting at the edge of her seat, glancing at the CSE report. She pointed to a paragraph above a large topographical map of the eastern Canadian Arctic, which took up half of the third page. "The US air base in Thule, Greenland is just across the Baffin Bay," she said, exchanging a glance with Johnson. "A little more than 124 miles from Ellesmere's coast."

Anna stopped taking notes on her yellow pad. "You mean these ships could be American?"

Carrie shrugged. "Why not? The Americans have never accepted our sovereignty over the Northwest Passage, and they still cruise it without our permission. They always anchor an icebreaker or two in Thule, and their claims over the Arctic are as aggressive as those of the Russians."

Johnson nodded. "I will seek clarifications from the US liaison officer in Thule." She scribbled in her notebook. "But, of course, the honesty of their reply will depend on the icebreakers' flag. I'm afraid if it's Stars and Stripes, we're out of luck."

Justin stared at the Arctic map. A red dotted line indicated the suspected route of the two unidentified icebreakers. It was in the southeast part of Ellesmere Island. At the bottom of the page, he noticed the cape's coordinates: North Latitude: 76° 59' 00"; West Longitude: 78° 15' 00". *How far is that from the North Pole? A thousand miles? Seven, eight hundred?*

Johnson rapped her blue pen on the table. "What are you thinking, Justin?"

Her voice brought him back from his calculations. "I was... I was just reading the map. I know we have few facts, since radio communications were inaudible and the RADARSAT-2 was experiencing problems—"

Johnson interrupted him, "Yes, I've already given hell to the DND, no offense to you, Colonel." She shifted in her chair, turning toward Alisha, whose face remained expressionless. "The DND blamed the thick layer of clouds, the whiteout, and an unexpected satellite upgrade for the blurry pictures in their report."

"Judging by their route," Justin said, "I'm trying to figure out something, anything, about the motive of this... this visit, if you will. See, initially, the icebreakers were sailing up to Smith Sound, north of Baffin Bay." He leaned closer to the map as his hand traced the icebreakers' course. "It resembles a patrol mission or an attempt to reach the North Pole. But, at this point, almost halfway through the Nares Strait, the icebreakers turn around, heading back." Justin's fingers stopped by Cape Combermere. "Here, they cross into our waters. This is the only place where this happens. Then they vanish."

"And your point is?" Johnson asked, a slight tone of impatience lingering in her voice.

"Perhaps the icebreakers had an accident and needed to anchor on our shores for repairs. Or maybe it was easier to navigate our waters. The visibility was better, fewer icebergs, a thinner layer of ice, so the need arose to steer around and zigzag to our side of the ocean."

He scrambled to correct his reply before her dismissive headshake. "I'm not trying to justify their behavior in anyway. I was drawing a deduction that may help us to understand better this situation."

"But their motives for crossing into our waters will not tell us anything about their identity." Anna raised her glasses to the bridge of her nose.

Johnson leaned forward before Justin could say a word. "I have to side with counsel on this one." She placed her copy of the CSE report back into one of her folders. "All the deductions in the world simply don't hold water in the face of empirical evidence."

Justin lowered his head and avoided Johnson's gaze. He threw a quick glance at Carrie, whose weary eyes had already accepted their fate. *We're up the frozen creek,* her face said. *And as usual, without a paddle.*

Johnson looked at each of them. "Since we're helping Marty and his Arctic unit these days, I've decided to dispatch a small team for a fact-finding operation." She stressed the last words a little more than necessary. "Because of our shared jurisdiction over national security and intelligence, as well as the DND's great assistance to our operations, I've accepted the colonel's offer to join this team. She brings years of experience in similar missions."

Justin wanted to blurt out his thoughts. *What great assistance? Their satellite was barely functional, and she's giving us nothing else. Maybe she can cough up more details, as the CSE receives them. But if she's already made up her mind these icebreakers are Russian, how can she be impartial?*

Justin knew from previous missions that as a career pencil pusher, Johnson had perfected the inter-departmental game of favors and back scratching. Assigning the colonel to the investigation team meant that the credit for resolving this case would go to both agencies, proving Johnson's competence in forging strong cooperation. The colonel would also serve as the scapegoat, single-handedly responsible for each and every potential failure. Johnson was covering all angles.

"And because of the sensitivity of this mission," Johnson continued, "and the CIS's increased concerns about our interaction with our own citizens, I'm adding the counsel to this mission. She'll provide her expertise during questioning of witnesses and collecting their testimonies." She gave Anna a nod.

Justin looked up in time to catch Anna's smile. Her eyes resembled a splendid sunrise over a calm ocean, with glitters of sunrays sparkling off the water's surface. *She's so excited, as if making the cheerleading team.* Justin suppressed a grin. *Poor girl doesn't know what she's getting into.*

Johnson looked at Justin. "You'll be in charge of this mission. Carrie will assist you in gathering the evidence about these ghost ships."

Carrie nodded after two long seconds, which, under the circumstances, was a considerable delay.

Johnson ignored Carrie's passive objection and returned her gaze to Justin.

His heart pounded in his chest. The opportunity for a field mission was finally in his hand. "You've got it, boss."

"I expect this team to cooperate fully with the Joint Task Force North and its Rangers in carrying out this mission. The Arctic is under their jurisdiction." Johnson tapped a folder with her index finger and pushed it toward Justin. "In addition to maps and pictures of the area, here's a list of useful contacts, Rangers, and local chiefs. Trustworthy sources that have proven themselves during our operations in the North."

Justin browsed through the folder, his eyes running through the names and the pictures, searching for a familiar face. Johnson was assigning him a sensitive mission, with two strangers, whose credentials were yet to be tested in the frigid Arctic environment. The support of a former partner would be extremely valuable.

He stopped on the fourth page and smiled. A middle-aged man, with thin lips and an even a thinner line of a gray moustache, a long curved nose, a pointed chin and almond-shaped brown eyes smiled from the portrait. Justin did not need to check the name of the Canadian Ranger typed under the portrait. The friendly face had refreshed his memory. "Kiawak Kusugak," he mumbled, "it's been a while."

Justin locked eyes with Carrie, reassuring her with a quick wink. Unnoticed by Johnson, who was writing in her notebook, the glint of his eye was caught by Alisha, who replied with a slick grin. *I don't want to be an outsider,* Justin translated her grin. *I will make my way into the inner circle.*

"Sounds perfect." He closed the folder and looked at Johnson. "I'll contact the JTFN right away and talk to one of their Rangers."

"I'm sure there's no need to remind everyone about the importance of this mission," Johnson said in an almost solemn tone. "It's a time-sensitive priority, but the need for secrecy trumps the need for a hasty completion. We're keeping this very low-profile. The populations of Ellesmere and Baffin are quite low, but the potential for mudslinging is still incredible, especially if things get out of hand. I don't want to be accused of interference or pressuring the locals into cooperation. This operation should be completed without any scandals. Understood?"

She lectured at the group but lashed her piercing glare at Justin and Carrie. *This is not Libya,* her glare told them. *Don't screw this up.*

They both nodded in unison.

"Great." Johnson stood up, and the team members followed suit. "Start preparations right away, with the goal of departing as soon as possible, hopefully by tomorrow. Based on your findings, we'll work on a course of action. Good luck."

She shook everyone's hand, and they left her office.

* * *

"Have you ever been to the Arctic?" Justin asked Anna as they headed toward the elevators. She was walking to his left, while Carrie was to his right, two steps behind the colonel, who led the group.

"Yes, Yellowknife. Last August, for a weeklong conference."

"Summers are a breeze there," Carrie said. "The winters, hmmm, not so much."

"I've been to Iqaluit and Nanisivik," Alisha said without waiting for anyone to ask her and without looking back. "Iqaluit in January, Nanisivik in July. A few years back, I ran the Midnight Sun Marathon, which takes place, of course, during the night, but when the sun is still very much shining in the skies, between Nanisivik and—"

"Arctic Bay," Carrie jumped in. "It's thirteen miles west of Nanisivik."

"Exactly," Alisha said. She slowed down and turned her head. "But that was quite a while back, oh, maybe twelve, thirteen years ago."

"Arctic winters are far from a walk in the park." Justin slowed down. "We get freezing snaps here too, but nothing like minus forty for months and months."

Anna flinched.

"He's right," Alisha said. "It's essential we dress warm, very warm. Plenty of Gore-Tex and many layers."

Carrie nodded.

Alisha picked up her pace. "I've got to run to another meeting, but send me an update on the preps."

"Sure," Justin replied. "Since Johnson wants the utmost secrecy, we'll fly commercial to Iqaluit, then charter a plane to carry us north. In order to avoid any unnecessary attention, we shouldn't land right near any of the communities of eastern Ellesmere or Baffin. Once I've confirmed we have a Ranger on board, I'll send you a draft itinerary."

"Good," Alisha said.

"Do you mind sending that to me as well?" asked Anna.

"Not at all," Justin replied.

"Thanks, I need to be in my office in ten minutes."

"I'll keep everyone informed on any new CSE reports," Alisha offered.

"That would be great." Carrie shook Alisha's hand, as they came to the painting of the explorers and their dogsleds.

Alisha gestured with her head toward it. "That's Sir John Franklin and his crew," she said to no one in particular but loud enough for everyone to hear. "He was a great explorer, but…. Oh, a sad story with a terrible ending."

"Why? What happened to him?" Anna asked.

"He starved to death," Alisha replied. "In the Arctic."

CHAPTER TWO

Ottawa, Canada
April 10, 6:50 p.m.

"When's Uncle Jim coming?" Olivier tugged at Justin's jacket. "It's so cold out here, and we'll miss the game."

"He'll be here in any second." Justin scanned the parking lot for Jim's white Honda and stroked the little boy's blonde hair. "We'll see the whole hockey game. Don't worry."

They were pacing in front of the main entrance to Scotiabank Place, the home of the Ottawa Senators, as the hordes of joyful fans swarmed towards the gates. The Senators were going to battle the Anaheim Ducks that night. In the words of five-year-old Olivier, they were going to roast some duckwings, instead of ducklings. Jim, a university classmate of Justin who had taken a different career path—financial advisor in a big bank—was supposed to join them for the game.

"Is he even going to show up?"

"Of course, he will. When Jim says he's going to do something, you can bet your life he'll follow through with it."

"Oookaaay." Olivier sighed.

He ran to the backlit decorative post featuring one of the Senator players performing a wrist shot. Olivier imitated the player's body positioning, as he flicked an imaginary hockey stick. The little boy wore the same red, black, white, and gold jersey as the Senators, a gift from Justin. The first time the Big Brothers Big Sisters local chapter introduced him to Olivier through their Mentoring Program, the gift-wrapped jersey immediately melted the ice, transforming Justin from a complete stranger to Olivier's best friend. The only thing that mattered to the little boy was wearing the colors of his dream team. When Justin was growing up, his older brother never took him to a hockey game. Justin tried to take Olivier to a game as often as his schedule allowed him.

"There he is." Justin pointed at Jim, who was jogging toward them.

"Yeaaaah, quick, hurry, hurry," Olivier cheered him on, and Jim broke into a sprint.

"Uh, eh, sorry… sorry, I'm late," Jim said, shaking Justin's hand and trying to catch his breath.

"Don't worry, Jim, this is Olivier. Olivier, this is Jim."

"Nice to meet you. Can we go in now?"

"Sure," Jim said.

They found their seats just as the teams were about to begin the game.

"I told you we wouldn't miss a second," Justin said. The little boy was to his left, Jim to his right.

"Ehe," Olivier replied with a mouthful of popcorn. "Why are we so far from the rink tonight?"

"We're not that far," Justin replied. "It's the center ice section, and we're only a few rows away from the glass."

"The kid's a real handful, eh?" Jim whispered as Olivier stuffed his mouth with another scoop of popcorn.

"You're right about that. He's afraid he won't see the puck."

"Yes, I can't see the puck," Olivier mumbled.

The start of the match put an end Olivier's to yawping, and he lost himself in the game.

* * *

Regardless of Olivier's cheering and the spectators' repetitive chants, encouraging the Senators to "charge," the first period was not very memorable. The occasional fights among the players could not make up for the overall slow pace and the discouraging lack of goals.

"Do you need to use the washroom?" Justin asked Olivier, whose sulking lips and sinking eyes showed his complete disappointment. The intermission had just begun, giving the players and the crowds a much-needed break.

"Oookaaay," Olivier replied.

"I'll get you another thing of popcorn," Justin said, but his words did not lighten up Olivier's mood. "You're coming, Jim?"

"Sure, I can't stand these Zambonis and the silly music from the nineties."

They struggled with the steady stream of people and made their way into the large halls. The fans had already begun to cluster around the concession stands.

"Do you need some help in there?" Justin asked Olivier when they came to the men's washrooms.

"No, I can do this all by myself," Olivier replied.

"I'm gonna grab a pop," Jim said. "You want anything?"

"Water, get me a bottle of water. Thanks." Justin waited a few steps away from the washrooms.

"You said there was something you wanted to tell me," Jim said when he returned. He handed Justin a bottle of water.

"Actually, it's a favor I need from you," Justin replied and took a sip from the bottle.

"Man, I knew there's no such thing as a free hockey ticket."

"It's a simple thing, Jim."

"I can't afford to run any credit checks, Justin, with or without a CIS order. One day, I'm gonna lose my job for pulling such tricks."

"It's nothing like that. I promised to go to Olivier's game this Saturday, but I can't make it."

"Oh, and you want *me* to babysit him?" Jim's voice suggested he would rather work through a stack of credit checks for a week.

"Only for the afternoon. His peewee league match takes place at 3:00 p.m. You pick him up, take him to the game, and then go out with him for supper at a burger joint."

"Hmm, I think I already have plans for the weekend," Jim said, the likely beginning of a made-up excuse.

"On the phone you said you had nothing going on because Susan is visiting her parents in Barrie."

Jim frowned, silently cursing himself for making that stupid confession.

"And when you signed up as an Alternate Mentor, you agreed to help me. You remember that?"

"Yes, I do, but I thought it was just a formality, to help you do your volunteering."

"It's only a couple of hours or so. C'mon, it's for the kid."

"OK, I sit through his game and cheer for his team. But what do I talk about when we go for burgers and fries?"

"Talk about your job, your life, your family."

"My job's too complicated for five-year olds."

"Not really. Say it's like playing monopoly, just with real money of other people."

"Exactly, that really covers it all. Very smart observation."

"You know what I mean. Make it kid-friendly."

"What did you tell him your work is like?"

"I told him it's like playing Risk."

"Ha. So, why can't *you* do this?"

"I'm going to be out of town on business for a few days." Justin took another sip from his water bottle. "I don't know when I'll be back."

"And you didn't know about this trip earlier?"

"No, I didn't. It came up today in a meeting. Look, I'm not trying to dump this on you and go golfing somewhere."

"Well, you kind of are dumping this on me, but… where are you going, if not golfing?"

"I can't tell you that."

"Europe?"

"C'mon, Jim."

"Who's going with you? Can you tell me that much?"

"Carrie's coming along. And a few other people."

"Aha." Jim's eyes flashed a wicked grin. His nod meant he knew something was going on. "Rekindling the old flame, aren't we?"

"It's nothing like that. It's been over a year since we broke up."

"Yes, that may be true, but the two of you keep falling into each other's arms."

"No, not really." Justin shook his head. "But we work at the same place, sometimes on the same tasks, and I can't help it that we end up in the same mission. But work was what got in the way in the first place. So I doubt it will reunite us at the end."

"You never know." Jim looked around for a trash can. He was already done with his pop.

"This time I know for sure. I'll never fall in love again with a co-worker."

"Then you'll remain single for life. Work is all you know."

"Look who's talking?"

"Hey, it took a while, but I married Susan. You need to go out more often and with a woman. Leave the national security to the old and grumpy kind of guys who can't wait to get away from their families."

"*Dating Tips from the Love Guru. Volume One.* Thank you."

"More like *Volume Ten Thousand*, but you never listen to any of them. Do you want another drink?" Jim eyed the closest concession stand.

"No, I'm good, thanks," Justin replied.

Jim disappeared into the crowd.

"So are you going to do me the favor?" Justin asked when Jim returned with another pop in his hand.

"What favor? Oh, that one about the kid? I thought you'd forgotten all about it. By the way, shouldn't he be finished by now?"

"Give the kid his time. Yes or no?"

"All right, I'll do it." He sounded like he was agreeing to a capitulation treaty. "But, man, oh man, you owe me big this time."

"Oh, I won't bug you for credit checks over the next month. That will do it."

"That doesn't even come close." Jim began coughing after taking a big gulp of his pop.

"Or I can give you a Heimlich so you'll stop choking."

"I'm fine." Jim regained his composure. "It's these kinds of favors that will kill me one of these days."

Justin consulted his wristwatch. "We'll have to get back soon to avoid the rush of people during the last minutes."

As he turned around, Olivier appeared out of the washrooms.

"Hey, little buddy," Justin said, "Uncle Jim will get you some popcorn while I use the little boy's room." He leaned toward Jim and whispered, "You two bond." He winked at Olivier.

"What do you do, Uncle Jim?" Olivier asked.

"Hmm, I am a fin... do you like monopoly?"

CHAPTER THREE

Nanisivik, Canada
April 11, 12:50 p.m.

The bright sun bounced off the hard sheet of ice covering the gravel road and blinded him for a second. Kiawak squinted. All he saw were yellow sparks and black dots. His Arctic Wolf sunglasses—coated for extra protection against the sunrays' sharp reflection from the snow—and the semi-tinted windshield of his Toyota truck were nearly useless. The permafrost, which had been agonizing under the weight of several feet of snow for months, mirrored all of the sunrays.

At minus two degrees—but driven down to minus thirteen because of the wind chill factor—the sun, although bright and blazing its way across the skies for sixteen hours a day, provided absolutely no heat. A man stranded outside, even with heavy protective clothing, could experience the first signs of the frostbite within minutes. The exposed skin would begin to freeze, the tissue turning red and burning at the lightest touch. Hypothermia would set in soon thereafter, and death could occur in the next hour.

Inside his truck cabin, however, the heater blasted hot air onto Kiawak's unshaven face as he drove around the corner toward his destination. Parting Waters was the only bar, restaurant, and grocery store in Nanisivik. Kiawak ran it with Joe, his best friend. Waters, as Joe called their joint venture, stretched over the length of three construction trailers. They were soldered, converted, and insulated to accommodate Kiawak's small apartment in the back and the business in the front. Waters was the right name for the joint, located on the edge of the old town site, overlooking the Strathcona Sound. The waters parted when icebergs in the spring and icebreakers in the summer cruised by the small town.

The truck let out a loud puff as Kiawak tapped on the brakes and turned right. The front wheels slid on the ice, but the truck responded to his command. Nanisivik used to have a lead-zinc mine, which spewed out enough ore to keep happy and busy about two hundred employees for many years. When the mine closed its doors, the managing company took away not only the jobs and the people, but also everything it could salvage: the machineries, the ship loader, and even some of the townhouses.

Recently, the Canadian government, alarmed by the so-called "black rush"—the race among Canada, Denmark, Norway, Russia, and the United States for ownership of the oil and the natural gas buried in the Arctic's permafrost and seabed—announced its Arctic strategy. It was a well-elaborated and multilayered strategy to bolster Canada's sovereignty in its northern territories. The strategy included the construction of the Canadian Forces Arctic Training Center in Resolute—two hundred and twenty miles north of Nanisivik—the expansion of the Canadian Rangers and the refurbishment and the expansion of the deep water port in Nanisivik.

Nanisivik was now crawling with DND employees surveying the proposed building sites, collecting samples, and carrying out environmental studies and technical assessments of the proposed work. New apartments and row houses were expected to start popping up. Kiawak had been flirting with the idea of investing in the promising real estate market and becoming a landlord.

For the time being, all these DND workers needed food, and Kiawak needed power to keep the kitchen running, the flat screen

TVs on, and the grocery refrigerators in working condition. The trip to Arctic Bay scored him a diesel generator, sufficient to power up all the equipment. The current propane workhorse of the Waters proved to be less than reliable because of a sudden snap of hellish weather the previous week that had dipped the mercury under minus thirty-one.

Three black GMC pickups were lined up in front of the Waters and Kiawak recognized them as DND vehicles. The orange Ford Explorer parked farther to the left looked unfamiliar. As usual, a beat up Arctic Cat snowmobile occupied the last available space in the gravel parking lot. Kiawak sighed as he slammed the front bumper of his truck in a snowbank and turned around, backing up by the front entrance.

"Hey, boss, how was the trip?" Joe waved at him from behind the counter.

"Good." Kiawak inhaled the warm air mixed with the appetizing aroma of fried pork chops as he entered the restaurant. Seven people sat around the small tables enjoying their lunch. Most of the patrons nodded at him.

"Where's Amaruq?" Kiawak asked while Joe poured him a large mug of hot coffee. Before Joe could answer, Kiawak snatched the hot drink out of Joe's hand. "I saw his Cat outside."

"Back in the office. Nina gave birth to a boy, Gabriel, last night and e-mailed him a few pictures. I opened them for him on your laptop."

"How are they doing? His sister and the baby?"

"Fine, I think. I mean, this is her fourth kid and according to Amaruq, everyone's doing great."

"Well, I'm happy for him." Kiawak drained the mug down his throat. "You and I need to install the generator today, after the lunch rush. Help me move it to the back."

"All right." Joe scratched his long gray beard.

He turned down the heat of the stove's burners, and put on his Taiga Gore-Tex jacket, the same as Kiawak's. He took a pair of heavy-duty gloves from underneath the counter, fastened a black wool toque with long earflaps over his gray hair, and followed Kiawak outside.

"Man, you shouldn't go out without a hat," Joe said. "Your ponytail will freeze."

"Oh, what about your Santa beard, eh?"

"I don't need any stupid scarves."

"It's nice now," Kiawak said. "The wind has died down, but it was quite strong in the Bay before I left."

Joe helped him untie the orange straps securing the generator to the truck. "How was Tania?"

"I don't know."

"What? You went all the way there and didn't see her?"

"No, I didn't." Kiawak waved his hand, as if to express his frustration with the tangled straps. In fact, he was getting annoyed at Joe probing into his personal affairs.

"Why not?"

"Joe, drop it."

"OK, fine. I'm just looking out for you, boss."

Kiawak snorted. "Thanks. Who's the pumpkin?" he asked, gesturing toward the orange Ford Explorer.

"Couple of researchers from Ottawa. They're doing some weather measurements, the humidity and such. Something about global warming."

"Oh, those things."

"Yes. You're ready?"

"I'm ready."

They lifted the two-hundred pound generator and slowly placed it on the gravel.

"I paid three Gs for it," Kiawak said, responding to Joe's curious stare at the gray metallic box, a little larger than the toolbox stretching the entire width of the pickup. "Brand new."

"Three point five kilowatt?"

"Yeah. The other one was seven, but way more expensive. This one's supposed to be economic and quiet and withstand up to minus forty."

They struggled and swore, but within a few minutes they had moved the generator to the back of the trailers. They set it on the raised wooden platform by the propane generator it was going to replace.

When they got back inside, Amaruq stood behind the bar counter, fixing himself a cocktail of dark drinks. Kiawak refilled his mug from the coffee machine before sitting on one of the stools next to Amaruq.

"You know you'll have to pay for that someday," Joe smirked at Amaruq. His tone sounded like a warning that Joe was going to take payment in kind. In fact, Joe could easily pounce on the feeble Amaruq, who hardly weighted one hundred and fifty pounds in his five-foot frame.

"Someday, someday, everyone has got to pay," Amaruq chanted in a weak voice that had a grouchy pitch while shaking both his head and his drink. "How's my good friend Kiawak?"

Joe squeezed behind them to get to the stove and check on the pork chops, his beer belly almost knocking over a teakettle.

Kiawak shook Amaruq's small, calloused hand. "Doing great, really great. How's the old wolf?"

Amaruq smiled. "Hanging in there."

"How's Nina and the baby?"

"In perfect health. And the proud godfather is drinking to Gabriel's long life." He took a sip of his brew then smacked his lips in satisfaction.

"That's his third drink today," Joe informed Kiawak. "In case you're wondering."

"Thanks for flipping my pork chops. They would have burned if I weren't here," Amaruq quipped.

"If you weren't here mooching off us, we could afford a real cook." Joe lined up four plates and hurried to take them to the waiting patrons.

"All this howling is making me miserable," Amaruq complained to Kiawak.

"Don't mind Joe. He's just worried about this place. I came back from the Bay, and we had to pop three thousand for a new generator."

Amaruq's eyes registered the dollar amount, and he seemed to ponder it. Kiawak's glance followed Joe as he fluttered between the tables, receiving more food orders. Two new patrons had walked in while they were moving the generator. Kiawak recognized them as Nicholas and Brian, two researchers working for the mining company. They showed up every year to monitor the contamination levels in the town site.

"So, you were at the Bay this morning?" Amaruq asked. "Why didn't you let me take you there?"

Kiawak snorted. "Don't you remember what happened the last time you drove a truck?"

Amaruq sighed. "Not fair. That was a long time ago, there was a snowstorm, and I was in a semi—"

"You went through the freaking ice, old wolf, taking with you the rig and a ton of dynamite."

"The herd... those damn caribou. I keep telling everyone. I was trying to avoid crashing into the caribou herd. That's why I lost control."

Kiawak shrugged. "It's not that I don't trust you. I just can't afford to lose my truck. And you need to see an eye doctor."

"My eyes are fine. I told you it was the caribou. But no one trusts me anymore."

Joe returned to the bar and began pouring beer from the tap into three large jugs. "Nick and Brian are here."

"Yeah, I saw them. Why are they early?"

"Something about a potential waste spill from one of the tailing ponds."

"Oh, crap," Amaruq whined and fired an angry stare at the two researches. Sitting at the far end of the trailer, they could not see his reaction.

"Keep it down, old wolf. Don't you start trouble now."

Amaruq raised his hands in resignation.

"There hasn't been a leak since the mine was sealed off. That's why these guys are here, to make sure it stays that way," Kiawak said.

"I get it." Amaruq turned around to face Kiawak and offered him a big grin. "Trouble's bad for business. By the way, how's the other business?"

Amaruq pointed his index finger above Kiawak's head at two framed photographs hanging on the wall. The first one showed a proud Kiawak in the Ranger's uniform, posing in front of the entrance to the Nanisivik port with the Canadian Minister of National Defence. The second was a shot of Kiawak's Rangers Patrol Group, thirty-three members in all, with the minister in their midst.

"You know what's missing there?" Amaruq's shaky hand kept stabbing the air as if he were trying to reach for the photographs.

"You?" asked Joe.

"No." Amaruq laughed. "Our Queen."

"Huh?" Kiawak asked.

"Your picture with the Queen. It would be nice if you had a picture of you and Her Majesty."

Joe laughed. The only time he agreed with Amaruq was when the old man threw out one of his punch lincs.

"The Defence Minister shows up only in August, the warmest month around here," Amaruq said, "I don't know how we can fire up this place much hotter for Her Majesty."

He lifted his voice in mock solemnity, and they all laughed aloud, attracting curious stares from the closest tables.

"Excuse me, but I need to refill my drink. From home." Amaruq lifted his glass one last time. A few drops trickled over his lips. He zipped up his jacket and hobbled out of the trailer.

"Talk to you later," Kiawak said.

Joe served his thirsty customers while Kiawak finished his coffee. He retreated to his office. It was slightly larger than a den, with a small foldable desk, two plastic shelves full of books and magazines, a file cabinet, and an office chair. He began reading the Nunatsiaq News website, his favorite English-Inuktitut weekly newspaper.

Joe showed up a few minutes later and stood by the door. "We really need to do something about Amaruq."

"He's a good old man, just poor and lonely. Can't you leave him alone?"

"I would, if he left *us* alone."

"Never mind him. Amaruq is always welcome here. My brother Julian, his soul rest in peace, owed him a huge debt that I can never repay. Remember when Amaruq found Julian almost frozen during the bowhead whale hunt? The occasional free drinks and meals are the least I can do for Amaruq."

"More like regular than occasional," Joe observed, his face showing he was unhappy with Kiawak's reply.

"In a year or two, the old wolf will find a job he can actually do. Maybe even this summer, if construction starts. He can drive a small Bobcat or help with dry walling, be kind of a gofer, things like that."

Joe remained unfazed, his left foot tapping nervously on the linoleum floor.

"Listen, starting tomorrow and over the weekend, I've got to work with some people from Ottawa. They're DND."

"What do they need you for?" Joe asked.

"They're flying an Otter here, and we're going for a research mission up north."

"Where exactly up north?"

"We're doing the regular triangle, Nanisivik to Pond Inlet to Grise Fiord and back."

Joe shook his head. "I can't believe this. Why do they have to do this now, in April? What's so important that can't wait till summer? July or August, when everyone flocks up there."

"Justin, one of the DND researchers, told me they have to collect the data right now. Ice thickness, ice movement, melting levels, and other stats."

Kiawak hated the fact he was lying to Joe about the reconnaissance mission. But Justin had insisted the mission remain top secret. If Joe learned about the real nature of Kiawak's assignment, the entire Arctic would be buzzing with gossip.

"Do you know these researchers?"

"Justin, yes. I've worked with him before. I don't know the other three. But they're landing here tomorrow around noon. After refueling, we'll take off."

"You'll not have to worry about this place," Joe said before Kiawak could offer any advice. "I will not turn up the heat, will not touch your truck, and will not tease Amaruq more than I usually do."

"OK," Kiawak said and nodded. He swiveled in his chair. "I've got to pay some bills now. Call me if you need a hand."

"OK, boss." Joe went back to the kitchen.

"Hey, Joe, two more beers, man," one of the patrons called to him.

"Right away, pal." Joe reached for two jugs.

CHAPTER FOUR

Nanisivik, Canada
April 12, 2:10 p.m.

The DHC-6 Twin Otter charter sat at the end of the hard-packed gravel runway of the Nanisivik Airport waiting for its passengers. Two mini-snowploughs circling around the aircraft had long conceded defeat to the flogging snowfall, which kept pouncing against their windshields and steel blades like a rabid beast. The drivers, sardined into their compact cabins, zeroed in on clearing a narrow strip of the runway. The Twin Otter was the only airplane scheduled to take off or land for the remainder of the day. The bush plane required a short but solid path for its swift ascent.

Justin's stared at the snow ploughs through the terminal windows and sighed. The snowstorm had left them stranded at the airport. His team was waiting for clearance from the air traffic controller.

His satellite phone chirped inside his jacket. He removed his right-hand glove and frowned as he glanced at the screen. *How did he get this number?*

"Who's dead?" he asked on the phone.

Carrie shook her head, apparently recognizing the only person Justin would greet in such a way: his dad, Carter.

"Justin, how are you?" Carter asked quietly.

"What do you want? I don't have much time." Justin turned his back to his team and took a few steps.

"Wanted to see how my son is doing."

"Fine. I'm doing fine."

An awkward silence followed for a few seconds.

Justin tapped his foot on the floor, staring at the small skywalk connecting the airport terminal to one of the hangars. Resting on high stilts, the skywalk resembled a bridge. At least in Justin's mind. He hated this bridge. In fact, he hated all bridges. It was a bridge that shattered his life when he was only eleven years old. His mother had gone off a bridge in her car. The police had ruled out suicide and instead blamed the icy roads for the accident. But Justin knew better. He hated the man he blamed for his mother's death. The man he would never call "dad" again.

"You're still there?" Carter asked.

"Sure. Now who's dead?"

"Sorry to disappoint you, but no one is dead."

"Strange. You usually call when a relative dies."

Carter sighed. "Can we... can we have at least one conversation without fighting?"

Justin kept silent.

"Your brother, Seth, was in car accident last night. It happened close to his home in Vanier."

Justin offered nothing but his uneasy silence. Seth, Carter's firstborn, had always been his favorite son. Even now.

"He's doing OK," Carter said after another deep sigh, "but he'll be at the Montfort Hospital for the next day or two. It would be nice if you—"

"I don't have time to see him," Justin snapped, "and I've got to go now."

He punched the End button on his phone and clenched it in his hand. A groan escaped his lips.

"Justin?" Carrie said.

"Yes?"

"Is everything OK?"

"Yes, everything's OK."

"I just got an update on the weather forecast. The snowfall is local and stretches for only a few miles. We're clear for takeoff."

"Great, let's go," Justin said.

After they got in their seats, Kiawak's abridged version of the flight safety instructions included two phrases: "No smoking during the flight" and "fasten your seatbelts for takeoff and landing." He gave them the distance to their destination, one hundred and thirty-five miles; the length of their flight, an hour, give or take; and the expected temperature upon their arrival to Pond Inlet, about minus eight degrees. Then he walked to the end of the plane, about fifty feet in length, and slammed the passengers' door shut.

"Now we're good to go." Kiawak returned to the cockpit. "Let me know if you need anything during the flight. If not, see you when we land."

Justin looked around the cabin. Anna, sitting across the aisle, was fumbling with her seatbelt buckle as if flying for the first time. Next to her, Carrie had taken a deep plunge into a thick folder spread across her lap. It seemed only an abrupt crash-landing would deserve her attention. In the seat in front of her, Alisha typed on her laptop, only occasionally peeking outside the small oval window.

The rumble of the airplane's twin engines shook the entire cabin. Anna dug her nails in her seat's armrest. Carrie rested a reassuring hand on her forearm. Alisha still hammered on her keyboard, ignoring the metallic rattle as if it were a faint whisper. The terminal faded behind a white curtain of thick clouds as the Twin Otter arrowed skywards at about twenty-five feet per second. The climb lasted about five minutes. Once the pilot reached his cruising altitude of eight thousand feet, Justin switched off the seatbelt sign. He waited a few minutes, a sufficient time for Anna to regain her composure, before turning on his laptop.

"I was reviewing the CSE report last night, and a couple of points made me wonder," he said. "It seems there were a couple of... how to put this... inconsistencies."

"Huh? What inconsistencies?" Alisha raised her left eyebrow, and her usual gruff voice rasped a bit louder than necessary.

Justin tapped on his keyboard, bringing up a scanned copy of the report on his laptop's monitor.

"On page 3, Stryker refers to what he calls 'unscheduled maintenance' of one of the Polar Epsilon satellite wings." Justin pointed at the screen, although neither Alisha nor anyone else could see the highlighted section.

Carrie leafed through her folder until she found Stryker's report.

"I checked with one of my contacts," Justin continued, "who knows about the upgrades of the RADARSAT 2, the satellite providing the feeds to the Polar. He had no information about any maintenance, scheduled or not."

Alisha shrugged and waved her hand in front of her face, as if to squash Justin's concerns like an annoying mosquito. "So? Your man wasn't aware of a problem. I'm sure you don't run to your boss every time something goes wrong in the field."

"This was not a small problem, as it caused the eye in the sky to turn blurry and the result was unrecognizable and useless pictures," Carrie said. "Someone should have filed a status report."

"I'm sure they have." Alisha stared deep into Justin's eyes. "And these pictures are not useless. They show these two ships, icebreakers, and the precise course they followed."

"The second discrepancy," Justin said, "is the weather report about the time of the incidents, when the icebreakers were crossing into our internal waters. According to Stryker's memo, 'an overcast sky hindered the satellite telescopes from zooming in the moving targets.' But other sources report that the clouds were small and scattered, not the best conditions for taking pictures, but sufficient for clear shots."

Alisha shrugged. "Who are these misleading sources of yours?" Her voice still carried a hint of menace, although she had dropped a few decibels of its volume.

"I can't tell you."

"In that case, what's the purpose of your allegations? To discredit the Associate Director's report?"

"Of course not. I have no reason to doubt Stryker conducted due diligence in assessing the evolving situation. I know he's a very skeptical kind of guy. Maybe someone has taken him for a ride."

"You mean somebody deliberately misled him?" Anna asked incredulously.

"That's complete nonsense," Alisha burst out, shaking her head and furrowing her brow. "The CSE provided accurate information, and we're expected to act upon that information. I'm not going to allow you or anyone else to throw mud over my colleague's hard work." She clenched her long bony fingers into a tight, threatening fist.

"I have no intentions of discrediting Stryker's report," Justin replied. "I pointed out what I consider some difficulties in explaining this situation. But then, this is why we've been sent here to investigate and to find out exactly what happened at Ellesmere Island."

A few moments of cold, awkward silence followed. No one was willing to concede defeat or declare victory. It felt like an unstable ceasefire.

Justin decided to take the first step toward peace.

"Our Ranger friend will guide us to the right people and the right places," he spoke softly, looking mostly at Alisha.

She seemed uninterested in his words and kept staring at her computer's screen.

"How long has he been a Ranger?" she asked.

Her question caught Justin off guard. *Her eyes may be elsewhere, but her ears are in the right place.* "Hmmm, oh, I don't know." He rubbed his chin and shrugged. "I think about ten years or so."

Carrie looked up from her folder. "What is he like?" she asked.

"Well, you saw he's a friendly kind of guy. He's very knowledgeable about the Arctic. His dad used to be a hunter. Kiawak was raised to find his way around and survive in the frigid landscape without any of today's gadgets. He has never left the Arctic for more than a few days."

"What's our itinerary?" Anna asked. The rose-tinted hue had finally returned to her face.

"First, we'll scout Pond Inlet," Justin said, "to check with residents to see if they've noticed anything unusual or suspicious around their area or the coastline. If we come up empty-handed, we'll fly over the coastline and hit Grise Fiord, the other community on the southern shore of Ellesmere. That's how far I've gone in planning."

Carrie nudged him with a gentle fist to his arm to keep talking.

"No, I didn't forget you," he said. "A chopper will be waiting for us at the Pond. One of the American geologist teams researching Devon Island has agreed to lend us one of their choppers, since we're their Canadian 'colleagues.'"

"I thought they did no research this time of year?" Alisha asked.

"They don't," Justin replied, "but they've stored a couple of helicopters in a hangar, waiting for the summer. The one we're taking needed some work on the rotor blades, but now it's ready."

"So what exactly are these Americans looking for in Devon?" Anna asked.

"Oh, who knows," Carrie replied. "We have no idea what they're doing or where they send their research teams." After noticing Anna's eyes blinking in disbelief, she added, "Well, other than what they tell us when they're kind enough to do that. Remember a few years back, when some illegal immigrant from East Europe showed up at Grise Fiord in a rubber boat?"

Alisha gave a small nod. Anna shrugged.

"Well, this guy had set sail from Greenland in mid-September. A week later, he pops up on our shores. One man, one single engine boat, one trip of a lifetime. We had no idea he was there, until he showed up."

Anna nodded thoughtfully.

"Keep in mind this was a lone man, very determined and maybe a bit crazy, but still only one man. This amateur sailor crossed into our waters entirely undetected by our satellite systems and our Coast Guard. And we've got more intrusions, foreign submarines, Russian bomber incursions. You would think the Russian and the American warships and jet fighters would be easier to detect, right? But here we have two icebreakers and no idea where they came from or where they went.

"Like Alisha said, we know the Russians are always either lurking underneath our frozen waters in their nuclear subs or looming overhead in their bombers. On the other hand, the Americans have always dismissed our claims that the Northwest Passage is a part of our internal waters, regardless of the fact that it cuts right through the heart of Arctic Canada. There is Pond Inlet and Arctic Bay to the south and Resolute to the north of the Passage. These are all Canadian towns. Their population may be sparse, but those are some pretty good numbers for the harsh conditions of these barren lands."

Carrie stopped to catch her breath. Justin nodded at her with understanding. She replied with a tired smile and a deep sigh.

"I didn't expect you to be so patriotic," Alisha said. "We'll have to make sure you're kept on a leash if we run into any 'comrades.'"

Justin held his tongue. There was no point in discussing the merits of her obvious bias.

"Won't be necessary." Carrie returned to her folder. "Whatever and whoever was there, they're now long gone. We'll be extremely lucky to find even a single trace."

Pond Inlet, Canada
April 11, 11:25 p.m.

"The pilot was shaking so hard, I thought he was gonna die." Kiawak raised his voice in order to overpower the shouting of his drinking mates. One of them, a skinny man who seemed to be losing his balance, slammed his beer jug on the table, splashing his buddies. They cursed and shoved him, and he cursed and shoved them back.

"So, you were... were you... man, you wanted to kill the pilot, ha, ha..." the skinny man pointed his empty jug at Kiawak and raised it to his thick lips. Disappointed that no happy portion flew down his throat, he yelled at the bartender for another beer.

"No, no," Kiawak replied, the only one sober in the wild bunch. "I wanted to put him to sleep for a few hours, so we could clean his wounds. He was allergic to the drugs or something."

Their chuckles echoed again throughout the small but crowded bar. Kiawak was telling some old hunting adventure, which became more entertaining when embellished with exaggerated details over a few drinks.

Qauins Bar and Hotel, at the southern edge of Pond Inlet, provided the overnight lodging for Justin's team. In the bar, Kiawak grilled his unsuspecting friends for information on anything out of the ordinary in and around town. With a little more than twelve hundred people, everybody knew the affairs of everybody.

Three tables down from Kiawak's, Justin kept an eye on the rest of the thin crowd. Earlier in the day, interviews with some of the residents and the courtesy visit to the Royal Canadian Mounted Police detachment produced no results. About two hours earlier, Kiawak had moved to Plan B: the Bar Operation. *In vino veritas.* Justin remembered the Latin expression he learned while attending McGill University. Vine, or whisky and beer in this case, the saying went, always brings out the truth, even in the best of people.

The wooden door of the bar squeaked as Anna rushed in. The little man at Kiawak's table ogled her figure, although she was wrapped in a thick Gore-Tex jacket and a black balaclava.

"It's… it's so… bloody, freezing cold out there." Anna sat at Justin's table, still shivering. She wiped the snow off her gloves and the hood of her jacket. Her nose was strawberry red, and tiny icicles adorned her thin eyelashes.

"Well, yeah. With the wind chill, it probably feels like minus twenty five out there."

"More like minus one hundred." She placed her balaclava on the table and straightened her hair. "The inside of my noise is frozen solid. I can't feel my nostrils any more. All this happened while I was out for no more than five minutes. Oh, I need some hot coffee to warm up."

"It's almost midnight. Will you be able to sleep?"

"I know I won't be able to sleep without warming up."

Justin called the waitress and ordered coffee. He noticed Kiawak gobbling a whisky shot, his last one. Five drinks and two hours were the agreed terms of the Bar Operation. Kiawak was getting close to his endgame.

"Where did Carrie and Alisha go?" Anna asked.

"Alisha whined about a terrible headache and left at about the same time you took off. Carrie wanted to get a good night sleep before tomorrow's long day. Did they know anything at the co-op?"

Anna blew carefully on the hot cup of coffee the waitress brought her and took a small sip.

"No, nothing useful. They wanted to talk to me about everyone and everything, but they knew nothing about icebreakers. The food prices were so crazy. I wanted to buy a can of pop and it was five dollars. Five freaking dollars."

"Well, do you think your coffee will be less? Everything is very expensive here, since most of the year they have to fly in the food."

The barman, a bald, middle-aged man, approached Kiawak's table and exchanged a few words with its patrons. Some loud cursing followed, and Kiawak picked up the tab. He escorted his buddies to the bar door and exchanged a bear hug with each of them.

"You're gonna lock up, Kiawak?" shouted the barman after he had cleared the rest of the bar from its drinkers, with Justin and Anna the only remaining customers.

"No, he will." Kiawak pointed to Justin, while meandering toward their table. "I've got to hit the sack right away."

"All right." The barman flipped a switch behind the counter, turning off the main ceiling lights. The bar sank into half-darkness. Justin's and Anna's shadows danced under the flickering lights of two floor lamps at the far end corner, near stairs leading to the hotel rooms on the second floor. Another faint blue light glowed behind the bar counter.

"Oh, Justin, always the unrepentant romantic," Kiawak said as he dropped in an empty chair next to Justin. Kiawak rested his hands on the table. They were now the only three people in the bar. "Enjoying some female companionship, eh?"

Justin chuckled. "Anything good come out of all that drinking, beside your sarcasm?"

"Nothing. Well, almost nothing."

"What is it?" Anna asked.

"This guy from Grise Fiord, a well-known con, is trying to fence some guns. Big guns."

"What caliber?" Justin asked.

"They didn't know. This guy and his partner, well, girlfriend, buy or steal weapons in the south and sell them here, all over the place. Usually, it's handguns and the occasional semi. This time, according to Mike, the little guy, it's large cal."

"Did he give you a name?" Justin said.

"Yes. Nuqatlak. That's the con's name. Ring a bell?"

"No. Should it?"

"I don't know. I hear he's a small fish, but I don't know whether the Service knows about him."

ETHAN JONES

"I'll call my office and see what they can dig up on this guy. What's his last name?"

"Beats me, but there can't be many Nuqatlaks in Grise Fiord. The whole place has only a hundred and fifty people."

"Do you think this man is somehow related to our mission?" Anna asked.

"I don't know." Kiawak pushed a few loose hairs away from his forehead and rubbed his puffy eyes. "I'm very drunk and very tired."

"Five shots and you're out?" Justin said.

"Five's the limit if you want me to remember names and facts. Anything on top of that and I won't remember my own name. Good night."

Justin looked over at Anna. Kiawak's steps creaked on the wooden staircase.

"Are you going to bed soon?" Justin asked Anna.

"Not that soon. What do you think of this guy, Nuqatlak?"

"He's not the focus of our mission, unless he's bringing in weapons from Russia, if we're to trust Alisha's hunch. But we asked Kiawak to find anything suspicious, and this increase in Nuqatlak's business is definitely worth a second look. We're on our way to Grise Fiord anyway, so tomorrow we'll have a chat with this guy. Before we do that, I'll see if the CIS has any files on him."

"Oh, now that I remember, I was thinking about what you said earlier, the discrepancies in the CSE report."

"Yes. What about it?"

"I was wondering about the odds of these 'coincidences.' The bad weather and the computer failure happened at the same time these two ghost ships turned into our waters." Anna leaned forward, resting her chin on her fists.

"Murphy's Law?" Justin said with a grin. "If anything can go wrong, it will."

"I know that, but these seem to work in favor of the ships. I can't help but think of the movie scene when the security cameras stop working just as the bad guys break into a bank."

58

"You think someone is trying to screw up our satellite defenses so these ships go undetected? That's a bold claim. If Alisha were here, I would have to break up a fight."

Anna drew her lips together, closed her eyes, and gave Justin a big headshake. "Oh, gosh." She sighed before looking up. "Don't even get me started. I can't believe you can stay so calm when even her presence angers me."

"Why does she bother you?"

"She's so difficult to work with and stuck in her old, strict ways."

"How so?"

"Well, she's so bloody arrogant and patronizing, like she already knows all the answers before even asking the questions. And for some unexplained reason, everything is somehow connected to those Russians she's so mad about."

"That happens to everyone. You work in a certain field and to you, everything is related to that. Since it's so important to you, it becomes your obsession. It grows and tries to take over your life. You see Russians everywhere and their influence in anything, as if they were, well, pretty much omnipresent."

Anna peered deep into Justin's eyes. "You talk from experience, I presume."

Justin hesitated a brief moment. "Yeah, I guess so, to some extent. But really, Alisha has no life outside her work. She's not married, has no kids, not even a pet."

"What the hell? How do you know that?"

"Professional hazard, maybe. But she has a great reputation at her work and a striking record. So we'll get this job done and leave all this behind us."

Anna nodded and covered a yawn.

"Hopefully," Justin said, "we'll cover more ground tomorrow when Carrie flies us in the chopper. Now we should try to get some rest."

"No, I'm still buzzed from the coffee. And I've got the munchies. Hmmm, I'm in the mood for something sweet."

"I'll get you some dessert." Justin stood up. "Strawberry shortcake? I think I saw some in one of the fridges. I'm sure the barman wouldn't mind if we dipped our fingers in the pie, as long as we pay for it."

"Sure." Anna smiled. "Why did you notice the shortcake? Is that your favorite dessert?"

Justin hesitated.

"Well… yes. No. It… it used to be." He struggled for the right words, the fatigue of the late hour and the fond memories visible in his flinching eyes. "It's actually Carrie's favorite dessert."

"And you served it to her as a midnight snack on your dates?" Anna dared to ask.

Justin did not answer. He walked behind the bar counter, although the fridge was on the other side. Anna stalked him, apparently determined to get an answer.

"It was a long time ago," Justin conceded after a long pause, leaning over the fridge. He dug out two plastic boxes and placed them on the counter. "We're still good friends."

Anna took a fork from a drawer underneath the counter and handed it Justin.

"Since you opened this door," Justin asked, "care to tell me about your midnight dates?"

Anna blushed and smiled.

"I haven't had any midnight dates for a while," she said with a sense of anticipation in her voice. She took a brief pause as if rethinking the rest of her reply. "Until now," she added under her breath. Her last two words were loud enough for Justin to hear, but soft enough for a quick denial.

Justin read between the lines. *I've promised myself not to fall for someone I work with. Besides, it's not the right time.* He pretended he missed Anna's not-so-subtle hint.

Anna shrugged and dug into her dessert. "Hmmm, this is so good," she said in a long moan. "Thank you so much."

"Oh, you're welcome."

"Justin, what made you wanna do this?"

"You said you were hungry."

"No, silly. I mean this job. Being a secret agent."

"In preschool, when playing hide and seek, I was very good at finding the other kids."

"Ha! Very funny. In that case you should have been a PI."

"This job is much more fun. What made you want to impress a jury?"

"I don't do litigation. Our section does research, analysis, and gives legal advice. I'm usually locked in the office for eight hours straight. On the rare occasions when I've seen the inside of a courtroom, it has been from a spectator's seat or the witness stand."

Justin nodded and licked his fork.

"But, you're right in a sense," Anna said. "I do want to impress someone. My father."

"What does he do?"

"He used to be a judge, for the Court of Queen's Bench, until he retired last year."

"Health problems?"

"Yes. How did you know that?"

"A simple guess." He shrugged. "That just happened to be right. Well, I have kind of a bit of insight, since I know a few people here and there, who can access certain databases—"

"No, you didn't?" She threatened him with a fork full of whipped cream. "You ran a background check on me?"

"Guilty as charged, your honor."

"You won't be smiling when I'm finished with you." Anna placed her box and fork on the counter, but Justin had already darted for the stairs.

"Don't forget to clean up," he said, keeping his voice as low as possible.

"Tomorrow, you'll pay for this, Justin Hall." Anna stabbed his image with her fork, but Justin noticed a joyful glint in her eyes. "And I'm not talking about the cake."

"Good night, Anna. Sleep well."

"Good night, Justin."

* * *

As he climbed up the stairs, Justin failed to notice a small shadow creeping next to the fire exit door, at the far end of the hall on the second floor: Alisha hiding in the dark. She had been eavesdropping on their entire conversation.

"Arrogant? Difficult to work with? Patronizing? Somebody's life is going to get extremely difficult, Justin. And I promise you won't even see it coming," Alisha mumbled as she tiptoed toward her room.

CHAPTER FIVE

Grise Fiord, Canada
April 12, 8:15 a.m.

"Neither Nuqatlak, nor Levinia, his longtime girlfriend, used their cellphones during the night or this morning." Justin handed Kiawak a printout, while whispering on his microphone. Aboard the Eurocopter NH90, the communication set earphones cancelled the constant rattle of the helicopter's engine. "So, even though we bugged their phones, there's no new intel."

Kiawak, sitting behind Justin on the second row of seats, glanced at the chart, full of rows of phone numbers, the time of the calls and their length, all from days ago. He shrugged, and passed it to Alisha, who sat across from him and next to Anna.

"We'll be on the ground in five," Carrie said and dropped the helicopter about ten feet.

None of the passengers were surprised by the stomach-twirling fall. The ride from Pond Inlet had been bumpier than if they drove a pickup truck without shock absorbers. But the helicopter had allowed the team to cross the two hundred and seventy miles separating the two towns in a little more than ninety minutes.

"Let's hope he's still there," she added.

"Well, the office confirmed Grise Fiord has been Nuqatlak's official address for the last three years," Justin replied.

"You've got a problem right there," Carrie said. "*Official.* Like his *official* job, which is a trucker."

"Well, his files at the CIS and the RCMP were pretty thin, so that's all we've got," Justin said. "If he's not there, we'll comb the town for clues."

Alisha analyzed the phone records Kiawak had passed her. "Who's Job?" she asked.

"Levinia's brother, I assume," Anna replied. She titled her head but could barely read the printout. Alisha was holding it close to her face. "They've got the same last name. He'll be our next stop, if a search of Nuqatlak's home turns up nothing."

Carrie tapped the helicopter's controls and the aircraft veered to the left. They had just crossed Jones Sound separating Ellesmere Island from Devon Island during the short summers but joining them with a thick ice cap the rest of the year. The ice floes, which had just started to melt, resembled large pieces of shattered glass. At the shore, the small houses of Grise Fiord came into view. Carrie gained some altitude, in order to climb over a series of cliffs over the town about five-hundred feet high.

"This should muffle the chopper's noise and give us the advantage of surprise," Carrie explained. "By the time they notice us dropping over the town, hopefully it will be too late."

She stared at the frozen plains and chose a suitable place for landing: a solid ice field, clear of ice boulders and with no visible, large cracks. She brought the helicopter down without any problems.

Justin and Kiawak jumped out of the helicopter only moments later.

"Here we go again in the cold," Anna whined in protest as she zipped her jacket and put on her gloves.

* * *

Anna had just set foot on the ground when a black snowmobile jumped over a tall snowbank and landed with a loud thud on one of the narrow trails leading outside the town. The vehicle coughed out a cloud of gray smoke and sprayed a storm of ice shreds from its rear. The driver headed south, toward Jones Sound. A second rider hung tight onto the driver as the sled bounced over the ice bumps of the trail.

"Who's that?" Anna asked.

"That's our target," Carrie replied.

Justin and Kiawak were running toward the town, in the opposite direction of the fleeing snowmobile. Knowing they would never be able to catch up to Nuqatlak and his accomplice on foot, Kiawak knocked on the door of the closest house. Justin stood by a Mazda truck parked on the driveway.

"What do *we* do?" Alisha asked.

"Can't follow them in the chopper," Carrie replied. "If they're armed and fire at us, a damaged chopper means the end of our mission."

"So, we're just going to stay here?" Alisha asked with an accusatory frown.

"No. Follow me." Carrie pushed the helicopter's door shut and gestured toward another house. "We'll go after them."

"Who tipped him off?" Anna asked, trying to keep up with Carrie, who began running. Alisha had already fallen behind, struggling with the slippery ice sheet covering the trail.

"Maybe one of Kiawak's buddies. But then, people caught up in these kinds of deals keep an ear to the ground at all times and live in constant fear. I mean, look, this guy bolted out of his home as soon as he heard the chopper."

Before Carrie could knock on someone's door, Kiawak tossed the Mazda truck keys at Justin. In an instant, they began their chase after the snowmobile. Carrie knocked again and the door opened.

"We need your snowmobile," she demanded from the sleepy-eyed man at the door. "I'm with the Rangers."

* * *

"Left! Turn left!" Anna screamed into Carrie's ear as she clung to her waist.

Carrie turned the handlebar to avoid crashing the nose of the snowmobile into an ice hill. They were airborne for a couple of seconds.

"I saw the damn thing too," Carrie yelled back. The snowmobile responded to gravity's call and landed on the packed snow.

"Sorry." Anna took a deep breath, loosening her grasp around Carrie, even though they were going faster. "It just seemed too close."

Justin and Kiawak had given up their chase. Nuqatlak was riding over the coastline. The ice was too thin to withstand the weight of a truck. It was dangerous even for the snowmobile, but Nuqatlak was apparently determined to avoid capture at all costs.

"Where are they going?" Carrie asked. "It looks like they're headed for the water."

Nuqatlak and the woman—Carrie was sure the passenger was female, since at one point they were so close her silhouette was very clear—were doing more than fifty miles per hour, extremely dangerous for the fragile terrain. Carrie and Anna were falling behind, but they were riding over a slope, at a higher level than the fugitives. They could see much farther away in the distance than Nuqatlak. The zigzagging trail of his snowmobile dodged crevasses, leads, and heaps of packed ice. Nuqatlak kept going toward Jones Sound where the melting ice floes filled the waters.

"Can't they see the water?" Anna asked.

"I don't think so."

"Let's tell the morons. We can't interrogate the dead."

Carrie eased on the throttle.

"Why are we slowing down?" Anna asked. "We need to catch up to them."

"I'm not sure we're riding over the ice sheet on the ground or over floating ice."

"What? But, in that case…"

"Yeah. We may go through the ice."

The open water leads, formed wherever sections of ice floes pulled apart because of ice shifting, confirmed their fear. The fugitives and their pursuers were both riding over a thin layer of ice. Ice hills had become less frequent, another sign of the dangerous conditions in the area. At some point, Nuqatlak must have clued into the fact that the ice might become too thin very soon. He eased back on his throttle lever and made a sharp U-turn. The snowmobile lost traction for a couple of seconds, skidded over the ice sheet, and crashed into a low snowbank. The woman almost fell off her seat.

"They're trapped," Carrie shouted. "Maybe we can get to them now."

Her hope was short-lived, as Nuqatlak's snowmobile pulled away from the snowbank and barreled toward Carrie and Anna. Carrie avoided a head-on collision by sliding to the left at the last possible moment. As the fugitives passed them, she noticed a sawed-off shotgun hanging on the side of the snowmobile.

"They're armed," Carrie said.

"Let's hope they don't start shooting."

Carrie had just turned around when Nuqatlak's snowmobile jerked to the right. The woman raised her shotgun.

"Shit," Anna shouted.

Carrie gripped the throttle lever. The snowmobile jumped forward, landing behind an ice hill. Lead pellets poured from the woman's shotgun and struck the brittle shield. Sharp ice slivers showered Carrie and Anna.

"The bastards are shooting at us." Anna squinted in horror as shreds of ice crackled against her helmet.

"Here." Carrie reached inside her jacket for the Browning 9mm in her waistband holster. "You know how to use this?"

"Yes, I do." Anna cocked the gun. "Grandpa used to take me to the range."

Carrie took a quick peek. The attack had given the fugitives a big advantage. She resumed the chase. Soon, Carrie and Anna were gaining on their target. Nuqatlak attempted a climb over a small ridge. The woman with him looked behind and raised her shotgun. Before she could point it at them, Anna pulled her pistol's trigger twice.

She missed both times.

"Shoot the bastards," Carrie encouraged her.

The snowmobile was almost over the ridge when Anna made her grandfather proud. She drove her third bullet into the woman's right shoulder. The woman was able to hold on to Nuqatlak, at least for a short time, and then she tipped to the left. The snowmobile dragged her until she brushed against an ice boulder and fell off.

Nuqatlak now flew over the ice floes even faster than before. He dodged a small crevasse by shifting the weight of his body to the right to avoid slamming into a heap of ice chunks. The left ski of the snowmobile lifted off the ground and shredded the sheet of powder covering the ice. Nuqatlak leaned to the other side and avoided tipping over. He looked over his shoulder. Perhaps because he noticed his pursuers were closing in, he pulled a small pistol from one of his jacket pockets. He continued riding in a crisscross pattern, struggling to control his snowmobile with his left hand, while trying to point the pistol with his right hand at Carrie and Anna, who were now less than one hundred feet behind.

Anna leveled her pistol at Nuqatlak's shoulders. She moved the sight of the gun a fraction of an inch, aiming for his right arm, before firing two successive shots. The first one missed. The second found its target. Nuqatlak leaned forward, very slightly, as if hitting an unexpected bump on the trail. Suddenly, he took a plunge along with his snowmobile. He rolled over the ice, his head slamming hard on a couple of boulders, as he went through a couple of three hundred and sixty-degree spins. Finally, he lay flat on his back a short distance away. Red traces of blood marked his path.

"That was great, Anna." Carrie stopped their snowmobile beside Nuqatlak.

His chest was barely rising, and his neck was twisted unnaturally to the left.

"Is he... is he still alive?" Anna whispered in a shaky voice.

Nuqatlak answered her question with a slight involuntary hand twitch.

Carrie dashed toward him. She slowly lifted up his head. Blood trailed down from his lips, his nose, and the left side of his head. His helmet was nowhere in sight.

"Don't worry." Carrie steadied his head in her hands. Nuqatlak coughed blood, and his entire body shook.

Anna checked his pulse. She shook her head at Carrie and mouthed, "Weak." She looked back down at the man. "You're going to be OK," she said with a whimper.

"No, I'm going to die." His lips hardly parted as his voice rasped. He struggled for strength to breathe and speak at the same time.

"We'll take you to a hospital. We have a chopper," Carrie whispered. For a second, she wondered if the end would have been different had she decided to use the helicopter for the manhunt.

"Too late," Nuqatlak groaned. "I won't make it."

Anna fought back her tears. Carrie knew a mountain of guilt must have been crushing her soul.

"Why... why did you run away?" Carrie asked, realizing they were running out of time.

Nuqatlak coughed blood again. "The guns. I know you came for the guns."

Carrie hesitated, pondering the next question. Nuqatlak's pulse was growing weaker by the second. "The guns... where did they come from?"

Nuqatlak's head fell forward, but he muttered no words.

"Where did you get them?" Carrie asked.

Nuqatlak's eyes moved toward the right. "North... northeast," he mumbled.

"What?" Carrie and Anna asked at the same time.

"Did you say north?" Anna asked.

"And northeast?" Carrie said. "That's Greenland. Did you get them from Greenland?"

Nuqatlak shook his head and closed his eyes. Even these simple gestures took a lot of effort.

"No..." his voice was weak and trailing.

"Then, where? Tell me where?" Carrie said.

Silence. His eyes remained closed.

"Nuqatlak, where did you get those guns?" Carrie placed her lips over his ear.

"Danish... Danish depot." He breathed the words between gasps, slightly opening his left eye.

"Where? Where's the depot?"

"Pig, pig..." Nuqatlak's breathing stopped.

"What? What was that? 'Pig' what?"

No answer.

"Where did you find the weapons? Where?" Carrie repeated.

His blank left eye kept staring at the gray sky.

"Nuqatlak, don't... don't you die," Anna muttered through her tears.

CHAPTER SIX

Grise Fiord, Canada
April 12, 9:25 a.m.

"There's at least a dozen *Let Støttevåbens*." Justin held one of the brand new light machine guns. It was equipped with a bipod and a night vision optical sight.

"Enough for a small army." Carrie examined her sample, her fingers running over the trigger and the sight on the barrel. "There's probably two thousand rounds in the den."

Nuqatlak's small kitchen had been turned into their command center. Kiawak made coffee and they were assessing their situation while sitting around a white dining table.

"Holy cow," Anna said. She almost dropped the gun Carrie gave her, not expecting it to be so heavy. "What were they planning to do with this? Shoot Moby Dick?"

"What troubles me is where these guns came from, and how many others are out there," Kiawak said. "*Slædepatruljen Sirius* uses this exact kind of weapon."

"Who's the Sla… Sirius?" Anna asked.

"The Sirius Patrol," Kiawak replied. "They're one of the best units of Danish Special Forces in Greenland. They use sleds, helicopters, and boats. They have bases at Daneborg, Nord, Mestrersvig, and all over Greenland."

"Why do I have a feeling the Sirius Patrol did not just lose all these weapons?" Anna said.

"It's too early to jump to conclusions," Alisha said. "We still don't know where these guns came from."

"Nuqatlak said he took them from a Danish depot," Anna replied.

"Did he really tell you the truth? Or you just want to believe it?" Alisha shrugged.

"Those were his last words," Anna said, "and I'm just repeating them. The man is dead, so that's all we have."

"Yeah, I know. You killed him."

"We told you what happened, Alisha. And I've had enough of your attitude that nothing anyone does is good enough for you." She got up and headed for the door.

"Wait for me." Carrie followed Anna to the door. "For your information," Carrie said as she turned around at pointed at Alisha, "she did well shooting him in self-defense. Otherwise we would be dead."

Justin decided to stay out of the squabble. Kiawak, however, apparently found no reason to be impartial.

"You need to watch your mouth," he growled at Alisha. "Those women risked their lives, but I haven't seen you do anything useful."

Alisha waited until Carrie slammed the door behind her. "We're on a cold trail right now because they killed the man who could explain the mystery of these guns. Now we're back to square one, and we have to explain the deaths of two innocent people."

"Nuqatlak was anything but innocent," Kiawak replied. "He was in possession of illegal weapons and was trying to fence them. We have two people who were shot at by Nuqatlak and had to respond in order to defend themselves. It's a simple thing."

"And now we know more," Justin said, bring their focus back to the team's objective. "We had no idea about a number of things until a few hours ago. Now, we have evidence: many guns, just like this one. We know they're Danish and Nuqatlak, the gun smuggler, confirmed their origin. We need to find where this depot is located, and how this ties to the Sirius Patrol and to those icebreakers, which most likely are Danish too."

"I wouldn't be so sure," Alisha objected. "These machine guns are made by Diemaco, the Canadian subsidiary of America's Colt. These guns *may* have been produced for Denmark and their armed forces, but that doesn't mean the Sirius Patrol or Danish icebreakers dropped them in Grise Fiord. They could have come from anywhere within Canada or the US."

"I don't think so," Kiawak replied. "There are way too many coincidences. Two unknown icebreakers cruising our waters and machine guns used by Danish forces pop up on our Arctic shores. Plus, the man himself said he found the weapons in a Danish hut."

"My other point exactly," Alisha said. "I know their huts are spread all over Greenland. Maybe Nuqatlak and his woman or other people snowmobiled to Greenland. They broke into one of these stations, which happened to be stashed with guns, instead of food or supplies."

"You're right about one thing," Kiawak said, "They have depots in East and North Greenland, but these weapons are on the wrong side of the pond. Besides, Nuqatlak said he found the weapons north."

"North Greenland?" Alisha said. "He took his last breath, so maybe he left out some words?"

"I don't know, Alisha, but I don't think so," Justin replied. "If this was really a Sirius Patrol depot, I think they would be guarding them pretty well, not leave them for Nuqatlak and his friends to take their pick. Plus, at this time of year, it's very dangerous to travel all the way to Greenland. According to Nuqatlak's file, last year he barely left Grise Fiord, but there was one time he flew to the Pond to buy pork."

"Pork? Pig meat? Pig?" Kiawak said. His eyes widened, and he scratched his head. "Why does the word 'pig' sound familiar to me?"

"Because women call you a pig all the time," Justin replied with a smirk.

Kiawak leaned back on his chair, holding both hands over his chest. "Oh, my heart. That hurt, Justin. I can't believe you would say such hurtful words…"

"It's because Nuqatlak called Carrie a pig after they shot him to death," Alisha said with a deep frown and a stern headshake. "Which was very polite of him given the circumstances, if I may add."

"Yes, yes, we know." Kiawak dismissed Alisha's comments by waving his hand in her direction. He tapped his forehead with his palm, as if wanting to push his brain into action and spark up the missing idea.

"Yes," he shouted a few seconds later, slamming his fist hard on the table. "Pig Fiord. Sverdrup, the Norwegian guy, the explorer who discovered this area more than a hundred years ago and later sold it to Canada." Kiawak was reeling off his words like a verbal *Let Støttevåben* machine gun. "Sverdrup named this place Grise Fiord, which translates as 'pig fiord' in his native language. Walruses used to live here at the time and their grunts reminded Sverdrup of pigs. So if Nuqatlak said 'pig' and 'northeast' when Carrie asked him where he found the weapons, he meant northeast of Grise Fiord. That's where Nuqatlak found the weapons cache. Some of the locals still call Grise Fiord by its old name, Pig Fiord."

Kiawak jumped to his feet as soon as he finished his rattling, a big smile glowing on his face.

"You sure about this?" Alisha raised an eyebrow and pointed at Justin. "You don't believe this nonsense, do you?"

"Well, there's only one way to know for sure. We'll fly northeast of Grise Fiord until we find the depot," Justin replied.

* * *

"The Sirius Patrol stocks over fifty depots, small huts they build during the summers," Justin said, taking brief pauses between his words. He was skimming through a few documents on his laptop. "Matthew from the office e-mailed me these documents a few minutes ago. These depots are all over the place, but they're supposed to be only on the Danish, I mean the Greenland, part of the Arctic. The troopers usually rest in tents, but they use these huts during extreme conditions when they need to repair their dogsleds or replenish their food supplies. According to Matthew's reports, some of these huts have hot showers, warm beds, and somewhat decent toilets."

"The Sirius Patrol still uses dogsleds?" Anna asked.

"Yeah, don't be surprised," Kiawak replied. "Dogs are more reliable than snowmobiles, you never run out of fuel and, if you're stranded without food—"

"Yuck," Anna interrupted Kiawak, her face squirming in disgust. "Yuck. Don't finish that thought."

"Well, you can't eat a snowmobile..." Kiawak mumbled. "Hey, check out the view at three o'clock." He pointed to his right. "Blue ice."

They looked out the large windows of the Eurocopter. Details of the layers of ice and snow were very crisp from their current altitude of three hundred feet. The area Kiawak brought to their attention shined with a baby blue color. It looked as if a careful mother had wrapped the ice slopes, cliffs, and crevasses in a warm blanket to shelter them from the cold.

"Cool, very cool." Anna dug into her backpack and pulled out a digital camera.

After a quick, curious glance, Alisha returned her gaze to the pilot. Carrie maintained a straight line, almost parallel to the Grise Fiord coast, which hacked deep into the southern region of Ellesmere Island. Two snowmobile or dogsled trails indicated someone had recently been travelling in this area, going north. Carrie flipped a few switches on the helicopter's control panel, and the aircraft swerved to the right.

"What are you doing?" Alisha asked.

"The fiord turns right about ten miles ahead. I'm going to take us over the ridges, so we can explore both sides at the same time," Carrie replied. "I don't think the Danes would dare to venture this far inland and come this close to Grise Fiord."

"Oh, now you're having doubts too?" Alisha said with self-satisfaction obvious in her tone.

"No," Carrie replied, "I'm just being realistic. If it's true that they built their depots in our land, they would set them along our coastline. That way, they have easy access to them and keep them far away from our communities."

"Yes, but don't you think they know the coastline is the first place we would check? It's the easiest place to reach," Anna said.

"That's true," Carrie said. "And that's why we're searching these inland regions as well. But I still think if we're to find something, it'll be along the shores, probably in a secluded bay."

"That's where I would hide my boats if we were out hunting, which, in a sense, we are," Kiawak said, a thoughtful expression on his face.

"The CSE report indicated these icebreakers came very close to Cape Combermere, which is exactly northeast of Grise Fiord." Justin pointed to a map on his laptop's screen. "If we put together the findings of the report and Nuqatlak's confession, something's definitely going on around that cape."

Alisha shrugged in a defiant silence.

They continued their flight over the next fiord and the one after it, maintaining their eastbound direction. At times, Carrie would study the blue map on the navigating screen to the left of the flight controls. The screen projected a detailed topographical map of the area underneath, the southeast part of Ellesmere Island, which resembled the flattened nose of a hammerhead shark. A red dot on the screen, just above the mouths of the fiords, indicated their helicopter's position.

Two other screens to her right, by the radar monitor, were the object of Carrie's occasional glance. The first one streamed enhanced real-time images from two powerful cameras mounted at the nose of the cockpit. These images were the most useful during summer flights because of the bright and sharp contrast between ridges and valleys, cliffs and plateaus. At this time of year, the staleness of the glittering snow and ice was blinding and mind numbing.

The second screen displayed photographs taken by two infrared cameras installed on both sides of the helicopter's fuselage. The infrared system enabled the detection of thermal energy emitted by all objects with a temperature above freezing. These waves were then converted into colored photographs. The higher the temperature of the target, the brighter the red dots in the pictures. A few miles past, the system displayed a few red dots, probably caribous or muskoxen, given their constant and rapid movement. A building, Danish or not, would emit a low and static amount of thermal energy.

* * *

Over the next sixty minutes, insignificant dots blipped occasionally on the infrared screen, but nothing worthy of a second glance appeared. The Arctic Cordillera mountain range gradually rose along the eastern shore of Ellesmere Island. Carrie was careful to keep a reasonable distance from the majestic mountain peaks. A few of their summits stabbed at the skyline with their steep cliffs, some of them over three thousand feet high. The helicopter crew admired glacial lakes, frozen rivers and rocky mountainsides. Everything was buried under snow blankets and ice caps. Baffin Bay was not yet in sight, but it was only a matter of minutes before they would marvel at the spectacular vistas of Ellesmere Island broken coastline.

"Where are we?" Anna asked, peering through the window. Her forehead pressed against the cold glass, and the vibration of the engines sent a jolt through her body.

"We're flying over the Manson Ice Cap, heading east, toward Baffin Bay," Carrie replied.

"How can you tell?" Anna continued. "All I see is white powder, with the occasional black mountain top poking from underneath."

Carrie smiled. "I've got the map in front of me. Plus, the chopper knows his way around these mountains."

They all giggled, except Alisha, who kept staring at her laptop.

"Once we're over the ocean, I'm gonna take us north, so we can search the coast. If we don't find anything, we'll turn around for another swipe of the inland valleys before—"

A few electronic beeps from the flight control dashboard interrupted Carrie. She glanced at the infrared screen, fumbled with a few switches, and zoomed in the right side camera.

"What is it?" Justin asked.

"I… I don't know. Let me check something."

The helicopter lost some altitude, and Carrie steadied the aircraft in order to focus the camera for a clear image. From their distance of six hundred feet above the coastal cliffs, she could not pick the details of a large mass of white-yellowish debris at the center of the small screen. At first, she thought it was a colony of seals, but the infrared screen remained relatively calm. *Could it just be ridges of exposed cliffs, after a windstorm scrapped the ice off their slopes?*

"We're dropping in for a closer look, at that point, right there." Carrie tapped one of the screens so Justin could follow her words. "There seems to be something tucked in at that little bay. Maybe, just maybe that's what we've been looking for."

Justin glanced at the helicopter's navigational screen, then at the topographical map of the island on his laptop, apparently comparing the curves. He took a quick look outside the window at the bay growing larger by the second underneath them.

"That's Cape Combermere, right?" he asked Carrie.

"Yes, that's right," she replied.

CHAPTER SEVEN

Cape Combermere, Canada
April 12, 11:10 a.m.

The debris was spread over a stretch of rocky ridges, about one thousand square feet. If it were August, Justin may have thought this was the shipwreck of some careless Arctic adventurers. But in mid-April, when the Arctic's frigid weather could stiffen a man in a matter of minutes, Justin was positive the rubble was not the result of a human error or a natural disaster.

The prefabricated, timber panels, although split into smaller fragments and scattered from one end of the site to the other, resembled the basic elements of a large shed. Two log pads created a flat platform over the hard-packed snow that was sheltered about two thousand feet inland and away from the sudden movement of menacing ice floes. High cliffs rose up on both sides of the narrow clearing, providing extra protection from the northern and eastern wind currents.

"What do you think, Kiawak?" Justin picked up a couple of the framed pieces, then scratched the snow surface with the tip of his boots.

"I'm sure this doesn't belong to Parks Canada. This area is not part of the Quttinirpaaq National Park," Kiawak replied. He crouched and inspected a few metal scraps next to the log pads. "It doesn't seem to be a research station. They're much larger and not so close to the ocean."

"Is it Danish?" Anna asked and followed Carrie. She took pictures of a few orange tatters that appeared to be fragments of a large tent.

"Who knows?" Kiawak shrugged. "If it's not Canadian, where did it come from?"

"Of course it's Canadian," Alisha said.

They all looked at her as she walked off the log pads. She stomped her feet on the solid snow. "Nuqatlak led us here and this was his stash, regardless of whether this stuff is Danish or not." She pointed at the rubble and at the orange tatters. A wind gust was trying to pry them away from the ice. "Nuqatlak's dead and the 'mystery of the depot' is solved. It's over. There's nothing more for us to do here. Let's go on with our mission."

"This *is* our mission," Justin said. "This is what Nuqatlak wanted us to find, and we found it, but we can't pack our bags and go. Not yet. The Danes stationed this depot here and stacked it up with their supplies. I'm sure when we dig down and discover what may still be there, we'll find evidence that the Danish icebreakers anchored here and left this... this 'present' behind. This evidence will convince whoever may still have doubts."

Justin looked at Alisha, but she did not take the bait. Carrie and Anna headed over to the helicopter. A minute later, they returned with a couple of pickaxes and a snow shovel.

"It's a waste of time and energy." Alisha stepped aside, making room for Justin and Kiawak, who took to the excavation. The only place Alisha would dig was in her pockets for a little extra warmth.

* * *

"Here's a flare gun." Justin handed his only decent find to Kiawak.

The first ten minutes of chiseling ice and spading snow had rewarded them with nothing but trash. Chocolate bar wrappings, empty water bottles, and wood fire ashes were clear proof of recent human activity on this site.

"Why didn't Nuqatlak take the flare gun?" Anna asked, staring at the orange pistol. She was shoveling away the snow Kiawak and Carrie had piled up in two large mounds.

"Maybe he ran out of space on his sled or left it behind for his next trip," Kiawak replied. "Or maybe he thought this hut would make a good hideout, at least for a while, away from everybody. Then a blizzard came and wiped it out. The snow in the area is fresh. The blizzard happened, two, maybe three days ago."

Justin lifted his pickaxe over his head and brought it down hard. A sharp snap, unlike the constant ice cracking under their sharp tools, responded to Justin's brute force. Tiny slivers, like glass shards, sprang up from the two-foot deep hole.

"What the heck was that?" Justin asked. He was glad the sharp slivers missed his face. The goggles and the black balaclava everyone wore constantly when outside for longer than a few seconds protected his entire face, but his nose and his mouth were still exposed.

"Easy with the axe," Kiawak said. "Anna, can I have your shovel?"

He filled the square blade of the shovel with debris from the bottom of the pit and carefully lifted it up. He placed the mixed mass of ice, snow, and mud over a clear section of the log pads, the display counter of their finds. Then he rooted nervously through the pile, examining each piece with care. Finally, Kiawak placed a tiny square-shaped transparent fragment in his left palm. He paraded it in front of Justin and Carrie.

"Is that what I just smashed?" Justin asked.

"It has to be, and it's definitely not ice," Kiawak replied with a smile. "I would say your axe smashed into a laptop or some other electronic gadget buried deep down there." He stared at the hole. "Something with a clear screen."

"Cellphone? Digital camera?" Carrie guessed.

"Could be," Kiawak said. He dropped to his knees and began to clear the hole with his black gloves. Carrie and Justin drew back to give him sufficient room.

"Why don't you take a drink of this?" Justin noticed Anna had begun to shiver and offered her a coffee thermos he fetched from his backpack. "Will warm you up."

Anna nodded and took a couple of big gulps.

"Do you want to wait in the chopper?" Carrie asked. Anna's lips were already chapped.

"No," Anna said. "I'll be OK. We're not gonna be here much longer, I assume, once we discover our little treasure."

"Well, here we go," Kiawak said. He had completed his excavation of the fragile article and gently brushed the snow from the black object, which fit easily on his glove. The object resembled a large cellphone, like those models from the eighties, but sleeker looking, with a leather coating and numerous buttons on the top and at the bottom.

"It's a multiband radio," Justin shouted over the rising wind. "A military radio."

"You're sure?" Carrie asked. "I haven't seen our army use them."

Kiawak flipped the radio over, scrapped a thin layer of ice from its backside, and read the white inscription. He shook his head. "Bingo," he shouted and passed the radio over to Justin.

"What's going on here?" Their excitement had drawn Alisha's attention, who stepped closer to the action.

"We've found the evidence. This is a Danish army radio," Justin said, his eyes focused on the radio.

"And how can you be sure of that?" Alisha's voice rang as an accusation.

"Because it says in the back, you whack job," Justin snapped at her and pushed the radio toward Alisha. "Read it for yourself. 'The Royal Danish Army' is stamped in large caps in the back!"

"That's not how you talk to a lady," Alisha replied and quickly, but calmly, withdrew her hand from one of her jacket pockets. Her fingers were wrapped around a pistol, which she pointed at Justin's head.

"OK, no reason to get angry," Kiawak replied, lifting up his arms slowly and gesturing for her to stop. "Put the gun away."

"Hands up. All of you," Alisha barked.

"What the hell are you doing?" Justin shouted back.

Alisha pulled the trigger. A bullet whistled by Justin's head. He dropped to his left side, raising his hand to check his ear. No blood, but his eardrum was almost shattered.

"Stay down and don't move," Alisha yelled, taking a step back, likely in case Justin decided to charge toward her gun. "You," she shouted at Carrie, who still was holding her shovel. "Are you fucking deaf or something? And you, the shivering beauty, hands up, turn around and face me!"

Anna brought her hands above her head, the left one still carrying Justin's coffee thermos.

"You're... you're going to kill us?" she muttered.

"What a bitch." Carrie threw the shovel to the ground.

Alisha grinned. "I told you, all of you, to stop dicking around with this Danish story and to stop looking for clues." Alisha brandished her gun, pointing at their heads. "Things would have been much easier if you would had listened to me and agreed the Russians were pulling the strings. But no, you didn't want to. What did you call me, Anna? Self-righteous? Am I being difficult, Justin? We'll see how difficult this will be for each one of you."

"So you work for the Danes?" Anna asked. "You're their spy?"

"The pay's much better, and I get to kill whoever gets in my way."

"Alisha, this won't work," Justin said in a shaky voice. "Whatever the Danes and you have been plotting, it will fail."

"Think about it, Alisha," Kiawak said, still kneeling by the pit. "This is your country, your home. This is Canada."

"On the map, yes, this is Canada," Alisha replied in a calm voice. "As for my home, that'll be wherever I want it to be. Justin, you had no idea what was going on here and even now, right before you die, you still don't have a clue. And you will all go to your graves as ignorant fools."

"Alisha—" Justin began.

"Enough," she yelled. "Give me your guns. Now!"

Justin removed his Browning 9mm from his holster inside his jacket. Kiawak hesitated for a brief second. Alisha took one firm step toward him, and his hesitation melted away. Carrie laid down her Browning pistol. Anna placed the coffee thermos in front of her feet.

"I don't carry a gun," she mumbled.

"It would have done you no good." Alisha smirked as she gathered their weapons. "But you have a satellite phone and a PLB. Drop everything on the ground. Everybody, do it! All electronics and anything else in your pockets. Empty them out! Come on!"

They placed all their satellite phones, personal locator beacons, pocketknives, chap sticks, keys, and spare change on the log pads.

"Your watches too." Alisha pointed at Justin's wrist. "It's not like you'll need that funny compass, but let's take no chances. Do it, or I'll blow your head off."

"What do you have in mind?" Justin asked.

"Can you fly the chopper?" Alisha asked Kiawak, gesturing toward the aircraft.

Kiawak nodded.

"Good, collect all that junk." She pointed at the team's belongings. "Stuff it in Justin's backpack and walk in front of me. *Very slowly!* To the rest of you, all I have to say is… stay warm."

Alisha began her retreat, carefully examining Kiawak's every move.

"You can't take off and abandon us," Anna shouted. "We're gonna freeze to death."

"Yeah, you're right. That's the idea," Alisha replied with another smirk, "but that's part of the plan. I would say it's about minus four now, which isn't that bad. I'll give you a couple of hours, but I would be surprised if you haven't turned into ice cubes by nightfall."

"Next time we meet, I'll tear your heart to pieces." Carrie jabbed the air with her arms and made violent gestures of ripping apart an object with her clenched fists.

"Maybe you'll meet me in hell," Alisha scoffed, "where you'll be dropping by tonight. Dressed in a cold, white gown, as if you were a pretty little bride."

CHAPTER EIGHT

Viborg, Denmark
April 12, 5:45 p.m.

"Has the jury reached a verdict?"

"Yes, Presiding Judge, we have reached a verdict."

High Court Judge Laurits Handel heaved a sigh of relief at the jury forewoman's reply. He nodded and removed his black-rimmed glasses without attempting to hide his smile. The appeal proceedings had consumed several weeks of time on an already overloaded court docket, and the judge was looking forward to the end of another intricate legal battle. The other two High Court Judges, sitting to Handel's left and right, impatiently swiveled in their chairs.

"What is the verdict?" the judge asked the forewoman. She stood behind the wooden rail separating the jury from the rest of the courtroom.

"On the two counts of assisting in a conspiracy to commit terrorist acts," the forewoman replied in a stern voice, her eyes fixed on the defendant's unshaven face, "by a majority of nine to three, we, the jury, declare the defendant, Mr. Sargon Beyda, guilty as charged."

Pandemonium exploded in the courtroom as soon as she finished pronouncing the word 'guilty.' Relatives of the defendant broke into angry barks, screams, whistles, and the occasional expletive. Joyful cries from police officers and numerous spectators, accompanied by a loud wave of applause, attempted to outdo the competition. The defendant, still in handcuffs, dropped his head in despair, despite his defense counselor's words of encouragement. In the second row, behind the counselor's seat, Lilith, the defendant's wife, began to weep quietly. Media photographers scrambled for the best shots of the defendant, adding to the overwhelming chaos.

"Order! Order!" The judge, already on his feet, shouted at the disorderly crowd. The other members of the court followed suit, but their voices were too frail. Three deputies, in charge of maintaining order and peace in the courtroom, stepped forward, their refrigerator-sized bodies barricading the enraged mob away from the judges.

"Clear the room," the judge instructed the deputies in a chirping voice. He made a quick exit through the doors behind the bench connecting to his private chambers. The other two judges used the same escape route. Two police officers, who escorted the defendant to and from the courthouse, snapped out of their standing guard positions and approached Sargon.

"Time to go, man," one of them said. The other lifted Sargon from his chair by his right arm.

"The court is adjourned," one of the gray-haired deputies boomed in a well-practiced, solemn tone, as if he closed with these exact words all trial hearings each time the court was in session. The other two deputies ushered the twelve members of the jury away from the emotional tide rising across the courtroom and toward the door to judge's chambers. Then the deputies proceeded to shove people out, starting with the journalists, who were tossing out questions at the runaway jury. In less than two minutes, the large Courtroom E of the High Court of Western Denmark was completely empty.

* * *

The two police officers pushed Sargon down the narrow hall leading to the west wing of the court, which housed administrative offices, press conference rooms, and a small cafeteria. A third one followed two steps behind them. Experience had taught the escort team they were most vulnerable during the loading and unloading of detainees. The courtroom disturbance had triggered the team's defensive instincts. Worried that Sargon's friends may have planned an escape, their eyes double-checked every door and questioned the faces of every person they passed in the hall.

"Look, mommy, the police... and a bad guy," a young boy blurted, pulling on his mother's arm. She stopped stabbing at her BlackBerry for half a second and whipped an angry stare at the boy before returning to her e-mail. One of the officers frowned at her indifference, but smiled at the little boy, who smiled back.

The escort team hurried down the last set of stairs, which opened into a small vestibule, and proceeded to the right exit taking them to the back of the building. Another police officer awaited their arrival in a Toyota Previa van parked less than six feet from the door. Two officers nudged Sargon into the middle of the backseats and sat on either side of him.

"We're good to go," the team leader said. He sat in the front passenger's seat, removed his cap, and placed it over the dashboard.

The driver nodded and glanced at the two officers in the rear-view mirror, as he put the Toyota in reverse. "How are you boys back there?" he asked over a microphone attached to the side of the dashboard. The bulletproof glass separating the front seats from those in the back was also soundproof.

"We're ready," one of them replied on a similar microphone embedded on the side door, as he fastened his seatbelt. The other officer nodded and rearranged his baton hanging on the left side of his waist. He inspected his HK pistol resting on his holster under his right arm.

The driver looked over at the team leader and asked, "Guilty?"

"Like Cain after slaughtering Abel," he replied. "His relatives raised some objections, and the judge kicked everyone out of the courtroom."

"I see." The driver turned left onto Gråbrødre Kirke Stræde, the road in front of the High Court building. "So, it's back to Horsens Pen?"

"Yes. For now. I'm sure they'll transfer him to *Københavns Fængsler*," the team leader said.

* * *

Sargon let out a whining yelp, like a puppy spooked while soaking sunrays on his front porch. He had picked up some Danish in jail and he knew the meaning of those words. *Fængsler* meant "jail" and *københavns* was "Copenhagen." It was the toughest prison in Denmark, beyond full capacity, ruled by thugs and flooded with drugs. Forget about the concepts of openness, normalization, and rehabilitation, held high and sought after at the detention center in Horsens. The center had a library, recreational facilities, water ponds, and separate units for conjugal visits. Any intimacy inmates could expect at the Copenhagen Prison would follow dropping the soap accidentally while sharing the showers.

Sargon groaned as the terror of spending twenty plus years in the Copenhagen rat hole began to boil in his mind. *Will it be twenty? Twenty-five years?* He remembered discussing the possible sentence with his defense counselor, but their legal strategy never envisioned a guilty verdict. After all, the public prosecutors could prove only that Sargon had been sending money to his brother, a fact established through witnesses during the trial. But the allegation of "conspiracy to commit terrorist acts" was a long shot, even though Sargon knew the money was for the financing of terrorist camps. Still, the jury had rendered a clear-cut verdict: he had supported terrorism. The court was pretty much at liberty to impose any jail term, even life imprisonment.

I'll never be able to see my children grow up. How will Lilith do it on her own? Sargon dropped his head between his handcuffed hands to hide his face.

* * *

"What does your wife think, Inspector?" the driver asked his team leader. They had just turned the corner to the Lille Sankt Mikkels Gade, the road taking them to Horsens, a city sixty miles south of Viborg. Lake Søndersø appeared on their left, between green trees and shrubs hedging around two-story, red-roofed houses.

"Huh, what?" the team leader replied. He was still watching the occasional vehicle appearing in the sparse traffic behind their van.

"The transfer. What does she think of your transfer?"

"Oh." The team leader glanced at the driver for a second before returning his gaze to the side mirror. "She doesn't like it. Her family lives in Århus, and she wants to stay close to them."

"But Horsens is less than an hour away."

"I keep telling her it's not that far, but she's so stubborn. Our kids are in good schools and all their friends live here, she says. As if children in Horsens are ignorant and unsociable—"

"Hey, guys," one of the officers in the back said, interrupting them. "Check out the Opel, just pulled in from the left. Two people in the car."

The team leader turned his head around to inspect the vehicle. The silver Opel Vectra was unremarkable but gaining on them. One of the officers involuntarily placed his hand over his holster.

"Is it going to pass us?" asked the team leader.

"I'm not sure, but it's getting really close."

The team leader checked his pistol, as the driver steered closer to the side of the road. This provided the Opel sufficient room to pass. The distance also gave the team an extra second to avert a crash. The driver kept checking his rear-view and left side mirrors, keeping both hands on the steering wheel, ready for any last second maneuver.

The Opel crossed over the white median dividing the lanes and accelerated. The team leader stared at the dark tinted windows of the sedan, trying to make out the features of the strawberry blonde woman in the passenger's seat sporting black sunglasses. Once both vehicles were neck and neck, the Opel lost its haste. The team leader saw something shining behind the passenger's window as the woman began to unroll the glass.

He pulled out his pistol. The driver clenched the steering wheel, gearing up to drive into the bushes along the road, if the shining object turned out to be a gun. But the sight of a brass badge, which the woman held in her right hand, signaled the escort team was not under attack. The team leader squinted, but the letters engraved on the badge were too small. The shield shape of the badge did not resemble any official symbol familiar to him.

"What does the badge say?" the team leader asked the driver.

"Her arm's shaking, but it looks like a MP badge."

"The Opel's unmarked," one of the officers said. "And who asked for the MP's support?"

"What's she saying?" asked the other officer. "Is she telling us to pull over?"

The team leader had interpreted the woman's finger jab as a pull over signal too. But he was not willing to take orders from unidentified individuals, military police or not. An unexpected stop would endanger everyone's life, including the detainee's. The unmarked car had contacted the escort team without any warning, use of radio or sirens, in breach of police procedures. The team leader reached for the radio to inform the Viborg police about the situation in progress and turned to the driver to tell him to keep driving. The sunlight hit the woman's badge just right, and the team leader could read the inscription circling a golden crown and three lions: *Politiets Efterretningstjeneste.*

"The Intelligence Service?" he asked. "What's the Service doing tailing us?" He frowned and decided to stop the van.

The Danish Security and Intelligence Service was part of the police force, forming Department G of the Danish National Police. Technically, they were the escort team's colleagues.

"Let's see what they want," the team leader said quietly. "Maybe it's a secret emergency, and that's why they couldn't radio it. They're probably from the Århus department."

The driver flipped on the turn signal light. He drove into Heibergs Alle road and found an empty stall in the parking lot, awaiting the arrival of the Opel.

"Keep your guard up," the team leader reminded everyone. "We're not sure they're really from the Service. Even if they are, we still don't know their motives for this stop."

Sargon was as alarmed as his guards. The woman's badge was unknown to him, and so were the identities of the people in the car. He had a gut feeling this story was just not going to end well.

* * *

The Opel entered the parking lot and rolled to a complete stop in front of the van under the watchful eyes of the escort team. The driver and his passenger came out of the car at the exact same time and strutted toward the van in quick steps. The woman was wearing a chocolate-brown suede jacket, a beige blouse, and a brown cashmere scarf. Her long slender legs were wrapped in black, skinny-fit denim, some designer's brand the team leader recognized, with a tongue-twister Italian name. The man had a navy blue, tweed jacket and matching pants, complemented by a black woolen sweater. The team leader noticed a large, leather banded watch around the man's left hand. *I'm sure they're both wearing guns, but they're hiding them very well.*

The woman lifted her sunglasses over her hair as soon as they stopped in front of the van, revealing her almond-shaped blue eyes.

The man waited until the team leader rolled down his window. At that time, he folded and placed his shades in his inside jacket pocket, before his small brown eyes gave the man a piercing glance.

"My name's Magnus Torbjorn. I'm a Special Agent with the *Politiets Efterretningstjeneste.* This is my colleague, Agent Valgerda Hassing."

Valgerda flashed her badge to the escort team. Magnus did not bother, since both the team leader and the driver were busy examining hers. Instead, he nodded at the two officers in the back, who were nervously staring at him. Then, he found Sargon's face and nailed him with an intimidating smirk.

"I'm Inspector Bruin Roby, in charge of taking a detainee back to his cell. Your intervention has threatened the safety of my men and of the detainee." Convinced of its authenticity, Bruin handed Valgerda her badge.

"Inspector, I believe we're starting with a wrong impression," Valgerda's voice rang out soft and smooth. "We don't intend, in any way, to interfere with your assignment."

"Well, your actions indicate a strong interest in my detainee." Bruin toned down the roughness in his voice.

"True. We need to have a chat with Mr. Beyda."

Sargon's face froze, in apparent recognition of his last name. Magnus was still staring at him, like a starving cat drooling underneath the canary's cage.

"Of course." Bruin nodded. "You can talk to him upon our arrival at Horsens Pen. And, if I may add, with Mr. Beyda's consent and in the presence of his defense counselor."

Bruin's reply distracted Magnus from his prey. His look told Sargon he was not off the hook, but at least he could breathe easier for a few moments.

"Inspector Roby." Magnus held Bruin's black eyes long enough to have his full attention. Then, he dropped his gaze to the officer's badge on the inspector's chest. "Since you seem to be an expert in our rules of engagement, I'm sure you're familiar with the structure of our national security. Anything that falls under the jurisdiction of the Service, like terrorism in this case, takes precedence over daily routines of the local police."

"You don't have to remind me of my job, Special Agent." Bruin frowned and his voice resumed its earlier gruffness. "And of our work relationship with the Service. May I see a court order that allows you to interrogate my detainee?"

Magnus smiled politely and tapped his jacket's outside pockets, as if to remind himself where he had placed the court warrant. Finding what he was searching for, he produced a BlackBerry and handed it to Bruin, who stared bemused at the palm-size device. *They've started to hand out court orders electronically?*

"The judge's number is on speed dial." Magnus encouraged Bruin to pick up the phone.

Valgerda contributed a big smile to contribute to Bruin's persuasion. "All you've got to do is dial 7."

Bruin hesitated. *Are they bluffing or has Judge Handel really authorized this interrogation, illegal as it is?* Bruin turned to the driver, but he just shrugged.

"The judge has already given us the go ahead," Valgerda said, "but if you must check…"

Bruin looked at the BlackBerry again and sighed. *I don't think they're bluffing.* "Fine," he conceded with a grunt, "but only five minutes. And we're supervising the interrogation." Setting those terms translated into a small victory for Bruin. He did not want to appear beaten in front of his men.

* * *

Bruin stepped outside the van, followed by the driver. The two officers opened the doors and brought Sargon out. Bruin's head gesture ordered Sargon to walk in front of them. They stopped about thirty feet away from a white pickup, the only other car in the parking lot.

"Not here." Magnus shook his head and looked across *Gammel Århusvej,* the street separating the parking lot from park land alongside Lake Søndersø. "We'll talk by the water. More privacy."

Bruin shrugged and took Sargon by his arm, leading him to the curb. Magnus stepped closer and coughed, in order to attract Bruin's attention rather than to clear his throat. "Inspector, I'll take over from here. You'll supervise from a distance."

Bruin opened his mouth to protest against such an idea. He wanted to listen to the secret agents grilling of Sargon, not babysitting while they played in the park. But before he could utter a single word, Bruin realized their conversation had to remain secret. Magnus and Valgerda would use the judge or some other jurisdiction trick to force him into obedience.

"We'll bring him back in five," Valgerda said, following Magnus, who already was shoving Sargon ahead of him.

They cut through the green-yellowish lawns, where tiny tufts of grass were struggling for revival after the long winter. Rows of apple, lime, pear, and chestnut trees surrounded the low, grassy shore, where small waves broke gently with quiet splashes. A little farther, a solitary boat was lazily crossing the ice-cold waters.

"Mr. Beyda, take a seat," Magnus said in English, a language Sargon spoke with difficulty, while pointing at the bench by a narrow pathway. Valgerda stood to their left, observing the parking lot where Bruin paced impatiently by the police van. Magnus sat next to Sargon, leaning close to his ear. Bruin could not see any facial expression or body gestures, neither of the interrogator, nor of the detainee.

"How are things going, Sargon?" Magnus asked with genuine interest.

"Good," Sargon said, his face giving a hint he was lying. "You worried for me?"

"No, we're worried about your future."

Sargon snorted and cleaned a few imaginary specs of dust from his gray suit. "Where's my lawyer?" he asked after a brief pause.

"You don't need one."

"You recording my words?"

"No. Our business with you is secret. Top secret. No records. No witnesses." Magnus gestured with his head toward the parking lot.

Sargon nodded his understanding.

"You won't say a word to your lawyer or your family about our meeting. But we want you to talk to your friends about it."

Sargon frowned and snorted at the same time. "What friends?" he asked gruffly.

"Yildiz, your brother. Saleh, your best friend. Fatimah, the landlady." Magnus was counting their names using his right hand fingers. "Ibrahim, the explosive expert. Bill, the computer techie."

Sargon kept his long face, showing indifference, annoyance, and contempt. Still, Valgerda noticed a tiny crack in his defensive façade. Sargon's left eye twitched slightly before he could control it, and his right hand turned into a fist, even if for a brief moment. A seasoned psychologist, Valgerda was trained to spot, read, and interpret the slightest clues of body language. She decided to exploit her advantage and placed a hand on Magnus's shoulder.

"I know nothing and say nothing to you." Sargon raised his shoulders and feigned disinterest.

"That won't be necessary," Valgerda said after Magnus gestured with his eyes that it was her turn. "We just want you to listen, listen very carefully."

"Eh, OK."

"We know about the Århus cell. We have detailed information about your associates and your plans. During the trial, in case you're wondering, it wasn't necessary for us to reveal this information. First, because your friends would hear about it and go underground."

Sargon suppressed a tiny smile. He thought about placing a call to his brother as soon as he returned to Horsens, but then he remembered Valgerda asked him specifically to *talk* to his friends.

"Second," Valgerda continued, without missing Sargon's lips twitch, "we still need more evidence to frame your associates."

This time, Sargon did not conceal his smile. "Aha! I snitch nobody," he blurted with a quick snap of his fingers.

"We don't need a snitch," Valgerda replied. "And you'll not get a chance to tell anyone in Århus about our plan. They're all being arrested as we speak. All of them."

Another piece fell off Sargon's emotional façade. Valgerda caught his left eye squinting and his right foot tapping lightly on the grass.

"Our courts have found you guilty. Twice." Valgerda began hammering Sargon, driving her words as if they were nails. "If I know anything about our criminal laws, and trust me, I do have a law degree, you'll most likely be sentenced to life imprisonment. Do you know what that means?"

Sargon nodded with a deep frown. "I do," he mumbled, his mouth suddenly turning dry.

"Life in jail, that's what it means. No escape. Ever."

She was bending the truth to fit her goal. Convicted felons in Denmark were entitled to a pardon hearing after serving twelve years of their prison term. Depending on a number of factors, they could receive their pardon. Besides, Danish courts rendered life imprisonment verdicts so rarely they were more of an oddity rather than the accepted standard of justice.

"You'll never touch your wife, Lilith, again," Valgerda continued. "You'll rot in jail."

Sargon buried his head in his hands. Valgerda smiled at Magnus, passing him the torch.

"Listen up, Sargon," said Magnus, taking over. "We're prepared to give you a pardon. Then you and your wife will receive political asylum, and eventually, the Danish citizenship."

Sargon looked up. He did not have to spell out the words. His glowing eyes did all the talking. He was ready to accept their offer, whatever it was they wanted from him.

"We want you to organize your old gang, once everyone is transferred to Horsens. We've got a job for you."

Sargon leaned forward toward Magnus, as if doubting his ears. "A job?"

"Yes. A big one. Keep your friendships alive. Stay in shape. And no word to anyone."

"Why? What do you want us to do?"

"We'll give you the details later. For now, convince them you have a way out for everyone. A legit one. The only one. Got it?"

Sargon nodded.

"I can't hear your head shake," Magnus said.

"I got it. Keep mouth shut, eyes open."

"Good, very good."

Magnus's BlackBerry chirped and he glanced at the screen. "Take him back. I have to make a call," he said to Valgerda after reading the short text message. "Remember, Sargon," he added, "if I hear rumors about our little chat, none of your family will mourn at your funeral, because they'd all be already dead."

CHAPTER NINE

Copenhagen, Denmark
April 12, 7:10 p.m.

The bronze statue of the Little Mermaid, sitting on top of a large
rock pile, looked weary eyed at the Copenhagen harbor, as if
wondering whether it was worth trading her soul for a pair of human
legs. Valgerda stared at the statue for some time, thinking if the
unexpected summons to Gunter Madsen, the Assistant Director of
the Danish Defense Intelligence Service, would result in the same
regretful exchange. Magnus, who had also been staring, likely had
the same thought. Secrets for their souls.

The DDSI headquarters were situated at the Frederikshavn
Citadel, better known as the *Kastellet,* a pentagram-shaped castle, a
stone's throw from the Little Mermaid. The castle, still functioning
as a military base, stood in a man-made island, surrounded by wide,
water-filled moats and accessible only through two bridges. Magnus
parked next to a pier, and they walked to the *Ved Norgesporten,* the
northern gate, where they presented their badges to the guards.

The evening air was cool, and a soft breeze toyed with their
hair. Their boots cracked on the gray cobblestones of the narrow
pathways. They glanced in silence at the red brick two- and three-

story barracks and warehouses as they made their way to the DDSI offices.

* * *

"Welcome. My name is Yuliya Novikov. I'm the Director of Operations and a close associate of Mr. Madsen. I'll accompany you to his office."

As they exchanged their pleasantries in the vestibule filled with dark, antique furniture, Magnus noticed Yuliya had a slight trace of a foreign accent. *Is that Polish? Russian?* A small-statured woman, Yuliya was dressed in a charcoal suit and moved gracefully in her black stiletto shoes. She had no problem pushing the heavy bronze-colored door, which opened into a large oval office.

"Welcome, Ms. Hassing and Mr. Torbjorn."

The man who spoke these words stood up from behind a black mahogany desk. Over six feet tall and of average build, the clean-shaven bald man was younger than what Magnus had expected, perhaps in his early forties. The large room seemed to amplify his loud, baritone voice. His face was as clean-shaved as his bald head. His small black eyes, seemed to search not only Magnus's face, but also his heart.

"I'm glad you were able to come here at such short notice," Madsen said. He shook their hands and returned to his seat.

Magnus and Valgerda sat across from him, on two armchairs in front of the desk. Yuliya made her way to the last empty armchair, the one closest to a tall bookshelf.

"We've been looking forward to this meeting, Mr. Madsen," Magnus said.

"Gunter. Call me, Gunter. May I call you Magnus? And Valgerda?"

"Of course," Magnus replied.

Valgerda nodded.

Gunter reached for a small wooden box on his table and offered it to Magnus.

"Care for a smoke?"

Smoking in public places had been outlawed in Denmark in 2007, but the ban had forgotten to knock on Gunter's door.

Magnus and Valgerda declined his offer. Gunter shrugged his disappointment and helped himself to a fat cigar from a brown box on his desk. Toying with it for a few seconds, he rolled it between his fingers, feeling for soft spots. He brought the cigar to his face for a closer look.

"This is Isabella," he said, when satisfied the cigar passed his inspection with success. "Private reserve, just outside Havana. They only make a thousand boxes each year. I can afford to buy only ten."

Gunter reached over and picked up an item from his desk. The sharp blade of a cutter, a small gold-plated replica of the French guillotine, flashed, as Gunter beheaded the cigar. He brought it to his face again and took a deep sniff of the tobacco. He lit it, while rolling it and drawing on it, making sure the match's flame did not touch the end of the cigar. No words were spoken until the Assistant Director had enjoyed the first few puffs.

"Yes, a genuine beauty." Gunter described his smoking experience. "But I didn't call you here to talk about cigars. We could have had this conversation over the phone, but one cannot be too careful. At times, spies have been able to breach even our most secure lines of communication."

Magnus nodded.

"How's the COP mission coming along?" Gunter asked, without specifying from whom he expected an answer.

Magnus exchanged a look with Valgerda. The anticipation was clear in her eyes and Magnus gave her the go-ahead with a head tilt.

"The Convicts Operation Project is going fairly well, sir." Valgerda glanced briefly at the manila folder resting on her lap. "The first stage of recruitment is near completion, with the last men being added as we speak. Agents will soon begin the hands-on training of the cons, and, once the wargame's ready, the unit will be ready for deployment."

"Great. What's our current number?" Gunter asked, dragging on his cigar.

"We have almost two hundred recruits."

"What's the risk one of these cons you've selected may threaten the secrecy of our mission?"

"They're all convicted felons, doing time for crimes they've committed, and for which they were found guilty," Magnus replied. "We're fully aware we're dealing with criminals, willing and able to backstab us and switch sides at a moment's notice. The information we spoon-feed them is very, very limited, provided on a need to know basis only. None of the recruits are aware of the exact nature of their duties, the coordinates, and the time of landing, or even the name of the country that is their target. All they know is that someone in the Danish government is requiring their hit men services."

"That's good. Let's continue to keep their knowledge about our operation to a minimum," Gunter said. "Now, since information is power, let me inform you of a few changes to our initial plans. One of our Assistant Directors of Operations, who was going to lead this mission on the ground, has been held up in Karachi taking care of an urgent task. I have talked this matter over with your Director, Mr. Kjær, and he shares my views about the new Chief of Operations for the Arctic Wargame. Magnus, the job is yours."

Magnus's face was calm. He knew where Gunter was going as soon as the name of his supervisor came up in the conversation. Valgerda congratulated Magnus with a big smile and a light pat on his shoulders. But Magnus found his promotion unusual. The DDIS had no shortage of capable Directors or Assistant Directors. *Why didn't the director tell me about this before going on holidays? Something doesn't feel right.*

"You have a very good knowledge of the background and most of the details of this operation," Gunter said. "Yuliya will brief you on those few technicalities withheld from you because of jurisdictional divides. She'll work closely with you in finalizing the remaining elements of the wargame."

Yuliya tilted her head and smiled at Magnus and Valgerda.

"Do they suspect anything about our true intentions?" Magnus asked.

"They had no clue we even existed until a few days ago," Gunter replied.

Magnus leaned forward. "What happened?"

"Nothing to lose sleep over. Three days ago, someone at the CSE detected our two icebreakers delivering military supplies to our provisional depots on Ellesmere Island. The DND and the CIS have dispatched a recon team to the Arctic."

"That's very serious," Magnus said. His eyes narrowed and his voice grew deep.

"It did have the potential to turn into a serious problem," Gunter said. "But we have an ace in the hole. One of the DND employees, with strong connections to the CSE, was able to manipulate the satellite images, blurring them into useless blotches. The same person is a crucial part of this recon team. This person will do everything, I repeat everything, to stop the Canadians from knowing what we're brewing up in the High Arctic."

The revelation took Magnus and Valgerda by surprise. They exchanged a skeptical glance, while Gunter savored his triumphant moment behind a thick veil of smoke. Valgerda withheld a cough, but the smoke in the room was causing her breathing difficulties.

"The chances of the Canadians finding any evidence incriminating our *Siriuspatruljen* are so improbable one has a better luck surviving naked in the Arctic," Gunter said. "But our mission is too important to leave anything to chance."

Magnus nodded.

Gunter placed his elbows over the black folders scattered over his desk. He said, "The Canadians have much less sovereignty over the Arctic's barren lands than us. We even discovered and first explored some of those islands. And now Canada claims them as theirs simply because they forced some people to go and live up there? The Arctic belongs to us."

He drew on his cigar, which had begun to die out. A couple of deep puffs and the sparkles of the burning tobacco were alive once again. "Once climate change has melted half the Arctic ice over the next few years, our patrol vessels will escort the merchant ships through the Northwest Passage. That passage will end up being more lucrative than even the Panama Canal, raking in billions of dollars each year. And all of that will belong to us."

Gunter stopped long enough to take in another whiff of his cigar and blow a large cloud of gray smoke. "Once our advance troops, led by you," he pointed at Magnus, "succeed in completing this mission, then our Greenland Command will establish a permanent presence along the Northwest Passage." He gestured with his left hand to Yuliya to take over.

"Our teams are made up of mainly hardcore criminals, from suspected Al-Qaida cell members and former Taliban fighters to gang members and bank robbers," she said. "They'll get the job done for the sake of their freedom. And we're going to be right there as well, to monitor every step of their progress and to make sure things end up the right way."

"So, I take it you're going with us and the advance troops?" Valgerda asked Yuliya.

"Yes, I am."

"I want to review the report on the final preparations by Saturday morning. Then, our assault should begin on Monday morning," Gunter ordered. "That's when we've told the Canadians our 'wargame' is taking place. They think we're just passing through international waters, showcasing our rescue mission skills. The fools won't even know what hit them until it's too late."

"We'll have it ready, sir," Magnus replied.

Gunter smiled. "Great. I'm not wishing you luck in this mission because Vikings don't need luck."

Copenhagen, Denmark
April 12, 7:40 p.m.

"Excellent performance," Yuliya said, looking out the window. She followed Magnus and Valgerda as they rounded the corner. "It seemed very convincing."

"I'd like to talk to my wife now," Gunter asked in a quiet, tired voice.

"That's not possible. One phone call a day. And you called her this morning."

"Bullshit. I need to talk to her." Gunter slammed his fist on the desk.

"You know the rules." Yuliya turned around to face him. "I don't make them. I'm here simply to enforce them."

"It's been a month. An entire month that you have taken my wife and I—"

"Your wife is safe, and she'll continue to be safe, as long as you continue to cooperate with us. You understand?"

Gunter opened his mouth then shook his head and folded his arms across his chest.

"You understand that?" Yuliya asked.

"Yes," came the weak reply.

"Good. Now that we've settled who gives orders around here, let's talk about Magnus. Do you think he suspects anything?"

"I tried my best to convince him everything's in order. That we, the Danes, are the only one planning and carrying out this crazy operation."

"That's what the Canadians and everyone else has to believe. But first Magnus and Valgerda need to believe it too. And Magnus seemed unsure. He looked like he knew you weren't telling him the entire truth."

"Don't know what else I can do to convince him."

"I have to keep a close eye on him. You know he wasn't my choice to lead this operation."

"I'm sure you can make your objections known to your FSB boss," Gunter said with a smirk, referring to the Federal Security Service of Russia, the real Yuliya's employer.

Yuliya walked over to his desk. "The FSB in general and my boss in particular do not like objections." Her Russian accent became much more pronounced as she spoke with a certain unease. "They see them as threats."

Gunter shrugged. "It had to be an outside man. My close associates know me. They know it's not my character to manipulate the system and unleash a bunch of thugs into a friendly nation so they can ravage it. They know I wouldn't betray my country and my duty to protect it."

Yuliya leaned over very close to Gunter's face. "But that's exactly what you're doing, aren't you? You're throwing your country into a war. And all because of your love of a woman. What is her name? Hilda? Helga?"

Gunter took in a deep breath and looked away. He put his clenched fists down, away from Yuliya's face. Punching the smirk off her face would not bring him back his wife Helma. "Fucking Russians," Gunter mumbled through his teeth.

CHAPTER TEN

Cape Combermere
April 12, 11:35 a.m.

"Damn it, damn it, you evil witch," Carrie shouted, kicking a snowbank. Their helicopter became airborne, turned into a small black dot, and disappeared behind a heavy gray cloud. "I should have seen it coming, the little bi—" She bit her tongue.

"Don't worry," Anna said. "I pressed the beacon's rescue button before that backstabber took it away. The rescue team should already be on their way."

"I wouldn't count on it." Carrie drew closer to Anna as if she could not hear her words. "Your distress signal went to Trenton, down in Ontario, more than twelve hundred miles away. By the time the Army gets a team ready and fly 'em up here, we'll be frozen solid corpses. Damn you, Alisha!"

"Save your energies," Justin whispered, as he joined them.

"For what?" Carrie asked and spread her arms with an annoyed shrug. Anna's head sagged, and she stood silent, staring at Justin's face.

"She left us here, *alive.* That was her first mistake," Justin said. "Her second was not taking away our pickaxes."

"Oh, great, so we're gonna dig our own graves, right?" Anna blurted out.

"We found a radio," Justin continued, unfazed by Anna's cry of despair. "Maybe there's another radio that works or that we can make it work. Another flare gun or something else we can use to indicate our position and call in help. Maybe there's something we can use."

"Something like what? A chopper? An icebreaker? Look at where we are!" Anna shouted, stretching her arms and completing a slow pirouette. "In the middle of nowhere. No, scratch that. In the middle of frozen nowhere."

"Enough, OK." Justin walked over and held her by the arms. "We can give up and die or fight and survive. You take your pick. As for me and Carrie, we've already made our choice."

Carrie slammed into the ice with one of the pickaxes while Justin was still speaking. He turned around and grabbed the shovel.

"Fine," Anna agreed, but her shaky voice showed her desperation. "What do you want me to do?"

"Carrie and I can handle the digging. See if you can climb that cliff, the tall one." Justin pointed to their left, where the rocks had formed a steep slope, about fifty feet high. "We need to gather our bearings as to our exact location and find the fastest way out."

"I remember seeing a small inlet with a broken coastline to the east," Carrie said in between gasps.

"You think we can walk back to Grise Fiord?" Anna asked, as she headed for the rocky ridge.

"No, absolutely not," Justin replied without looking up, driving the shovel deep into the snow. "Too far away."

"So, what exactly am I looking for?" Anna shouted, while searching for a suitable ledge on the rock wall where she could plant her hands.

"You're looking for water," Justin replied. "Water that's not covered by ice floes."

* * *

The rugged surface of the cliff was extremely cold and slippery. The snow had turned into a thick layer of ice, covering the rocks in a wax-like film. Anna pushed her body up by digging shallow holes in the ice layer for her gloved hands and the tips of her boots. Already shivering and experiencing the familiar numbness in her extremities, she avoided pressing against the rocks to keep her clothes dry.

Her progress was slow and, at times, uncertain. Her strength was draining out of her body quite rapidly. Every inch she advanced upwards came at a hefty cost. She was losing precious body heat through the tiny droplets of sweat covering her face and her upper torso. She agonized over the chances of a timely rescue, her judgment when volunteering for such an assignment, and the doom looming over them, as she fought her way to the flat top of the cliff. *How long did that take? Was it fifteen, twenty minutes?*

Justin and Carrie were still busy, burrowing like moles. They had dug out a few piles of frozen snow and ice chunks, each about four feet high, and had uncovered a couple of large wood panels. They were thicker and wider than the other boards they had already found. *Those panels formed the wall structure of the depot, probably. Oh, only if they could find something useful.*

She looked to the east, squinting hard to discern anything else but the whitish blinding blanket covering her entire field of vision. A few miles to the southeast, she found a small hill, which was partially uncovered by the snow and the ice. It soared a few hundred feet high. A little further to the east, her eyes found a tiny strip of a dark blue color that surfaced out of nowhere, right at the bottom of the hill.

Anna muffled her screams of joy, unsure of whether she really spotted the water or whether the scene was an optical illusion or a trick of her hopeful imagination. Lifting her goggles for a clearer look and squinting so hard her eyes began to water, she double-checked again.

"Yes," she shouted, "that's water, clear water."

A small section of the ocean, without any deadly icebergs or flimsy ice floes, was only a mile away. *OK, I found the water, but how is the water going to help us?*

Copenhagen, Denmark
April 12: 8:20 p.m.

Yuliya nodded at the waiter holding a bottle of Lois Latour Bourgogne Rouge. He filled her crystal glass, and she took a quick sip of the pinot noir. She smiled at the great taste and looked at the shadows cast by the black iron sconces on the restaurant's red brick walls. The hushed voices of the dining patrons and the large white candles on every table added to the unmistakable ambiance of an ecclesiastic location.

In truth, the seven hundred year-old building used to be the Saint Gertrud Monastery during medieval times. Since 1985, the establishment began serving wine no longer as part of the Eucharist, but a la carte and at extravagant prices. Gradually, the Saint Gertrud Monastery became one of the most luxurious rendezvous in Copenhagen.

Tonight, Yuliya had reserved a table for two in the Confession Room and was awaiting the arrival of her diner date when her cellphone rang.

"Good evening, Ms. Novikov. I'm sorry to bother you, but there have been some negative developments," Alisha spoke slowly on her satellite phone.

"I thought the whole point of hiring you was to avoid any negative developments," Yuliya replied.

"I have everything under control," Alisha broke down her reply by separating and stressing each word. "I'm just updating the Command, as I've been instructed, on the most recent situation."

"I'm listening. Go on and update me."

111

"The Canadians discovered one of the depots set up by the *Siriuspatruljen.*"

"What?" Yuliya's hand trembled. A droplet of red wine trickled down the glass, staining the crispy white tablecloth. "How the hell did that happen?"

"Here's the condensed version. Some of the locals found and looted all the weapons and began selling them. Soon enough, word got around, and Justin heard about it. He tracked down two of the locals, and a member of his team killed them in a shootout. But one of the looters didn't die instantly, but was able to cough up the truth and led Justin to the depot, despite my constant stalling tactics. So, I had to come out in the open, and I left three members of the team, Justin included, stranded about one hundred and some miles northeast of Grise Fiord."

"You left them alive?" Yuliya struggled to keep her voice a quiet hush. She gulped down the contents of her glass. "What about the fourth member?"

"I needed someone to fly me back out of that freezing hellhole. Plus, it would be difficult for me to explain a bullet in their head if it ever came to—"

"Nobody will be asking questions once our plans succeed," Yuliya interrupted her. She snapped her fingers to call the waiter. The impolite gesture was out of place in the posh restaurant but in sync with her feelings.

"*If* it does succeed. One depot has been discovered and, who knows, the security of the others may have been compromised. The weapon depots were supposed to have been hidden exceptionally well."

"Are you having second thoughts?" Yuliya covered her cellphone with her hands and ordered another glass of wine. The waiter disappeared very quietly, in the same manner in which he had materialized at her table.

"No, but I have a few concerns about the implementation of your plan. We need to be even more careful, especially in light of these events."

"Do you have any actual suggestions?"

"Yes, I do. I will stall the RCMP investigation and the spreading of the news about the casualties in Grise Fiord and the lost members of the recon team. You need to speed up the planned landing. I suggest a change in the landing coordinates. Ellesmere Island is too hot for action. There's a very high probability of unnecessary exposure."

"I'll talk to the boss about it, but you know how much he hates last minute changes."

"In that case, let's not call this a change of plans, but an improvement to an already excellent plan. Nanisivik has a good airstrip and very few residents at this time of year. It will be a great place for landing your troops."

"Nanisivik? Isn't that on Baffin Island?"

"Yes, but still far away from civilization. Once you control both sides of the Northwest Passage, you'll practically be invincible."

"All right, I'll talk this over with the boss, and I'll inform you of his decision. Where will you be over the next two hours?"

"I'm going to spend the rest of the day in Arctic Bay. Once I know of the improvements to your plan, I'll adapt my travels accordingly."

"OK. Talk to you very soon."

Yuliya flipped her cellphone shut and looked up. Grigori Smirnov, her boss, entered the Confession Room. Smirnov was widely known as an oil tycoon. Very few people knew he was also a Deputy Director of Operations with the Federal Security Service of the Russian Federation. He marched with long steps toward her table at the end of the hall, paying extra attention not to disturb the other patrons or the hovering waiters.

"I have some bad news about our Arctic operation," Yuliya said, "but nothing that can't be fixed."

Smirnov frowned. "How bad?"

"One of our depots has been compromised, so we'll have to make some improvements to our initial plan. I'm afraid our transportation will have to be aerial, since the naval option, seemingly, is no longer on the table."

Smirnov's frown covered his entire forehead. He leaned forward and whispered to Yuliya, "Give me everything you have."

Arctic Bay, Canada
April 12, 13:35 p.m.

"Distress signal? What distress signal, Constable?" Alisha asked, her sweaty palms as slippery as the tone of her voice.

"One of the geologists in your team, Ms. Anna Worthley, initiated a dire emergency SOS signal this morning at 11:30 a.m.," Constable John Bylot of the Grise Fiord RCMP detachment said.

Alisha bit her lip.

"The MCC, that is the Mission Control Center in Trenton, received this signal, and they're preparing a rescue team," the constable said, "which should be dispatched... hmmm... as soon as the weather conditions improve, hopefully as early as tomorrow morning. Do you know anything about this incident?"

"Oh, yes, Constable Bylot, now that you mentioned the right word, incident, it was an incident. A mistake, I mean. Ms. Worthley accidentally pressed the button on her PLB while unloading her backpack and her personal effects." She bit her fingernails. *C'mon sucker, buy it.*

"A mistake you say," the constable replied. "The signal, according to the Canadian Forces Base in Trenton, came from Cape Combermere. The beacon transmitted for a few seconds and then disappeared."

"Shit," Alisha swore under her breath. *I should have kept the beacon going, but it would have pinpointed the chopper's location.*

"Yes, we deactivated the beacon, in order to interrupt the signal, since, like I said, it was a big mistake. We didn't want to bother the rescuers with a false alarm, you see?"

"Well, once the signal is emitted, the rescue team will have to go ahead with their mission."

"By all means, Constable. I'm not trying to stop anyone from doing their job. I'm just reassuring you and your colleagues that Ms. Worthley is safe and sound." Alisha stood up from her chair and looked out the small window of her hotel room.

"Oh, is that so?"

"Yes. We gathered our data and completed our trip. Everyone's doing well."

"Where are you right now?"

"Arctic Bay. Hunters and Trappers Lodge."

"May I talk to Mr. Hall?"

You don't believe me? Alisha reined in her thoughts. She stood up paced around the room barefoot. "Sure. As soon as he returns."

"Where did he go?"

"I think he went out with his friend, Kiawak," she said, staring at the bathroom door.

"Oh, yeah, Kiawak," John let out a quiet laugh. "He's got a couple of friends there, even a girlfriend I hear, although he'll never admit it."

"Really?"

"Oh, yeah. So, they'll be out for a while, I guess."

"They said something about coming back in the evening. But you can try Justin's cellphone, if you want." Alisha tapped the side of the table, where she had locked all personal belongings of her team members in two of the upper drawers.

"I may do that. I'll contact the Trenton Base and see if I can get the rescue mission cancelled, especially since they haven't dispatched it yet."

"OK, thanks," Alisha said.

"On another issue, my partner, Heidi, told me Kiawak is requesting that we wait for a while before we release the news about the deaths of Nuqatlak and Levinia. Strange, don't you think?"

"Well, I recall Kiawak talking about potential accomplices that the victims may have had relationships with. Releasing the news may damage further investigations."

"I understand. I will use ultimate discretion in this case."

"Thank you. Anything else, Constable?"

"No, that will be all. Thank you for your help, Ms. Gunn."

"It was a pleasure. If you need anything else, call me."

"I will. Good bye."

"Bye."

Before Alisha even closed her cellphone, a low vibration came from the drawer where she had placed Justin's phone. "Son of a bitch," she blurted. "That constable is a real pain in the ass."

She ignored the ring, which replaced the vibration, and looked outside the double-glazed window at the snowstorm. The walls and the roof of the one-story mobile structure squeaked and groaned under the whip of the blowing snow and the strong wind gusts. *So, my friends were able to ask for help by using a distress signal. And they did this under my own freaking nose! Stupid beacon! I wonder what else they're doing instead of freezing and dying. Stubborn little bastards! I should have shot them in the head.*

She cursed her choice and swore that if the weather did not kill them, she was going to make sure she finished her job with her own hands. She walked to the bathroom and kicked open its door. Kiawak lay on the floor, blindfolded and handcuffed to the bathroom radiator. Alisha removed his blindfold and checked his eyes. They were droopy, bloodshot, and narrow because of the injection she had administered to him twice in the last thirty minutes.

A small doze of the sodium-based sedative cocktail impaired the target's judgment, numbing his senses and instincts. Most importantly, it proved to be a reliable source of harvesting information from unwilling subjects. The substance destroyed all defense mechanisms in the victim's brain, releasing every true fact and detail stored in their memory.

"Kiawak, Kiawak," Alisha whispered next to his ear.

"Hhhh," Kiawak groaned, his head jerking left and right, and his eyes rolling up and down. "What? Who?"

"It's me, your grandma. How are you, my boy?"

"OK, OK, grandma, but it is cold, a little cold."

"Your girlfriend called earlier. She wants to see you."

"Tania? She's here?"

"No, she wants us to visit her. Can you tell me where she lives?"

"Eh... eh... I don't know."

"Please, Kiawak, where does she live?"

"OK, her house is the second from the..."

CHAPTER ELEVEN

Thule, Greenland
April 12, 2:30 p.m.

Domingo, one of the technicians on duty at Satellite Tracking Station Four, was returning from his coffee break. The only thing in common between the cafeteria's coffee and the Starbucks gourmet he used to enjoy back at his home in Seattle was the color. Two weeks into his new job as a Satellite Communications Assistant, one of a few dozen civilian contractors in the 821st Air Base Group in Thule, he was still suffering withdrawal from his preferred espresso dark roast.

"What's up, hombre?" Technical Sergeant Bryan greeted him, as soon as Domingo stepped inside the station's control room, a small, windowless cube. An array of cables snaked around two tables covered with electronic gadgets and notepads. He fought with them for a place to lay his paper cup, before stumbling into his chair.

"Crazy time to get this... this dark piss they call coffee. Anything interesting happen while I was gone?"

"Nope, nada." Bryan pointed at the monitor on his workstation that displayed data signals from satellite dishes mounted above the station. "As you can see, it's too cold even for Russian bears to roam outdoors."

Domingo gave the screen an indifferent glance. "Do you ever wonder what we're doing here?"

"Work. For a living."

"No, I mean, our troops here in the air base. The 12th Space Warning Squadron, the Security Forces Squadrons, these ballistic missiles all over the place, and a thousand or so people working like ants, day and night."

"Do you want me to repeat our patriotic mission statement?" Bryan sat straight up in his chair but did not bother to stand up. "Our mission here," he said, deepening his voice, "is to perform support for tracking and commanding operations of the United States of America and—"

"No, not that. I want Bryan's no-bullshit answer."

"All right then, since you're asking for it. But no complaining after I'm done, if the truth hurts."

"Give it to me straight, buddy."

"We live in the new oil rush era. We're literally sitting on a pot, no, millions of pots, barrels, of black gold. It's all about the oil, baby. We're here so Uncle Sam can claim it."

Bryan put his feet up on the corner of his table, ignoring a notepad whose pages began to crinkle under the heel of his boots and crossed his hands behind his head.

"That's it?"

"No complaining. I warned you."

"That's your *best* explanation?"

"Sorry, my poor dreamer from Seattle, but that's the only *logical* explanation. What else do you want me to tell you? The Russians are going to attack us? If they held back when that crazy Khrushchev was doing the Cold War dance, why would they start a war now, when they're not even half as powerful? Besides, you know how much defenses and satellites we have in place here? No? Well, let me tell you."

Bryan lowered his voice. "I've been here three years and I've seen every corner of the base. This place's a fortress. It was built in just three months in 1951 in total secrecy. The Blue Jay operation they called it. The base was built extremely fast but also exceptionally well. Some of the buildings, this one included, we still use today. At the peak of the Cold War, in 1961, this place had ten thousand people, ten thousand trained soldiers and airmen. Can you imagine all that? Jet fighters, icebreakers, a full army. We were ready to begin our assault against the Soviets and send enough bombers to blast Moscow like it was the apocalypse. The Kremlin would be pulverized before a comrade could ask, 'What the hell was that?'"

Domingo soaked up Bryan's explanation, acknowledging his attention with the occasional nod.

"On the other hand, our DEW, the Distant Early Warning system, had over seventy radar stations, communication centers, radio signal interception towers, the works. From Nome, Alaska in the west, and all the way to Thule, Greenland in the east, no snow goose could flap its wings without beeping its position on our radars. Regardless of the ongoing dismantling, we still have countless eyes in the sky, our stealthy satellites. So, what do you think?"

"Fascinating, but I still think we're here for a higher mission."

"Dude, the only thing high here is you." Brian deepened his voice again and dragged his words as he said, "You sure that's only coffee in your cup, and you didn't sweeten it up? Huh, you know what I mean?"

"You're hilarious, you know," Domingo replied with an annoyed groan.

"I thought you were acting stupid when you first asked your question."

"The one about what we're doing here?"

"Yeah, bro, yeah, that one," Bryan continued in his mocking voice.

"No, I'm really curious. I wonder if the Russians are ever going to make a move. If this is, as you say, the new oil rush, shouldn't they be here already, to beef up their claims?"

"Oh, the Russians are here, all right. There's always a submarine or two in international waters and sometimes in the Canadian waters. They're just like sharks, circling around their prey, waiting for the right moment to clamp shut their jaws. I've no idea when and if all hell will break loose, but I hope it's not on my watch. The thing is the Russians know it's a war they can't win. We'll kick their ass in the end, of course, but the blood cost will be so high, I don't think our generals we'll send us into battle. Unless, the Russians throw the first punch, but, like I said, that's unlikely."

"So, what about the oil then?"

"Oh, the Russians are trying their hand by launching all kinds of scientific expeditions, geological, topographical, measuring the continental shelf, and all that science bull. They're playing nice, for the time being."

Domingo reluctantly took a sip of his coffee, and his distorted face showed its bitter taste.

"If it's so bad, why do you keep drinking it?" Bryan asked.

Domingo swallowed his poison and opened his mouth to explain the long-term effects of caffeine withdrawal. But the phone ringing on Bryan's table took away his chance. Bryan rolled his eyes, waited until the third annoying buzz, and punched the hands-free button. "Yes, Dave, what can I do for you?"

"Bryan, what's the hold up there? You playing Solitaire?"

"Dave, step out of your cave, and into the digital age. Solitaire was hip in the eighties! Call of Duty, baby. It's all the thrill now."

Dave snorted. "Makes sense. The only weapons you'll ever shoot are in video games. In real life, you troubleshoot our network and fight viruses. That gets your blood pumping, doesn't it?"

"You got it, Dave. What's your trouble today? Can't find your computer's start button?"

Domingo grinned, suppressing his laughter. Technical Sergeant Dave Manning called them—or 'badgered' them, as Bryan considered the calls—every time he needed some assistance with the communication satellites of the base.

"I found the start button just fine. Thanks for your concern. We've noticed some movements earlier today over the coastline of southeast Ellesmere. Helicopter flights."

"Yeah, you didn't read the memo?"

"What memo?"

"The one about the Arctic wargame. Denmark's engaged in some High Arctic military maneuvers over the weekend and next week, depending on the weather conditions."

"Do you know what gear they're bringing?"

"A few planes, Lynx choppers, and two icebreakers. They may carry out a few missile tests overland. Nothing of interest to us, since we're not invited to their party. Too bad, 'cause it would have been lots of fun and a good break from this monotony."

"The chopper in question is not a Lynx, and it's flying over Canadian airspace."

"Maybe it's a Cormorant of the Canadian DND?" Bryan suggested.

"It can't be. Our radar imaging shows something of a smaller size, probably a civilian chopper."

"Isn't it too early for expeditions this year?"

"I don't know. There's always a crazy son of a—"

"All right, all right. I'll point one of our satellites in that area for close-up shots," Bryan said and tapped the mute button on the speakerphone. "Most likely it's nothing, but I'll do it, or he'll badger us all day," he said to Domingo, who shrugged with indifference.

"We last traced this chopper over Cape Combermere. We lost it soon afterwards because of a heavy overcast in the region."

"Cape Combermere? That's only one hundred and forty miles east, so it shouldn't be too difficult to get some images, if the chopper's still around."

"Bryan, I was thinking it would be a good idea to send in a drone."

"Why do you want a drone if I'm gonna get you the shots through the satellite?"

"In case the thick clouds don't let you get clear images."

"You'll have to run this by the commander. He's responsible for dispatching aircraft, whether they're remote controlled or not."

"I know, but I'll need your support, in case he asks for your opinion, which I'm sure he will."

"OK, I'll back you up on this, Dave, but only 'cause you're asking nicely, and I'm getting curious. The last two weeks have been so dull. A little excitement would make me feel alive again. What do you think, Domingo?"

"Whatever you say, boss," Domingo replied with a nod.

Cape Combermere, Canada
April 12, 1:10 p.m.

It was quite an exaggeration to call the two wooden pieces secured together with polyester fabric paddles. Still, at the bow of the raft, Justin rowed as fast as possible, careful not to splash Carrie and Anna sitting at the stern and sculling through the icy waters. The only useful objects salvaged from the Danish depot were a few logs and wooden boards, in addition to an abundance of tent liners. Justin and Carrie had built a makeshift raft, barely buoyant, but sufficiently stable to carry the weight of the crew. Steered by their determination and helped by the current, they were flowing southbound, about one hundred and fifty feet from the closest ice floes.

"Push away from the ice, quick," Justin said, moving his paddle to the left and pulling hard on it.

"Careful, easy," Carrie said, counterbalancing Justin's swing by leaning to her right.

They avoided the collision with a large piece of drift ice. The waters were open, unlike a few miles farther back, when the narrow leads in the ice floes meandered in sharp curves. They had seen two icebergs so far, fairly small and a few hundred feet away. The raft was holding up against the fast moving current and the occasional high wave. Still, their rafting downstream was not without problems.

Justin had dipped his hands a few times in the ocean by mistake and was suffering from the bitter bite of the frigid waters, in addition to the general numbness in his hands and feet. Anna could hardly control her shivers.

"How long... how long has it been?" Anna's voice was controlled by her jolts.

"About an hour or so," Justin guessed. "I'm sure we have done several miles. The current is carrying us south pretty fast."

"So... how much... how much longer do we still have?" Anna asked.

"A little more," Justin replied. "Just a little more."

"We may need to stop soon for a short break," Carrie said.

"That may not be wise."

"I know, Justin, but it may be necessary."

"I don't see how, since we'll not be any warmer on the ground."

"We can make a snow shelter."

"No, we can't waste time. Things won't get better if we make a shelter, and it's only gonna get colder as the night falls. We have no food. Our only hope is to paddle."

"Paddle to where?" Carrie drove her paddle into the water and pulled it towards her with a long, powerful stroke.

Anna coughed a wheezing gasp and fought to keep her fingers wrapped around the end of her paddle.

"South. Toward people. Toward safety."

"Really? You really think we can make it?"

"Yes, Carrie. We've got to hope, OK? We've come so far. We can't give up now. We've got to keep trying."

"Let's stop for a break. Just ten, fifteen minutes."

"No, we can't. It will be difficult to anchor the raft on the fractured floes. In the water, we're out in the open and more visible than if hiding in a shelter."

"Visible? You really think someone is actually going to rescue us?"

"Justin, can we stop, please?" Anna whispered, tilting her head to the left.

"How about we go on for another half an hour or so?" Justin asked.

"I guess... I feel kind of warm now, so... yes, we can continue," Anna replied.

"No," Carrie said and leaned over to Justin. "She's sinking deeper into hypothermia," Carrie whispered in his ear. "We may lose her. We need to stop. Now!"

"Hey, look at the bird, a cute little bird," Anna said playfully, pointing straight ahead.

"Maybe it's already too late," Carrie muttered, shaking her head. "What bird, Anna?"

"There... oh," she whimpered. "It's already gone. But where did it go? It was right there, right there in front of us, just, just two seconds ago."

"Keep paddling, Carrie," Justin said.

"Shhhhh," she said. "What's that noise?"

"Noise? What noise?" Justin asked. "I can't hear anything."

"The buzz, the electronic buzz," Carrie insisted. "There, look there." She pointed high above her head.

Justin peered into the sky and saw nothing but endless gray clouds. "Carrie, it's going to be OK," he said. "I'll take care of you and—"

"No, I'm not going crazy," Carrie shouted. "Right there, at two o'clock. The bird Anna saw a minute earlier, it's probably the same bird."

Justin's eyes caught a quick glimpse of the bird, hovering at roughly fifty feet to their right and maybe fifteen feet over the ocean's surface. It resembled a grayish-white fulmar, and it was about the same size as the gull-like bird. Its wingspan was about four feet, but there was no wingbeat. The bird simply glided in midair, as if riding an updraft.

Suddenly the bird screeched a loud, electronic beep. It fluttered in small circles over their heads with uneven motions. At some point, it stood still, before dropping a few feet, quite mechanically as if someone was pulling it with an invisible string. Justin wondered for a brief moment, unsure if hypothermia was playing a trick on him. Then, he noticed the bright green eyes of the bird blinking twice. *That's not a fulmar, it's a machine. It's a drone.*

"That's a drone," he shouted.

"A what?" Anna asked. A quiver shot through her body.

"A machine," Carrie said. "The bird you saw is an aircraft without a pilot."

"So, is that… is that our rescue?" A faint glint of hope marked Anna's trembling voice.

"The airplane will transmit our coordinates to whoever sent it, and rescue will be on its way," Carrie replied.

"Great, it will be nice… to be safe… and warm," Anna mumbled.

The drone disappeared into the clouds abruptly, as when they first noticed it.

"Maybe we should wait for the rescue team onshore," Carrie suggested. "Since they have our current position, it's not wise to drift further south."

"Good idea." Justin nodded. "Let's look for a landing spot."

He scanned the ice floes for a flat area, away from the water current. A small inlet would have been the ideal choice. But this part of the coastline offered nothing of the kind. The edges of the ice floes were tall and sharp. Small sections of drift ice made their landing attempts even more difficult.

"Push to the left, harder," Justin encouraged them.

The raft gained a few precious feet, but the current dragged it further than their intended dock. They were forced to swerve around a chunk of drift ice.

"There, that's a good place." Justin pointed at the spot where two ice floes had collided, pushing over and under each other, forming a finger rafting. The ice sloped gently into the water, and it was clear of any loose debris. Carrie clenched her teeth and held a tight grip on her paddle. In quick, short strokes, she doubled her rowing. The raft moved closer to the shore.

"Careful, the current's stronger here," Justin shouted.

His warning came one second too late. The waves carried Anna's paddle away.

"Carrie, one last good paddle," Justin said. "One more time."

She flexed her shoulder muscles and biceps, jolting the raft to the right. Eight more feet and they could anchor their raft to the ice shore. Justin kept paddling furiously, realizing he was testing the limit of his strength and the balance of their raft.

"Huh," he panted, feeling a burning sensation between his first two ribs. The end of the paddle had slammed against his chest.

The pain tolled the bells of panic in his brain. This was their last chance to step ashore; otherwise, the current would drag them to the open ocean. Justin took a deep breath and paddled faster and harder than the entire trip. He smiled to himself, surprised by this unexpected strength, as well as the hoped-for result. The bow of the raft rubbed against the ice floe but Justin did not stop driving the paddle into the water until half of the raft was on the shore. He helped Carrie drag Anna's unconscious body away from the slippery edge of the ice. Then he fell on his knees, praying for the quick arrival of the rescue team.

CHAPTER TWELVE

Søndre Strømfjord, Greenland
April 13, 5:10 p.m.

The discovery of the Sirius Patrol weapons cache in Cape Combermere highlighted the urgency of the wargame. Gunter did not like the rush. It increased the risk of the entire operation being discovered by his close associates. But his hands were tied. The Russians were pressing hard.

The FSB wanted immediate concrete results, and Gunter had no other option but to follow their orders. He pulled in all favors, made promises he could not keep, threats he could not carry out, all for the purpose of pleasing his wife's kidnappers. He was in constant agony over any exposure, as the circle of senior officials to whom he was lying grew by the hour.

Finally, the platoons' aerial transport was authorized and the two-stage Arctic Wargame began. At exactly 1:00 p.m. local time, three C-130J Super Hercules airplanes, part of the Squadron 721 of the Royal Danish Air Force, took off from their Transport Wing center in Aalborg, Denmark. True to their motto *"Ubicumque, Quandocumque"*—Anywhere, Anytime—the pilots of the Squadron 721 completed their trip on time and without any problems. The Air Force Command Post barracks in Søndre Strømfjord became the temporary stopover for the contingent force, while Gunter awaited FSB orders about the second stage of the operation.

Søndre Strømfjord, situated at less than one hundred and twenty miles inland—at the head of the fjord by the same name—offered easy access to Davis Strait separating Greenland from Canada's Baffin Island. At its narrowest point, the strait was one hundred and eighty miles wide.

Gunter was confident Alisha was taking care of sabotaging the Canadian surveillance. But there was a certain amount of danger in being detected by the United States spy satellites. At more than seven hundred miles southeast of the 821st US Air Base Group in Thule, and tucked away between impenetrable mountains, Søndre Strømfjord stood at a supposedly safe distance from the US prying eyes in the skies. But Gunter's troops would become vulnerable to radar detection during their short flight. He could only hope their Hercules airplanes would go unnoticed.

* * *

Magnus glanced at the snow-covered fields and the Tarajornitsut Mountain ridges in the distance. At the main command post—a revamped, whitewashed military barrack—he was assigned a small office, with small windows, but large desks and comfortable chairs. Valgerda was typing a status report on her laptop, while he paced back and forth, the constant thuds of his boots interrupting her concentration.

"You're still thinking about Gunter's choice, aren't you?" she asked without looking up.

"I can't help it."

Valgerda sighed. "We went over this. Twice. He thinks you're the right choice to lead this op and so do I."

"OK, so why is he sending us a babysitter? I heard he may take over the operation himself. Something's up. He doesn't trust us?"

"Gunter's a control freak." Valgerda stood up and walked toward Magnus. She placed her hand on his shoulder. "He trusts you. He just wants to make sure nothing goes wrong."

"Nothing will go wrong."

"I know, I know. We've done such ops many a time. But we've never worked with Gunter before this mission. And trust only goes so far in our business."

Magnus's BlackBerry began playing the first notes of Beethoven's Fifth Symphony. He walked over to his desk. "It's her," he said after a quick glance at the smartphone's screen.

Valgerda sat on the other side of the desk. Magnus picked up the phone. "Hello, Yuliya," he said.

She replied in a pleasant voice, "Hi, Magnus. How was your trip?"

"It was great. Has Gunter made a decision yet?"

"He's still talking to senior officials as we speak. It seems very likely they'll agree to an air operation."

"I'm glad to hear that. The information provided by your agent in the Canadian Army, has it been confirmed by other sources?"

Yuliya's voice turned cold. "Negative, Magnus. We don't have another source. The area's too hot, and there's no time to develop another asset. We trust our agent and her information. Did you encounter any difficulties at the base?"

"Not at all. The folks here didn't exactly roll out the welcome wagon but also didn't lock us up. Is there any change to our 'standstill' orders?" Magnus glanced at Valgerda, placed his BlackBerry back on the table, and put Yuliya on the speakerphone.

"That's correct. Maintain your positions and make sure our pack of dogs is behaving decently."

Magnus smiled.

"They are," Valgerda replied.

"Oh, hi, Valgerda," Yuliya said. "I didn't know you were listening in. That's great. I'll be on the next plane, and I should land shortly after midnight. Call me right away if there's anything new. Anything else?"

Magnus swallowed. He was afraid of the answer, but he could hold back the question haunting him all along. "Is Gunter coming here?"

Yuliya hesitated for a second. Magnus crossed his fingers and muttered a silent wish.

"Gunter and I will be on the same plane."

Her words cut deep, but Magnus held his cool. His throat and his lips became suddenly dry.

"There's... there's nothing else," he said.

Valgerda shook her head.

"OK, see you tomorrow."

"Bye," said Valgerda.

"Rumors fucking confirmed," Magnus blurted after turning off his phone. "The big wig is coming to hold my hand."

"It could have been much worse if the wargame was cancelled all together," Valgerda replied with a sad look in her eyes.

"I don't know which one is worse: sitting here doing nothing or fighting a battle out there with Gunter's strings around my neck."

"It's not like that. He'll realize soon enough he can trust you completely."

Magnus said. "I hate delays and hesitations."

"Tomorrow morning, hopefully, we'll be good to go. We can take a few hours to relax before that. I last checked on our recruits about half an hour ago, and I'll make another round in a couple of hours. The barracks' west wing is completely secured and perfectly isolated from the rest of the complex. I don't anticipate any problems overnight."

"Have you double-checked their surveillance bracelets?"

Valgerda nodded. "I have. They're all fully functional. I installed the monitoring software on my laptop, and I've transferred all data from our office network. We know the exact location of each and every recruit at all times."

Magnus stood up and walked to the window. He squinted, his eyes staring at the sun, barely visible over a high ridge at the end of the horizon. He guessed there were a few good hours of light before the fiery disk burned out for the day.

"I'll take your advice and try to relax," he said, still looking at the sun. "Tomorrow, we'll have no time."

Thule, Greenland
April 13, 1:40 p.m.

The angel had gray-blue eyes like Carrie, but black hair like Anna. The musical voice of this heavenly creature whispered sweet words into Justin's ears. Her warm, soft hands began massaging his forehead, slowly and gently, in such a delightful way he felt his entire body responding with a soothing feeling of deep relaxation. Justin stretched his legs, enjoying the coziness of the fresh sheets, the warm blanket, and the overall comfort of his soft bed. His pillow felt much smoother than the ice where he recalled resting his head the last time he fell asleep.

The ice! The ice floe!

As he began remembering the ice floe, Justin's memory started the unpleasant and irreversible vortex. The angel's face became blurry, the pampering stopped, and the sweet voice disappeared. The image faded quickly, its pieces falling as if from a jigsaw puzzle. When he opened his eyes, all he could see was a white wall. His entire body felt a constant chilling pain.

"Welcome back, Mr. Hall."

There's nothing angelic in his voice. Oh, what a dream. Justin sighed. Then, he smiled. *At least they brought me out of the freezing cold. But where did they take me? Who are they?*

"I see this is some kind of a hospital and you're a nurse," Justin spoke softly to the young man in scrubs.

He was lying on a bed, in an emergency room, connected by a wire to a cardiac monitor. A couple of gel pads were placed on his left arm. Intravenous lines were attached to his hands. Two metallic shelves, stashed with a variety of medical boxes and bottles, were lined up along the other wall. "Where is this place?" Justin asked.

Before the nurse could answer, he glanced beyond the glass door and noticed a Stars and Stripes flag on a mast in the hall. "That's the American flag. Are we... is this the United States?"

"Technically speaking." The nurse replied. "We're in a territory under the jurisdiction of the US. The US military, to be exact."

"The military? And where is this territory?"

"We're at the air base in Thule, Greenland," the nurse replied. "How are you feeling?"

"OK. I feel like I have a hangover. My entire body aches, especially the joints."

The nurse nodded. "That's normal. You're recovering from frostbite. I'll let your regain your strength. I'll be back in an hour or so." The nurse headed for the door.

"Wait a second. How did I get here? Where are Carrie and Anna?"

"That's the rest of your crew, I imagine." The nurse turned around. "You were rescued on the coast of Ellesmere, somewhere south of Cape Combermere. Everyone is doing well. Relatively well, considering your body temperature had dropped to ninety-three degrees when our rescue team found you. We stabilized everyone in the medical chopper before the flight back.

"When you got here, our only option was to perform active and passive core rewarming procedures. I'll save you the medical lingo, but all I'm saying is that you were almost dead, but now you're no longer in danger."

Justin lifted his arms to look at his hands, carefully not to detach the intravenous tubes. He disturbed the injection site on his left arm and winced in pain. The catheter's sharp bevel pierced his skin.

"Stop. Don't do that." The nurse reached for Justin's hand and rearranged the catheter and the tubing.

"Sorry, I didn't mean to. I was just checking for frostbite blisters."

"There are none. Hypothermia seems to have left no physical scars on your body. The same is true for your friends. No hemorrhagic blisters, no dead tissue, no permanent damage to your skin or muscles. I guess you're a lucky crew. A few days of rest and, if there are no complications, you should be on your way. However, not before talking to our commander. I don't guarantee you'll come out without any psychological scars after *his* interrogation."

CHAPTER THIRTEEN

Thule, Greenland
April 13, 5:30 p.m.

Colonel Richard Clark was the commander of the 821st Air Base Group at Thule. The man in charge of the entire base, who had ordered the rescue mission, and saved the lives of Justin's team. The commander's receding hairline had spared a few bushy, white patches around his large ears. His crisp navy blue uniform, white shirt, and matching blue tie indicated his utmost attention to detail. When Justin had asked earlier, the nurse had described the man with a few words, concealing the fact that his short stature matched perfectly his short patience.

"I'm glad to see you're doing well," the commander said. His deep voice was warm, and his black eyes displayed a real concern about Justin's condition. "The doctors have done a great job."

"Thank you, Commander, for everything you've done." Justin rearranged the pillows behind his back. He adjusted the angle of the bed frame, in order to sit up straight when talking to the commander.

"Can you tell me what was it you were doing in the middle of the ocean?"

Justin had anticipated the question, fearing the commander would be able to see through his well-planned lies. As a CIS operative, he could disclose neither his profession, nor the nature of his Arctic mission.

"Our boat capsized and became useless. So we scrambled to build a raft." Justin worded his reply brief and kept it vague, tricks he had learned since the early days of the CIS training.

"Uh-huh," the Commander said and squinted, as if checking the truthfulness of Justin's words by studying his facial expression. "And you were sailing the High Arctic for what purpose?"

Justin swallowed before replying. "We were collecting data on a research project, Commander."

"I see. And whom do you work for?"

"I'm with the CRI, that's the Canadian Research Institute, out of Ottawa." One of the front organizations the CIS used for cover operations.

"So, you're scientists, you and your colleagues?"

"Yes, we're geologists."

He paused to think about Justin's reply. "And you were gathering data on…"

"Our project is related to… hmm… the study of ice thickness and its melting rate over the last year."

"Oh, I see."

The commander's eyes continued to search Justin's face for any hints of pretense. Justin wondered why he was taking so long to call his bluff. The odds of Carrie and Anna concocting the same exact tall tale were slimmer than being struck by lightning in a submarine.

"I don't believe I asked you for your name." The commander began pacing at the end of Justin's bed.

I hope he's not starting the interrogation from the beginning.

"My name is Justin Hall."

"What was the purpose of your mission to Ellesmere Island?"

Justin blinked and did a double take. *That's exactly where he's going, back to the beginning.*

"I told you, Commander, we were gathering information on our research project on—"

"Geological ice thickness. I heard you lie to me once," the commander interrupted him. He leaning over Justin's bed, drawing closer to his face. He was so close Justin noticed a thick blood vein pulsating on the commander's right temple.

Justin flinched. In a flash, he was back in his Libyan prison cell, the interrogator's hands clamped around his throat.

The commander's voice erupting in a stern roar brought Justin back to reality. "Here, I'm measuring the thickness of your bullshit."

"Huh, what?" Justin spread his hands, his face feigning utter confusion. "I don't understand, sir."

"I took the same crap from your associates. They fed me the same lies about your boat crashing or sinking or capsizing, while three helpless geologists or meteorologists were working their asses off collecting data on ice thickness or weather patterns, depending on which one I chose to believe."

Justin shrugged in silence. He decided to make a last-ditch effort to cover up the truth. "We struck a piece of drift ice and that's why our boat—"

The commander cut him short. "Enough with this crap! Your story doesn't add up. It doesn't explain the fact that your clothes were dry when my men found you, and why there were no IDs on any of your crew members. No radios, no PLBs, no satphones, nothing. It looks like someone robbed you and left you to die."

Justin took a deep breath before opening his mouth, but the commander held up his right hand as he stood tall again. "I'm not finished. I don't know many geologists or meteo-whatever-logists who from scrap can build a fully functional raft, manage to keep it afloat in ice-infested waters, at seventy-seven degrees North latitude, and guide their team to safety until rescue arrives. I don't know about in Canada, but, back home, we have a name for such folks. We call them 'special agents.'"

Justin tried to voice his objection, but the commander shook his head. He asked, "Are you Canadian, Justin?"

"Yes, and let me explain—"

"Are you a Canadian secret agent?"

"No, I'm not a secret agent."

"Don't lie to me!"

Justin drew in a quick breath. "Sir, if what you're saying is true," he said quietly, "about the odds of simple geologists surviving an Arctic shipwreck then you know I can't admit anything to people without a security clearance."

A tense silence hung in the small room. For a moment, Justin found it hard to breathe, as if all oxygen had been pumped out of his lungs. A nurse knocked on the glass door and made her way in, dragging a meal delivery cart. She sensed the tension and looked at the commander for instructions.

"Leave!" he ordered her with a dismissive glare.

The nurse pushed away her cart.

The commander said after waiting until the nurse slid back the glass door, "you can't tell me who you are or what you were doing freezing to death. Can you give me anything about your situation?"

The moment of truth, but not of the entire truth.

"We're in grave danger, Commander." He chose his words carefully and pronounced them in a friendly tone. "And we desperately need your immediate help."

The commander's thick eyebrows arched back. He asked, "Who is we? What grave danger? Can you be more specific?"

"Canada... and the Unites States. The immediate threat comes from Danish troops—"

"Danish? Seriously?" the commander burst out in a good-spirited laughter.

"Yes, Commander, I'm not joking. I'm talking about Danish troops. We've always waved them off as a little more than a political pain in the butt. But they have the capacity of launching a military attack against Canada, and they've already started their attack."

Seriousness returned to the Commander's face. "Do you have any evidence to back up your allegations?" he asked. "Are you aware that my air base is on Danish soil, and three Danish senior officials are a crucial part of my staff? I can't allow you to drag their good reputation through the mud."

"That's not at all my intention, sir. With all due respect, I don't think those officers would know anything about these plans."

"Lieutenant Colonel Eichmann with the Royal Danish Air Force is not a simple officer."

"It doesn't matter, Commander. I believe the Danish operation is top secret. Very few people would know about it."

The other man folded his arms across his chest. "Let me ask you again, Justin, what is your evidence?"

"The raft. We built the raft out of logs found in the debris of a Danish depot. The *Siriuspatruljen*, which store supplies and—"

"I've met a few of the *Siriuspatruljen* brave men, and I know about their excellent job. What were they doing on Ellesmere Island, if that's what you're insinuating?"

"We found a military radio and other rubble, which assert that Danish troops have, at the very least, violated the Canadian sovereignty, by setting foot in our land without authorization."

"Where is this alleged radio? Or did you lose it when your boat tipped over?"

Justin sighed and bit his tongue. He could not tell the commander how Alisha had backstabbed them. It would raise more questions and doubts on the commander's already skeptical mind. "I don't have the radio any longer, Commander."

"So, let me clarify this: All you have is a far-fetched story about a disappearing military radio, on which you base a mountain of crazy accusations. You know what I have? I have three uninvited and unwanted guests, who require extensive and expensive medical attention, lengthy reports and explanations to my superiors and to the Canadian authorities about my search and rescue, and this nonsense about an invasion from Denmark, of all places."

Justin decided to reveal another piece of information, in an attempt to persuade the commander. "We've found a lot of weapons.

Danish machine guns, *Let Støttevåbens*. They're planning an attack against Canada. I'm absolutely sure about this."

"Now the plot is getting thicker. Let me guess the answer to my own question, you don't have any of these guns, do you?"

Justin heaved a sigh of defeat. "They... hmm... I know where they are."

"Did you find these machine guns in the depot?"

"No, but witnesses have confirmed the origin of the weapons, which is Denmark, the Royal Danish Army."

"Are these witnesses available for questioning, and will they corroborate your story?"

"No," Justin said, shaking his head. "I'm afraid they're not."

"No? Why not? Have you *lost* them too?" The scorn was very clear in the commander's voice.

"The witnesses are gone. They're dead."

"You know, Justin, you would make a great storyteller. You're just making up this entire story to distract me from whatever you and your associates were cooking up in Ellesmere, aren't you?"

"No, no, of course not. You've got to believe me. This is real. It's all true. The Danish are not stupid. They wouldn't start an all-out war. Difficult to keep that a secret. The probability of being detected by the Canadians or the Americans is reduced to a minimum if the Danish Army is planning a single and isolated attack."

"So, why are we bothered if this is only one man, albeit a strong man?"

The scorn burned him, but Justin brushed it away. "I'm not saying we're facing a one-man team, but the size of the Danish attack may be considerably smaller than we anticipate. Something that will not draw attention to itself and will not look like a movement of troops ready for war. Something that looks legit. Canada's Arctic territory is sparsely populated, and these areas are very isolated and very remote. A few hundred men, properly trained and equipped, can take over strategic positions in the blink of an eye."

The commander shook his head. "That's none of my concern, Justin. I've already done more than enough." He began walking toward the door.

"You're involved in this matter now, and you know as much as I do," Justin said. "I need your help with this."

"The doctor tells me you should be healthy enough to fly in a couple of days. My staff will make arrangements to take you and your associates south, first to Søndre Strømfjord, and, from there, to Ottawa. Your government or agency, whatever it is, can take over this crazy situation of yours."

"Commander, you're going to leave and do nothing with the information I gave you?"

The commander turned around. He stepped closer to Justin's bed, raised his right hand, and pointed it at Justin's face. A moment later, he shrugged and produced a big smile. "You know what?" he said with a grin. "You almost pulled me back into this useless argument. I've already lost a lot of precious time. Good bye, Justin."

"In that case, I need to make a few phone calls. And I need to talk to Carrie and Anna."

"What do you think this is, the Sheraton?" the commander replied without bothering to look back. Instead, he tapped on the glass door. A tall man in a military uniform appeared and stood at attention. "Sergeant Brown, make sure this patient doesn't go anywhere without an escort."

"Yes, sir. I will, sir."

The man's strong voice, his broad frame, and vigilant eyes were clear hints to Justin about his chances of sliding through the glass door undetected.

* * *

Five minutes later, the same nurse the commander had thrown out of Justin's room wheeled in the meal cart.

"You hungry?" she asked.

141

Justin nodded and the nurse, whose lab coat nametag read "Moore", gave him his dinner. Grilled chicken parmesan, vegetable broth, and canned nectarines. Everything was served in white plastic tableware. A set of utensils—spoon, fork and knife—also white plastic, were wrapped in a red, white and blue napkin.

Justin closed his eyes and frowned, as he chewed on the first bite of the cold chicken breast. *Great. Once I'm finished with the soup, I can use the spoon to dig myself a tunnel out of this place.*

CHAPTER FOURTEEN

Thule, Greenland
April 13, 6:00 p.m.

Emily Moore was a young nurse who also served meals to patients recovering in the intensive care unit since the air base hospital employed a small staff. At the same time, she was a sergeant with the Seventh Flight of the 821st Support Squadron, which was responsible for the medical care of the air base personnel. Emily's pink lips, although adorable, were sealed tight. Justin tried to charm her into telling him the location of Carrie's and Anna's room or slipping him a cellphone for a quick phone call. She did reward him with bright smiles, hushed giggles, and a definite no.

Moving on to Plan B. Make a weapon out of anything you can find in the room. He began to look around, while Emily copied in her notepad a bit of data from the cardiac monitor. In a matter of seconds, Justin was forced to scrape his idea. The door opened and two uniformed men, followed by Sergeant Brown, barged in. They exchanged a few whispers with Emily, and, after her nods, they proceeded to remove every piece of equipment that could be used to even remotely facilitate an escape. Emily detached Justin's intravenous lines and cardiac monitor wires, and the officers wheeled out the machine, the liquid medicine dispenser, as well as the defibrillator. They emptied the metallic shelves of all sharp objects, glass bottles, and boxes of syringes. The commander had anticipated Justin's armed rebellion and had decided to deal a strong pre-emptive strike.

After Emily was gone, Justin convinced Sergeant Brown to allow him to use the washroom. It was two doors down from his emergency room. This was the first time Justin ventured out in the hospital hall.

The short reconnaissance mission produced a few useful results. Shuffling his feet as slow as possible, he located the fire exit at the far end of the hall. He identified another possible escape route, the elevator next to the washrooms.

A quick sweep of the three bathroom stalls yielded nothing useful. *Unless I attack Sergeant Brown with a roll of toilet paper, there's not much to work with in here.* The door leading to the janitors' closet, adjacent to the washroom, was locked. His three attempts at prying it open were unsuccessful. Disappointed, he stumbled back to his room, under the scolding glance of his escort.

Justin paced around his bed to stretch his legs and also to energize his thought process. The emergency room had no windows. The door was going to be his exit point. *I have to figure out how to get past the guard, but first I need to find out where they're holding Carrie and Anna. I need to get out of this room, but this time, for much longer. But with what excuse?*

He stopped pacing and glanced at the bare walls. His gaze wandered from the floor to the ceiling and found his dinner leftovers on the plastic tray at the end of his bed. He walked over to the tray and dumped its contents in the garbage can. But he saved the unused plastic knife. *It's not much, but maybe I can find a use for it.*

When Emily returned for a routine checkup and to retrieve his meal tray, Justin complained of severe chest pain. Emily took a closer look at his eyes and his face for any signs of foul play, but his expression showed real signs of acute pain. She agreed to inform a doctor about his new condition but not before completing a preliminary examination.

Justin coughed and winced while Emily listened to his chest and his back. Her conclusion was that there was nothing wrong with him. Insisting he may suffer from internal bleeding, as the pain stabbed from inside his chest, Justin scored a small victory. Emily agreed to arrange for an x-ray exam. Unfortunately for Justin, it was going to take some time.

* * *

Justin decided the best way to use that time was to fine-tune his escape plan, which was a little more than an idea. He did not blame the commander for refusing to lift a finger and give them with any help. The case against the Danes, from the commander's perspective point of view, was pure speculation. *I wouldn't help someone in my shoes either. First, I need to find Carrie and Anna. They shouldn't be far away, since we all suffered frostbite, and Anna was in the worst condition. But how do I fake the need further medical attention if I can't find them this time? I don't even have any frostbite marks on my hands or feet.*

He stretched his legs, and his knee made a popping sound.

"Voila!" he exclaimed with a big smile and snapped his fingers. *A wheelchair! I'll complain of leg pain, and Emily will have to get me a wheelchair. It will slow me down and give me extra time to look around. It will also give me a reason to ask for other tests.*

"The doctor will see you now." Emily walked in and interrupted his line of thoughts. Justin made no attempts to leave his bed.

"You didn't hear me? I said we can go."

"I can't. My legs… my legs hurt so bad."

Emily gave him a suspicious glance. Justin's eyes were pleading for help, and his face was contorted in pain.

"I think I snapped my kneecap while stretching my legs. I might have pulled a muscle or something."

"You can't walk at all?" Emily asked with a deep frown, placing her hands on her hips.

"Barely. How far is the lab?"

"Two floors down… uh… about three hundred feet."

"Yeah, too far. I don't think I can do it."

Emily shrugged, pursing her lips. "All right, since the doc's waiting, I'll get you a wheelchair."

"Thanks. Can you arrange for someone to have a look at my knee?"

"I'll see what I can do."

Five minutes later, Emily rolled in an old wheelchair. A musty stench rose up from the black fabric of the seat, overpowering the chemical smell of the emergency room.

"Our troops don't use them too often," Emily said. "The men, *our men*, tend to suck up the pain."

Justin ignored her sharp words and lowered himself into the wheelchair, feeling the cold aluminum of the armrests against his hands and his body. At first, he struggled with the manual wheels, then began to follow Emily.

"I'm taking him for x-rays," she said to Sergeant Brown, who began to follow them, marching three steps behind the wheelchair. "This way, Justin."

They turned left, passing by the other emergency rooms. Justin had suspected his room was the last one in the intensive care unit. His doubts were confirmed.

He moved slowly, poring through every glass door. The first two rooms were empty, but the blinds of the third one were pulled shut. A dim light glimmered inside that room, and Justin wondered if that was the one. The fourth room was also occupied. Its blinds were drawn only halfway down. Someone was lying on a bed. Justin could not make out the patient's features, since the lights were off.

"You OK?" Emily asked him, as she turned her head. The wheelchair's squeaking noise had ceased.

"Yes, I'm fine. One of the wheels got stuck for a second."

146

"Let's move it," Sergeant Brown growled.

Justin pushed on the wheels. The last emergency room was empty and the door left open. They turned the corner by the fire exit and approached the second elevator of the floor.

So it's either door number 4 or 5, Justin thought. *Unless they moved Carrie and Anna to another unit somewhere else in the hospital.*

* * *

They went past the Immunizations Laboratory and the Pharmacy, before arriving at the Radiology Unit, at the other end on the first floor. Emily left Justin under the watchful eye of Sergeant Brown, and they lingered in the waiting room. Justin wheeled back and forth, trying to peek out of the small windows.

A thick darkness had veiled the entire landscape, but for the air base grounds, which were well lit. The contours of a few, six, maybe seven "golf balls"—huge protective covers for satellite dishes—were visible in the distance. The tarmac of an airstrip reflected a blurry moonlight. There were two large hangars to the right, about three hundred yards away from the hospital.

What's that noise?

Justin felt the vibration of the waiting room walls. The entire wooden structure trembled under the violent wind bursts.

"Chill out," Sergeant Brown said, looking at Justin's confused face. "It's just a storm delta."

"Huh?"

"An extremely strong blizzard. Wind blowing, snow drifting, and all that white crap. Cuts down your visibility to almost non-existent, even in daylight."

"I guess that means no flying?"

"No flying, no driving, no working." Sergeant Brown pulled out a folded newspaper from one of his jacket pockets and spread it over his lap. "Last April, it happened twice. When it's early morning, the command tells us to stay in," he added, flipping one of the newspaper's pages.

Justin moved closer to the window for a better look. Two men seemed to be moving in and out the furthest hangar, the one with the smallest entrance.

"Somebody's working late on their planes." Justin motioned with his hand for Sergeant Brown to come to the window.

The officer shrugged, his only gesture. "That's the Maxwell Brothers, working on the medevac chopper."

"Medevac?" Justin tried to hide the sudden burst of interest in his voice.

"Yes. The Bell chopper of Greenland Air."

"What's their chopper doing on US soil?"

"US base. The land's not ours, we're just using it. Anyway, we have this agreement with Greenland, with their government, to give medical care to their folks living around here. And sometime even stupid Canadian geologists who end up lost and wash up almost dead."

"I see," Justin said, thinking about how to change the conversation.

"Well, you may have been out cold, but that chopper saved your ass, when you and your crew were as frosty as a polar bear's balls."

A small man appeared out of the Radiology Unit. His presence cut short the sarcastic lashing Justin was enduring.

* * *

Of course, the x-rays would reveal nothing unusual about Justin's abdomen. But the trip to the Radiology Unit had enabled him to decide on one of the crucial elements of his getaway plan.

Now, if I can only find out where they're holding Carrie and Anna, we can be on our way out of this place, Justin thought, as the small man led him back to the waiting room.

Sergeant Brown wasted no time in demanding their prompt return to the Intensive Care Unit. Nobody was walking down the halls, but Justin felt he had enough to set his plan in motion.

* * *

Sergeant Brown allowed Justin to close the blinds in his room. At almost 8:00 p.m., the sergeant felt he could afford a single act of kindness. His babysitting chores would be over in an hour.

Once sheltered behind the blinds and away from the vigilant eyes of the guard, Justin had no difficulties dismantling the wheelchair, despite the near darkness in his room. It took longer than he had planned, but by using the tip of his plastic knife—which he had safely hidden inside his pillowcase—Justin was able to loosen the flat tip screws. Once the wheels came off, he dissembled the armrests, the cross braces of the frame and its backrest rails, which he set aside to use as future batons.

* * *

"Oh, crap," Justin shouted.

Even if his voice was not loud enough, the noise of the wheelchair crashing against the wall was a good enough reason for Sergeant Brown to jump to his feet. He slid open the door and barged into the room, stepping right into Justin's trap, who welcomed Sergeant Brown with a blow of an aluminum tube to the back of his head. The sergeant took a plunge next to Justin's bed.

"Sorry about that, Sergeant," Justin whispered, leaning over the sergeant's body. "I just need your clothes, sir. And your gun."

CHAPTER FIFTEEN

Thule, Greenland
April 13, 8:25 p.m.

Justin had finished changing into the sergeant's uniform and was buckling the belt when Emily appeared in the doorway.

"Don't make a sound," he said softly, reaching for the M-9 pistol on his hip.

Emily held her breath. "Oh, did you… did you kill Tom?" she said, staring at the sergeant's body lying in Justin's bed, covered with the bed sheets and the blanket.

"No." Justin walked over to her, his pistol pointed at her chest. "And I won't kill you either. He'll be unconscious for a while. I've got to get out of this place, and this seemed to be the only way out."

"Oh, really? You didn't think to ask?"

"I did. Your commander placed me under arrest, chaining me to Sergeant Brown even when I went to the washroom."

"It's for your own good. This is a US military base, not a rehab. You can't just wander anywhere you please."

"I won't try to convince you. I know you're loyal to your country. But you have to understand I have to be loyal to mine. Where are Carrie and Anna?"

"Four doors down."

"Take me there. Slowly. And for your own sake, be quiet."

* * *

Emily unlocked the door of the room 4A without knocking or otherwise announcing their arrival.

"Who's there?" Carrie asked, flicking on a nightstand lamp. She did a double take at the unexpected sight of the pale-faced nurse and the tall, uniformed airman, whose face looked familiar, in spite of the dim light.

"It's me," Justin said, staying two steps behind Emily. "Just different clothes."

"Finally." Carrie stood up from her bed, ran to Justin and gave him a big hug. "I see you took some time for grooming." She rubbed his arms.

"I had a guard dog at my door, and I needed to distract him."

"Hey, Justin, you're back," Anna said, holding back a yawn. "I guess I must have dozed off. You look good in uniform."

"Thanks. Now, change out of your gowns. We're getting out of this place."

"Where are you going?" Emily asked. "It's a blizzard out there."

"We'll figure it out," Justin replied.

Carrie glanced around the room, but there was nothing on the coat hanger by the door. "What happened to our clothes?" she asked.

"Someone must have taken them down to the laundry," Emily replied. "They were wet and gross, probably."

"Where's the laundry?" Justin asked.

"Downstairs. First floor."

"Take us there," Justin ordered Emily and headed for the door.

"No," Carrie said. "The base is small, and someone will clue in you're not one of them. I'll go with her." She gestured toward Emily. "Do we have a car?"

"I said it's a blizzard, a snowstorm, out there," Emily said in a loud, annoyed voice. "Why isn't anyone paying attention to me? You can't drive anywhere!"

"You're right about that," Justin said. "I won't, but you will."

"You're crazy. I'm not going anywhere."

"Oh, I think you will," Justin brandished his gun.

"You said you weren't gonna kill me and now—"

"He might have said that," Carrie said, "but I've made no such promise." She took the pistol from Justin's hand. "I'll go with her to get our clothes back. Wait here."

* * *

Five long minutes passed after Carrie's departure. Justin and Anna endured every second in silence, hoping and praying for her safe return. Occasionally, Anna would take a quick peek through the blinds, but nothing disturbed the tranquility of the empty hospital hall. Each moment that passed increased their fear someone had detected Carrie, Emily may have let out a scream, or somehow things had taken a turn for the worse.

"Where is she?" Anna asked, after taking another glance. "Why is it taking so long?"

"Relax," Justin replied. "It's only been a few minutes. Carrie will be back as soon as she can."

"What if she's been discovered or caught?"

"Let's not worry about that."

Anna sighed and paced around the room. She sat at the end of the bed and toyed with the edge of her white patient gown. Justin placed a reassuring hand on her shoulder, and she looked into his eyes, searching for a glint of hope. Finding what she sought, she replied with a big, hopeful smile and stood up.

"They're here," she whispered.

Justin opened the door, and both Carrie and Emily entered in.

"Our clothes weren't ready yet, so I grabbed whatever was there," Carrie said.

She was wearing a pair of black jeans, a gray sweater and a brown jacket. Emily had changed into a red cushion jacket, two sizes too large and baggy blue jeans.

"Take this and hurry up." Carrie handed Anna a black laundry bag stuffed with clothes.

Anna pulled out a blue Gore-Tex jacket, a pair of green and black camouflage pants and black boots. Justin got an orange and black leather jacket, with the Harley-Davidson logo and an angry wing-spread eagle on the back. He turned around, as Anna changed into her new clothes.

"I checked two different phones on the way to the laundry room," Carrie said. "The lines are dead."

"Happens often in storms like this," Emily said.

"That means we can't inform Johnson and can't call in help." Justin changed jackets. "At least at this point."

"I'm ready," Anna said after a few seconds. "Let's go."

"OK. Where did you park?" Justin asked Emily.

"In front, where I always park. My truck's a red Ford. The third one to the left of the main entrance."

"Too risky," Carrie said. "The main door will certainly have guards or at least receptionists."

Justin nodded. "Take us to one of the back doors," he said to Emily. "The closest one. We'll walk around."

She gave them a bold stare, holding everyone's eyes for a brief second, as if deciding which one of them to take down first. Carrie gestured with her pistol toward the door. Emily led them down the hall and to the left, toward the elevators.

They rode in a tense silence to the first floor and followed Emily, as she turned right. They continued in the opposite direction of where the nurse had brought Justin for his x-rays and passed by a series of closed doors.

"Where's the back door?" Justin asked.

"Over there." Emily pointed further ahead and to their right. "Around the corner."

"You're not dragging us deeper into the hospital?" Justin said.

"No," Emily replied, "you're the ones dragging me into your crazy schemes."

"Keep your voice down," Carrie said.

As they rounded the corner, the hall opened into a small lobby, where three different halls connected. Emily proceeded for the one to the right, just as a woman in a white doctor's coat walked into the lobby from one of the other halls, about thirty feet away from the group.

"Emily, I need your help in the lab for a muscle biopsy," she said, while studying their faces and their mismatched clothes.

"Sue, help me," Emily shouted. She tried to break away from Carrie's tight grip around her left arm.

"What's going on here?" Sue took a few steps toward them as Carrie and Emily began to struggle.

"Help me, help me," Emily screamed, and dropped to the floor, to stall Justin's attempt at hauling her away. Carrie's pistol was now visible to Sue.

"Oh my gosh!" Her eyes widened. In apparent panic, she flipped a fire alarm switch on the wall. The high-pitched scream of the siren cut through the silence like a surgeon's scalpel slicing through soft tissue.

"Crap." Carrie released her grasp on Emily. "Run."

"No, we need her." Justin kept pulling on Emily's right arm, this time using both hands.

"For what? I'll drive."

"In case someone goes nuts and starts blasting us."

Carrie raised an eyebrow, but there was no time to argue. Justin wrapped his arms around Emily's waist. She kept fighting, kicking her legs, and spinning her arms, taking swings at his chest and head. Her punches mostly missed their target, but succeeded in slowing them down.

"Stop or I'll shoot you," Carrie threatened her. Emily kept up her resistance, calling their bluff.

"Turn around, we've got to go this way," Anna said.

She pointed ahead at a couple of patients looking at the bizarre scene. Over the loudspeakers, a man's calm voice instructed the staff and the patients to leave the hospital premises in an orderly fashion.

"Go ahead and bring her truck to the door," Carrie shouted over the deafening screech of the alarm. She threw the keys of Emily's truck to Anna, and she began to an through the hall.

"Hey, what are you doing there?" said a strong voice.

A patient stood about fifty feet behind them. The hospital gown looked a few sizes too small on the big man.

"Stay the hell back," Carried raised her pistol and aimed it at him.

The man stopped and glanced at the gun for a moment. Then, he shook his large head and kept moving forward toward them. "You ain't shooting nobody," he boomed, sounding much closer than he actually was.

Carrie lowered her gun and grabbed Emily's kicking feet. The nurse was airborne now, and it was easier to carry her through the halls. As soon as they got to the elevators, Emily's scuffle subsided. She realized there was not much hope someone would actually come to her rescue.

They reached the reception desk and heard the rumbling of a truck's engine. A Ford's tailgate lights glowed bright orange in the thick haze outside the main entrance. Carrie pushed the doors open with her back, and they rushed outside. Justin shoved Emily in the back seat of the truck and dove in beside her.

"Go, go, go," Carrie shouted, as she slammed the front passenger's door.

Anna stomped on the gas pedal. The front wheels spun, the engine coughed, and the truck jerked before bolting ahead. It sprayed a small cloud of mud and ice at two men who ran outside and gave chase behind it.

* * *

"So, where do we go now?" Anna asked.

Justin glanced through the rear window. No one was following them. At least, for now. "Let me think," he said, while turning around in his seat and squinting at all sides.

They hit a patch of ice on the road, and the front wheels of the truck drifted to the right. Anna steered in the same direction for a second, and then slowly turned to the left, to correct the slide.

"Straight ahead, go straight ahead," Justin said. "The hangars are that way."

"The hangars?" Emily asked. "You're going to hide in the hangars?"

"I can't see anything," Anna complained, bobbing her head and wiggling left and right in the driver's seat.

She drove at the edge of the road, in order to gain some tire traction over the snowy powder. The gray fog had reduced the visibility to just a few feet, concealing the landscape in a dazing blur. The bright, long headlights could hardly penetrate the pitch-black night. The winter storms had formed high snow windrows along the narrow trail, in some places higher than the truck's roof.

"Slow down," Emily yelled. "You're gonna kill us all."

The truck jumped over a snow bump, the metal frame rattling as if it was going to fall apart at any moment. Anna squinted and noticed a row of dim lights to her left.

"That's the airstrip," Carrie said. She was looking in the same direction.

The road curved slightly to the right. Anna eased off the gas to avoid another slide. The haze had dwindled a bit, and she could see two flashing lamps mounted over the hangar doors. A third one, smaller and fainter, lit up a sign on the blue wall. THULE AIR BASE was written in large white letters. Anna parked the truck underneath the sign.

"Who the hell are you?" a man howled as he stormed out of a door next to the hangar's entrance. He was holding a large pipe wrench in his right hand, and he paraded it menacingly in front of his chest.

"Mr. Maxwell," Justin said, trying to calm him. "My name is Justin—"

"What are you doing here? Emily?!" Maxwell exclaimed.

"Help me," she screamed, throwing a punch toward Carrie's face.

Carried dodged it easily and twisted Emily's arm in a submission move.

Emily moaned, "Aaaaah," while trying to kick back.

Maxwell needed no further explanations. He raised his improvised weapon, the pipe wrench, and launched himself for Justin's head. Justin fell back. The wrench barely missed his face, swinging about an inch in front of his nose. Justin felt the air move in front of his eyes.

Bang, bang.

Two warning shots stopped Maxwell's second attempt at a second blow. He stared at Carrie, who was holding her M-9 pistol at his head. Her face was covered in a thin white veil from her heavy, warm breath rapidly condensing upon contact with the freezing air. Out of options, Maxwell threw the pipe wrench on the tarmac.

Justin picked it up. "Open the hangar doors," he ordered Maxwell.

"Why? What do you want there?" Maxwell resisted.

Justin gave him a strong shove.

"Do we need to explain ourselves?" Carrie waved her pistol. "Hurry up," she added.

"A chopper? You're planning to take off in a chopper?" Emily blurted out.

"This is totally nuts. You'll crash before you even reach the bay," Maxwell said.

"The keys, man." Carrie pressed the muzzle of her pistol against Maxwell's thick chest. "Nobody asked you to predict our future."

"Someone's coming," Anna warned them with a shout.

CHAPTER SIXTEEN

Thule, Greenland
April 13, 8:40 p.m.

Carrie turned around in time to see a yellow Dodge truck plowing through a snowbank then fishtailing over the tarmac. It was coming from the direction of the hospital.

"All of you get inside," Justin said. "Carrie, the chopper. I'll keep them busy."

He took her pistol and ran for cover behind their truck. He pointed the M-9 at the fast approaching Dodge, waiting for the right moment. As the Dodge neared one of the lampposts and its blue glow covered the truck, Justin leveled the sight of his gun with the wheels of the yellow truck. He fired two quick shots. The bullets found their target, piercing the truck tires, and bringing the Dodge to a stop. Two men jumped into the snowbank, scrambling out of the line of fire.

* * *

Maxwell fumbled with the door keys, but he eventually let them into the hangar. After flicking some light switches, the entire warehouse was showered by bright, powerful lamps hanging from the vaulted ceiling. Carrie began to admire the helicopters and airplanes in storage, six in all, lined up on both sides of the hangar. Her only dilemma was deciding which aircraft to choose for their getaway flight.

"Is Justin gonna be OK?" Anna asked. The sudden burst of gunshots had brought back her panic shivers.

"He'll be fine," Carrie replied, "as long as we're out of here soon. How about this beauty?" she asked, disappearing behind the aircraft at the far end of the hangar.

* * *

Justin wondered why Carrie was taking her time. He knew it had hardly been two minutes since she entered the hangar, but the unnerving standoff with the two men from the Dodge stretched every waiting second. Another vehicle—he was almost certain it was a Humvee—was approaching his position from the right. No one had returned fire yet, but he knew orders were being transmitted over the communication lines. A firestorm was just around the corner. Justin hoped they would not find themselves in the dead center.

A Bell 212 helicopter rolled slowly over the glistening tarmac with the distinct splutter and fizzle of its engine. It turned left and headed away from him, its rotors still unengaged. Justin found the pilot's behavior very strange. Was Carrie trying to stop the Humvee? *That's unnecessary if we're flying right away.*

Before he could draw a conclusion, a much louder rattle shook the entire hangar. Justin felt the ground rocking underneath his feet. He could not believe his eyes as he stared at a large military helicopter appear through the hangar doors. It rotated heavily over the tarmac, its silver grayish skin reflecting the tall headlights of the incoming Humvee. Two Hellfire missiles were affixed on each side of the helicopter, and a 7.62mm machine gun was mounted on the left side of the fuselage.

A second later, the machine gun blasted a hailstorm of bullets, raising endless sparks a few feet in front of the Dodge. *Carrie.* She maneuvered the helicopter, completing a one hundred and eighty-degree pirouette, and sprayed a similar torrent of fire against the Humvee. The Humvee skidded over black ice while dodging the helicopter's barrage, and it flipped over before crushing deep into a snowbank.

Justin dashed for the helicopter, which was hovering about seven feet over the runway.

Anna slid open the metallic door on the right side of the cabin and gestured for him to climb aboard. "Come on. Hurry up."

Justin went for the doorsill, but all he could grasp was the cold, slippery wheel of the landing gear. "It's too high." He motioned for Carrie to lower the helicopter.

Anna relayed Justin's message to Carrie, and she dropped the helicopter another foot or so. Justin sprang upward and grabbed Anna's stretched hand. She gave him a strong pull, much stronger than he had expected, and he was able to drag half of his body inside the cabin. He saw one of the crew seats by the door, and he went for its closest leg. He wrapped his fingers around the steel post, and he dug his elbows on the cabin floor.

"I'm good to go," he shouted. "Good to go."

The helicopter gained altitude, and Carrie veered to the left, giving Justin a helpful nudge. The shifting force threw him against the crew seat. As he clenched his teeth in pain, Anna slid the cabin door shut.

"Welcome aboard, Justin," Carrie greeted him.

He struggled to catch his breath, while throwing a quick look around the cabin. Gray and black equipment racks and operation consoles stood against the navy blue walls. Emily was crouched in the co-pilot's seat in the cockpit, next to Carrie. Anna sat next to him. Once their eyes locked, she gave him a warm hug.

"I thought you were going for the med chopper," Justin said after fastening a helmet he fetched from one of the crew compartments and adjusting the volume on its earphone.

"Why settle for an ugly duckling, when you can have a gorgeous swan?" Carrie replied. "Or in our case, a hawk. A S-70 B Seahawk."

"Wow," Justin said, as he brushed his hand over the leather seats and kept gazing at the helicopter's interior design. "I've always wanted to fly in a Seahawk. Maybe not in such a crazy situation."

"Don't get too excited, 'cause we aren't going too far," Emily said. "The blizzard will force us down for sure."

"Not too worried about the breeze," Carrie replied with a grin. "The chopper has so many sat-nav gadgets, we can fly blindfolded all the way home."

Thump, thump, thump. The sound resembled heavy hammers viciously pounding against a massive anvil.

"What was that?" Anna asked.

"The Americans are shooting at us," Carrie replied calmly, checking the control panels. All navigational instruments and screens did not seem affected by the sporadic gunfire.

She tapped the throttle, and the helicopter jerked forward. A second later, the vehicle began a quick ascent, climbing about fifteen feet per second.

Carrie said, "The chopper's built to resist small arms fire. In a minute, we'll be out of their range anyway."

"We won't crash?" Anna said. The pouncing had stopped, but her voice was still shaky. She was blinking rapidly, holding on to Justin's arm.

"There's no real danger coming from outside," Carrie replied. "The Seahawk has isolated control systems, separate for each rotor blade. Even if one system is damaged, the other will allow the pilot to maintain full control of the chopper."

"Oh, really?" Emily sneered. Then, she shouted, "Watch out for the mountain."

"What mountain?" Carrie asked, sitting up in her seat.

"The Dundas Mountain. That freaking one!" Emily shouted even louder, pointing directly ahead of them. "We're gonna crash!"

Carrie squinted. Through the clearing haze, she noticed the rocky cliffs, gray and black, ragged and huge, and growing larger by the second. The helicopter was headed straight for them at about one hundred knots. She flicked on a couple of switches. Two powerful light beams swung over the knifelike surface of the mountain.

"What? You didn't turn the lights on?" Emily shouted.

"We were an easy target even in the dark. We took a few bullets, in case you didn't notice," Carrie replied. "And I wasn't expecting a mountain right off the base but hold on," she shouted needlessly over the microphone, "we'll climb it."

She tapped the throttle and held it while pulling back. The engines screamed. The Seahawk soared upwards, faster and faster. Carrie veered the helicopter to the right, attempting a ninety degree turn. Wind gusts were stronger alongside sharp slopes like these ones. They were capable of throwing down even large aircrafts during blizzards.

Their distance from the mountain was getting smaller and smaller.

A hundred and fifty feet.

A hundred feet.

Fifty.

One of the screens beeped an alarm sound, informing Carrie of the dangerous distance between their helicopter and the obstacle. She wrestled with the controls and the throttle, as the Seahawk angled off, further to the right, struggling to complete the tight turn.

She cursed under her breath.

The tail rotor blades swung toward the cliffs, as Carrie pulled on the throttle, hurling the aircraft sideways, in a last, do-or-die spin. The alarm kept screeching its distress signal. The terrifying sound of doom pierced throughout the panic-stricken cockpit. Carrie ignored

Emily's screaming. As she turned her head to the left, the flat-top surface of the cliffs sank below the helicopter.

"We're clear. We're above the mountain," she said over the microphone.

Emily had stopped shrieking, but her mouth was still wide open, and her eyes were clamped shut. She raised her eyelids, one at a time. Her eyes bounced back and forth, shifting from Carrie's face to the control panels, the cockpit floor and finally, at her own arms and hands.

"We're OK." Carrie placed her hand on Emily's head, stroking her short blonde hair. "Everything's OK."

Emily nodded silently. Carrie glanced behind her seat. Anna gave her a shy smile and a nod of approval. Anna had not uttered a single whisper, let alone a shriek or a scream during the entire ordeal. Justin, on the other hand, had kept silent, because he knew Carrie was going to do the impossible to save them. He also knew you can have only one pilot in a helicopter at a time.

"Great job, Carrie," he said. "You're the only one I know who could have pulled it through." He raised his right hand, making a thumbs-up gesture.

"Thank you, Justin," Carrie replied.

Carrie's gave Justin mischievous smile, as her gaze caught both of Anna's hands wrapped tight around Justin's arm.

CHAPTER SEVENTEEN

Ten miles east of Saunders Island, Greenland
April 13, 9:10 p.m.

A few minutes had passed since their narrow escape, and the blizzard had grown wilder. Strong wind gusts and heavy snow blasts were tossing the small bird in all directions. Carrie grasped and released the throttle and worked the control panel, using every trick in the book to keep the helicopter in the air. The Seahawk kept rocking to the left and to the right, constantly dropping and climbing. At four thousand feet over the ocean, the view from the cockpit was a dense curtain of gray fog, twisting and twirling in a restless vortex.

"Do you have any idea where we are?" Emily asked.

"We just passed over Saunders Island," Carrie replied. "My goal is to keep us in a straight path, as much as possible."

As if to object to her claim, a strong downdraft pushed the helicopter a few feet to the left like some sort of gigantic flyswatter was trying to whack the Seahawk down to the waters.

Emily snorted. "Straight like that?"

The high frequency radio on the control panel crackled with a static sound. Carrie tapped a couple of switches. "This is HAC Carrie O'Connor," she said, after muting the audio feed to the rest of the crew.

She guessed it was the air base back in Thule, and she wanted to keep their threats or pressure to herself, at least for the time being. Despite the fact that piloting was not her profession, she decided to switch to aviator's lingo. HAC stood for Helicopter Aircraft Commander. "Identify yourself," she continued over the radio.

"This is Colonel Richard Clark, Commander of the 821st Air Base Group in Thule. I'm ordering your immediate return to my base." The colonel spoke in a clear and confident voice.

"Commander, I see you missed our departure. I'm sorry we had to leave without saying good bye."

Justin knocked on the side of Carrie's seat. Carrie raised her hand and made a stop gesture without turning her head.

"Carrie, if you keep flying, you're doomed," the commander said. "You're barely fifteen miles off the coast. Come back, and we'll ensure your safe landing."

"Safe landing? Where? In the den of lions? Our chances are better if we keep our current course."

"You can't be serious. It's impossible to make it across the ocean in this kind of weather. You're going to kill everyone on board."

"I don't think so. We're gonna make it, or at least try to, since we have a choice up here, unlike when we 'enjoyed' your hospitality."

"What did you expect me to do?"

"We expected you to act as a trusted ally of Canada, with whom the US shares more than just a border. Commander, we asked you for simple courtesies, which you denied us. You practically locked us up in our rooms, as if we were dangerous felons."

"You would have done exactly the same thing. Think about it for a second. Suddenly I'm responsible for three people who've been rescued in high seas. They're on their deathbeds, but doctors are able to treat them, saving their lives. Instead of a simple 'thank you,' these ingrates bullshit me about a Danish invasion and request my intervention in the internal affairs of another sovereign country—"

"Oh, please, Commander," Carrie said. "The US is notorious for sticking their nose into other countries' businesses, especially those who don't like to kiss a Yankee's ass. If we had more time, I wouldn't mind lecturing you on the US foreign policy, since you seemed to be out of the loop."

"Enough," he barked. "Don't forget that you asked me to do the same exact thing for which you're accusing my country."

"Wrong..." She bit her lips as the Seahawk wrestled with an air pocket draft, which threw the helicopter a few feet upward. Carrie checked the altimeter and a few gauges and screens. "Sorry about the interruption, we're fighting small turbulence here." Carrie had resumed talking after making sure the helicopter kept jerkily but steadily to the established course. "That's it, Commander. Now, I've got better things to do."

"Wait," the commander spoke faster, his voice sizzling with anger. "You've kidnapped one of my people, and you've stolen my fifty-million dollar Seahawk. You started by lying. Now you've added these crimes to your list. You wonder why I don't trust you folks."

"Sir, my compliments for loading Hellfire missiles and filling up the chopper's auxiliary tanks. This way, we'll have enough fuel to make it back home. Oh, and thank you for the emergency flotation system also. A very nice finishing touch. I just hope we won't need to use it."

The commander grunted at Carrie's sarcasm.

"Seriously, Commander, I'll make sure both Emily and the chopper are safe, if you lay off our back and don't try to force us to return to your base."

He still did not utter a single word.

"I'll take your silence as approval, Commander. Thank you."

She flicked a switch to end their communication and another one to return the audio to the crew's earphones. "That was the commander," Carrie informed them officially, even though their eyes indicated they had paid close attention to her every word. "He demanded our return to his base, but as you heard me, I refused."

"Do you think he'll take your advice?" Justin asked.

"I'm not sure. He didn't strike me as a daredevil, but that was before we stole one of his people." Carrie glanced at Emily "And his chopper." She returned her gaze to the Seahawk's control panel.

The helicopter sunk a few feet, tipping to the right. Carrie pressed a few knobs and buttons, leveling the aircraft.

"Do you really think we'll make it in one piece?" Anna asked.

"Of course, we will," Carrie replied. "I'm flying us at a safe altitude, and the navigation system points to the right way at all times. On top of that, the search radars will alert us about any incoming human aircraft from all directions. The blizzard should have also grounded any stubborn or confused birds."

"Where and when do you plan to land?" Anna asked.

"We need to figure that out, our landing destination I mean, keeping in mind Alisha and the threat of…" Justin stopped. His gaze rested on Emily.

"You can say it," Carrie said. "Emily's going to be with us until this is over."

"Who's Alisha?" Emily asked. "What threat are you talking about?"

"Alisha's the reason we ended up half-dead, washed ashore Cape Combermere, where the rescue team found us."

"The b…" Carrie suppressed her swearing.

"Well, she used to be on our side," Justin continued, "I mean the Canadian side, but she betrayed our country. She's working for the enemy now."

"What enemy?" Emily shrugged.

"We found a Danish weapon cache on our shores," Carrie said. "We suspect the Danes are planning an attack on our coastline. I'm not sure about their exact intentions, but I know they're not coming to ski."

Emily blinked. "Really? So, what were the reasons the commander didn't help you?"

"He didn't believe our story," Justin replied. "I mean your base is on Danish soil."

"Maybe it was plausible deniability," Carrie added. "If the commander distances himself from our story, dismissing our claims as ludicrous, in a sense he's washing his hands of all responsibility. If there's ever an internal investigation or an embarrassing media scandal, he's untouchable, using his ignorance as his stay out of jail card. With the base being in Greenland, under Denmark's sovereignty, any rumors about suspicious activities of Danish troops would be considered a stab in the back."

Carrie checked a few controls. According to the horizontal indicator, the helicopter was titled at a fifteen degree angle to the horizon, so she steadied the Seahawk.

"This is one of those situations when the wrong move ends a career," Justin said. "And I couldn't give the commander everything we have, so I don't really blame him. Now back to Alisha. She forced Kiawak to fly her away. Where would she ask him to take her?"

"I don't think they went back to Grise Fiord," Anna replied, while Carrie battled a new air pocket. "Too many witnesses, and someone would have noticed our absence."

"Those reasons eliminate Pont Inlet also," Justin said. "Kiawak knew many people there, who would invite him for a few beers once they saw him... If they saw him."

"Hey," Carrie said, "Kiawak's still alive. He knows how to survive and, as long as Alisha thinks he's useful, she'll let him live."

"Yes, but once they're on the ground—"

"No, Justin. After landing, she'll still need intel from him."

"We've got to find him soon," Justin said.

"We will," Carrie replied. "Nanisivik is also out of the question, because that's Kiawak's hometown. That only leaves two other places, Resolute and Arctic Bay."

"Resolute has a lot of military traffic, since the Army began building their training center. A civilian chopper landing there would definitely make the military ask questions," Justin said.

"So, you all think this woman, Alisha, has gone to Arctic Bay?" Emily asked.

"Positive," Justin replied.

"Justin, what exactly do you think she's up to?" Carrie asked.

"No idea, but she's not a small-time player in this game. She didn't think twice about dumping us like garbage. Alisha seemed to know a lot about the Danish plans."

"She may know a lot about their plans," Carrie said, "but she has no clue we're still alive. And she doesn't know we're coming for her."

CHAPTER EIGHTEEN

Six miles east of Arctic Bay, Canada
April 14, 00:07 a.m.

The Seahawk's navigational lights streamed two powerful beams, which were supposed to assist with the helicopter's night flight. But the thick waves of the unrelenting blizzard absorbed almost every ray of light. Carrie was forced to squint and blink continuously, trying to follow the two small faint dots bouncing over mountain tops, hill slopes, and highlands. She was surprised at her own abilities in handling the rough ride with only a couple of close calls. At the heart of the storm, the wind currents reached a speed of fifty knots, and the visibility was almost nonexistent. At times, Carrie prayed that God would just take over the helicopter's flight.

Emily had not said much during the trip. Justin and Anna had tried, time after time, to reach the Coast Guard, the Canadian Forces, or anyone else over the radio. The vast distance and the relentless storm ensured only constant static was all they received.

The helicopter approached their destination, Arctic Bay. Carrie focused her entire attention on landing the Seahawk safely. It was going to be a tricky maneuver. She would have to complete a smooth descent from their current altitude of three thousand feet to almost ground level. She could not afford to make any mistakes when assessing the strength of sudden wind gusts and performing the actual landing.

"We're coming up to the Bay," Carrie announced, glancing at the controls. The night was pitch-black, and she doubted her crew could see anything on the ground. "I'm going to drop gradually, then hover in search of a decent landing."

"Are we going to descend over water or land?" Justin asked.

"Over land. The Seahawk's control system has a great topographical map, detailed and updated, which takes into account typical snowfalls and other winter conditions. Approaching the Bay from over the water would be extremely dangerous, almost a suicide."

"I thought our entire trip was an attempted suicide." Emily snorted.

Carrie let her sarcasm slide. "I'm getting some good readings from the airspeed and the angle sensors. Hopefully, the visibility will improve once we're closer to the ground."

She veered the Seahawk, and her crew felt the fuselage take a sharp nosedive. The fall continued for about thirty seconds. Carrie steadied the Seahawk, hovering at the same altitude for a few moments. She repeated the same diving maneuver, this time followed by spiral downward movements.

"What are our chances of actually landing in one piece?" asked Emily.

"Greater than hovering forever without trying," Carrie replied. "We have sufficient fuel for two, three attempts, maybe. But I'm worried about damaging the rotor blades, so I hope to make it the first time."

She continued to drop the helicopter into the frightening descent, following the direction of the wind gusts and taking advantage of any breaks, no matter how small, in the blowing snow. Her eyes kept leaping between the control panel and the windshield, since clear isolated patches began to appear in the fog. She could see some details of the mountainous landscape.

"There, do you see the King, at ten o'clock?" Justin asked Anna.

They were falling through a quasi-transparent veil of mist. Carrie tried to take in as much as she could of the rugged terrain. She recognized the flat shape of the King George V Mountain top. A little further, she noticed the vast opening of Adams Sound. A large iceberg was wedged between the ice floes. As she titled the Seahawk to the left, dropping a few dozen feet, she was able to see the first houses of Arctic Bay, clustered along the coastline of the inlet.

"I see the school," Justin said.

"Yes, I do too," Carrie replied. "It's great some places still have their lights on."

The Seahawk continued to draw nearer to the town.

"I'll try to take the chopper there." Carrie pointed to her left, toward a small clearing far away from the mountain. "It's a good distance from the closest houses. Just in case someone may be listening for strange noises." She remembered the last time they landed in Grise Fiord.

"I wouldn't worry about the noise," Emily said. "Just get us down there safely."

"Yes," Carrie replied, "but then we'll have to chase Alisha if she hears us coming."

They dropped another hundred feet. Suddenly a dense layer of fog concealed the ground.

"What happened?" Emily said, her voice filled with panic. "I can't see anything."

"We've got to crash-land," Carrie replied. "Just when I though we got a break, as if it weren't enough to fly blind…"

She slowed their fall by decreasing their speed and spinning the Seahawk around in a small circle. The altimeter showed there was still one hundred and fifty feet between the helicopter and the frozen land. A fierce crosswind could still push the helicopter away from the intended landing area. Carrie tried hovering in one spot, while coming down slowly. The ice blanket covering the permafrost glistened under the Seahawk's powerful light beams, revealing for a few seconds the shape of the clearing. Carrie estimated the height of the snowbanks and the ice mounds, the angle of the hill slope, and the distance the heavy Seahawk might slide when sinking into the snow.

"Get ready," she shouted. "We're touching down in ten."

Emily clung to her armrests.

Justin and Anna locked hands.

Carrie held the throttle, manipulating the controls with utmost care, as if they were made of crystal. She knew any wrong move could cost their lives. After slowing their descent even further, she battled the last wind gusts blasting white powder at the windshield. A moment later, she realized the helicopter was the source of the snowstorm swirling around them. Air currents caused by the helicopter's rotors were lifting snow and ice chunks from the foothill. As they touched down, the helicopter shook, bouncing twice off the ground before sliding to the left.

"Crap," Carrie shouted, tapping the control panel.

Her efforts paid off. The Seahawk reluctantly obeyed her commands. It gyrated on its axis, slower and slower, while Carrie kept it stable on the ground, avoiding a deadly rollover. A sharp crash came from the tail rotor. The blades cut through hard-packed ice. The blades survived the impact, but the Seahawk slid another couple of feet. Finally, it rested next to a snowbank as high as its windshield.

"Welcome to Arctic Bay," Carrie announced then turned off the Seahawk's main controls.

"Thanks, God," Anna finished aloud her silent prayer.

"Let's find Kiawak," Justin said. He took a deep breath and slid open the cabin's door.

Arctic Bay, Canada
April 14, 00:32 a.m.

A young man in his early twenties, dark-skinned, but sporting a blonde goatee, opened the door at Justin's first knock.

"Yeah, what's with the chopper?" he asked, dragging his words like heavy boots through thick snow. The young man was fully awake and held a PlayStation controller in his hand. His eyes flashed a sincere excitement about their sudden appearance. "You guys Army or something?"

"Eh, no, no. We're... we're friends of Kiawak," Justin replied.

"What Kiawak?"

"Kiawak Kusugak. The guy who owns the bar in Nanisivik. Parting Waters."

"Oh, Julian's bro. The Ranger."

"Yes, that one. You've seen him today, I mean yesterday or the day before?"

The young man passed his left hand over his long, black hair tied in a ponytail. "No, I don't know, man," he said with a slow shrug.

"Where does Kiawak stay when he comes to town? Who are his buddies?"

"Oh, buddies. Well, Mike, the Mountie. Abe, the honey trucker and Paul, the guy at the Safelife Co-op."

"Great, can you show us to these guys' places?"

"Now?" the young man asked, shaking his head. The ponytail whipped the air behind his head from side to side.

"Right away. It's urgent."

The young man glanced beyond Justin, at Anna. She was waiting at the end of the driveway. Then his eyes rested on the helicopter. "Is this some kind of a secret mission?" He returned his gaze to Justin. "You guys are cops? National security? Like in Global Ops?"

"Something like that," Justin replied. He had no idea what Global Ops was, a movie or a game maybe, but they needed the young man's help.

"All right, let's do this," the young man said. He turned around and disappeared inside his house, leaving the door ajar.

Anna stepped closer to Justin. "Is he coming out?" she whispered, trying to control her shivering.

"I hope so," Justin replied, fighting the cold wind by moving his arms up and down.

They waited at the doorsteps. Carrie and Emily had stayed behind with the Seahawk, in case Alisha had noticed their arrival and launched an attack or made a runaway attempt. At the same time, Carrie could keep an eye on the aircraft and on Emily.

"Let's go, buddy. This way." The young man showed up at the door. He was wrapped in a heavy duty trucker's jacket. He led them to his garage at the back of the house. "Ned, that's my name."

"I'm Justin, and this is Anna," Justin said. He rode shotgun in Ned's souped-up Land Rover. Anna hopped in the backseat, after pushing away a pile of hockey sticks, skates, and helmets.

"Sometimes I coach our teens," Ned said in justification of the mess in the backseat. "But what's the rush with your friend?" He started the Land Rover, and they took the road snaking downhill, toward the ice-covered Adams Sound.

"Kiawak may be in danger," Justin said. "We think he's been kidnapped."

"Kiawak? Kidnapped?" Ned snickered. "Who would dare to touch a Ranger?"

"Some really bad people," Anna replied. "Any ideas where he may be? I'm sure Alisha wouldn't drag a tied up Kiawak into a hotel."

"Kiawak tied up by a woman?" The scorn was clear in Ned's voice. "What kind of weed have you guys been smoking?"

"No, seriously," Justin said. "Alisha's really dangerous, even for Kiawak."

"Well, usually Kiawak crashes at Mike's, but if I had a hostage, that's the last place I'd go. I don't think the trucker's back from Iqaluit, so, first we'll check out Paul's house, the guy of the co-op."

Ned sped up. The Land Rover hopped over natural speed bumps on the road formed by frozen ice blocks. The ride on the uneven road was very bumpy. The haze was dwindling, and the Land Rover's bright headlights offered a clear view of the road ahead. They swung around a couple of curves, as they drew closer to the bay shores.

"Paul lives at the other end of town," Ned said, "but we'll get there in a couple of minutes."

They drove by two log houses, and Ned tilted his head to the left, observing them closely. "That's where Abe lives, the house in the dark. He's still gone, I guess. But Tania, she's still up? What, she's still grading papers?"

"Tania?" Justin asked. "Who is she?"

"Kiawak's ex."

"What?" Justin shouted. "Stop, stop the car, right now, here. Why didn't you mention this earlier?"

"Because they kind of broke up." Ned pressed slightly on the brake, steering toward the edge of the road. "About a month or so ago. There's no way he's there without everyone in town knowing about it."

"Alisha can use Tania to squeeze information out of Kiawak," Anna replied.

Ned stopped and Justin jumped out. Justin switched off the safety on his M-9 pistol and tiptoed toward the snow-covered wooden stairs leading to the back door of the house. Overcast clouds hung over the town, but the snow reflected a considerable amount of the grayish light, giving him sufficient guidance for a stealthy approach. He noticed small footprints on the snow along the wall of the house. *A single set of footprints. Let me guess who they belong to.*

Justin tried to make as little noise as possible as he slithered up the slippery staircase. Gun drawn, he advanced with small, silent steps. Once he reached the landing by the door, he stopped for a moment and listened for noises coming from inside the house. After hearing nothing but the howling of the sharp wind, he proceeded to turn the doorknob. It yielded, and he pushed the door open.

As soon as he had taken the first step inside the house, a flashlight blinded him. A sharp object hit him squarely on his forehead. Justin saw bright stars, then his eyes rolled back in their sockets. He felt a warm liquid dripping from the wound down to his lips. It tasted like copper. *Blood.*

"Don't move," Justin shouted. He leaned against the wall, raising his gun and squinting in search of the invisible attacker.

Floorboards cracked under heavy footsteps, but he could not see anyone. A second later, he noticed a small shadowy silhouette running toward him. Before he could make out the person's face, a swift kick to the stomach knocked the air out of him. The shadow overtook him. Two strong arms lifted him and shoved him through the door.

He looked up just as Alisha's left fist closed in on his right temple. His body smashed through the staircase rail. He became airborne for a second or two before dropping into the three-foot deep snow covering Tania's backyard.

The fresh snow softened his fall, and the icy feeling on his head and neck pumped up his surviving instinct. Feeling dizzy and noticing his vision was blurry, Justin threw a handful of snow on his face. He repeated the motion again, until the fuzzy curtain covering his eyes began to fall. As he climbed back to his feet, Alisha was shoving someone who looked like a small-statured woman toward a nearby pickup truck.

"Anna! Ned! Where are you guys?" Justin shouted at the top of his lungs. "Don't let her go."

He searched in the snow for his pistol and found it by his feet.

"Anna! Anna!" he kept shouting, while struggling to step out of the slushy, slippery snow.

Lights came on in one of the houses across the street. The truck turned the corner and vanished around a downhill curve.

Justin swore and jogged to Ned's Land Rover.

"Oh my gosh," Anna cried upon seeing Justin's bruised and bloody face. "What happened to you?"

"Turn around and go left," Justin instructed Ned. "Alisha took me by surprise. She's gotten hold of Tania."

Ned nodded without any of his usual wisecracks. The Land Rover roared and slid, but his experienced hands kept the car on the road. He made a quick U-turn, ramping up one of the smaller snowbanks and gave chase.

"There are paper towels in the glove box," Ned said. "Alisha hits like a man."

"And she'll die like a man," Justin vowed, cocking his pistol. He crumpled a couple of paper towels and dabbed at his forehead. The blood had started to coagulate, and his finger rubbed against the rising bump.

Ned kept snaking from one street to the other, always going east, but there was no trace of Alisha's truck. Lights began to shine inside a few houses, as the rumbling car stirred up the sleeping town. As Ned eased around the corner next to the Health Center, almost slamming into an ice heap, a truck appeared ahead of them.

"There she is." Justin tightened his grip around his gun. "Get closer."

"I'll try." Ned pressed on the gas pedal. The Land Rover skid over a stretch of black ice for a couple of feet. Ned controlled the car, aiming toward the snowbanks to the right, to increase the tire traction.

"Where's she going?" Anna asked. "We're out of town."

"Victor Bay," Ned replied. "It's about two miles south."

"Maybe that's where she hid our Eurocopter," Justin added. "Speed up!"

"It's not safe to go any faster," Ned replied.

"Why not? She'll get away."

"She may, but we're not gonna die trying to catch up to her."

"Just gas it up, Ned."

"Listen, I know this road. I drive it every day. It's paper-thin."

"What do you mean?"

"The ice cover. Look, right there on the shore. The erosion has been eating away at the ground. In the summer, we drive around these huge holes, six, seven feet deep. The snow and the ice fill them all up in the winter, and the road's safe for small trucks going at low speeds."

"So, we're driving over the bay waters now?" Anna asked.

"Yes, we're on pure ice."

A loud crack exploded under the Land Rover's tires, confirming Ned's words. He slowed down even further. The taillights of the truck grew larger and glistened brighter. Alisha had finally found a use for her brake pedal.

"She's slowing down," Justin said.

"Yeah, but she's still too fast. Way too fast," Ned replied.

The distance between the Land Rover and the truck was about eighty feet now. The fog was quite thin, allowing for the blurry contours to be somewhat visible to the attentive eye.

Justin blinked in disbelief, as he thought he saw the square shape of the truck box fishtail very unusually. "What... what is she doing?" he asked.

Before anyone could reply, he got his answer. The truck twisted and turned, skidding and sliding on black ice. It seemed Alisha was able to regain control because the truck drove in a straight line for a couple of seconds. Then, it resumed its winding. A moment later, it slammed into a couple of ice blocks and bounced over a pressure ridge. It came down hard, plunging through the thin sheet of ice.

"Oh, crap, crap, crap," Justin shouted, watching the truck nosedive into the frigid waters. Unless they were very careful, they could meet the same fate.

"Are they... are they dead?" Anna asked.

"No... I hope not," Justin replied quickly, "but they will if we don't pull them out."

Ned stopped at a safe distance. The Land Rover's headlights lit up the scene of the accident. The truck had already vanished underwater. Small ice crystals were floating over the open pit. They could still hear loud cracks. *It's probably the truck sinking deeper.*

"How deep's the water here?" he asked, stepping out of the Land Rover. He removed his leather jacket.

"It's not supposed to be deeper than seven, eight feet, but if it gobbled up the truck like that..."

"You're not thinking—" Anna shouted.

"It may already be too late, but I've got to do this." Justin treaded slowly toward the pit.

"No, you don't." Anna followed him, reaching for his arms. "Don't go. Don't do this."

Justin sat down on the edge of the pit. The ice sheet cracked and bent under his weight.

"Stay back," he shouted at Anna. "The ice is cracking."

She nodded and moved back.

He took a deep breath and whispered a quick prayer. Then, he let his body slide down into the dark pit.

* * *

The sharp claws of frigid waters tore at his skin. The water crept from all sides, filling his boots and climbing up his pants. Justin felt the numbness starting to petrify his hands. The feeling pressed on him the urgency of the rescue. His entire body jerked in a series of throes, his muscles beginning their involuntary contractions.

He lunged downward, blindly searching with his hands and feet. He did not open his eyes, afraid the seawater would instantly freeze them. He spun around and dove deeper, frantically thrusting his arms to all sides. All he could feel were broken ice pieces. *Where did the truck go?*

He felt the strong water current pushing him underneath the ice sheet and realized the truck had been dragged away. His feet struck something hard, which felt like rubber. *Is that one of the tires?* After a back flip, he stretched his hands toward the bottom of the pit. *Yes, that's a tire,* he thought after touching the hubcap. His breathing became difficult, and he swam back to the surface.

"I've… brrrr… I found it," he could hardly mumble, as he lifted his head over the slushy water. "Now… I should… pull… pull them out."

"Justin," Anna called. "Come out. You're gonna freeze."

"One… more… try." Justin quivered as he took another deep breath, his muscles tensing. He braced himself for the return dive to the frozen hell.

This time he kept his eyes open. He blinked rapidly to fight the sharp needles of water puncturing his eyeballs and intensifying his jackhammer headache. Justin clenched his teeth and carried on, reaching the bottom of the pit. He found the truck tipped to its left side. Hypothermia was slowing his limbs movements and was shutting down his brain. *What do I do now? Oh, yeah. Open the door. The passenger's door!*

As he reached for the door handle, a sudden movement inside the truck's cabin startled him. He heard a weak thud and a horror-stricken face pressed against the window. Justin did not recognize the terrified eyes buried deep in their dark sockets, but he knew she was not Alisha. He read the terror in her lips. She was crying for help, shoving the door with her hands and her shoulders.

Justin tried prying the door open, but his vicious yanking was in vain. He gestured for the woman to lean back and stepped on the glass. He stomped his feet. The water was softening the impact of his boots. The glass was resisting his repeated attacks.

The woman's motions were dwindling away. Justin wondered whether she was resigning to her fate. Maybe he was experiencing the early symptoms of hallucination. Suddenly, he felt a sharp object jab him on his hip. He lifted the bottom of his shirt, fearing an ice fragment had stabbed him. It was his M-9 pistol, its metallic barrel stuck to his skin.

The gun! I can use the gun to break the glass!

In a single, swift move, he pulled the gun from his right side, ripping a chunk of his skin. He slammed the gun muzzle against the glass as hard as he could, but there was no crack. After the fourth failed attempt, he gestured to the woman to hide behind the door frame. He placed the gun muzzle at the center of the glass and pulled the trigger.

Twice.

The first shot would have been enough for the job. The glass shattered, fragments raining over the woman's head. Justin finished clearing the leftover glass pieces on the truck's window frame and stretched his arms toward the woman. She grabbed his hands, and he pulled her out of the cabin. Once her body was outside the deathtrap, he lifted the woman by her waist. They swam together toward the blurry headlights gleaming over the water surface.

* * *

"Quick, let's get them both somewhere warm," Ned instructed the two men standing next to him.

Awakened by the noise, a large group of curious onlookers were observing the rescue mission.

"Our home," said one of them, lifting Justin's left arm.

The other man moved to the right side, dragging Justin's almost unconscious body to their truck.

"OK," Ned replied. "We'll bring Tania." He helped Anna carry the gasping woman to his Land Rover.

"What about Alisha?" Anna asked, as they laid Tania in the backseat.

"She's... she's dead," Tania mumbled. "The crash..." She broke into a violent cough.

"Don't talk." Ned started the car and followed the ttruck. "Save your energy. You can tell us everything later. Once you're better."

CHAPTER NINETEEN

Thule, Greenland
April 14, 01:00 a.m.

The commander fumbled with his wristwatch. He was awaiting the arrival of a captain who was visiting five of his men in the hospital. They were wounded during the shoot-out with the Canadians. He looked around the table, trying to read the thoughts of his colleagues. The superintendent of the air base was writing on a yellow notepad in front of him. The commander was unsure of his reaction. Before the commander could fix his eyes on the other two men sitting to his left, he heard quick footsteps coming from the hall.

"I apologize for my delay," the captain said as he entered the conference room.

The commander gestured for the captain to take a seat. "How are the men doing?"

"They'll all make it. No one is in danger of their lives."

"Good, I'm glad to hear that. So, what do we have?"

"The Seahawk handled the storm without a scratch. The pilot, Ms. O'Connor, did a damn good job riding the blizzard," replied one of the men at the table.

"Where did they land?"

"We lost our tracking signal when the Seahawk was about six miles east of Nanisivik, Canada."

"They did four hundred miles in the blizzard?" the superintendent asked. "Who are these people?"

"The blizzard, like most Arctic storms, was localized mainly around our air base. The tail end of the storm stretched over Ellesmere Island," explained the same man who had earlier expressed admiration of the Canadian pilot. "Still, it's quite an amazing feat."

"Which confirms my initial suspicions these Canadians are anything but geologists," the commander said. "Special Forces? Rangers? Canadian Air Force?"

"Whoever they are, sir, we should dispatch immediately two rescue teams," said the deputy commander in a terse voice. "Then, when we find them—"

"Wait a second," the commander said, trying to calm him, "we need a plan for the rescue."

"We're here for this purpose, sir, to draft a plan," the deputy commander replied. "If they made it through the snowstorm, so can our pilots. We know their coordinates, and we'll find them. Then, we'll engage these people and force them to release the hostage and return our helo."

"There are so many issues with your suggestion," one of the other men said. "First, the difficulties of a night flight in the blizzard. I'm not saying our troops are incompetent, but it's just too great of a risk to order them into a doomed mission before they even take off from the tarmac."

The deputy commander opened his mouth to begin his objections. The commander stopped him with a stern gaze.

"Second, it's clear from the data that we know only the possible destination of the helo, not the exact coordinates of its landing. And that's their position as of what, thirty minutes ago?"

"Fifty minutes ago," said another man.

"Yes, thanks. They could be anywhere, and our teams will have trouble locating them. Third, the Canadians took a Seahawk, a helicopter this air base is not even supposed to have. And we're planning to go after them with what, other Seahawks that shouldn't be in Greenland's airspace? Fourth, we'll be sending our troops into Canada, our ally. Can you imagine the repercussions of such an action?"

The deputy commander shrugged. "Since when do we worry about 'repercussions' of our acts? We carry out missions like this on almost a daily basis all over the world. Somalia. Pakistan. Colombia. These renegades kidnapped one of our soldiers. That act should not go unpunished."

"It will *not* go unpunished," the commander spoke softly, setting an example of the tone he expected from his men. "As it was pointed out accurately, we will not jeopardize our relationship with a strong ally by wreaking havoc in the Arctic. We revert to the use of force as a last resort, by targeting a precise location. Canada is not like the countries you mentioned. Our first step will be to inform the Canadian government about this crisis and to seek to resolve it through diplomatic means."

The deputy commander raised his metal-framed glasses to the bridge of his nose and scratched his fully shaved head. "Yes, sir," he mumbled.

"Good. I'll contact our Chief of Mission to Canada, and he will follow this matter further through diplomatic channels."

"Is that... is that all we're doing, sir?" asked one of the men in a faltering voice. He was Support Squadron Commander of the airbase. Sergeant Emily Moore and Sergeant Tom Brown were two of the people in his team.

"Of course not," the commander replied. "Emily is my highest priority, and we'll do everything we can to bring her home. I had a chance to interrogate the Canadians, when they were still recovering in the hospital. While I may have misjudged their abilities, they didn't strike me as vicious criminals."

"That's an understatement, sir," the same man replied. "Sergeant Brown's skull is fractured. He was tied up and left naked on the emergency room floor."

"It's all because of that stupid radar signal that notified us about these people in the first place," another man blurted out. "If those technicians would stop messing around with their toys, we wouldn't even be here at this graveyard hour."

"Whoa, whoa," said another voice. "If it weren't for my team, we would have three dead people in our conscience. Three dead people, which we could have saved. There was no way for anyone to know about this turn of events."

"Oh, is that so? Well, my conscience is already burdened with a head split sergeant and a kidnapped sergeant, held as hostage who knows where."

"Gentlemen," the commander shouted, silencing their bickering. "There's no gain in figuring out who's to blame. Let's focus on solutions, rather than accusations."

Some of the men nodded in agreement.

"I was saying the Canadians seemed like decent folks," the commander said. "I know Hall mugged Sergeant Brown, and I don't condone his action. I'm simply accepting it as a fact, regrettable as such, yet still notable, since it tells us about his determination. It also testifies to his character. Hall is not into overkill, but precise, controlled use of physical force, in correct proportion with the needs of the situation."

He looked around the room. "I'll explain myself, since some of you seem lost. When the Canadians had a chance to fight back, their machine guns blasted tarmac chunks, not the flesh of our soldiers. I'm sure they're not going to hurt Emily. They did not kid... take her for ransom or to pressure us into submission or negotiation. Hall was afraid we were going to pulverize the chopper. The bastard was right; I may have issued the order to shoot down the Seahawk, if it had nothing valuable on board."

There were some nods around the table.

"Now, my question is: Why were they in such a hurry to go back? What was so important that couldn't wait, not even three, four days, until their health improved, and we could escort them safely back to Canada?"

"They were trying to hide something," one man guessed.

"Rushing to get rid of their tracks of whatever illegal scheme they were working on," the deputy commander said.

"Hall claimed they had secured evidence confirming their suspicions about Danish soldiers attacking their Arctic territory."

"What?" the superintendent asked.

"Really? That's a clever one," the deputy commander said in a mocking tone.

"Yes, a fascinating claim," the commander said. "I dismissed it offhand as nonsense. But after their death-defying stunt, I'm not so sure. I want to check yesterday's satellite monitoring records for anything out of ordinary, in terms of Danish aircraft or icebreakers heading toward Canada. Hall talked about some isolated maneuver Denmark may be carrying out. I remember seeing a memo a few weeks back, when they were planning a training exercise, but I don't recall its details. At the time, it looked pretty harmless. Find me anything recent about the Danish preparations for this exercise. I also want the other Seahawks on standby for a rescue mission at a moment's notice. Pilots and armaments should be ready, awaiting my orders."

"Sir, hmmm…" the superintendent began, "those choppers, the Seahawks. We'll have to anticipate a considerable backlash from the Danish government if news about their existence at our base appeared in the media."

The commander thought about the superintendent's words for a few moments. "I'm quite aware of our agreement with Denmark on the expansion of our base. I know it prohibits the presence of sophisticated and heavy armed fighter aircraft. But thank you for the reminder. Now, allow me to remind everyone around this table we're the only people in possession of this secret. If the Danes start asking about our Seahawks and whether they're in violation of our treaty with their government, I'll start an investigation of the leak. I will not hesitate to court-martial anyone who leaks the information. Is this clear?"

The commander waited until everyone had nodded their acknowledgment before continuing. "I'll make sure our personnel are informed about our official position on the situation. We're actively pursuing a diplomatic solution with the government of Canada. At the same time, we're working to ensure the return of our airman. I'll address the troops over the radio as early as this morning. Hopefully, we'll have more positive news by then.

"One last thing, I want all our eyes on the Canadian coast. Nothing flies over or swims in or under the waters separating Greenland from Canada without me, personally, knowing about it."

Arctic Bay, Canada
April 14, 01:47 a.m.

"He's a lucky bas..." Nilak's voice trailed off.

He stood up, as Anna entered the small spare bedroom. She tiptoed toward the bed, where Justin was buried underneath a mountain of sheets and blankets. His pale face was the only uncovered part of his body. His eyes were closed, and his breathing was heavy.

Iluak, who was sitting on a small wooden stool next to his twin brother, asked Anna, "How's Tania doing?"

"The nurses are still with her." She gestured toward the hall leading to Iluak's bedroom, where Tania was wrapped in warm blankets. "They say her exposure to the freezing water was not severe, so no internal rewarming is necessary."

"I remember they were saying something about a hot bath," Iluak said.

"You're right. They did that already. Has Justin said anything?"

"Not much. He complained about being cold, ten minutes ago, so I turned up the heat. It takes some time for the house to warm up, since it's so damn cold outside," Nilak replied.

"What did the nurses say about his arrhythmia?"

Nilak rolled his eyes. "I don't think they mentioned it. But how do *you* know so much about this?"

"Just recovered from some serious hypothermia of my own."

"You did?"

"Yes. All thanks to the one who's frozen solid at the bottom of the Bay."

"Alisha, she's such a f..." He stopped and offered an apologetic smile.

Anna shrugged.

"So, why did Alisha do that?" Iluak asked.

"Oh, it's a long story. A very long story."

Anna looked at Justin's face. One of the nurses had combed his hair to the side and had attended to the wound on his forehead, which was now dressed neatly in clean gauze. She reached over to remove a loose hair from his eyelids, but her warm breath on his face disturbed his light sleep.

"Carrie," he muttered, his eyes still shut. "Is that you?"

"No," she whispered in his ear. "It's Anna."

"She gave you the kiss of life, and you're confusing her with another woman?" Nilak wondered aloud, quite loud, for the small room.

"Yeah, man, what's wrong with you?" Iluak said with a smug grin.

"I... I don't know... maybe because I'm exhausted," Justin replied with a wheezing sigh, which turned into a loud cough. "And dead, if she had to revive me," he added after his hacking stopped.

Anna helped Justin to sit up. Nilak straightened Justin's pillow and blankets, forming a soft support against the headboard.

"Did you really kiss me?" Justin whispered, reaching for her hand.

"Why? You really don't remember?" Anna replied, her left fingers toying with a few curls at the back of his head.

"I was going to say 'get a room,' but you already have one," Carrie said, interrupting their ill-timed romance. She stood at the doorway, staring at Justin and Anna, as their fingers parted ways.

"Gentlemen," Carrie said to Nilak and Iluak. "Thank you for your help. We need the room to go over a few things."

"We're at the Health Center to talk to Kiawak," Iluak said, speaking for himself and his brother. "Call us if you need anything. Mi igloo es su igloo," he added, the usual smug grin returning to his face.

"Gracias." Carrie closed the door behind them. She sat on one of the stools. Anna kept standing at the left side of the bed.

"What did Kiawak say?" Justin asked.

"He hasn't said a single word, other than painful grunts," Carrie replied. "The two nurses at the Health Center and Emily are doing what they can to detox him. That psychopath shot him with a bunch of 'truth serums' as they call them, so Kiawak would do whatever she wanted. The nurses are cleaning him up pretty good. Liver, kidney, blood. When he wakes up, he'll feel like a new man. What about you?"

Justin smiled. "I'm doing well, just very, very tired. But don't worry about me. What did you find at the inn?"

"Alisha's laptop. That traitor kept track of all our moves, but she was vague about the Danish schemes. But we know they're planning to take over our Northwest Passage."

Justin nodded as his eyes lost some of their hopeful glare. "As I suspected," he mumbled.

"D-Day is tomorrow, well, today, April 14, 8:00 a.m."

"We're gonna turn it into their Day of Defeat, I promise." Justin clenched his teeth.

"Calm down, Rambo," Carrie said. "We don't know where they're flying or sailing from, but I'm a hundred percent sure it will be somewhere in west Greenland."

"It can't be Thule," Anna said. "Too close to the Americans for a secret mission."

"Wherever they're coming from," Carrie said, "at least we know where they headed. Nanisivik."

"Nanisivik?" Justin asked with clear amusement.

"Yes. According to the traitor's notes, Nanisivik is supposed to be their landing point. It's far away from Grise Fiord and Pond Inlet, and it has a good deep-water port. And she could have flown there in the blink of an eye."

"Before we talk about our defense strategy, can you get me some painkillers, please? Whatever they have; my head is exploding."

"I'll get you some aspirin," Anna said, heading for the door.

"Maybe even something stronger," Justin said.

Once Anna had stepped outside the room, Carrie whispered, "I think she's in love with you."

"Puppy love." Justin shrugged and looked away.

"Listen up." Carrie leaned closer to his face, so he could not avoid her eyes. "Don't make the same mistake with her like you did with me."

"What mistake?"

"Allowing your career to kill your passion. Never underestimate the love of a woman. Learn something from our mistakes."

"Oh, now they're ours?"

"Yes, they are. We're both responsible for our relationship failing. But…"

Carrie heard the door crack open, and Anna entered, so she changed the topic. "Once you start feeling better, we'll come up with a plan. Oh, you're back already," she turned to Anna, who handed Justin his painkillers and a glass of water.

CHAPTER TWENTY

Søndre Strømfjord, Greenland
April 14, 06:00 a.m.

Gunter frowned at the first ring of his BlackBerry. He threw a casual glance at it, annoyed rather than curious to learn the name of the caller. GS were the initials on the screen. Grigori Smirnov of the FSB. What did he want? His office in the Air Force Command Post had suddenly become very small. Before the BlackBerry could chirp its second ring, Gunter reached for it.

"Yes, Smirnov," he said, leaning back in his chair.

"I believe you and I have some unfinished business," Smirnov said in an impatient tone.

"As I told you last night, I'll provide you with timely updates if anything worth mentioning occurs."

"Patience is not my virtue, Gunter. And rumors travel faster than your reports."

"What rumors?"

"The US Chief of Mission to Canada, a certain Abraham Locke, is asking questions about our wargame. He's has been talking to senior Canadian officials. We can't have anyone stick their nose in our unfinished business."

Gunter moved the BlackBerry away from his mouth as he muttered a few curse words. He took a deep breath, before asking, "How come the Americans are so suspicious all of a sudden?"

"The US Chief has a deep interest in our activities in the Arctic. That's because the Commander of the US Air Base in Thule rescued three survivors in international waters by Ellesmere Island. They were Canadians, and they repaid him by stealing one of his aircraft."

"Really? The Canadian way to say 'thank you' for saving us?"

"It's not funny. You're really not aware of this?"

"No, I'm not, and I don't see how it affects our mission."

Smirnov sighed. "Exposure, Gunter. Unnecessary exposure. The Americans are going to be on very high alert. Their teams may circle the area. And they're also going to monitor everything that happens in there."

"You don't have to worry," Gunter offered his assurances, while fishing for the other BlackBerry on the inside pocket of his jacket. "We're going to conduct our wargame as planned. The Americans' prying eyes are not going to find us. However, if you're having second thoughts, we're still on time to cancel our show." He typed a quick message to Yuliya by using only his left hand. *My office, now!*

There was a brief but tense pause. Gunter knew Smirnov was not going to back down simply because the Americans had some vague concerns. It was not the Russians' way.

"No, we're not going to cancel it, but reduce the force to the bare minimum to finish the job. That's it."

"I'll get it done," Gunter replied over the knock on his office door. "Come in," he said, after covering the BlackBerry with his hand to muffle his voice.

Yuliya walked in.

"Great," Smirnov said. "You should, if you expect to see you wife alive again."

Gunter sizzled on the inside but did not let his rage show up in his voice. "I'll keep my end of the deal, and you'll keep yours."

"Of course, we will, Gunter. Let me know if you run into any complications."

"I'll be in touch."

Gunter took a deep breath as he ended the call. "That was your fucking boss, Smirnov," he shouted at Yuliya standing by the door. "Why the hell didn't you tell me about this call?"

"Mr. Smirnov wanted to inform you personally about the situation," Yuliya replied calmly.

"I don't understand this. You know I'm not the only one who's going to lose if our mission goes to shit. You need to talk with me and tell me everything you know."

"Smirnov called me five minutes ago. He insisted I didn't tell you anything until you heard it from him."

"Well, here's what I know. The Americans in Thule have lost an aircraft. Justin and his crazy bunch are still alive and causing trouble."

Yuliya nodded. "Alisha should have followed my clear instructions and killed them. I told the fool not to spare anyone's life."

"She didn't. The Americans rescued Justin, and in turn, he made away with some kind of aircraft."

"Yes, that's what Smirnov told me too. Did he tell you anything about Justin's whereabouts?" Yuliya asked.

"He didn't say."

"Thule has Twin Otters and medical helos, so Justin and his gang made out in one of the two. How does this affect our plans?"

"Smirnov wants a smaller contingent, enough to do the job."

"What if Justin organizes some kind of resistance?"

"I'm not worried about that. By the time the CIS investigates, and the DND dispatches their troops up there, it will be over. Have you heard anything from Alisha?"

"No, not since late last night. I tried her sat phone, but no answer. Not even a busy signal. It's like she fell off the face of the earth."

"Let's make sure she's knows about Justin's escape. He may have informed his supervisors about her betrayal and the evidence they found at the depot."

"I'll keep ringing her until she picks up her damn phone," Yuliya said.

Arctic Bay, Canada
April 14, 05:25 a.m.

"What the hell?" Justin stared at the satellite phone on his hand. "They hung up. They hung up on me. The stupid DND officer said they're aware of environmentalist nut jobs trying to come up with bogus stories to create trouble in the Arctic. I guess Alisha was afraid Kiawak might escape and notify the DND, so she took care of that by creating this disinformation." He set the phone on the nightstand by his bed.

"I'm not surprised," Anna replied. "Even if Alisha had not contacted the DND, this mess is so unreal. I can hardly believe it myself."

"And I can't get through to our office. For some reason, the connection fails every single time."

"Does e-mail work?"

"No, nothing works."

"How come we can talk to the DND, but no one else?"

"The Army uses special satellites, dedicated solely to their communications."

"If we can't convince the DND that the Danes are using a wargame to cover up their real intentions, and we're completely isolated from the rest of the world, how are we going to stop this attack?"

Justin did not reply but began to stand up from his bed. He placed both hands on the nightstand for support.

"You OK?" Anna stood up from her chair.

"Yes." Justin struggled to find his balance, like a toddler taking his first steps. He shifted his weight from one leg to the other, pressing his heels on the floor.

"Where are you going?" Anna asked

Justin shuffled his feet and walked toward her.

"Nowhere. Just wanted to see if I can be of any use. Pacing helps me gather my thoughts."

"You're going to fall."

"I'm not. I made it to the bathroom a couple of times during the night. How's Kiawak doing?"

"He's OK," Anna replied, her eyes attentively following Justin's unsteady gait.

"Still unconscious?"

"Yes. The nurses are convinced he's not gonna die, but they fear there may be some internal damage."

"When can we talk to him?"

"I don't think we can. I mean, he can hear us, but he'll not respond to our words."

"Is Carrie back from Resolute?"

"No, not yet."

"Is her flight delayed because of the storm?"

"Not sure. But it may take a while to convince the top brass at the Army training center about the Danish threat."

"OK, so Kiawak is out of the play, and we still have to hear from Carrie." Justin leaned his arm against the window. The storm had grown weaker over the last two hours. At the moment everything was quiet. A gray-white glaze was hovering above the houses. "What can we do against the Danes?"

"Not much, unfortunately," Anna conceded. "If the information we've obtained from Alisha's laptop is accurate, about two hundred and fifty Danish troops are going to storm Nanisivik in less than two hours. Who knows what they'll do next? By the time our offices in Ottawa will open for business, Danish flags may be flying over the entire Arctic."

"Oh, no, Anna." Justin resumed pacing, "I'm not gonna let that happen."

"Why, what are you going to do? We've come to the end of the line, Justin. We're telling our Army, our defense forces, there's a real danger here, and they're shutting us out. Nobody cares we're losing our Arctic."

"Well, you and I do care, and we're not gonna sit here and watch the Danes take over our country. How many RCMP officers do we have here?"

"We've got two Mounties and about a hundred able men, at the most."

"There're all patriots. They would die for their land before they see it taken away in front of their own eyes. Count them all in."

"OK, let's say we enroll the entire Arctic Bay. Then what?"

"Nanisivik can come up with about twenty other people or so. If Carrie brings another twenty, we're up to, oh, I would say a hundred and fifty."

"Yeah, soldiers armed with knives and rifles. Alisha's notes talk about an icebreaker." Anna dug in her backpack for a small notebook. "Listen," she said after flipping a few pages, "HDMS Knud Rasmussen, type of ship, blah, blah other characteristics. Huh, oh, of course. Here, two hundred feet long. Armament. Two .50 cal Browning machine guns and missile launchers. The Evolved Sea Sparrow Missile kind."

Justin shook his head.

"No, I'm not finished. Don't forget that Rasmussens can be fitted with larger caliber weapons, as if .50 cal wasn't sufficient, and torpedoes."

"Great, you've completely given me the jeepers." Justin snorted. "Just for your information, our men have Lee Enfield rifles. The Rangers' weapon of choice, very reliable and powerful. A single shot can stop a charging polar bear. Those missiles you're talking about are for anti-aircraft warfare and—"

"Well, that eliminates any surprise Seahawk attack on our part," Anna interrupted him.

"Who said anything about attacks? I'm talking about setting up a defense perimeter."

"What? What are you trying to say?"

"Anna, it will come down to a man-to-man fight. Alisha and the Danes underestimated us, and we'll take advantage of their mistake. We'll set up a defense perimeter around Nanisivik's shores and await their arrival. Once everyone's on the ground, away from their big guns, we'll pick them out one after the other."

"That's our plan?"

"Pretty much. We'll wait until Carrie's back before beginning our march. Alisha's notes indicate the invasion is expected to start early morning. We'll prepare and wait for the dawn."

"Don't we have other options? Why can't we keep calling our office?"

"It's impossible to get a reliable signal. Even if we did, there's not much time left," Justin said. "Even if we talk to them, by the time the cavalry gets here, it will be too late."

Anna shrugged. "I don't know," she said.

"It's our last resort, so we better pray it works." Justin turned toward the door. "Let's going check on Kiawak and get some food. Then we need to gather our troops for battle."

CHAPTER TWENTY-ONE

Arctic Bay, Canada
April 14, 06:00 a.m.

The meeting took place at the Arctic Bay School gym. It was the preferred location for most public events, from court sessions to dances to funerals. Heated indoor space was scarce and the people were pragmatic in their choices.

Pacing with difficulty under the basketball stand, Justin smiled as the small court began to fill with people, mostly young men. Some of them were talking casually to one another, as if this were a sport tryout. A small group approached Nilak and Iluak, who were standing next to Justin. They pulled the twin brothers aside and began whispering and gesturing, mostly with their heads, toward Justin, Carrie, and Anna.

"You know that's unnecessary," Justin mumbled at Carrie, turning his back to the group. "The whispering, I mean. I don't understand Inuktitut."

"Right, but they don't know that," Carrie replied. "When are we going to start?"

"We'll wait a few more minutes," Justin said. "After all, it's only six in the morning."

"If only those cowards in Resolute would have listened to me," Carrie said, "and sent over men and choppers, we wouldn't need to bother these people."

"You did your best to convince them. Some people just aren't persuaded that easily," Justin said.

More people appeared in the doorway. Some strutted in, eager to take up arms, Justin thought. Others dragged their feet, looking like they regretted getting out of bed. There were very few women. Justin counted only five out of about fifty people in total. *Not bad,* he thought, *but now let's see how they feel about me calling them into battle.*

"Ahem, ahem," he cleared his throat, but his voice came out raspier than he intended. His cough drew the attention of almost everyone, especially those few who had already been measuring him up. Nilak and Iluak reluctantly walked toward Carrie, who was standing to the right of Justin. They stopped a few steps away from her, a clear indication the twin brothers were not a part of Justin's group.

"Welcome, welcome every one of you," Justin said in a strong voice. A big smile adorned his face, and he stretched out his arms toward the people. "I appreciate you coming out so early in the morning."

He noticed an old man nodding and a few people taking a timid step forward.

"My name is Justin Hall, and I've already met some of you. These are my colleagues, Carrie O'Connor and Anna Worthley. We all work for the federal government. We're part of Canada's security services. This is—"

"You cops?" asked one of the young men who had been chatting with Nilak and Iluak.

"No, no, we're not the police," Justin replied quickly, as a quiet mutter rose up from the crowd. He looked at the young man and tried to read the white letters embroidered in the young man's bandana. All he could make out was a white skull. He added, "We're—"

"What then, spies?" interrupted another young man, standing next to the bandana young man. He was wearing a gray hooded shirt with the words Ecko stamped on the front.

"No, of course not," Justin answered his question before any grumbling from the crowd. "We're with the defense forces."

"The Army?" an old man asked. Justin could not see his face, but his voice had a feeble ring to it.

"Yes, today, here, we're the Army," Justin replied. *I wish Kiawak was here*. Justin let out a small sigh, before continuing. "As some of you are aware, we flew here last night, I mean early this morning, looking for our friend, Kiawak Kusugak."

A few people nodded as he mentioned Kiawak's name. Justin understood the clue.

"Kiawak Kusugak, one of my best friends and a courageous Canadian Ranger, was kidnapped by someone, someone who has chosen to sell out our country to the enemy."

Justin allowed time for his words to sink in. The crowd grew weary and agitated.

"Sell out our country?" a woman's high-pitched voice came from the back of the hall.

"Our land?" shouted another old man.

"Enemy? What enemy?" asked other people.

"Let me explain," Justin raised his voice in order to silence them. "This person had struck a deal with the Danish military forces to enable their entry into Canada through our waters, so they can take control of our Northwest Passage."

The crown erupted in a loud noise.

"What?"

"You've got to be kidding!"

"Is this true?"

"Yes." Justin limped toward them and tried to calm them with hand gestures. "The Danish troops are going to attack us, right here in the Arctic, in our homes."

"The Danish troops are not our enemy," said one man. "They're our allies. They have troops in Afghanistan to fight terrorism and Canada trades goods with the Danes."

"Yes," the bandana young man said, "I had some Danish for breakfast."

Noisy laugher roared among the people. Some young men were shaking their heads in disbelief.

"Any help would be appreciated," Justin whispered at Carrie and Anna.

"I've got nothing," Carrie replied. "If I open my mouth, I'll make matters worse."

Anna raised her shoulders. Justin glanced at Nilak and Iluak, but they were staring at the ceiling.

"Listen," Justin tried again, "I'm telling you the truth. The Danes are launching their attack under the pretense of a training exercise. We need your help to stop this attack."

"Wrong choice of words, Justin," Carrie muttered under breath.

"Training exercise? All this brouhaha for some training?" The squeaky voice had the unmistakable hint of scorn.

"You're the Army, right?" An old man pointed his shaky hand at Justin. "Why don't you call for reinforcements? Why do you need us, eh?"

"Yes, why?" other people joined him.

"Oh, I'm out of here, bro." The young man in the Ecko shirt threw his hands up in the air with a snort. He turned around to leave. Justin tried to remain calm. Other people followed the young man.

"Where the hell are you going?" A stern voice echoed throughout the entire court, suppressing everyone's whining and mumbling.

The crowd went still for a moment. Then it began to divide right in the middle. A low, screeching sound, resembling the metallic rattle of rusty door hinges, was the only thing breaking the silence. People were making room for a man to walk through. *Not walk, roll in.* A woman pushed in a wheelchair holding a man wrapped in blankets. *Kiawak! Yes, that's Kiawak!*

"It's great to see you, man." Justin tapped Kiawak on the shoulder. His pale face was the same color as his blankets.

Carrie and Anna offered pleasant smiles. Kiawak nodded back. The woman, who Justin realized was Emily, turned the wheelchair around so Kiawak could face the crowd.

"I can't believe it's you who brought him here," Justin whispered at Emily. "I thought you hated us."

"I used to, but he convinced me you're actually the good guys." Emily gestured toward Kiawak.

"Maybe he can convince them, as well," Justin mumbled, taking a few steps back.

Kiawak faced the curious and angry stares of his own people.

Søndre Strømfjord, Greenland
April 14, 07:40 a.m.

"Why the handcuffs?" Sargon asked.

Magnus ignored his question. He marched past the man and the other recruits scurrying to form five rows of ten soldiers each inside the wooden barrack. Magnus's team, four people in all, was handcuffing the hands of every man in front of them, refusing to give more than one line answers to their questions.

"Hurry up," Magnus barked at a skinny man fumbling with his shirt's buttons. "We're out of here in less than thirty minutes."

"What's the rush, boss?" asked a large man with a thick voice. A few steps away, he straightened the ear flaps of his woolen hat.

"The special op, for which you've been preparing for so long, is finally under way." Magnus stopped in front of the man and asked, "Jack, right?"

The man nodded.

"Jack, and everyone else," Magnus shouted, while scanning the faces of the disorderly bunch, "the handcuffs are for your own protection. This mission is extremely important. We don't want it to be threatened by your emotions, which, at times, have triggered your violent responses. In this way, your aggression will be focused at the right target."

"Great mental shit, boss," Jack replied. "We still don't know our target or any details about this *important* mission."

"Mr. Madsen, our Commander, will soon inspect this platoon. He'll explain these final details." He stood toe-to-toe with Jack, whose defiant grin swung from one corner of his lip to the other.

"Platoon my ass," mumbled a man from the last row. "We're being tied like prisoners."

"You *are* prisoners, but this mission will make you free, each and every one of you. That's why your minds and your bodies should work toward accomplishing this mission."

"Which we still don't know," retorted the disgruntled man.

"I'll tell you exactly what it is," Gunter replied, standing at the entrance of the barrack.

The recruits scrambled to complete their lines. Magnus and his team turned to face the commander and stood at attention. Gunter strutted in with Yuliya in tow. She was followed by six armed guards Magnus was seeing for the first time.

Gunter stopped in front of the platoon. "Soldiers, my name is Gunter Madsen, and I'm the commander of this operation. Soon we'll embark on a short flight, a mission to defend our country's sovereignty in a much disputed region, the High Arctic. It is our duty to march forward as the leading unit to secure these Danish territories." Gunter kept pacing in front of the platoon, his voice reaching a crescendo with the rhythm of his speech. "We will fight, and if need be, we will shed our blood, so that our land may be prosperous and secure."

"Did he say shed our blood?" a small man in the fourth row whispered to a tall recruit to his right. "We were told this was a patrol mission, to confirm Denmark's presence in the Arctic."

"Shhhhh," the tall recruit replied.

Gunter paused and scanned their faces with his bright eyes. "In terms of exact details, you'll be flying in one of the Hercules that brought you here. Our destination is Nanisivik, a small Canadian settlement at the northern tip of Baffin Island. Once on the ground, you'll take over the town. When the area is secured, we'll continue up north, to Resolute. At the same time, another group will take over the town of Arctic Bay, another insignificant obstacle in our way to control the entire Northwest Passage."

Loud mumbling broke through the crowd, mostly from the back rows.

"Weapons will be given to you after landing," Gunter continued, pacing to his right and then turning around. "Resistance from the enemy is expected to be pathetic, at best. Still everyone is urged to take this mission very seriously. You should make every effort to accomplish it victoriously. May God bless you all."

"Hmm, Chief," a scratchy voice called from the back row. "We're all chained up here, like mad dogs."

Gunter tilted his head and looked for the man. He found him standing at the far end corner of the platoon.

"I've got this." Yuliya held Gunter's arm and marched toward the scratchy voice. Two of the guards unknown to Magnus followed her. "Chained up you say?"

"Yes, don't you see the handcuffs?" the man lifted up his arms.

"I see an attitude." Yuliya replied. "An attitude of disrespect toward authority."

The man snorted with a big shrug.

"Mr. Madsen's authority is not to be questioned, neither by you nor—"

"I'm saying, if we're heroes and that bullshit, why don't you trust us?"

"You interrupted me. But maybe you're right. Maybe we're asking too much of you, and we're seeing things that just aren't there. Maybe it's all bullshit, as you say, and there are no heroes among you." Yuliya nodded to one of the two guards behind her. "Yuri, what is Mr.—"

"Villadsen, Pedar Villadsen," the man replied. He stood straight and tall with a natural pride when giving his name.

"Yes. And Mr. Villadsen's reason for being behind bars?"

Yuri swung his HK MP5 submachine gun behind his shoulder and tapped a few keys on his BlackBerry. "Murder," he said after a few seconds. "Mr. Villadsen was convicted for murder and has served half of his fifteen-year sentence."

"Murder. Interesting." Yuliya circled around Pedar. "An innocent man?" she asked.

Pedar remained silent.

"What's going on here?" Magnus asked Gunter, who was observing the exchange, his arms crossed in front of his chest. "What is she up too?"

"I have no idea," Gunter replied coldly. His gaze seemed distant, detached from the scene taking place in front of his eyes.

"Tell me. Was he an innocent man?" Yuliya asked again.

"Nobody's innocent," Pedar replied.

"Quite so," she said.

She took Yuri's BlackBerry and skimmed through the pages of Pedar's file stored in the device. "You shot a liquor store clerk, after tying and blindfolding him."

Pedar nodded, his crooked teeth flashing an evil grin.

Yuliya stepped closer to him. She removed her HK USP 9mm pistol with a swift gesture and pressed it against Pedar's left side, wedging it tight in the man's ribcage. "I'm doing you the same favor, you son of a bitch," she sputtered.

Pedar stumbled backwards and began to raise his arms. Yuliya was fast on the trigger. A single bullet pierced through Pedar's clothes and skin. He was dead before his body hit the cement floor.

Magnus's hand went for his side weapon, but the corner of his eye caught a quick glimpse of Gunter's emotionless face. *Why is he not intervening? What's going on here?*

"Shit," shouted the man standing next to Pedar, glancing at the pool of blood forming around the body. "You've killed him, you—"

Yuliya pointed her pistol at the agitated man, in case he attempted a stupid act of revenge. "Yes, and I will not think twice about punishing any form of disobedience."

She returned to the front of the platoon, followed by Yuri and the other guard.

All Magnus could do was stare in disbelief, as Gunter took a step back, giving Yuliya the floor. Some of the recruits shook their heads. Others stared at the floor.

"Maybe the commander was thinking too highly of you maggots, when he tried to lighten up your condemned souls. Maybe we're miscalculating your thirst for evil. Well, here it is in simple and clear words: You do what you're told, or else I'll kill you all with my own hands. Is that clear?"

A couple of shy nods came from the third row.

"I can't hear anything," Yuliya shouted. "Do you get it?"

"Yes, ma'am," a few half-hearted replies came from the crowd.

"What? I can't hear you!"

"Yes, ma'am," the platoon roared in a single voice.

"Great, that's much better. Back to you, Commander." Yuliya placed her pistol in its holster.

Gunter sighed and took a deep breath before speaking in a wavering voice. "Magnus, take the platoon into the Hercules. I'll complete the inspection of the other barracks. Follow me, Yuliya."

"Yes, yes, sir," Magnus replied. *I've got to figure out what the hell is going on here, and who is actually in charge.*

Arctic Bay, Canada
April 14, 6:25 a.m.

"My father, Pukiq, was a hunter." Kiawak's voice was shaky, like his hands, and mixed tinged with nostalgia as he began to speak to his people in their native language. He had asked for Justin's help, and he had sat him on the floor. Everyone in the crowd had followed his example, forming a semi-circle. "Pukiq's father, Saghani, he was a hunter too. He liked to hunt seals in particular, and he liked it when my grandma Kenojuak cooked them for him after he returned from long voyages."

"What is Kiawak saying?" Justin whispered to Nilak, who leaned over and began translating for him in a hushed voice.

"Our ancestors roamed Baffin Island," Kiawak continued, "from east to west, as far as the caribou and the polar bear wander, when the land froze and when the snow melted, and when the long dark nights were replaced by endless daylight. As far as our forefathers remember, this place, these mountains and oceans, rivers and lakes, these were always our home. We built our villages, and we hunted our food. We lived and we died. We married, and we raised our children.

"It was a time when there was no government, no Canada. We had no enemies, but our own forgetfulness, which, at times, came with the high price of famine, shortages of supplies or sicknesses. The White Wolf was our guide, and the Polar Bear our wise and powerful friend. The land gave us food, and the iceberg gave us water."

Kiawak's words had begun to calm down even the loudest people in the crowd. The young man in the bandana removed it, and his eyes showed he was deeply entangled in the fascinating world Kiawak was taking them. Other men had closed their eyes or were blinking constantly, trying to envision the beauty and the serenity of the time far gone.

"Summers and winters played tag with each other. Our children had children of their own, and our elders fell asleep and joined their fathers. But when the white man came, he brought division and fighting. He pillaged our land, stole our values, and crippled our spirits. He took away our names and gave us numbers, confining us to earthly dwellings, and separating us from our freedom. A country he made for us, towns and cities, promising us prosperity and security. Instead, we found misery and isolation, abandonment and rejection."

Justin squinted as if to come out of his trance and glanced at Kiawak. *Where's he going with this?*

"But not all white men are the same. Like fingers on our hand, they are all different. Two great women we have in our midst, our nurses, Liana and Marietta, who save lives and take good care of us. Our teachers, Sebastian and Vladimir, are great mentors to our children, as they mold their young minds. We have wonderful pilots, who fly us fast to faraway places, where it would take us weeks to get on our own."

Justin felt Kiawak's feeble hand resting on his shoulder. "This hunter, Justin, one of my best friends, saved my life and rescued Tania from the claws of death. He's a great defender of our people. He will never abandon his own. Now that our freedom is once again threatened by the white men coming from across the Great Waters, our only reaction is to take up our arms to fight. We need to unite. We need to be one, in our goal and in our mind. Just as a single man leads his group during a hunt, so shall we go into our battle and return victorious. We will fight and win this battle. Every one of us, all of us, will join the fight."

Kiawak's last words, shouted in a strong, loud voice, brought the expected reaction. People applauded, some in tears of joy and some in cheerful cries. A few young men raised clenched fists, waving them in the air.

"Thank you, Kiawak," Justin whispered, shaking Kiawak's hand.

"No, thank you, my friend. If it weren't for your determination, I would have been dead."

"Determination? Some people would call it craziness."

"Not me, Justin. I call it what it really is."

CHAPTER TWENTY-TWO

Twenty-five thousand feet over Baffin Island, Canada
April 14, 07:00 a.m.

The cockpit of the C-130J Super Hercules felt warmer and Gunter ordered the pilot to turn the temperature down. The glass-enclosed cabin provided ample room for five people. In addition to the second pilot, Magnus and Yuliya sat next to Gunter behind the pilots. Valgerda had been assigned to the cargo compartment, along with one hundred and fifty combat troops. The contingent was almost a hundred men short from the original plan. Alisha's unavailability and Smirnov's paranoia had reduced the front unit to the bare minimum.

"We're flying over Pond Inlet, sir," the pilot informed Gunter, who kept fiddling with his BlackBerry Bold.

"Ehe." He nodded. He squinted in order to read the small inscription on one of the screens of the aircraft's control panel. The number, 137, showed the distance in miles from their destination, Nanisivik. "What's our ETA?" he asked.

"ETA is twenty-eight minutes, if we keep our current cruising speed of two hundred and fifty knots," the pilot replied. "Plus five, ten minutes, depending on conditions at destination."

"Alisha's pictures showed the runway at the Nanisivik airport as clear and suitable," Yuliya said. "The meteo data confirm favorable conditions for landing."

Gunter nodded.

Yuliya smiled at him. "Why don't you give your wife a call, sir?" she asked.

Gunter peered at her. "I called her earlier this morning, before leaving." He did not say the words, but his eyes asked whether there had been a change in FSB's one call a day policy.

"Oh, I'm sure she would love to hear from you again," Yuliya said. "Today's the big day and once everything's done—"

"Then, I'll call her when we land," Gunter said. "We'll do our job here perfectly, and then I'll give her the good news."

"All right," Yuliya said, exchanging a quick glance with Gunter.

Magnus's frown grew larger. He was supposed to be the chief of this operation, but Gunter and Yuliya were blindsiding him on every step. He had told Valgerda about the cold-blooded murder he witnessed in the barracks and how Yuliya, not Gunter, was in fact in charge of the Arctic Wargame. Magnus and Valgerda had agreed to watch each other's back. They could no longer trust Gunter or Yuliya.

Arctic Bay, Canada
April 14, 7:20 a.m.

Kiawak's speech had revived the warrior spirit among Arctic Bay's residents, and their response was overwhelmingly patriotic. Everyone, young and old, men and women, even children, wanted to take up arms and fight the Danish invasion. Justin and Kiawak were very selective in their recruitment and only enlisted those who could actually be of help in the nearing battle. Eventually, around one hundred people were loaded in half as many pickup trucks and Suburbans. They took anything that could be useful: coils of rope, shovels, boxes of dynamite and ammunition, and as many firearms as they could carry.

As she stood inside the Health Center, Emily's eyes followed the long convoy of the ragtag militia trailing south toward Victor Bay and then heading for Nanisivik. She moved away from the window and retreated to the kitchen for a warm drink. The coffee she made was bitter and weak, but steaming hot, which was the only thing she cared about. She blew gently on the cup and took another sip.

After gulping down half of the cup, she felt much better. With everyone gone, the Health Center was empty. This was the first time she could enjoy a few moments of silence and peace since Justin had forced her at gunpoint to take him to Carrie's and Anna's room. From that moment on, everything had taken a scary downward spiral. At times, Emily felt like she was clinging to life by the skin of her teeth. *Yes, like the time the chopper was being shot at. By my own people! Or when we almost crashed into the Dundas Mountain. And the time when Seahawk's rotor blades sliced through the ice hill. Man, I could have been killed so many times. Then, the resuscitation of Justin, the constant care for Tania and Kiawak. It was all so crazy!*

She shook her head in disbelief and finished her coffee in slow sips. She stretched her legs and arms while still sitting on her chair. Her entire body was tense, and she felt her head pounding. Emily began to massage her neck muscles, which were completely stiff, while turning her head to the left and to the right. Then, she paced in the small hall.

After about ten minutes, she reached for the cordless phone mounted on the wall and dialed a cellphone number from her memory. It took her a few unsuccessful tries to realize the phone line was dead. She glanced out the window at the clear blue sky and the bright sun. The view gave her the determination she needed to keep dialing until she got a free signal. As she heard the dial tone, she quickly punched the number.

"Hello, this is Bryan," the familiar voice replied after the first ring.

"Hey, Bryan, it's me," Emily spoke fast, afraid the line might go dead at any second.

"Emily, you're OK, sweetheart? Where are you?" Technical Sergeant Bryan asked, all in one breath.

"Arctic Bay. North of Borden Peninsula, on Baffin—"

"I know where it is. Are you OK?"

"Yes, I'm fine. Can you guys come and get me?"

"Well, the commander wasn't sure if we could violate Canada's sovereignty."

"What? Tell me you're kidding."

"Unfortunately not, but I'll get him on the line. Now that we know where you are, it shouldn't be difficult to get authorization from Canada for a rescue mission."

"Hurry up and… thanks."

"OK, you just hang on in there. We'll come and get you."

Her nervous pacing, while holding the handset pressed to her ear, lasted less than a minute.

"Sergeant Moore," the commander asked. "Are you doing well?"

"Yes, sir," Emily replied. "Just eager to come home, sir."

"Have they mistreated you?"

"Negative. Other than the horrors of battling the blizzard and crash-landing blindfolded on an ice field, I'm doing well."

The commander let out a laugh of relief. "You don't have a gun pointed at your head as we speak, do you?"

"No, no. Everyone's gone."

"They left you alone? Where are Justin and the others?"

"Oh, they're off to battle."

"What did you say? Battle? What battle?"

"You know the Danish attack they were mumbling about when at the base?"

"Yes, the wargame. Denmark has made plans for military exercises over the next couple of days."

"Well, Justin and his gang are convinced the Danes are hostile, and they're going to land in Nanisivik, believe it or not, to take over the Northwest Passage. This place, Nanisivik, they told me it's about an hour from here. Justin and his men gathered around a hundred people to meet the Danes there and give them a real taste of the Canadian hospitality."

"Nanisivik? You sure about this?"

"Absolutely sure, Commander. The town there has a deep sea port, and Justin has information about a Danish icebreaker that is going to anchor right there, in the Strathcona Sound."

"That's strange because our satellites show no images of sea vessels. Instead, a large footprint of a transport aircraft, possible a Hercules, is beeping on all radar screens."

"Hercules? Where's the airplane headed?"

"I thought it was Resolute until you mentioned Nanisivik. If you put together this and the bogus information about the icebreaker, everything makes perfect sense."

"I don't understand," Emily said.

"If it's true the Danes are carrying out an invasion, they have done an excellent job masking their true intentions. They've circulated false intel on seaborne maneuvers, but they're mounting an air attack."

"Air attack? Didn't you just say the footprint was of a cargo plane?"

"I said it was a transport aircraft, since these Hercs are used mainly for supplying equipment and refueling, but also for transporting troops and weapons. These monsters can easily carry more than a hundred combat troops in their belly. Who knows what else, in terms of weapons, the Danes may have stored inside the plane, if it's theirs."

"You're not sure whether this is a Danish plane?"

"Correct. Our identification capacity's limited because of the great distance between our base and the target and their possibility of the pilots intercepting us. Besides, the Canadian Forces have a few of these planes. In any case, you don't have to worry about anything. We have a few choppers on standby, and I'll dispatch one right away to extract you. What exactly is your position in Arctic Bay?"

"I'm at the Health Center."

"OK, stay there. Shouldn't take long before our boys will come to get you."

"Thank you, sir. What about Justin and his battle?"

"It doesn't involve us, Sergeant." The commander's sudden change of voice, from a warm to a strict tone, expressed his feelings about the matter much stronger than his words. "It's not our battle."

"But if this Hercules is Danish that means it's probably carrying a company of soldiers," Emily said. "And if Justin and his men are making their stand at the seaport, instead of the airport, then—"

"Sergeant Moore," the commander did not let her finish her sentence. "I'm ordering you to stay put until our Seahawk's arrival."

"Where's the airport? Nanisivik's airport?" she asked.

"Why, what's that got to do with anything?"

Emily kept silent.

There was some paper shuffling on the other side of the phone line, then the commander spoke again, "The airport is southeast of town, about eighteen miles south."

"Eighteen miles," Emily repeated. "South, that's behind their back. Justin will not see the Danes coming until it's too late."

"As I said, Sergeant Moore, this is not our fight." The commander spaced his words equally, pronouncing them with a pause in between.

"I can't just let them die, slaughtered like lambs, Commander. You don't know, but Justin saved a woman's life, bringing her out of the freezing ocean. He risked his own life and almost died while saving her."

"So? He risked your life a thousand times, and he wouldn't lose sleep over it if he did it again."

"That may be true, but I have a chance to save his life and the lives of all his men and women, brave people, sir, who're not afraid to fight for what they know is right."

"I don't believe—"

"The goal," Emily said, "the goal justifies the means. You'll send your men here to save my life, why not save the Canadians as well?"

"Not my call."

"I'm sorry, sir, but I can't just sit here and let them die."

"Then use a damn phone to call them."

"Phones don't work all the time in this place. Plus, I'm sure they can use an extra shooter. And they can use many more, sir."

"For the last time, Sergeant—"

"You're breaking up. I can't hear you, Commander? Commander?" She placed the handset back on its wall-mounted base.

What the hell did I just do?

Nanisivik, Canada
April 14, 7:45 a.m.

"We've got the guns." Kiawak brought his walkie-talkie closer to his mouth, as he looked through the door of the Parting Waters door at Strathcona Sound. Carrie had taken him, Joe and a few other men aboard the Seahawk, to prepare for the Danish invasion. "Joe's setting up a perimeter in the hills around the seaport. As soon as those bastards set foot ashore, we'll give 'em hell."

"That's good," Justin replied on his radio. He held tight to the door handle, as the Land Rover slid to the left.

"Sorry," Anna, the driver, mumbled.

The gravel road connecting Arctic Bay to Nanisivik was coated with a thin layer of fresh snow. It provided sufficient tire traction for most of the trip but also concealed slippery ice patches.

"Don't worry, you're doing a great job," Justin said to Anna. "Kiawak, is the Otter back from Grise Fiord?"

"Yeah, got here ten minutes ago. He brought those Danish rifles we found, and we're gonna use them to pierce new holes in their butts."

"Is Carrie with you?"

"No, she dropped us off at my place, and she's been looking for a vantage point but hasn't made up her mind yet."

"Did any of the contractors stay?"

"Hmmm, less than what I thought. A handful or so."

"Better than nothing," Justin said, "since we didn't get anyone from Resolute."

"I guess. How far are you?"

"Ten, fifteen minutes, maybe."

"OK, we'll see you when you get here."

"All right. It's all falling into place." Justin glanced at Anna, then at the Toyota truck in front of them. Their Land Rover was the third car in the fifty vehicle convoy. "Kiawak just got those *Let Støttevåbens* we found in Nuqatlak's place in Grise Fiord. Those should greatly increase our firepower."

"Great," Anna said, struggling with the steering wheel.

The radio crackled. "Justin, can you hear me? This is Ned," said the driver of the lead car in the convoy. "I've got some bad news."

"What is it?" Justin said.

"Emily just finished telling me we've got the wrong place. Our plan, our defenses, our entire operation is wrong."

"OK, calm down and tell me what you mean?"

"She says the Danes are not coming by sea, but they're landing at the airport."

CHAPTER TWENTY-THREE

Nanisivik, Canada
April 14, 07:55 a.m.

"Are you sure about this?" Kiawak asked over the radio, trying to curb the anger in his voice.

"Absolutely," Justin replied. "Emily, I mean Sergeant Moore, is so convinced this intel is true, she's coming to join our forces."

"That's what I call conviction. We should move our positions to the airport."

"Yeah, right away. The Danes have probably realized their mole has been caught, and they've changed their plans."

"When did Emily say the Hercules is landing?"

"I don't know. I don't think she knew. Could be anytime."

"The terrain around the airport isn't great, lots of small hills and very little cover," Kiawak said. "We may still have the upper hand, especially if we get there before the Danish troops spread out. We're moving there right away."

"OK, we're turning the convoy around as we speak," Justin replied, then hung up.

"What are you thinking?" Kiawak asked Carrie, who was gazing at the ceiling of the Parting Waters.

"I'm thinking how it would feel to drive two Hellfire missiles deep into the guts of that Hercules."

"I'm sure you'll get your chance to do that. Now, let's buckle up."

Nanisivik Airport, Canada
April 14, 8:15 a.m.

The aft ramp lowered slowly onto the packed gravel airstrip. The freezing wind swept around the doorway, its loud howling protesting the arrival of the C-130J Super Hercules airplane. The recruits stared at the snowstorm brewing outside. Gray clouds hung over the hills on both sides of the runway.

"Soldiers, welcome to Nanisivik," Gunter's voice echoed over the intercom system. "Everyone knows his job, so let's go out and do it."

Magnus appeared at the small door connecting the cockpit to the galley and the cargo compartment. The latter had been configured for maximum seating capacity, and the troops were packed in tight rows. They were stretching their legs and chatting with each other.

"How was the trip?" Magnus asked Valgerda.

She stood up from her seat, the first one to the right of the galley. "Manageable." She straightened her hair. "They behaved, well, mostly."

"Time to go, soldiers," Magnus shouted. "Form a single file when exiting the plane and line up to the left in platoon formation. We'll hand out weapons once my team's ready. The terminal is our first target. Secure a perimeter and take control of the Otter and the two Bell choppers in the hangar. Don't wreck them, since we'll need them for our next missions."

"Magnus," Gunter's voice came over his earpiece. "A hostile truck is approaching the plane. Take care of it."

"Right away," he replied on the small mike incorporated on his Kevlar helmet.

"No, I've got it," Yuliya said and moved in front of Magnus.

She unzipped her white Gore-Tex jacket and removed her sidearm—the easily concealable HK MP5—from the holster wrapped around her shoulder. Then, she ran across the cargo compartment and jumped off the ramp. Her heavy combat boots crunched on the gravel. She ignored the wind gust and stared at the incoming vehicle, an old model Ford. It was still about three hundred feet away. Yuliya guessed it would take the driver about twenty seconds to reach the airplane.

She turned around and gazed at the gravel airstrip. The airplane's nose wheel had stopped a few feet short of the end of the runway. Both pilots had fought with the airplane's controls to complete the wheel brake operation. A large snowbank lurked over the cockpit, casting a shadow feet away from its front glass. *This is probably the largest and the heaviest airplane to ever land here.* She shook her head at the deep ditches the Super Hercules wheels had dug into the runway.

She looked up at the approaching Ford. The driver—maybe in his sixties—did not seem too impressed, judging by his burning eyes.

"What the hell are you doing here?" the old man spit out his words. He stopped the truck and got out.

"Get lost," Yuliya shouted back.

"Who do you think you are?" The old man began to walk toward her.

Yuliya waited until he was at point blank range, before bringing out her gun from behind her back. The old man gawked at the weapon. She jabbed its short barrel into the old man's chest and squeezed the trigger. His shriek was muffled by the gunfire and the thud of his dead body collapsing to the ground.

"The coast is clear," Yuliya whispered on her mike, turning around to face the aft ramp. "Aegir Rise!"

As soon as she shouted the code words, waves of recruits burst out of the airplane, like the God of the Sea in the Norse mythology rising with rage from the watery depths. They formed four platoons with wild hoorays. Four men from Magnus's team carried out two large containers, the weapon caches. As soon as Gunter stepped off the plane, every recruit was ordered to pick up a Gevær M/95 automatic weapon, the standard assault rifle of the Danish army, along with four magazines, each containing thirty rounds. They also picked up a side weapon, the small Sig Sauer P210, and an extra magazine for it. Two men in Magnus's team were armed with Barrett M95 sniper rifles. The the other five, including Valgerda, carried Gevær M/95s specially fitted with a 40mm grenade launcher.

Valgerda joined Magnus, who was standing by the Ford, and jumped into the truck box of the old Ford.

"Let the rookies drive," she said.

Magnus nodded. "Sargon, Vince, Ali and Dominique," he shouted at four men in the front row of the closest platoon to him. "Step forward. You're coming with us to be the leading unit as we take over the terminal. Hurry up!"

The recruits obeyed his order. Sargon and Vince climbed in the cabin. Ali and Dominique sat across from Magnus and Valgerda.

"Man, it's so freaking cold," Ali, a small bearded man complained, as he leaned against the side rail.

"No worries," Valgerda replied. "We'll light up this place so it's blazing hot."

* * *

"They've overrun the terminal," Joe said. He was scanning the windows of the one-story building through his powerful binoculars. "Some blonde guy is having a smoke by the hangar." He adjusted the zoom, swinging his head to the left. "Other people are moving toward the road, about a mile to our left."

"Shit," Kiawak swore and spat on the ground, "Herman's probably dead. I see someone else driving his Ford. Now the sons of bitches have another airplane and two choppers, besides the one they flew in and they're heavily armed."

He counted up to fifty silhouettes, mostly in winter fatigues, each brandishing an assault rifle. He tossed his binoculars on the passenger's seat of his Toyota and plodded for the truck box. Their small convoy of five vehicles was parked next to a small ice hill, which seemed to provide them sufficient cover from the airstrip.

"What are you doing?" Joe followed him.

"I'm out for revenge, what do you think I'm doing?" Kiawak lifted the black tarpaulin cover, pulling out one of the *Let Støttevåben* machine guns.

"You're gonna just run down there and kill everyone?"

"Save it, Joe. I'm not gonna stay here and wait."

He slammed a 100-round C-Mag drum into the receiver and pulled back the bolt. His action slid a round from the magazine into the gun's chamber. The weapon was ready. All Kiawak had to do was tap the safety switch, which he did with a flick of his finger.

"We need a plan." Joe blocked Kiawak's path, who sidestepped around him and went through a tall heap of snow. "We need a strategy."

"We don't have time for that." Kiawak turned around. "We planned our defenses at the inlet and see what happened?"

"That's because we had the wrong place. Now we know where the enemy is."

"I'm going downhill," Kiawak shouted at the other eight men, who were standing quietly around their vehicles. "Who's coming with me?"

"Kiawak, you're a hunter. Think like a hunter," Joe said. "This is like chasing a polar bear."

"Yes, kind of. Here we have our chase dogs, our snowmobiles, and then hunters surround the polar bear. Oh, wait, we can't really surround these sons of bitches because they completely outnumber us." Kiawak raised his voice as he spurted out his last words.

"My point is that you need hunters, you need many people for a successful kill. We've got to wait for Justin and the rest of our men."

"How far are they?" Kiawak asked after a deep sigh.

"Can you check how long until they're here?" Joe called at one of the men.

"We can stop their advancement. We can do this." Kiawak took his binoculars and glanced at the airstrip. Then, he spat on the ground.

"What now?" Joe asked.

"More black flies scattering around the runway. I'd love to swat the bastards." Kiawak pointed his weapon at one of the Danes and gently stroked its metallic trigger.

"Even if everyone was here, they're still out of range for our guns," Joe replied, looking thought his own rifle sight. "They're probably a thousand yards away, maybe even a little more than—"

A metallic bang cut off his words. It sounded like a heavy hammer striking a steel barrel. Joe glanced to the right side of Kiawak's truck, less than four feet away from his position, and noticed a bullet hole the size of his fist. Before he could say another word, the window glass shattered, spraying a storm of slivers around him.

"Hell," Joe yelled, dropping into a snowbank. "They may be out of *our* range, but we're getting hammered by their snipers."

"Justin says they're about two miles and a half south," a man shouted, while crawling for shelter behind one of the Suburbans.

"That's maybe five minutes," Joe said.

"Where's Carrie?" Kiawak raised his head from the pool of slush where the sniper shots had sent him and ran his eyes over the horizon.

"She's behind the ice ridge." Joe pointed to his left. "I guess she anticipated sniper fire."

"Well, when's she coming out to fight, 'cause we—"

He was interrupted by a deafening blast, as the Seahawk arrowed through the sky, a few feet above ground. As it descended over the runway, rapid reports of machine gun fire from the Seahawk began mowing down the Danish vanguard that had begun climbing the hills.

Kiawak saw a few silhouettes falling to the ground. His men shouted battle cries with every rattle of the Seahawk's weapons.

The air assault lasted for a few seconds and then, as suddenly as it had appeared, the helicopter vanished, taking cover behind the ice hills, a few hundred yards away from the trucks.

"There you go girl," Kiawak yelled. "Give 'em hell."

* * *

"What's the casualty count?" Gunter stomped out of the airport terminal. Yuliya followed two steps behind him.

"We're still checking, but we've confirmed four dead," Valgerda replied over the radio. She was crouched behind the Hercules's nose wheels, clutching her assault rifle. "The attack was uncoordinated and—"

"I saw the attack," Gunter interrupted her, "and how it was or it wasn't carried out. But how come these idiots have Seahawk choppers? And how the hell do they know of our change of plans?"

Valgerda knew better than to offer a guess.

"We're setting up positions, sir," Magnus replied. He was digging up a small trench in the snowbanks by the runway. His men, the foremost unit of the Danish troops, had suffered two casualties, both recruits. "There will be no more surprises."

"Support sniper fire with machine guns from one of the Bells," Gunter commanded.

"I've got it," Yuliya said. "Yuri, Alexei, come with me," she called at two of the guards. They left Gunter's side and began to jog toward the hangar.

"We've got to take that hill. Now!" Gunter said. "I don't want to get pinned down here while they call in reinforcements."

"We'll take the hill, sir," Magnus replied. "It won't take long."

* * *

The machine gun rattle greeted Justin even before his convoy took the last couple of turns snaking down the airport road. As soon as they stopped, about thirty yards behind Kiawak's truck, two bullets struck the hood of their Land Rover.

"Crap," Justin ducked instinctively. "What the…"

A Bell 204 helicopter was hovering in the sky, to the east of the runway.

"Get out of the car, quick," Anna shouted.

Justin shoved open his door and crawled behind the Land Rover's front wheel. He held his M4 carbine with his right hand. Anna sat next to him.

"You're OK?" Justin asked.

"Yes. I'm good," she replied.

They stared at the rest of the convoy in front and behind them. People had dismounted their vehicles and were scrambling for cover, alongside their vehicles, in snowbanks or behind the ice hills.

"Ned. Ned," Justin yelled, as the hammering continued from the Bell's gunners.

There was no answer.

"I don't think he can hear you," Anna replied.

Ned was less than fifty feet away, but the gun blasts made their communication impossible.

Justin's walkie-talkie chirped. "Yes," he answered it.

"Hey, Justin," Kiawak said quickly in a loud voice. "We're getting slammed here. Your men have any long range guns?"

"No. All we've got are assault rifles," Justin replied. "M4s and the like."

"Too far. The chopper's too far away."

"Half a mile?"

"Yeah, I think so."

"Has Carrie tried an assault?"

"Yeah, she did. A few minutes ago," Kiawak said, "but we're saving her Seahawk for a rainy day."

"This *is* a rainy day. It's hailing bullets." Justin pressed his back against the Land Rover's tire.

More rounds clang against his truck and the other vehicles.

Kiawak said, "Yeah, I know Justin, but the battle has just begun."

CHAPTER TWENTY-FOUR

Nanisivik, Canada
April 14, 09:00 a.m.

"OK, so what do we do now?" Kiawak asked.

Their small group was huddled behind the ice ridge, next to the Seahawk helicopter. Though they had managed to gather together, they had done little to deal with the enemy's air advantage in the air.

"Well, there are no reinforcements," Justin said. "So, whatever we plan, it's entirely up to us to do it."

"Their strongest points of attack are the snipers and the Bell chopper," Carrie noted. "Our defenses aren't gonna hold forever if we don't eliminate them."

"Their sniper attacks came from only two positions." Justin began to draw on a patch of snow. "Here and here." He stabbed the snow at two points. "One by the terminal and the other to the left of the plane. The chopper usually strikes from the right, with two gunners. But everyone's beyond our gunfire range."

"So, we've got to get closer," Anna said.

"That's easy to say," Joe replied. "Their snipers have us in their crosshairs at all times. If we attempt to advance, it's certain death."

"There's got to be another way," Justin said.

Carrie shook her head. "There isn't. I have to agree with Anna. We need to push forward."

"But how?" Kiawak asked.

"We need to move at the same time and at the same pace. The Danes have no idea how many men we have. But we know they have no more than two hundred of them. It's impossible to squeeze more troops in that plane. I propose we begin a slow, motorized attack, one man driving a vehicle, with another one forcing their way in through constant shooting. I'll cover from the air."

"Wait a second," Kiawak said. "The sloped terrain is very difficult for our vehicles, especially SUVs with no rear-wheel drive."

"We'll use all-wheel drive trucks only," Justin said.

"I don't know about throwing our entire force into battle all at once. We have about a hundred people, roughly," Kiawak said.

"Thirty/sixty," Carrie said. "We'll prepare thirty trucks with sixty men, who will attack first. The second wave will be the rest. They'll pour downhill once the front units have gained good positions."

"If they make it," Joe mumbled. "OK," he added after a brief pause. "Let's do it."

"I'm going in the front line," Kiawak said, "and you're not coming with me. The men need you here." He pointed his finger at Justin.

Justin smiled. Changing Kiawak's mind was a lost cause. At least in these circumstances. "I'll lead the second battalion, General." Justin saluted Kiawak.

* * *

"What the hell are they doing?" Gunter barked, noticing ten trucks plodding through the snowbanks and sliding downhill toward the runway. The ruts they left behind in the snow looked like scratch marks of a giant's hand. "They're... they're attacking us?"

"Negative, sir, we're not taking fire," Magnus replied over the radio. "But they're advancing to gain strategic positions. My men are shelling them with heavy fire."

Magnus's two sharpshooters, Hobart and Soren, had burrowed trenches halfway between the runway and the hillside. They were taking aim indiscriminately at the approaching vehicles. Magnus raised his binoculars to his eyes just as Hobart clipped the right mirror of the front truck, a Ford 350. The driver steered to the left, but his rear wheel mired in an ice rift. The truck came to a halt. A man peered from the truck box and fired several shots from a light machine gun. Hobart corrected his aim by a few millimeters and his .50 caliber bullet blew away the right side of the shooter's chest.

"One down, no, two down," Hobart said with a smirk. Soren's slug pierced a large hole through the driver's door.

"Great job, guys," Magnus congratulated them. "Keep it up."

The Danish soldiers were shooting at the other vehicles too. Their firepower had stopped a Dodge Ram, but its driver was still blasting round after round. His machine gun bullets snipped ice chunks and raised snow dust in front of the Danish troops.

"Luigi and Benito, move forward!" Magnus called at the troops. "They're still too far."

Luigi looked back at Magnus, who was standing by the Hercules's cargo door, and shook his head. Benito also ignored Magnus's words, keeping his head down and flattening his body against the snow.

"Fucking mafiosi," Magnus cursed.

"Sir, I've got it," Hobert said.

He turned his sight to the right, toward the Dodge. A few rounds coming from a white truck to his left reminded him there were closer targets that needed his attention. Before he could take a shot, Soren pulled the trigger of his sniper rifle. The white truck kept inching downhill regardless of the hole Soren's bullet drilled in its windshield. Hobert had no clear shot of the driver from his position. He aimed at the right front wheel and planted his bullet at the intended spot, blowing out the tire. The white truck sank in the snow and began to tip over, until it rested dangerously on its right side.

"Is the driver still alive?" Soren asked.

"I don't know," Hobert replied. "I don't see any movement."

"Let me handle this," Valgerda whispered over the radio.

She began plowing through the knee-deep snow, avoiding rifts and crevasses. She tried to keep to the trail set by other troops who had marched through before her. Cutting to the left, toward her target, she noticed the muzzle of an assault rifle flashing at the rear end of the white truck. Valgerda lay on her stomach and began to crawl through the snow. She pushed forward for about sixty feet, and stopped when a couple of bullets slammed into an ice block less than four feet from her head.

She raised her Gevær M/95 rifle. Once the truck was exactly in her crosshairs, she pulled the trigger very slightly. The grenade launcher screamed, and a gray cloud of smoke engulfed her. Two seconds later, the warhead exploded in the white truck's cabin tearing it to shreds.

"That's it," Magnus said. "Watch and learn, guys."

Three other trucks began descending down the hill to their right flank. Magnus's binoculars identified six men aboard the trucks.

"Hobart, Soren," Magnus said. "We've got more visitors."

"I'll take care of them, sir," Hobart replied.

"Sargon, Vince, and Ali," Magnus ordered another group of recruits, "support Hobart and Soren by attacking these targets." He glanced at the group. They were standing about one hundred and fifty feet away from the runway. "Onward, soldiers!"

"Sir, they're shooting shit at us from all sides," Ali replied over the radio. "It's not safe to go any farther."

Sargon and Vince dug their heels in as well.

"Soldiers," Magnus hissed. "Move ahead as ordered. Now!"

Ali refused to respond to the command, but Magnus had no time to convince his defiant men. A metallic bird of prey materialized over the ice hills and began slaying the soldiers with its steel talons.

The Seahawk poured a torrent of bullets over the frontline positions of the snipers before taking a sharp dive to the left and out of sight. The surprise attack had given the Danish force no time for any counteracting fire.

"Kill that damn pilot," Gunter screamed over the radio.

Magnus adjusted the volume of his earpiece before suffering permanent damage to his eardrum.

"Bring down that bloody chopper," Gunter shouted.

"Where the hell is Yuliya?" Magnus asked.

"I'm on my way," she replied. "It took me some time to turn the Bell around, since this rusty piece of junk doesn't work well."

Magnus's binoculars followed the flight of the Bell helicopter. It hovered over the runway for a few seconds before it went screaming toward the battlefield.

"That should take care of that problem," Valgerda said.

"I hope so," Magnus replied. *I've got my own problems to resolve.* He glanced at Ali's group still rooted in their trench.

* * *

"Fire! Fire at the chopper!" Justin shouted.

The Bell roared, circling above their heads.

"We are." Joe slammed a fresh magazine in his *Let Støttevåben.* "But the beast is moving so fast."

He cleaned the snow from his face with the ear flap of his toque, and straightened his gloves before resuming shooting.

"Maybe we should have Carrie dogfight this," Anna suggested between sporadic shots. Justin had given her a crash course on how to use his M4 carbine. The weapon rested heavily on her arms. The firing recoil jerked the metal stock against her shoulder.

"Carrie's ammo's running low," Justin replied. "We have to ride this on our own."

"Doesn't she have Hellfire missiles or some rockets?" Joe shouted.

A volley of bullets sprinkled the Land Rover. Anna gritted her teeth. Justin offered her a reassuring smile, but her eyes showed their defense needed a more powerful boost.

"Ned," Justin called at the man lying fifteen feet in front of him, "status!"

"Two men critically wounded," he replied. "Nilak tells me they have three dead and ten wounded, two of them in serious conditions."

"That's beside the guys lost down in the field," Joe added. "Seven or eight, I believe."

"Can we afford another attack?" Justin asked.

"Not until the flying monster's dead," Joe replied. "Or at least down on the ground."

Justin peeked through a couple of holes in the Land Rover's doors. The Bell helicopter completed a downward pirouette and was rising up toward the ice ridge. The Seahawk was hidden behind it.

"Well, the pigeon's going to the hawk." Justin pointed out the obvious. "Is Carrie ready?"

"She better be," Joe replied.

* * *

As soon as the enemy helicopter appeared over the hill, the Seahawk broke into a long volley of machine gun fire aimed at the Bell's tail rotor. The Seahawk hovered a few feet above ground, swinging slightly to the sides.

As machine gun bullets slammed into the Bell's rotor blades and pierced its tail boom, the helicopter pivoted to the right. Yuliya's mission had been turned upside down. She struggled to regain control of her helicopter and avoid a nose-first crash into the fast approaching ground.

The Bell responded to her commands and regained its earlier altitude but only for a few moments. Sharp electronic beeps erupted throughout the cabin. Flashing red signals on the control panel urged

Yuliya to perform an immediate emergency landing. But landing behind enemy lines meant death or capture. She attempted a one hundred and eighty-degree turn.

The unsafe maneuver brought the helicopter dangerously close to the ice-covered hills. At the last moment, the Bell jerked upwards, the damaged tail rotor barely missing a huge rock jutting out of the ice ridge. Yuliya steadied the helicopter and headed back to her camp.

* * *

When Carrie fired her shots, she intended to disable the Bell helicopter and force the pilot to land within easy reach of Justin's men. The crew of the downed helicopter would serve as bargaining chips. Once Carrie realized the pilot was escaping her trap, there was no point in holding back.

The Seahawk pitched forward until it was about a hundred and fifty feet above the ridge. Carrie tapped the joystick mounted on the center console, which controlled the machine gun. The powerful rattle returned. She spread out her bullets evenly over the entire length of the runaway target.

Soon enough, the Bell was swallowed up in a thick cloud of smoke. Carrie eased on her trigger, waiting for the inevitable explosion. A few seconds passed. The Bell helicopter appeared on the other side of the gray cloud, still airborne, but swaying to and fro like a duckling during its first flight.

Carrie closed her left eye, once again focusing on her target. She wondered whether she should launch one of the two Hellfire missiles.

"C'mon," she yelled. "C'mon! Go down, you son of a…"

The Bell swirled around a couple of times, dropping a few dozen feet. Then, it jerked upwards, regaining its lost altitude. But when the pilot had steadied the helicopter, its main rotor blades stopped spinning. The helicopter took a downward plunge, fast and hard.

The helicopter was doomed. Some of the Danish troops scurried in panic as the large fuselage of the Bell helicopter crashed into the permafrost. The impact shattered the ground. The ensuing explosion hurled huge blocks of ice and rocks in all directions and tore open the ice shield. The crater swallowed the helicopter's wreckage, as dark waves slammed against the edges.

"Holy crap!" Carrie stared in awe.

Narrow crevasses stretched like cobwebs for tens of feet on both sides of the pit. It looked like when a rock cracked but did not shatter window glass.

* * *

"The Danes are over a lake," Justin yelled over the jubilant shouts of the men around him, "over a lake whose ice cover is busted open."

"Yeah," Nilak added. There are two ponds by the runway. Tim used to complain that water from melting ice would flood parts of the runway."

"Why didn't we think of this earlier?" Justin said. "The solution is right in front of our eyes. Call Kiawak and the rest of the people back."

"Eh, what? Why?" Joe asked.

"Our best defense is the natural one, the lake. We'll blow off the top, breaking apart the ice sheet and sinking every one of these jerks."

* * *

"Sir, Yuliya's gone, sir," Valgerda mumbled over the radio.

"I can fucking see that," Gunter exploded.

Valgerda removed the receiver from her left ear. She could still hear him blurting obscenities and ordering four men to prepare the DHC-6 Twin Otter airplane for the fight.

"Magnus, where are you?" she shouted and began to look around. "Magnus?"

"I'm here, down here," he replied with a groan.

She followed the sound of his weak voice until her eyes found him lying on his back. He was about fifty feet away from the helicopter's grave. She noticed a trickle of blood over his right pant leg and a long tear, about four inches, on his shin.

"Fuck," Magnus cried, as he tried to get back to his feet.

"It's not broken, is it?" Valgerda asked.

Magnus placed his heel carefully over the slippery ice. "A damned ice sliver almost cut off my freaking leg. What was Yuliya thinking?"

"I guess she wasn't. And neither is Gunter." She pointed at the terminal. "He just ordered the Otter in."

"Yeah, I heard it." Magnus took an uneven step, leaning on Valgerda's shoulder.

Whizz.

A bullet screeched over their heads. They both ducked. Magnus's leg failed him. He plunged into the snow, cursing and rolling downhill. Valgerda returned fire at the closest truck from where the shots were coming. A couple of trucks farther up the hill were struggling to retreat from their initial positions.

"They're falling back," she said over the mike. "The enemy's falling back. All troops, fire at will, fire at will."

The gunfire from their recruits was not as loud as she expected. Valgerda repeated her order. More recruits joined in, but their firepower had diminished, and their shots were sporadic.

"You're OK?" Valgerda stopped shooting to check on Magnus.

"Yeah, I'm fine. Lost my footing there and avalanched down the hill."

He gasped for air and flattened his jacket. Then he dusted off the snow.

She glanced at his leg. The skin was now completely exposed, and his pants had ripped in another place.

"I'll get that checked as soon as we're over this bump," he said. "What were you saying about those trucks?"

"They're moving back. Or at least it looks like that."

"Maybe they're regrouping."

"It could be."

"How are we doing?"

Valgerda looked around then dug out her binoculars from inside her jacket. A brief surveillance of their troops gave her the bad news. "We're retreating, too."

"What? Who gave that order? Gunter?"

"I don't remember hearing it."

"Cowards. It's those damn cowards." Magnus lifted himself to his knees. Valgerda placed her arms around his waist.

"What are you talking about?"

"I noticed insubordination even before the helo crash. I've got to fix this myself."

He staggered to his feet. Realizing they were out of enemy fire range, they both kept their heads up.

"Hey, you," Magnus shouted at a man smoking a cigarette and chatting with other recruits, their backs turned against the battle hill. They were standing about a hundred feet away from the runway, at a very safe distance from the gunfight. "Ali, right?" Magnus asked with a grimace.

"Yes," Ali replied. "Wanna smoke?"

Magnus shook his head, his hand groping for his submachine gun. Once he found the trigger of his MP5 still hanging in its holster, he pointed the gun at Ali.

"Hey, man, what you doing?" Ali spread his hands, taking a step back. The half-smoked cigarette fell out of his mouth.

Magnus caressed the trigger, jamming the gun into Ali's throat.

"Don't try it," Valgerda barked at Ali's companions, who scrambled to pick up their guns. She kept her rifle lined up with their heads. "Unless you want to bang seventy virgins tonight."

"Relax, I'm not going to shoot you," Magnus said coldly. "But next time you disobey my orders, I'm gonna kill you all, one after the other. When I tell you to advance, you do it, or I'll blow you heads off. Now get your asses there, all of you, and use those guns in *that* fight." Magnus gestured with his head toward the hill.

The group took up their weapons and reluctantly headed for the battle. Valgerda followed their every move, in case someone decided to become a martyr. No one did. She sat across from Magnus, on a heap of frozen snow.

"I'll get the first aid kit and do what I can." She pointed at his wound.

"Fine," he said with a shrug. "I'll update Gunter on our status. We'll need more men. Maybe all of them."

CHAPTER TWENTY-FIVE

Nanisivik, Canada
April 14, 10:23 a.m.

"So, that's your plan?" Anna rolled her eyes. "Drive to their flanks, plant the explosives and kaboom, it's done, just like that."

Joe's face remained calm. Kiawak looked at Justin, who was sitting with his back against the ice ridge. They were back in the small clearing, their improvised headquarters away from the battlefield.

"What do you think?" Justin asked Kiawak. His words sounded more like a plea for support rather than a simple question.

"It... it may work," Kiawak replied, unsure about how to word his hesitant approval. "I mean, the frontal attack isn't working, and we're still counting our losses. This is probably our last attempt."

"It will work," Joe said strongly. "We *will* make it work."

"You'll need a lot of suppressive fire," Carrie noted. "We also have to take the Otter airplane out of the equation before we sneak any men down to the lake."

"I'll go with my own truck," Kiawak said, ready to stand up. Justin placed his hand on Kiawak's shoulder.

"I'll go with you," Joe said.

"Wait a second," Justin said. "Let's not rush things. Carrie, you were saying about the Otter?"

"The airplane's last attack left us with three wounded. I don't want Kiawak and Joe or anyone else out in the open while the Otter's still overhead. We've got to trap him or engage him head on."

"Plus, the Danes have launched another attack, this time with twice as many troops," Anna said.

"Which makes it even more pressing for us to act now." Kiawak spread his hands. "If we keep sitting here and talking, they'll climb up the hills and we're all be dead."

Anna squinted as Kiawak spat out the word "dead." They were under the threat of incoming bullets at all times. But the way in which Kiawak uttered the dreaded word, in a cold, flat tone had a powerful effect on her doubts and fears. She asked, "Where do we start?"

"I'll take on the Otter," Carrie replied. "My big gun is almost out of ammo, but if I calibrate the Hellfire missiles properly, I should easily bring down the airplane."

"I'll have everyone hammer their soldiers, so they'll have no time to fire at you," Justin said. He turned his head in Kiawak's direction. "You'll need more than Joe for this thing to work."

Kiawak nodded thoughtfully. "Of course. I'll take two, maybe three other guys. I'll drive, two guys will set the charges, and a fourth man will slam the Danes with continuous fire."

"I'll do the same on the other side," Joe said. "We need to advance at least halfway to the bottom of the hill, about half a mile. We'll use the chopper's pit as a central point, since the ice sheet has already cracked around it. I wonder how big each explosive charge should be?"

"How much dynamite do we have?" Kiawak asked.

They all chuckled.

"No, seriously," Kiawak continued. "Like Justin said, this is our last stand. We can't afford any miscalculations."

"All right," Joe agreed, noticing the head nods of Carrie and Justin. "We'll use all we've got. In terms of distance, I'm sure fifty feet apart should do the trick."

Anna asked, "How thick is the ice sheet?"

"About two feet or so," Kiawak said, "but I can't be sure. We don't want to just break the ice along the perimeter. We want to break apart the entire sheet over which these bastards are positioned, so they'll all sink and die, drowning and freezing to death. Fifty feet between charges is about right."

"That will require constant pounding for twenty, thirty minutes," Justin estimated.

"Yeah, that sounds reasonable," Kiawak replied.

"What do you think?" Justin asked Carrie.

"I think the battle will be over either way, but I hope it will swing in our favor."

"I'll round up the men." Kiawak stood up. Joe followed behind, encouraging him with a shoulder tap.

Justin gazed at them for a long time, wondering if he would see them again.

* * *

"We'll be in position in five," the pilot of the DHC-6 Twin Otter airplane informed his two gunners kneeling by the rear cargo door. They had attached their safety harnesses to the handles inside the compartment, in order to withstand the rough flight, as the plane took sudden turns and steep dives. "Try to get the chopper this time," he added.

"What about those trucks?" asked the first gunner, pointing at two vehicles rolling down the hill. They were off to the sides, and it seemed they were avoiding a direct clash with the Danish troops.

The pilot glanced at the suggested targets and shook his head. "Negative. The land forces will handle them, and they don't seem like an urgent threat to me. Our sole objective is the helo."

"Roger that," replied the first gunner, cocking his Gevær M/95 assault rifle.

The pilot tapped a few controls, and the airplane climbed about three hundred feet. The maneuver gave the pilot an unobstructed view of the ice ridge. The usual hideout of the Seahawk was right behind it, but the flat clearing was empty. The helicopter was nowhere in sight.

"Where did the helo go?" asked one of the gunners.

"I have no idea, but I'm… there," the pilot said, pointing at a small black dot on one of the control panel screens. "Two o'clock. Looks like our hawk's trying to fly away."

The pilot stared through the windshield at the horizon. He squinted hard and spotted the helicopter in the distance. "That's our target," he said. "Let's get him, boys!"

The airplane picked up speed and altitude at the same time.

"Wow, buddy," one of the gunners shouted. The swift acceleration threw him against one of the walls. He juggled his gun, nearly dropping it through the open door. "Take it easy. And shouldn't we let the commander know about this change of plans? The pilot of that chopper is pulling us away from the combat zone."

"I'm a pilot and *the sky* is my combat zone," replied the pilot. "Our order was to take down the helo, and that's what we're doing. Hang on tight there."

* * *

"First stop," Kiawak shouted at Nilak, Iluak, and Sam, who had volunteered for the explosive setting mission. "Hurry!" Kiawak pulled on the hand brake.

The brothers replied by jumping out of the truck box.

Sam stayed behind, lying next to a wooden box full of dynamites, blasting caps, detonators, and wires. He gazed at the enemy through the scope of his M-16. The Danes had yet to take any shots at their vehicle, even though they were trailing slowly to the flanks of the platoons. A single truck was too little of a worry for the Danes, since Justin and his men were hammering the Danish positions with heavy fire.

"We're almost done here," Nilak said in a loud voice, chipping at the snow with his ice pick, digging a small, but deep hole.

Iluak scooped out the snow, then planted four eight inch long dynamite sticks. Kiawak had already bundled them together and inserted blasting caps on each one.

Nilak inspected the copper wires to ensure they were connected properly to the cap.

"Good to go," he shouted, once satisfied with their work.

They climbed back into the truck box, and Kiawak pressed the gas pedal.

Nilak held the dynamite wire roll steady as they proceeded downhill. He counted for thirty seconds then called on Kiawak to stop. The brothers were once again on the ground, setting another explosive charge.

* * *

"What's that truck doing?" Magnus asked over the mike, pointing at the white truck descending over the slopped terrain. "This is their fourth stop."

Valgerda raised her binoculars slightly over the ice sheet. She ducked immediately to dodge a bullet that ricocheted less than two feet away from her head.

"You're hit?" Magnus asked.

"Nope, I'm not hit," she replied with a sigh. Her voice was shaky, like her hands. "But it was close."

She fired her weapon toward the enemy positions, two vantage points on the side of the road. Then, she looked at Magnus, who had taken cover behind a thick ice boulder.

"Cover me," she said. "I'm coming there."

Magnus peeked over the boulder and fired his assault rifle a few times. When he looked back, Valgerda rolled next to him.

"You're OK?" he asked.

"Yeah. Running low on ammo though." She tapped on her ammunition belt around her waist, fetching another fresh magazine. "These bloody Canadians are tougher than we thought."

"We're advancing, but very slowly," Magnus said.

She glanced through her binoculars at the white truck Magnus had pointed out earlier. "I'm not sure if they're trying to run away or surround us," she said with a snort. "If it's the first, they're going the wrong way; the second, they're just pathetic."

"I don't think it's a maneuver to attack us on our flanks or try to box us in. There's another truck, a white Toyota, to our right," Magnus said between sporadic shots. "There, I got one of the dirtbags," he said, watching as a human silhouette fell off a black truck.

"Great shot," she said. "I wish the rest of our troops were getting somewhere."

"Oh, c'mon." Magnus shrugged. "He was just standing there, out in the open."

Valgerda tilted her head in a whatever-you-say pose. "What do you think those trucks are for?"

"I don't know," he replied, while unloading his Gevær M/95. "Maybe they recon, to determine our numbers."

"Can't they see from atop the hill?"

"Yeah, but they don't know if the Herc's empty or how many are back at the terminal."

"A recon team you say?" Valgerda pondered his words.

"Could be. I don't think they've started to fire at us yet, but I'll order our men to gun them down."

"Only if they have clear shots. No use in wasting our last rounds."

"Of course."

Valgerda surveyed the white truck one more time. Two men jumped out of the back, dug briefly in the ground, then hopped back in their place. "I don't know," she said. "They keep getting stuck, and two men dig in the ground. But it's behind the truck and to the sides, not in the front. What's going on?"

"It's only seven people, and they can't do much harm. I'll tell my men to wipe them out. And just for good measure, I'll inform the Herc's pilots and Gunter at the terminal."

Valgerda squeezed her rifle's trigger. "I think I got one too." She raised her binoculars to confirm the kill. "Yes." She grinned. "Five down, a hell of a lot more to go."

"It would be easier if we had some aerial support." Magnus looked up for any sign of the Twin Otter airplane. "Where did the pilot go?"

"Gunter sent him after their chopper. I guess that's where he went."

"Yeah, but I don't see the Seahawk either. Where are they?"

* * *

"Someone's coming." Ned stared at the cloud of snow nearing from the north, the direction of Nanisivik. "I thought we had everyone willing and able to fight."

Justin turned around, his assault rifle ready for action. "Let's make sure it's hostile, before we blast him," he shouted.

Anna and a few others followed Justin's cue. If a Danish soldier were riding in the middle of the snow cloud, he would be greeted by a hail of bullets as soon as he showed his face.

Ten long seconds dragged on, toying with their nerves. Then, the profile of a snowmobile became visible, as it came to a jerky halt on the wrong side of the road. Justin looked sideways but did not recognize the feeble-looking man wrapped in a white parka. He had black gloves, a red toque, and a large pair of ski goggles.

"Who's that guy?" Justin asked, noticing Ned was grinning and had already lowered his weapon.

"False alarm," Ned replied. "That's Amaruq, one of Kiawak's old buddies."

"What's he doing here?"

"I have no idea."

Before Justin could say anything, Amaruq had removed his goggles. "What the hell?" he blurted at the welcome wagon, but staring mostly at Ned. "You're fighting without me? Why didn't anyone tell me about this party, eh?" He staggered toward Ned, his shaky feet sliding over ice patches on the road.

"You're drunk, man." Ned shook his head in disgust. "What good are you to us? Go back home."

"Oh, get out of my face." Amaruq waved him off. "If I'm drunk, which… which, OK, I am, then you… you're stupid, yes, you are."

Ned turned around, heading toward his fighting position.

"Yeah, get lost, move it," Amaruq yelled at Ned. "You're not in charge anyway."

"But I am." Justin took a step forward. "What do you want?"

Amaruq peered at Justin's face then at the assault rifle in Justin's hands.

"I want to fight. I got up this morning and one of the guys told me everyone was fighting some Swedish badasses—"

"Danish," Anna corrected him.

"Ehe, yeah, Danish. So, I'm saying to myself, what the hell, they forgot me?"

"You can fight?" Justin asked.

"Hell, yeah. I've been hunting before you were even born."

Amaruq's breath stunk like an Irish pub. Justin doubted it would be a good idea to give a gun to him.

"I… I don't know," Justin said, worried about enraging the old man any further. "You can help with the wounded down there."

"Do I look like a nurse to you?" Amaruq spewed out, taking a step forward. "I'm a... I'm a hunter and yes, I do drink. Sometimes. I... I ran out of Listerine today and I needed... needed to wash my mouth. Verbal hygiene's important, you know."

"Oral hygiene, you boozer," Ned shouted. "Send him home, for Pete's sake, before he kills one of our guys."

"You shut up or else..." Amaruq charged in Ned's direction.

Justin held out his hand. "Whoa, whoa, hold it! The battle's down there, soldier. If you want a gun, I need to know you'll follow orders. Can you do that?"

"Yes, sir. I can, sir." Amaruq attempted a standing guard position. His right arm trembled as he brought it up to his temple.

"OK, I'll get you a gun." Justin gestured at Anna, who brought him a Lee Enfield rifle from a stash of boxes behind them. "You know how to use this?"

"Bring it here." Amaruq snatched the rifle from Justin's hand. "I fired rifles before you were even born."

Yeah, I know, you said that earlier. And I know I'll probably regret doing this. "Shoot only when you can hit the target. That's the only mag you'll get. And stay close to me."

"Yes, sir," Amaruq replied. This time he did not bother with the military salutation. He cocked his rifle and ran toward the closest truck set up as a barricade.

"I said..." Justin began to talk, but realizing his words were useless, he hurried behind Amaruq. "Don't go anywhere else," he shouted. Amaruq nodded and pointed his rifle at the Danish positions.

* * *

Carrie did not have to consult her radar screen to determine the location of her tail. The Twin Otter airplane was visible in the horizon, as she hiked her way up, and pivoted to her left. The airplane was tailing her at a distance of about two thousand feet. It was within her missile striking range, as indicated by the Remote Hellfire Electronics system incorporated into the control panel.

The Twin Otter would have no chance of survival once Carrie fired the laser-guided missile. She would push a button and forget about it, while the airplane disintegrated into a million pieces. As she flipped the switch encasing the weapon activation button, another thought crossed her mind.

She remembered the Bell helicopter smashing through the ice sheet and wondered if she could orchestrate the crash of the Twin Otter over the combat lines of the Danish troops. It would lend a helping hand to the explosives planting mission. Even if the airplane crash did not burst open the ice sheet, it would trample the soldiers and demoralize the rest of the troops.

Carrie grinned. She imagined the gray, metallic bird gravitating toward the ice surface after she had clipped both its wings. She slid the cover over the missile launch button and tapped the throttle, propelling the Seahawk into a swift ascent. *Never bring an otter to a dogfight.* She smiled to herself.

CHAPTER TWENTY-SIX

Nanisivik, Canada
April 14, 10:57 a.m.

Kiawak, the driver, felt pain jolting upwards from his leg at the same time he heard the metallic clunk. The bullet pierced through the door of his Toyota and landed in his right shinbone. He glanced down. The first trickle of blood seeped through his ski pants. He tried to ease up on the gas pedal but realized he had lost control of his right foot. A second later, the truck slammed into an ice boulder.

"What the hell, man?" Nilak yelled from the truck box. The impact had thrown him against the rear window. He saw sparks coming from the tailgate. "Freak, we're getting shot at."

"I can see that," replied Sam. A foot away from Nilak, he was laying on his stomach on the truck bed and blasting his gun at the Danish recruits.

Iluak peered at the cabin through the small window. "Are we stuck?"

"Shit," Kiawak replied.

He tried to lift his foot from the gas pedal. The Toyota roared and jerked, going nowhere.

"What's going on?" Nilak asked.

"We're not stuck. I've got a bullet in my leg. I can't move."

"I'll come and get you out," Iluak said.

He jumped from the truck box and landed in a snowbank. He lost his footing, slipped and fell on his back, just as a bullet shattered the passenger's window. Other bullets rained on the stalled vehicle.

"Shit." Kiawak pushed the driver's door. "Iluak, stay down," he yelled.

"Kiawak, we're sitting ducks here," Nilak shouted. "Do something!"

"I'm trying." Kiawak pressed his shoulder against the door, gritting his teeth and dragging his leg. "Get out of the truck, both of you," he shouted. More bullets hammered the vehicle.

"Sam, Sam," Nilak said and began shaking the unresponsive gunner. Sam's head was hanging to the side, and Nilak saw a large wound in the man's chest, as he rolled over the lifeless body. "Kiawak, Sam's dead, Ki—"

"Nilak." Kiawak was halfway out of the truck, when he heard a thud from the truck box. "Nilak."

"Is he OK? Is my brother OK? Nilak," Iluak shouted from the other side of the truck.

"Stay down, stay down there," Kiawak shouted back. "He'll be fine. Still got your walkie-talkie?"

"Eh, yes, I think… I think so," Iluak replied, searching for the radio in his jacket pockets.

"Call Justin and tell him we're hit. Ask him to get the other men out of here. Tell him… tell him it's over."

* * *

"I was wondering why they were staying there," Joe shouted at Justin over the radio, while Neville and Max, his team members, kept alternating their shots.

On the other side of the hill, Joe's team had advanced deep into the enemy's right flank. The terrain sloped at a much softer angle, and the three-man team encountered little resistance. With the

Danish army largely destroyed and the suppressive fire from the Canadian positions up the road, Kiawak's vehicle had been the main target of the enemy's sporadic fire. Until now. Once the Danish shooters stopped the advancement of the Toyota, they turned their attention to Joe's Mazda.

"There we go, whoa." Neville exchanged a quick fist jab with Max, celebrating another casualty in the enemy ranks. "What's going on, chief?" Neville asked Joe. "Are we gonna do this or not?"

Joe looked at the adrenaline-pumped young man, a white skull bandana draped around his head. He flashed Joe an evil grin, while checking the status of a rifle magazine by tapping it lightly against his head.

"Kiawak's shot," Joe replied. "Sam's gone."

"Oh fu—" Max bit his lip, as a bullet drilled a deep hole in the front bumper, sending a few metal slivers above his head. "That numbskull almost whacked me."

"You're a lucky dude." Neville snorted and fired two rounds. "So, we're out of here or what?"

"I'm not sure. I'm still talking to Justin." Joe frowned at Neville, who shrugged and kept pulling the trigger of his *Let Støttevåben*. "You were saying, Justin?" Joe said, his back pressed against the truck's front wheel.

"Kiawak's wounded. Nilak may be dead by now." Justin sighed heavily. "I need to get them out of there."

"Are we going on with the explosion?"

"How far along are you? Three, four more charges?"

"Actually, it's only one more, but we can blast 'em right away, if need be."

Justin paused to mull over this information. "Even if you do set them off, the chances of the ice shattering all the way around are not that good, are they?"

"I don't know," Joe replied. "We'll cause a huge blast on our side, but without Kiawak's explosives I doubt the ice sheet will cave in entirely. Can't Kiawak fire them up from where he is?"

"He said he could do that, but they're three charges short."

"That's a hundred and fifty. Crap!"

"Yeah, I don't think it's gonna work."

"How about sending someone else to finish the job?"

"The area's too hot," Justin replied. "At this point, I can't send other men. Even a rescue mission is going to be difficult. Hey, where are you going?"

"What?" Joe asked, confused about Justin's question. "I'm still here."

"Come back here," Justin shouted.

"What? What did you say? Whom are you talking to?"

"I've got to call you back, Joe."

"No, wait, what do we do? Huh? He's gone." Joe groaned.

Neville looked up at Joe for a second. "My girlfriend does that to me all the time, hanging up on me and shit." He placed his left eye once again on his machine gun's scope.

* * *

"I ordered you to stop." Justin followed Amaruq, who kept marching toward his snowmobile. "Where the hell do you think you're going?"

"I'm saving Kiawak's ass, since no one else seems to give a damn about him."

"What are you talking about?"

"I heard you talk to Joe on the radio about the rescue being difficult and all that bullcrap."

"I didn't say we're not gonna help him."

"Yeah, right. You stay here and talk, while I'll show you how it's done." He turned his back to Justin, proceeding to start his snowmobile.

"Amaruq, I can't let you do this. It's suicide." Justin stepped in front of the snowmobile. Amaruq was busy tying his rifle to one of the saddles.

"Well, in that case, you have to shoot me 'cause I ain't staying here and watch my friend die."

Amaruq fired off the throttle. Justin sighed, staring at the M-16 in his hands. He held Amaruq's dark blue eyes for a moment, realizing he was powerless against the storm brewing in the old man's soul.

"Fine." Justin began to move aside. "Just pick up Kiawak and his men and get back right away. Don't even think about—"

His last words were lost amidst the snowmobile's engine blast. Amaruq hacked his way into a snowbank and down the steep hillside.

* * *

Amaruq avoided the crooked trails plodded by the trucks' tires. He cut through the snow as far away from the Danes as the broken and rugged permafrost would allow him. At first, he slalomed in a regular pattern, with slow, circular turns and rare jumps, as he dodged ice hills, rock boulders, and snow crevasses. Aware of his vulnerable position as he approached the enemy flanks alone, Amaruq picked up speed. At the same time, he shifted into a largely dangerous and mostly improvised descent. Sharp S curves, swift zigzag maneuvers and random leaps over rifts, as well as increased cover fire from Justin and his men, allowed Amaruq to swoop unharmed close to Kiawak's jammed truck.

"Fifty more feet, you can do it," Amaruq whispered to himself, hanging onto the handlebar while the snowmobile sprang over a pressure ridge and landed on an ice patch. "Crap," he swore, his body bouncing on the seat.

The snowmobile kept sliding and swerving, in danger of tipping over at any moment. His fingernails clawed through his gloves, as he tried to cling to the tottering vehicle. The left ski had broken off as a result of a bad landing. The sled was now tilting to that side. He steered to the right to counterbalance the drag and felt the snowmobile losing traction. *The rubber's probably broken or one of the lugs is damaged.* He was not in control of the snowmobile any more.

A barrage of bullets scrapped the ice a few feet in front of him. Amaruq ducked. His head was at the same level as the snowmobile's windshield. He released the throttle and tapped the brakes, seeking cover behind a tall mound of ice boulders. Then, he screamed in pain from a sharp stab in his right arm. A bullet struck him by the elbow.

"Ah."

It was all Amaruq could grumble before finding himself airborne and rolling to his side in midair before plunging head first into a deep snowbank, a few feet away from a large crevasse in the snow.

* * *

Carrie completed a small circle around the Twin Otter. The airplane needed a much larger space to perform any rotational maneuvers and a much longer time frame. On the other hand, the Seahawk could change its direction in a matter of seconds. But the airplane had the upper hand if it came to a straight-line pursuit because of its two powerful turboprop engines.

Understanding the Seahawk's weakness, Carrie zigzagged left and right, climbing and dropping constantly, avoiding a fatal fall in the crosshairs of her pursuers, and always maintaining a safe distance of no less than three thousand feet. Beyond the maximum fire range of medium-caliber weapons, she felt relatively confident when playing cat and mouse with the airplane. *If they had any rockets or missiles, they would have launched them by now.*

The altimeter locked the Seahawk's position at nine hundred feet above ground. Carrie searched the entire battleground for the best location to bury the enemy airplane. She noticed two trucks far to the sides and assumed they were the teams of Kiawak and Joe. Carrie looked through the helicopter's camera mounted at the tip of the fuselage. The image on the screen was grayish and somewhat blurry, but she recognized human silhouettes spread out in fighting positions in trenches or stretched without moving on the snow.

She veered to her left, dropping about eighty feet and glanced at her radar screen, looking for the Twin Otter. It was still behind her. She glanced again at the field below, this time through the windshield, and noticed a quick moving dot darting over the snowbanks and the ice mounds. *What on earth is that?* Puzzled by the discovery, she dove in for a better look. At three hundred feet, the shape of the object became clear. *A snowmobile is all Justin has for backup?*

Carrie tapped the throttle and the Seahawk responded with a swift ascent. The Twin Otter repeat the same maneuver, but at a slower pace. She reached for the radio just as the snowmobile slammed right into a snowbank, dropping out of sight. *What the hell just happened? Did he get shot or lost control of the sled?*

"Hey, Justin, come in."

"Carrie, where are you?" Justin replied.

"About half a mile to the left of the field. Can you see me?"

"I can't see anything. We're being hammered here and almost out of ammo."

"I hear you."

Carrie made a quick right turn.

"I was planning to drop the Otter over the enemy to help with the explosion."

"No time for tricks, Carrie. Kill these bastards now before they wipe us all out. And the explosion plan failed."

"Repeat your last," Carrie said. "Did you say it failed?"

"Yes, unfortunately."

"Got it," Carrie replied. "Did you send the snowmobile to extract them?"

"Kind of. Don't know if Amaruq made it."

Carrie swallowed hard before breaking the bad news to him. "Justin, he didn't make it. I saw the sled crash into a snowbank and almost fall into a crevasse."

"What?"

"Yeah, I'm sorry."

"And the driver? Amaruq?"

"I didn't see him, but I'm getting closer. Let me take another look."

The Seahawk circled at about two hundred feet. Carrie tapped a few controls, pointing the camera and zooming in on the snowmobile.

"Wait a second," she shouted. "Justin, I think he's alive. This guy, he's alive."

* * *

Amaruq found it impossible to tell whether his dizzy head was spinning around or his body was still rolling on the ground. In any case, he drove his hands deep into the snow, scrapping the ice layer underneath, desperately searching for something to cling on and stop his fall. The burning pain coming from his arm did little to deter his efforts. He grabbed at the edge of a rock jutting above the ice and stopped sliding.

He stayed there, lying on his back, staring at the gray clouds in the sky. A minute or two passed, as Amaruq tried to catch his breath. He noticed a bloody slush around his right elbow by the bullet wound. His left glove was missing, and his fingers were already beginning to suffer the frostbite. *At least I'm alive. But where exactly am I?*

He stuck his head up after brushing snowflakes and ice chunks off his face. The crevasse was about two feet to his right.

"I barely missed it," he mumbled, wondering about the depth of the pit.

A couple of bullets landed within arm's reach. Their screech helped Amaruq by pointing him in the right direction. He crawled to his left and saw Kiawak's Toyota, less than thirty feet down the hill.

"Kiawak," he shouted, as he began crawling toward them. "Kiawak, Kiawak."

"Amaruq? What are *you* doing here?" Kiawak's voice was so feeble Amaruq wondered whether it was his imagination or he really heard Kiawak's words.

"I'm saving your sorry ass," he replied. "Since no one else was willing to take the job."

"Good for them. Is Joe out of this hellhole?"

"No, they're waiting for you to light the fuses."

A bullet slammed against the side rail of the truck.

"It's over, Amaruq. Let's get out of here."

"What about the explosion?"

"It's over, get it? My freaking leg it's broken. Sam's dead, Nilak's dead."

Amaruq stared at Kiawak. A pool of blood had gathered around his left side. Iluak sobbed next to his brother's body.

"You'll be fine." Amaruq reached to give Iluak a reassuring pat on his shoulders. The man's empty stare showed he was transported to another reality. "Both of you are going to be fine. I'll get you out of here. I wonder if the truck's still working."

"You're not touching my truck."

"I have to. I've got to finish setting the explosives."

"No, it's not gonna work. You'll get yourself killed."

"Oh, shut up! I've heard that enough for one day. Nothing bad will happen to me."

"You're already bleeding like a walrus." Kiawak pointed at Amaruq's arm.

"Flesh wound, nothing big. But, if Joe and I don't set off the charges, we'll still have to deal with these Danes."

A few metallic thuds against the truck confirmed his words. Amaruq slid into the trench dug by Kiawak and Iluak.

"How many more are left?" Amaruq asked.

"You're drunk, man," Kiawak replied. "How can you—"

"What? Save your ass while drunk? I don't know. You tell me, since it was your whisky that gave me the courage to drive from Nanisivik."

"*Courage* was not the word I had in mind."

"Whatever it was, don't say it, unless it's 'thank you.' How many more explosives are left?"

"Twelve sticks for three charges."

"How far apart?"

"Fifty feet."

"Is the truck stalled?"

"No, it shouldn't be. I hit the ice block when I got shot. You'll have some trouble backing it out."

"If I drive down, it shouldn't be that difficult."

"Don't forget to double-check the wires. I've already placed the caps on the dyno sticks. At the end, once you're ready, give Joe the signal with the flare gun. You know how to use that, right?"

"Yes, you know I do."

"Just making sure. Take care, old wolf. Don't get yourself killed."

"I won't."

Amaruq peeked from underneath the rear tire. He waited for a few seconds, glided over the ice and pushed himself up. At first, he clung onto the truck step then climbed up and reached the driver's seat.

"I can't believe I'm letting you drive my baby especially now that it's full of explosives."

"Don't worry. I won't make a dent."

A bullet skimmed over the hood of the truck at that same instant.

"See," Amaruq said with a grin. "What was I saying? *I* won't make a dent."

CHAPTER TWENTY-SEVEN

Nanisivik, Canada
April 14, 11:21 a.m.

Carrie held her left thumb over the firing button of the Seahawk machine gun as she flew over the front lines of the Danish troops and gave them a fierce pounding. The helicopter completed a daring descent over the runway. She brought up the Seahawk to escape any backlash from the troops her onslaught had spared. Several metal-on-metal clunks came from underneath the helicopter. The Seahawk was hit. Flying instruments issued no warnings about any noticeable damage. *Time to bring out the big guns.* Carrie smiled.

She leveled the Seahawk at a thousand feet. The Twin Otter was far behind over the airstrip. Carrie surveyed the Danish troops for the place where a Hellfire missile would cause the most casualties. There was some movement at the center of the vanguard, a few men pressing ahead. She tapped a couple of switches, calibrating the missile for air-to-ground combat. Entering a series of numbers, she set the striking coordinates for the laser-guided weapon. Then, she flipped a switch to the right of the throttle.

"May God have mercy on their souls," she muttered and pressed the missile launch button.

The missile screamed as it whooshed off the left launcher of the weapons pylon. A dense cloud of white smoke swallowed the underside of the helicopter. The missile tore the sky's veil with its orange glowing trajectory. Less than a second later, the Hellfire missile stabbed right through the heart of the Danish camp. The blast fragmentation warhead exploded with a hailstorm of metal shrapnel, brash ice, and rock fragments, scattering everything outward in a wide ring of death. The missile blew a large crater in the ice sheet— about fifty feet wide—as well as many smaller pockets. Nothing seemed to be moving around the explosion site.

Before Carrie could savor her success, two electronic alerts beeped throughout the Seahawk's cabin. She grasped the throttle, jerking the helicopter upwards, before glancing at the control system.

"Crap," she shouted.

The tail rotor had taken a hit.

One of the crossbeam blades was clipped severely, and the rotor shaft was also damaged according to the control panel instruments. Once the tail rotor blades stopped spinning, the Seahawk's airborne balance was at risk. There was nothing else left in the helicopter to counteract the torque force of the main rotor. The Seahawk would pinwheel its way to a crash because of its downward yaw movement.

The altimeter needle swung sharply to the left. The helicopter plunged tens of feet in a single second. Carrie pressed the throttle, trying to keep a high speed while flying forward. This maneuver could allow her to use the helicopter's tail as if flying an airplane, while she picked a safe area for the crash-landing. As soon as she began this emergency maneuver, the radar informed her the Twin Otter had closed the distance. The enemy airplane was tailing the Seahawk at the unsafe distance of less than a thousand and five hundred feet.

Carrie had no time to blurt out a string of curses. The left side window cracked, the bulletproof glass stopping the incoming bullets.

More bullets clobbered the helicopter's metallic frame. The alarms blared from almost all the control panel sensors.

"I get it, I get it," Carrie yelled at the machine. "We're gonna crash. We're gonna freaking crash. But not yet. Not yet."

She silenced the angry alarms with quick gestures of her hands, and prepared to launch the second Hellfire missile. She fed into the system the coordinates and pressed the launch button without any further delay.

"Take that you pricks," she shouted.

The Hellfire missile darted forward for a brief second. Then, it took a left turn and aimed for its target. Carrie pirouetted to her right, just as the missile slammed into the cockpit of the Twin Otter. A million pieces of scorched debris rained over the ground.

Carrie allowed herself a brief moment of celebration. A new electronic beep, sharper and louder than the previous ones, warned her of a new failure. This time, it was coming from the main rotor. Other bullets had damaged its blades. The Seahawk dropped fast, spiraling about thirty feet each second.

A controlled crash-landing had become impossible. The Seahawk pirouetted another time, gravity driven. For the first time in hundreds of hours of flying, Carrie began to feel dizzy. Her eyes became blurry. She tapped buttons and switches and levers, uncertain of the one controlling the emergency jettison of the pilot's door.

Her efforts failed. The door's lock mechanism was damaged and had jammed the door. The ground approached. The helicopter plunged fast, swinging uncontrollably while falling to its imminent crash.

Carrie cursed the door, realizing it was useless to try and pry it open. She reached for her Browning 9mm pistol. With the Seahawk taking its last twirls, she aimed the gun at the door latch and pulled the trigger. She emptied the thirteen bullet magazine in a rapid burst of fire. The latch and the encircling glass burst into pieces. Carried threw her body against the door.

The door swung open.

She found herself falling through the air and the black smoke. The helicopter swept across the sky. Its main rotor blades wheeled slower and slower, while the ground approached faster and faster. The helicopter took another final twirl before crashing into the ice sheet. Carrie plopped into a deep snowbank, just as the Seahawk's explosion rocked the entire hillside.

Sharp metal pieces from the helicopter's wreckage, ice, and rock slivers flew all over the field. Then, the freezing waters of the crater devoured the Seahawk's burning remains. The ice sheet began cracking with a blaring noise, eating up adjacent hills, ridges and snowbanks.

* * *

Kneeling by the Toyota truck, Amaruq held the orange flare gun in his left hand. He double-checked to make sure it was loaded properly. He glanced at the last charge of dynamite he had just finished connecting to the electrical detonator box by his feet. The only thing left to do was to signal Joe by firing the flare gun.

Amaruq pulled the trigger and watched the yellowish trace arch over the Danish camp. A similar flare rose up from the other side a moment later, indicating Joe was in position and the blast was forthcoming. He reached for the detonator controller, a yellow plastic box, which fit easily in his palm. He pressed a white button labeled CHARGE and held his thumb on the switch. The device began creating the necessary electrical charge to light up the detonators.

Amaruq was not certain if Kiawak had synchronized the blasting caps for a simultaneous explosion of all charges or if the long row of dynamites would go off one charge after the other. In any case, he would have to cover at least two hundred feet, to escape the explosion's range and to survive the blast of the dynamite charges.

His thumb pressed hard on the detonator switch, Amaruq began crawling toward safety. But he was exposed to the enemy, who had noticed his bright signaling flare. Bullets circled around him. He kept moving forward, his head a couple of inches off the snow, his body half sunk into the snow.

"You're almost there, keep going," he encouraged himself. "Right behind—"

A bullet ricocheted off an ice boulder, striking Amaruq in his left foot. It skimmed over his pants, carving a flesh wound. He brushed it aside. But the next bullet hit him in the shoulder, pinning him to the snow. He screamed and turned sideways, trying to push his body deeper into the snow. A third bullet snuffed the air out of his lungs.

Amaruq looked at his bleeding chest then glanced at the detonator. His fingers were still wrapped around it in a fierce grip. The red indicator light was steady. It meant the explosive charges were ready for the blast.

He tried to lift his right shoulder, but a gut-wrenching pain zapped through his entire body. He was running out of breath and he could not even crawl an inch. He was stuck within the deadly range of the explosion. Another screaming bullet shattered his knee cap, forcing Amaruq to make a decision.

With great strain, he slid his trembling index finger until it rested over the DETONATE button, while keeping his thumb over the CHARGE switch. He took a deep breath, knowing it was his last. Once he was certain his fingers were not going to fail him at the last moment, he pushed the DETONATE button and began the countdown in his mind. *Five. Four. Three. Two. One.*

* * *

The simultaneous explosions made the earlier Hellfire blast and the helicopter crash resemble fireworks at a New Year's party. Kiawak had coordinated the blasting caps to detonate all at once. Joe's team set off their string of dynamite charges at the same time. The explosion not only split open the entire ice surface of the lake, but also blew away rocks from its bottom. The ice sheet caved in piece by piece, starting at the sides and dragging underneath everything and everyone still over it.

CHAPTER TWENTY-EIGHT

Nanisivik, Canada
April 14, 11:47 a.m.

"Amaruq? Has anyone seen Amaruq?" Kiawak shouted at a couple of men carrying him to a safer area on higher ground, away from the ice edges collapsing into the lake.

Their only reply was a sad headshake, as they placed him in the back seat of a truck.

Kiawak glanced to his right and saw a man running toward him. "Justin, where's Amaruq?"

"I have no idea. "Carrie…" he could not finish his thought.

Kiawak said, "She's still alive. I have this feeling she's still alive."

Justin nodded without conviction. "How are you doing?"

Kiawak coughed before answering, "I'll make it."

Justin looked at Kiawak's left side. The wound still bled over his clothes. "Our plan worked." Justin tilted his head toward the lake.

The scene resembled a catastrophic shipwreck. Some of Justin's men were helping the Danes who had survived the explosion. They were getting them out of the freezing waters. "I think it's over."

"Is it?"

"Yeah, it is. Whoever's left of the Danish troops that are not turning into ice cubes is making a run for the Hercules."

"Don't let anyone get away." Kiawak raised his head to observe the situation through the truck window. "And send someone to look for Amaruq."

"I'll look for him. Joe's taking care of the runaway and the Hercules."

"I'll stay with him," Anna whispered to Justin. She had just arrived with a group of men carrying more wounded in makeshift stretchers. Anna sat by Kiawak and tried to catch her breath.

"OK." Justin stood up and began plodding through the snow, treading a few feet away from the broken shores of the lake. "Carrie, Amaruq," he shouted, his hands funneled in front of his mouth. "Amaruq, Carrie, where are you?"

* * *

On the other side of the lake, Neville, Max, and other men were helping out the Danes who could swim to the shore. Joe and Ned had begun the final sweep against the remaining Danish troops. They had encountered a few pockets of resistance around the airport terminal and next to the Super Hercules airplane.

"So, why are we stuck here saving these pricks?" Max gestured toward a blond in a white jacket clinging to a large, floating ice chunk.

"Because, now they're POWs," Neville replied. "And because Joe ordered us."

"These sons of bitches were trying to kill us less than ten minutes ago. Now, we're supposed to save their lives?"

"We're not saving their lives. Do you see us get wet? No. We simply stay here, and if they wash ashore, then we pick them up."

The blond struggled to lift his body over the slippery edge of the shore, but his efforts were unsuccessful. After the blond's second try, Neville stepped forward very carefully. He offered the stock of his assault rifle to the survivor. He thought it was ironic that the same rifle was shooting bullets toward the blond and his band of brothers. The rifle now served to save the Danish recruit's life.

* * *

"Get this plane in the air. Right away!" Gunter screamed at the pilot, who was already scrambling with the airplane's flight controls. "You too." Gunter turned to the second pilot. "Hurry up!"

The Super Hercules began to rotate at a slow pace. The mammoth airplane required a few minutes for the jet engines to reach the takeoff speed. The gravel airstrip and the unfavorable positioning of the airplane—at the far end of the runway—were turning the routine step into an almost impossible goal.

It did not help that half a dozen men were pounding the flight deck with countless rounds of firearms. The cockpit's windshield and side windows were bulletproof, capable of resisting heavy barrages from all kinds of small-caliber weapons. Nevertheless, spider-web cracks made the pilot's task very laborious.

The increasing tension had eaten up all of Gunter's patience. "Hurry up; hurry the hell up," he shouted at both pilots.

He marched through the door connecting the cockpit to the cargo compartment. Two men were shooting sporadically through a few broken windows. These five people aboard the airplane were the lowly remains of the Danish contingent. Gunter and the two men had made it safely through the shootout ordeal to the airplane. It was the last resort for their escape, their flight out of hell.

"More men are closing in, sir," one of the shooters said. He reloaded his Gevær M/95. "I'm down to my last mag."

"All I've left are seven bullets," the other man said, raising his Sig Sauer pistol. His empty assault rifle lie discarded on the floor.

"Hold them back for another minute or so," Gunter shouted over bullets battering the metallic walls.

The airplane jolted forward and began rolling on the gravel.

"There we go," Gunter said with a sigh.

He hurried back to the cockpit, as the airplane picked up speed. "How long until we're airborne?" he asked the pilots.

"Soon, very soon," replied one of them. He flipped some switches and checked a few gauges in the control panel. "All systems are fully operational. No considerable damage to the wings or the engines."

"How much fuel do we have?" Gunter asked with a considerable amount of pleasure in his voice. The jet engine rumbles boosted his confidence.

"Sufficient to take us out of here," the other pilot replied. "Still, we may need to make a stop on the east shore of Baffin Island."

Gunter counted the seconds in silence, as the airplane defeated the gravity and began to climb up, slowy at first, but picking up speed with every passing moment. The gravel runway, along with the carnage, fell behind them.

Gunter took a seat and closed his eyes. *What a defeat. What an incredible defeat. I hope the Russians will still release Helma. They will have to. I did what I was told and the results... well, I can't control the results. We were prepared, but we made mistakes. We rushed our attack. We did not have enough people. I followed the FSB's orders. They wanted a swift, but small attack. We underestimated the Canadians and their reaction. They discovered our plans and ambushed us. Yes, that's what I will say, and the Russians better accept it. I'll not allow to be jerked around by them anymore.*

* * *

"Carrie, Amaruq. Carrie," Justin kept shouting, as he reached the end of the hillside. He had searched the nearby area twice, without finding any trace of the Carrie. Amaruq had disappeared as well. "Carrie, Amaruq, can you hear me? Carrie, Amaruq, where are you?" he repeated his shouts.

He noticed a large metallic object jutting out from the snow. He dropped to his knees and began sifting through the snow. Debris from the crashed helicopter was littering the area. Justin was careful to avoid any cuts by the sharp edges. He lifted some twisted parts of what seemed to be the helicopter's passenger door. He almost jumped with joy because of what he found underneath the wreckage. After brushing the snow to the side, he uncovered a Kevlar helmet. He stared at Carrie's ice-cold and pale face.

"Carrie," Justin whispered in her ear. He felt at the side of her neck for a pulse. He found it, barely throbbing, slow and irregular, but still beating. "Stay… stay with me," he whispered. "Don't die on me now." He drew in a deep breath. "Help," he shouted, but his voice wheezed out slightly louder than a whisper. He coughed to clear his throat before trying again, "Help, help. I need some help here. Help."

A couple of men sprinted toward him.

"I've found Carrie," he said. "Let's get her out."

"The chopper's pilot," one of the men mumbled.

"Yes," the other man replied quietly.

"Let's be gentle when we move her," Justin said. "Take the clips out, and make a stretcher with those rifles."

A third man arrived to lend them a hand. They threw their jackets over two rifles and used scarves and belts to form a somewhat sturdy stretcher. They placed Carrie over it and began to tread slowly toward the runway.

"Hey, hey, driver," Justin shouted at a man in the driver's seat of a truck by the airport terminal. "We need your truck. Hurry up!"

The man stepped on the gas and rolled the truck to a stop by Justin's feet.

"Open the door, the back door," Justin said.

They placed Carrie in the back seats, her head resting carefully on a jacket rolled up as a pillow. Her arms and feet hung unnaturally.

"I'll take over from here." Justin dismissed the men and climbed in the driver's seat. "Hold on, Carrie," he said. "I will *not* let you die."

Only if we had a doctor out here.

CHAPTER TWENTY-NINE

Nanisivik, Canada
April 14, 11:54 a.m.

"Emily, what in the world are *you* doing here?" Justin could not contain his enthusiasm in seeing the nurse awaiting their arrival at the top the hill. She was holding a box in her left hand. The words FIRST AID and a large white cross were embossed on its side.

"I told you I was coming. But it seems I missed most of the party. Then they told me you were bringing up a patient." Emily hurried to the other side of the truck. "How is Carrie doing?"

"I don't know. She's unconscious."

Emily looked for Carrie's pulse at the side of her neck and began to check her vitals. She lifted Carrie's head up to make sure there were no obstructions in her airways. Then, she leaned closer to Carrie's mouth, feeling for any sign of respiration.

"Unzip her jacket and lift up her sweater," Emily said.

The skin of Carrie's neck and upper chest had turned a yellowish-gray. It felt numb and frozen. Her chest was rising and falling, but very slowly and scarcely noticeable.

"Her breathing's shallow, but her lungs are getting some oxygen," Emily said. "Which is good, at least for now."

Justin's eyes were glued to a blue blister on Carrie's neck.

"Cryopathy, I mean frostbite, hasn't set in yet," Emily said after catching Justin's gaze. "Once we warm her up, the skin will be fully restored, since superficial frostbite is reversible."

Justin nodded in silence. Emily listened for a heartbeat.

"The heart rate is slow, very slow and irregular. What exactly happened to her?"

"She was in the chopper, piloting the Seahawk, when it was shot down. She had to jump out of the chopper."

"Ouch."

"Yeah, it was quite a distance."

Emily examined Carrie's arms and legs, paying special attention not to move her, and focusing mostly on her joints.

"At first sight, it looks like her legs are fractured, but I can't be sure. There may be internal bleeding in her chest and also in the abdomen, since the ribcage is easily affected by blunt trauma."

Justin swallowed and looked away.

"Carrie's alive," Emily said, "but we need to take her to a hospital as fast as we can. I have a few things in the truck to stabilize her for a while, but we've got to get her to a hospital. ASAP."

* * *

Joe arrived in his truck when Justin was getting ready for the drive to Nanisivik. Ned was riding in the passenger's seat. His eyes were puffy and red, bearing the clear marks of tears, even though he had tried to dry them out. "How's she doing?" Joe asked, while Ned stared out the window.

"Still out of it," Justin replied and walked over to Joe's truck parked a few feet away from his. "Emily, the nurse, says she's gonna make it, but we've got to rush her to a hospital."

"Arctic Bay?"

"No. Emily just drove from there and said they don't have the necessary equipment. Carrie may have broken ribs and fractured legs. She'll need surgeries. One of the defense contractor's choppers is in Nanisivik, so I'm heading that way. Our Eurocopter is still in Arctic Bay, so that will be our last resort. But I don't want to lose that much time."

"I wish I could tell you to use that Bell." Joe jabbed his finger toward the airport terminal. A red helicopter stood outside the hangar. "But it got damaged in the fight. We couldn't save it. And I couldn't stop those jerks from taking off in the Herc."

"No worries. We've won the battle, and that's the important thing."

All of a sudden, Ned broke into a low sob.

"What's the matter? Amaruq's d..." Justin stopped in mid-sentence, as Joe's rested his arm on Ned's shoulder.

Ned's weeping grew louder. "I called him names... but he, he just saved us all. I'm... I'm so stupid."

"Don't say that," Justin said. "You were trying to look out for him."

"No, no, I... I screwed up."

"Amaruq lived a hunter's life and died a warrior's death," Joe said. "Ned, we should be proud of him, instead of shedding tears. Amaruq, he would want us to do just that."

Justin nodded. "That's right. Has anyone told Kiawak yet?"

Joe and Ned shook their heads.

"He's not doing that well either," Joe said.

"What's our death toll?" Justin asked.

"I'm not sure. I don't have all the numbers. Could be somewhere between twenty and fifty, dead and wounded. The Danes, on the other hand, were wiped out completely. We only saved, what?" Joe turned his head toward Ned, who was trying to appear composed. "Seven, eight guys?"

"Seven," Ned replied. "The eighth is a woman. Her name is Valgerda."

"See, he's good with the gun and also has a perfect memory." Joe tapped Ned on his shoulders.

Ned replied with a shy, broken smile. "She surrendered when we took over the terminal. Her partner claims to be the tactical commander of their operation. His name is Magnus. Magnus Torbjorn."

"Magnus," Justin repeated.

He had hardly finished breathing the man's name, when a great explosion flashed in the sky. Far away, at the point where some white clouds were floating over the horizon, the bright yellow glow of an airburst flamed for a few long moments.

"What the hell was that?" Joe asked.

"Isn't that where the Herc was headed?" Ned said.

"The Super Hercules? You think that son of a gun found his doom up there?" Joe rubbed his long beard thoughtfully.

"Fire raining down from heaven?" Justin said. "A lightening rod up the Hercules's aft?"

They all laughed.

As their chuckle dwindled, another loud rumble came from the sky, from the same direction of the explosion. This time it was constant and ever increasing.

"Airplanes?" Ned wondered.

Joe shook his head. "It sounds like choppers, two, maybe more." He reached for his binoculars in the back seat of the truck. "Yeah," he added a second later, "three choppers."

"Canadian Forces?" Justin asked.

"Stars and Stripes." Joe handed Justin the binoculars. "They look to me like the one Carrie was flying."

"Seahawks?" Ned shouted. "American fighter helos? What's this turning into, the Third World War?"

Justin gazed through the binoculars at the approaching Seahawks. Other men had spotted the helicopters, and they were gathering around Justin's truck.

"How do the Americans know where we are?" Joe asked, stepping out of his truck.

"No idea." Justin stepped out of the truck, still peering at the helicopters. "Maybe there was a GPS transmitter in Carrie's chopper."

"Or maybe someone radioed them in," one of the men suggested.

"We've got to get ready," Joe shouted, holding up his M-16 in his right hand. "Ned, set up positions—"

"No!" A woman's voice interrupted them.

Justin turned around and saw Emily waving her arms in the air, striving to push her way through the group of men and reach Joe's truck. "They're not here to fight," she shouted.

"Oh, really? So, what do they want?" Joe asked Emily.

"It's Richard," Emily said to Justin. She got closer to him. "Colonel Richard Clark. You remember him. Commander of the Thule Air Base."

Justin nodded. "Did you call them?"

"Yes. I asked… I begged him to help you, to send in troops, but he refused. I'm surprised they're showing up here and now, but… hmmm, at least they can take Carrie and the other wounded to a hospital."

"Really? They come in peace?" Joe said. "Like the Danes?"

"Joe, calm down," Justin replied. "Emily has no reason to lie. She didn't have to come here. We left her in Arctic Bay, and if she wanted to save herself, she could have asked the Americans to come and rescue her there."

"She's seeking revenge for the time you kidnapped her," Joe said. "That's why she called Uncle Sam."

Emily frowned and shook her head. "Of course not. If I wanted revenge, I would have stayed in Arctic Bay. The helicopters would have dropped bombs over your heads as we flew over. I helped Justin and Kiawak and your other wounded friends. What a great way to seek revenge!"

Joe swallowed and looked around. A few men were nodding in approval of Emily's words. Some of them held up their gauze-wrapped arms.

"Well, maybe *they* want revenge, this Richard guy," Joe said. "I still say we need to set up positions."

Justin looked up at the helicopters. Their shape was now visible to the naked eye. Flying in a triangular formation, their rumble began to shake Justin's eardrums.

"How about this," Justin said. "Joe, you set up a defense line, while I go and meet up with them."

"I'll go with you," Anna said, stepping up beside Justin.

"Take Ned and a few other guys," said Joe. "In case things get ugly."

"I'm staying here," Emily said, moving to the driver's seat of Justin's truck. "Carrie will be in good hands."

Justin nodded. "Thank you. I appreciate it."

"Now, just to let you know, the commander, if he's there with the copters, may be slightly pissed off." Emily placed her hand on Justin's right arm. "At first, the commander didn't want to violate Canada's territorial sovereignty. But he was more than willing to order a rescue mission when I called the base from Arctic Bay. As we were talking, I learned from him about the Danish airplane landing here, like I told you earlier. But what I didn't tell you was that he ordered me to stay in the Bay. Obviously, I disobeyed that direct order. Besides," Emily bit her lip before continuing, "in the heat of the moment, I may have called him a coward."

"What?" Anna blurted.

"Yes, exactly that." Justin pointed at Anna.

"He wasn't going to lift a finger, and he wasn't coming to your rescue. I was trying to challenge him, in hopes he would change his mind."

"Well, your insult did work, since he sent three choppers here," Justin said. "Late, of course, but better late than never."

"I wanted you to learn this from me, in case Richard's in there, and comes charging at you about this."

"Trust me. He has many, many other reasons to be furious with me. Just keep an eye on Carrie, and I'll take care of this."

Justin looked over across the road. The three Seahawks were touching down over the permafrost. A cloud of snow dust surrounded them, as their blades began to slow down. "Let's go, guys." He gestured toward the Seahawks and led a group of ten men.

Anna followed one step behind him, her rifle ready to shoot at a moment's notice.

CHAPTER THIRTY

Nanisivik, Canada
April 14, 12:03 p.m.

Colonel Richard Clark was dressed in the same navy blue uniform as the first time Justin had met him, with a black felt overcoat that hung down to his knees. A deep frown was carved in his face.

"Commander," Justin said with a respectful nod.

His team stood at about fifty feet away from the commander and his men, seven people in all, who were lined up in front of their helicopters. They were carrying assault rifles and looked more like a SWAT team than a rescue dispatch.

"I owe you a big apology," Justin said.

The commander gave Justin a smirk.

"OK, two apologies. I took Emily with me, and I borrowed your chopper. But it was for a very noble reason."

"Go on, I'm listening."

"I have the evidence to convince you of the Danish attack. We've just survived a long and harsh battle. Many good men are dead or gravely wounded. We have captured a few of the Danes, who will testify to their evil plans, reasons, motives, and whatever you want to ask them."

"You don't have to convince me of anything." He gestured with his hand to his troops to relax their position. "I'm sure Sergeant Moore told you about the landing coordinates of the Super Hercules," he said in a quiet voice, although a certain degree of anger was still evident in his words. "Otherwise, you wouldn't be here. In a way, you could say she did you all a big, big favor."

"She did, you're right. In fact, I can truly say she saved our lives, a great number of our lives."

"I'm glad we agree on something. As soon as we intercepted the Hercules, we contacted the Canadian Forces to establish the identity and the objective of this plane. After confirmations that the plane was not Canadian, we demanded clarifications from Denmark. Their replies were vague, at best. They had scheduled a wargame for later in the week, but it was supposed to take place in international waters and airspace, not deep into Canadian territory. After we received this information, and as soon as the Canadian Forces authorized me to fly into the Canadian airspace and retrieve one of my own, I rushed in."

"Did you blast the Hercules to smithereens?" Anna asked.

"No. The airplane exploded all of a sudden."

"We tried to stop it from taking off. I guess our firepower must have damaged its flying systems," Justin said.

The commander shrugged. "I'm up to my neck in a matter that doesn't pertain to me. You and Canada can clean up *your* mess."

Justin nodded and exchanged a quick glance with Anna. "OK. The Seahawk was shot down and the pilot, Carrie, is unconscious, fighting for her life. I will kindly ask for your help to fly her and my other wounded men to a hospital. The closest one is in Iqaluit."

The commander took one step forward. "I guess this battle has taught you how to ask politely when you want something, huh? My clearance does not involve the transportation of Canadian army troops or irregular militia."

"I'm sure you have access to the right channels to ask for such an authorization. Many people are gravely wounded. They will die if not provided immediately with extensive medical attention."

The commander held Justin's pleading gaze for a brief moment. "All right. I'll get the necessary authorization, and we'll take your people on board. The only restriction will be the one imposed by the choppers' capacity."

"Thank you. I'm very much obliged."

He dismissed Justin's gratitude with a wave of his hand. "I don't see Emily among your people." His tone of voice expressed clear disappointment.

"Hmm, that… yes… about Emily." Justin chewed the words in his mouth.

"Is she dead?" he asked without any emotion. "You can tell me the truth."

"No, she's not dead."

"So, where is she? Didn't she recognize the Seahawks?"

"I was… I understand you and Emily exchanged some… some harsh words."

The commander moved closer to Justin. "Harsh words is a euphemism." He lowered his voice to a harsh whisper. "Sergeant Moore disobeyed a clear and direct order. She was willing to put my own life and the life of my men in great danger and force us into a war we have no part in. Now, where is she hiding?" He looked over Justin's shoulder toward a cluster of trucks further down the road.

"Emily has been a tremendous help to us and—"

"Save it, Hall. If she's a hero for Canada, then honor her bravery with a medal. But she disgraced her country, and she'll be lucky if she doesn't get court marshaled."

"Commander, I'm sure we can come to an agr—"

"Yes, an agreement. Hand over the traitor, and I'll save your girlfriend and your wounded friends."

Justin shook his head. "I don't think that's going to cut it. Emily deserves praise for her bravery, not punishment for taking a stand. I'm not going to let that happen."

Ned moved his M-16 rifle a little farther from his chest and settled his finger on the trigger.

"Maybe that's how you do things here in Canada, stealing copters from allies, kidnapping their soldiers and using them as human shields. In the US—"

"In the US you like to force other countries to agree to military bases in their land, like the one you run in Greenland, under the excuse of space surveillance and defense operations, joint security initiatives and other bullshit like that."

It was the commander's men's turn to tighten their grip around their weapons.

Justin raised his right hand, gesturing to his men to stay calm. "Those helicopters, the Seahawks behind you, were stationed in Greenland without the knowledge and the authorization of its government authorities. This is in clear violation of the treaty for the expansion of your base. It's in your own best interest and in the interest of the US that your secret about these violations does not end up on the cover of New York Times."

A somber mood fell over the commander's face. "I have… I have no idea what you're talking about, Hall," he stuttered, waving his arms in agitation. "And you're badly mistaken if you think you're in a position to impose your terms on me."

"We're simply negotiating a peaceful and acceptable solution to everyone. We'll be tight-lipped about your choppers. You have our word."

Anna nodded and so did Ned. The commander began pacing back and forth. Justin focused his attention at the men standing by the Seahawks. A shootout was going to be nobody's victory. Justin hoped the commander would make the right decision.

"What does she want?" he whispered in a low voice. He avoided Justin's eyes, staring instead at the slushy ground around his boots.

"Emily, Sergeant Moore, will have to agree to these terms, but I believe an honorable discharge or a transfer to a detail equal to her current position is a fair deal." Justin delivered his proposal in one quick sentence, before the commander could change his mind about reaching a compromise.

The commander entertained the proposal for a minute in his mind. At some point, he opened his mouth, but then shook his head, snapped his fingers and said nothing. He hesitated another second, then spoke in a quiet voice, "We have a deal. You'll forget about the Seahawks, and she'll get a transfer to Alaska or some other God-forsaken place."

"Thank you," Justin said.

"Thank you, sir," Anna said with a respectful nod.

"Don't mention it." The commander turned around and swaggered toward the helicopters. "My men will help you bring in the wounded. We'll leave as soon as everyone's loaded up."

"This way." Justin guided the American soldiers. "Follow me."

* * *

Ten minutes later, Emily had set up a temporary medical center in the second Seahawk. Kiawak's stretcher was the first one to be lifted up there.

"The old wolf fought well." His voice was weak and shaky. A bloody cough made his breathing very difficult.

"That he did," Joe said. "A brave man. A true warrior."

"He gave his own life to save ours," said Kiawak. "That is… eh… amazing that is."

"Both of you gave your best too," Justin said. "The battle was won because you guys and the rest of the men gave their best."

"Eh." Joe waved off the praise with a shrug. "Get well, Kiawak. I'll be missing you, and so will everyone else in town. But most importantly, someone very special is already waiting for your return in Arctic Bay."

Kiawak rolled his eyes.

"Uh-huh." Joe reached for Kiawak's arm. "I will not let you go until you promise me you'll talk things over with Tania. She's too good of a girl to lose. Promise me!"

"Joe, I need to give Kiawak some morphine," Emily said.

"Sure, in a minute," Joe replied. "C'mon, buddy."

Kiawak mumbled something that could be interpreted as anything but a promise.

"I'm not kidding," Joe insisted. "You've got to make things work with Tania. You owe her a second chance."

Emily raised a tall syringe with the exposed needle for everyone to see then brought it close to Joe's hand. "Last warning. I'm not kidding either."

Joe ignored her words.

Kiawak mustered a feeble smile. "I do. I promise."

Joe withdrew his arm, and Emily administered the painkiller injection. Justin waved at Kiawak, whose bloodshot eyes grew heavier. He was no longer able to keep them open.

"Justin, you didn't have to pull that miracle with the Commander," Emily said, jumping off the helicopter. "But, thank you." She gave him a tight, warm embrace.

"It's the least I can do. Like I keep saying, without you, I don't think I would be alive. I don't think most of us would be alive at all."

"Oh, stop it," she said with a smile. "You're making me blush."

"It's the chilling wind. Thank you again and sorry for everything."

Emily shrugged. "Don't worry about Carrie. I'll take care of her as if you were sitting next to her bed, holding her hand." She gestured toward Carrie. Her stretcher was being lifted into the helicopter.

"I don't think she would want me to do that anymore." Justin stroke Carrie's hair. "I mean the holding of hands. I'll be in the next flight. We still have a chopper in Arctic Bay."

"Oh, yeah. If I knew how to fly it, I would have brought it here. It would have been much quicker."

"You came just at the right time," Anna said and gave Emily a gentle hug. "Thank you."

"No problem," she replied. "Goodbye."

"Sergeant Moore, it's time to go," one of the sergeants whispered in her ear. "The commander wants to get the hell out of here now."

"OK, I'll be ready in a second," she said in a cold, dry voice. She waved at Justin and Anna. "Take care, friends." She hesitated a second before adding the last word, but once it came out, she reinforced her thought with a friendly smile.

A minute later, the three Seahawks were airborne.

CHAPTER THIRTY-ONE

Nanisivik, Canada
April 14, 12:31 p.m.

"Magnus, that's your name, right?" Justin asked the prisoner, shoving him into the backseat of the truck, next to Anna. The makeshift handcuffs fastening Magnus's arms behind his back made his climb into the souped-up truck a bit difficult, since he was already limping. Joe started the truck, and Justin sat behind the driver, to the left of Magnus.

"Where are we going?" Magnus asked.

"Arctic Bay," Justin replied. "So tell me. You're Magnus Tornbjorn?"

"Yes," Magnus replied. He winced as he lay back in the seat.

Emily had done a great job of treating the cuts and bruises on his face, but his back and his legs had suffered severe trauma during the explosion. With not much external bleeding and given the limited space in the helicopters, Magnus was out of luck. Besides, Justin wanted to have a quiet little chat with him before flying to Iqaluit.

"OK, Magnus, what was the objective of the Danish Security Service?"

"You mean the Danish *Defense Intelligence Service*, who designed, executed, and finally botched up this operation?"

Justin snorted. "Come on, Magnus. We know you're the biggest fish of our catch."

"You're right about that. The whale, the big whale, got away. But after all, his blubber blew up to pieces in the Hercules explosion."

"What are you talking about?"

"The mastermind behind this mission, coded *Arctic Wargame*, is Gunter Madsen, an Assistant Director with the Danish Defense Intelligence Service."

"And you're just a simple foot soldier, is that what you're saying?" Anna asked.

"Of course not, although the idea crossed my mind." A small grin appeared on Magnus's tired face. "I was Chief of Operations. I was in charge of the tactical preps for this mission."

"And?" Joe asked. "Go on. Keep talking."

"*And* I have nothing else to say until we agree on the conditions of my release."

"Huh?" Anna said.

Joe and Justin shook their heads.

"I don't think you're going anywhere," Anna said. "We know how you planned the takeover of the transport plane, and we know about your plans for this and other terrorist attacks in Canada. We know everything." She was making things up to provoke a reaction from Magnus.

"Anna, that's more than enough," Justin said.

"Well then, if you know everything, why are you asking me? If you're so confident you've caught a terrorist, this case is closed. Hand me over to the Americans. During the flight to Egypt or Jordan, to one of their extraordinary rendition bases, I'll tell them my side of story. Maybe they'll show some interest in hearing *my* version of the facts and meet my request for political asylum."

What does he think he has up his sleeve? And why would he want political asylum? What's he afraid of back home?

The truck hit an ice bump. Ammunition boxes rattled in the back of the truck.

Justin rubbed his eyes with his palms then stroked his chin, replaying Magnus's words in his mind. "Fine," he said. "Let's hear it, but there are no strings attached. No preconditions, no ultimatums." He waited for Magnus to acknowledge his understanding, which he did by nodding. Justin continued, "I need credible evidence that what you're claiming is, in fact, true."

"The black box. Let's begin with the Hercules's black box. Once you retrieve the box and the bodies of Gunter and the two pilots, you'll have more than you need to doubt the 'official' version of the story you may have heard."

"Clever move," Joe said, gazing at Magnus's face in the rear-view mirror. "The plane exploded over the freezing waters of the Inlet. It will take months and a crap load of money to find anything, and that's if we're lucky, very lucky."

"I'm sure you have something else, let's say, more concrete and at hand," Justin said.

"All right, how about transfer records of prisoners? A quick search of transfers in the main prisons in Denmark will reveal a common trait. The most dangerous criminals were transferred to a separate facility, with, I guess now you know what mission."

"You mean the Danish troops were common criminals?" Anna asked.

"Well, not exactly 'common,' but they weren't regular army either. Bank robbers, terrorists, murderers, arsonists, you name it. Most of them I handpicked myself."

"This sounds more like a stalling tactic than useful information," Justin said.

He stared attentively at Magnus's face. The prisoner's eyes were clear and focused, their gaze steady and determined. He did not stutter when talking, and he expressed his thoughts concisely and without pauses. *I can't tell if he's making this up. If he is, he's doing a great job keeping it all together. Will making him nervous reveal anything?*

"These facilities, prisons, they are in Denmark, outside our jurisdiction," Justin said, "I can't think of any good reason for your government to accept our request or to issue clearances for us to inspect these records or visit these places."

Magnus frowned. He winced, as Joe cut through a curve a bit faster than necessary. The truck bounced over a cluster of ice bumps on the road.

"Well, I don't know what else would convince you," Magnus said. "You can ask Valgerda, but you'll think she's my partner, so, of course, she'll try to save me. And herself. You can ask the other men, but they also have a personal interest in this matter, and they're hardcore criminals, so there goes their credibility."

Magnus's voice had no hint of desperation, just resignation. "One of them, a man called Sargon, whom I recruited personally, will confirm my words. But then, he's a convicted terrorist staring at a life sentence, so there you have it. At some point, you'll have to decide whether you want to trust me or not." Magnus jerked up his shoulders and turned his head first toward Justin, then toward Anna.

"I want to trust you," Justin said. "But after trying to kill me and my friends, trust doesn't come easy."

The next few minutes they drove in silence, broken only by Joe's occasional cursing at the slippery patches on the road. Justin looked out the window at the rolling ice hills, followed by short segments of flatland, and by more rolling ice hills. He kept the prisoner within the corner of his eye, and every so often observed Magnus's behavior for any signs of surrender. He found none.

"You know what," Justin said, "I don't think I can trust you. Unless you give me some facts: names, numbers, places, you'll keep wearing those handcuffs."

Magnus grinned and kept staring ahead. "Tell the Americans I prefer to fly business."

"Oh, no." Justin shook his head. "You're not going to the Americans. I'll take you to one of *our* secret locations. Once we've arranged for your return back to Denmark, I'll take you back to Copenhagen. Always wanted to see the Round Tower and the Latin Quarter." *He should start to feel trapped, now. I need to keep him worried and in panic, so that he'll see the need to bargain with me. He doesn't want to go back to Denmark.*

"You're bluffing," Magnus said, but without conviction. "You need me, so you can learn what we're up to, our next moves, our future plans."

"Is Kronborg open at this time of year? You know, Anna," Justin said and looked over at her, "Kronborg is a fascinating castle, right on the shore of this place... hmmm, I don't remember its name..."

"Helsingør," Magnus offered with an uneasy smirk.

"Yes, exactly. On a clear day, from atop the castle one can see all the way across the waters to Sweden. In one of the castle halls they have this statue of one of their great heroes..." Justin gestured at Magnus with his head for the name he was looking for.

"Holger Danske."

"Yes, that one. According to the legend, his marble statue will turn into a human being, flesh and blood, if Denmark is ever in danger, and it will rise to fight for the country's freedom." Justin stared into Magnus's eyes. "I wonder what would Holger Danske do if Denmark was the aggressor toward another country that is an ally and a friend?"

Magnus closed his eyes and shook his head. "I thought you were going somewhere there, you had a point or something," he said, his eyes still shut.

"I have a point, which is *I* will enjoy Copenhagen's best, while you, well, I'm sure your authorities will decide on how best to handle you."

"You think they're going to kill me, do you?"

"Oh, no, I think they'll give you a promotion. Maybe they'll give you the position of this Gunter character. You seem to know or at least pretend to know all about the Arctic Wargame mission. I wouldn't want you to be unhappy and go around blurting out secrets to who knows whom. I would make sure you remained silent. For good."

Magnus opened his eyes and stared at Justin. He seemed unsure whether Justin was being sarcastic or not. Magnus looked left and right, as if he were waiting for the right moment to make a run for it. But his face was calm, his breathing regular, and his overall composure quite relaxed.

"And who knows," Anna said with a head tilt and a slight shrug, "maybe we'll have better luck with Valgerda."

"Oh, you want to talk to her?"

"Yes, now that you have placed all the blame on her in order to save yourself, of course we're going to interrogate her."

"I haven't said… oh, I see, you're trying to play us against each other," Magnus said in a mocking tone. "She's not going to take the bait."

"We'll see about that," Justin said with a confident nod.

Joe's cellphone rang. He glanced at the screen, checking the caller ID. "It's Ned," he said, handing the phone to Justin.

"Hi, Ned, what's up?" Justin said.

"Not much, just cleaning up the terminal. Listen, we've finally got through to someone from the Canadian Forces. They've dispatched a couple of Cormorant helos to check things out here, after military officials from the US and Denmark began asking all kinds of embarrassing questions."

Justin pressed the cellphone to his ear, so Magnus and the other passengers could hear only his side of the conversation. Ned's unexpected call had given him an idea.

"Who's aboard the helos? I mean from the Danish side?"

"Nobody, there are no freaking Danes in there, the bastards. It's the Canadian Forces, our army, can't you hear me?"

"Yes, I hear you. Anyone I may know?"

"They didn't give me any names."

"But they're from the Ministry of Defence, right?"

"Yeah, they call it the Department of National Defence, the DND. But you know that."

"Do you think they would be interested in picking up one of their own?"

Justin released his grip on the cellphone. He guessed Ned's reply and wanted Magnus to hear for himself the words that could seal the deal.

"Of course, they will, when they go back."

"OK, Ned. Tell them to meet me in Arctic Bay, and that I have something for them. The man for whom they came this far is sitting with me in the truck as we speak. Bye!"

Justin flipped his cellphone shut. Before he could say another word, Magnus leaned toward Justin.

"Hey, move back." Anna shoved her pistol into Magnus's side.

Magnus sat up straight.

"It's OK," Justin said. "I think he wanted to whisper in my ear."

"I want a deal," Magnus said, his voice low and unsteady. "Don't hand me over to the Danish troops, whoever they may be."

"What do you want?" Justin held Magnus's eyes. Panic had begun to replace the courage in the man's heart.

"Political asylum and a new identity. Both for me and Valgerda."

"That's a steep price. Your secrets are really worth that much?"

"They are. Trust me, you're the one getting a deal here. I'll give you everything about the Arctic Wargame, the players, the story, everything."

"Start talking."

"Do I have your word?"

"A lot of people will have to sign off on this, but as far I am concerned, I'll do my best to get it done."

. "That's good enough for me, I guess," Magnus agreed with a deep sigh.

"OK, I'm listening," Justin said.

"No, you said it yourself that talk is cheap, and I know you're a difficult man to convince. Find me a computer, and I'll show you everything. E-mails, photos, plans, coordinates. Everything."

CHAPTER THIRTY-TWO

Arctic Bay, Canada
April 14, 1:13 p.m.

Magnus's watch looked like any other wristwatch. Its only remarkable feature was the black dial, which had four yellow dots representing the numbers three, six, nine, and twelve. There was nothing special about its leather band either. But as Magnus flipped over the watch, Justin noticed a small clasp in the casing, right next to the switch for setting the time. Magnus inserted the tip of his fingernail underneath the clasp, popping out the pin of a USB connector.

"It's a jump drive," Justin said. "What a great idea."

Magnus shrugged, as he handed his watch to Justin. "Its capacity is 64 GB. I keep it as a backup for confidential materials. In this case, it turned out to be my insurance policy."

Justin turned on the desktop computer and looked out of the living room's small windows. Ned had allowed them to use his old Compaq.

"What's in there?" Anna asked, pacing around the desk, waiting for the computer screen to light up.

Justin was sitting in the only chair in the room, in front of the monitor, while Magnus stood to the right of Justin, his back against the wall.

"You'll see. Pictures, maps, names, numbers. The entire Arctic Wargame operation at your fingertips."

"So, you just happened to be carrying around the operation's database?" Justin asked, fumbling with the keyboard. The computer was still going through the stage of scanning the hard drive for startup errors.

"No, of course not. I planned it well in advance. I sensed at some point things were not as they seemed in this operation. I had this unsettling feeling that Gunter was not telling me everything, and I was being set up. Maybe he needed someone to blame in case things went wrong, like they did. I know Gunter is very close to our Defense Minister. Then, just before the beginning of our mission, I saw…"

Justin looked up at Magnus. "What did you see?"

Magnus remained silent. He wanted to tell Justin how he saw Yuliya kill in cold blood one of the recruits, how he ran a background search on her but could not find a record of a Yuliya Novikov ever working in the Danish Defense Intelligence Service or anywhere else in the security establishments of Denmark, about Yuliya's slight trace of a foreign accent, and how Gunter was not really in charge of the Arctic Wargame. But Magnus did not trust the Canadians. Not yet. After all the paperwork was signed and he received his new identity, he would tell Justin everything he knew.

"Magnus, what did you see?" Justin asked again.

"Eh… I realized that… that most likely things were going to turn ugly… We had very few soldiers and against my better judgment, I still went on with this mission."

Justin thought over Magnus's reply for a few seconds. "Here. It's working." He pointed to the screen lit up by a Caribbean sunset picture set as the wallpaper.

"Once I began to feel uneasy about the whole deal," Magnus said, "I began backing up anything I could get my hands on. I figured the information might come in handy if my survival was at stake. If not, it was hidden so well that your own men missed it."

Anna nodded. "It's very clever. Hidden, but still in plain sight. I would have never thought these things even existed."

"They do, and for a couple of hundred bucks these days you can get larger capacity models."

"OK, let's see what secrets you actually have in here," Justin said once the computer was ready. "Let's start at the beginning." Justin selected the oldest folder, "March 30."

Three other folders were stored inside it, named respectively "To Do", "In Transit" and "Completed." A simple method of keeping records of the mission's daily progress. He accessed the To Do folder. The screen was flooded with an abundance of files. JPEG and PDF files, as well as Word documents. The first picture he clicked on was a blown-up map of Cape Combermere in Ellesmere Island. There was another satellite picture, showing crystal clear details of a rocky beach and a structure that looked familiar to Justin.

"Do you know what that is?" Magnus asked.

"A Sirius Patrol depot," Anna replied.

"Yes, very good," Magnus said.

"We were there actually right here." Justin tapped the monitor with his index finger and pointed at the wooden hut. "The depot was pillaged by some of the locals, but we still found leftover items, evidence of your patrols landing and stashing weapon caches."

"Really?"

"Yes. We retrieved some of the looted *Let Støttevåben*. Come to think about it, we used your own weapons against you."

Magnus's face grew pale, and he looked away.

"What's this one?" Justin asked.

The image he was referring to was a topographical map of Ellesmere Island's east coast. A series of red and green dots were scattered all over the area.

"Green dots are possible locations for other Sirius Patrol depots. Red ones are places where we actually set up weapons and supplies caches."

Justin began to count the red dots.

"There are seven," Magnus said, "minus the one that was discovered. Once we learned that area was too hot, Nanisivik was suggested as an easier point of entry because of the deep-water port and its considerable distance from the hot area."

"Alisha suggested Nanisivik, didn't she?" asked Anna.

"Yes," Magnus replied with a nod of defeat. "I guess you know everything about her."

"We do. But you changed your plans at the last moment and that threw us off," Justin said.

"Yes, we were worried because the Americans were sticking their nose into our business, as they usually do. So we didn't want to send icebreakers, opting instead for an aerial assault. So, we left our Rasmussens anchored in Søndre Strømfjord."

Justin shook his head.

"So, are we worth the witness protection?"

"Every byte of it," Justin replied, pointing at the screen.

"I've got a question," Anna said. "Why are you so loyal to Valgerda?"

"If you're asking me if we're lovers, the answer is no. Valgerda is an excellent agent, but after this mission, her career is over. Her life will be in danger, as well. I'm just doing my duty as her commanding officer and looking out for my teammates."

"What about the other survivors?" Anna said.

"They're all felons, and they didn't keep their end of the deal. I have no obligations toward them. Jail them or deport them. It's up to you."

A loud, rattling thunder announced the helicopters arrival. A quick glance outside the windows and Justin recognized them as the Canadian Forces. "OK," he said, getting up quickly. "You," he said, pointing at Magnus, "you died during the fight. Valgerda, she's dead too and, of course, your bodies will never be recovered."

Magnus nodded.

"Joe will hide you both for now. Once the DND is gone, we'll fly you to a safe place, after I make a few phone calls. Anna, call Ned and tell him to bring Valgerda here very discreetly. Give him a few details, but nothing they don't know already. Something about her being a potential witness and that we need to take her into custody. That should be sufficient."

Anna nodded.

"I've got to meet the military." Justin leaned over the keyboard and closed all documents still open in the computer. He fastened Magnus's watch to his left wrist. "We'll make sure Magnus and Valgerda are all set," he said to Anna. "Erase the history of this computer, and make sure there are no traces we ever used this station."

"Yes, I'll take care of that."

Justin extended his hand to Magnus, who readily shook it. "You made the right decision," Justin said.

Iqaluit, Canada
April 15, 9:07 a.m.

"Where did you get that?" Carrie muttered in a throaty voice, pointing at a box of chocolates Justin was holding in his left hand.

"You weren't supposed to see that, and the doctor said you should be sleeping." Justin closed the sliding door of Carrie's emergency room and sat on a low stool by her bed. Her left arm was connected to numerous intravenous tubes, while her right arm was completely wrapped in white gauze, from her wrist all the way to her shoulder.

"When every inch of your body hurts like it has been run over twice by a train, it's impossible to even close your eyes, let alone sleep."

"Do as you wish. You always do, anyway."

"Yes, and it works. Well, most of the time."

"It may work when it doesn't involve jumping out of helicopters, you crazy nut job."

"Eh, jump, shjump," Carrie said. She sighed and coughed a dry, deep hack.

"You're OK?" Justin leaned over her bed.

"I'm... I'll be fine. You know I had another visitor earlier today."

"Who? Johnson?"

"No. Mr. Carter Hall. Your dad."

"No, he didn't..."

"Yes, he did come to visit. He was actually looking for you."

Justin frowned. "I'm not really in the mood to argue with him."

"He's worried sick about you. Your brother came with him too. You should talk to them both."

"Look, Carrie, if I want your advice—"

"I know you don't want it, but I'm giving it to you anyway. You need to make peace with your family, OK? Don't let the past haunt you any longer." Carrie looked deep into his eyes. "I know you want to see your old man again."

"What, you're an oracle now?"

"I'm just saying they're staying at the Welcome Inn, in case you change your mind."

Justin nodded, then gave her a shrug.

Carrie sighed. "Oh, I'm so tired. Everything hurts, and the doctor says it will not get better for a few more days."

"There's no rush. Take your time and get your strength back. Our job is done."

"Kiawak told me a few things about what happened after the explosion, but his version was sketchy."

"You're not going to believe what I have to tell you and show you," Justin said, unfastening his wristwatch.

"That's new. Where did you get it? At the gift store?"

"No. This watch belonged to Magnus Tornbjorn, the Danish Chief of Operations for Arctic Wargame."

"What?"

"Yes, you heard me correctly. This watch is not what it seems. Actually, nothing in this story is as it seems."

CHAPTER THIRTY-THREE

Federal Security Service Headquarters, Moscow, Russia
April 16, 8:15 a.m.

Grigori Smirnov stared for a long time at the Lubyanka Square. His weary eyes followed the black Mercedeses, Porsches, and other expensive vehicles zooming around the traffic circle. A stream of pedestrians flowed from the Metro station, heading for their offices, braving the chilling breeze and the first snowflakes blanketing the streets.

Smirnov sighed and frowned. His day had begun as chaotic as the traffic outside his office. It had been over twenty-four hours since he last communicated with Yuliya, just before the beginning of the Arctic Wargame. Smirnov hated silence. Silence meant bad news. Bad news meant mistakes, blame, and scapegoats. Especially since his superiors had started asking questions. Questions to which he had no answers. Or worse, questions he could not afford to answer.

He allowed himself a small grin. Yuliya had disappeared and he wished she was dead or somehow incapacitated. She and her silence had become a liability. And so had become Helma, the kidnapped wife of Gunter Madsen. *The prick. Botching up a perfectly good operation.*

He sighed again. His breath fogged a small section of the window glass. The view became blurry, and the cars and the people disappeared from his sight. He turned around and walked to his desk, determined to erase all traces of his involvement in the Arctic Wargame, his brainchild, and cut all his ties to this operation.

There was a knock on his door. Smirnov grinned. He was expecting the man behind the door. The man who was going to fix all his problems. The man he should have sent in Yuliya's place. "Come in, Vladimir."

A lean man in his late thirties entered his office. Vladimir was Smirnov's assistant for overseas clandestine operations and the man who was personally involved in the kidnapping Gunter's wife.

"Hello, boss," he said and remained standing by the door.

"Take a seat."

"OK."

"There's bad news. Arctic Wargame failed. We need to pull the plug."

"OK."

One of the reasons why Smirnov loved Vladimir's work was his complete disinterest in the motives. When he was told to do something, he got it done, no questions asked.

"Yuliya Novikov has become a problem to this office and to our country," Smirnov said.

"Shall we eliminate her?"

"She is most likely dead or out of the game. I need you to contact her family. Inform them in clear terms that if Yuliya is alive and starts singing, unfortunate events may take place in their lives."

Vladimir nodded.

"If Yuliya is alive," Smirnov said, "she's probably in Canadian custody and highly protected. Difficult for us to put a hit on her. But we can ruin her reputation here, so if she says anything, no one will ever believe her. You know what to do."

Vladimir nodded.

"Next issue, Helma. Can she make you or the other men?"

"No, she can't."

"Are you sure?"

"Absolutely. We wore masks when we grabbed her and she was blindfolded most of the time."

"She can recognize your voice?"

"Never talked to her."

"The voices of the other man?"

"Perhaps. But they entered Denmark as tourists and ran into her at a market center. That's not much evidence."

Smirnov frowned and thought about Vladimir's words for a few seconds. "It's still evidence. If the Danes or the Canadians begin to connect the dots, I don't want anything tying those men to you or me."

"Shall we eliminate them?"

Smirnov nodded. "Unfortunately, we have to."

Vladimir's face remained void of emotions.

"Clean up the apartment where you held her. Fingerprints, DNA, sanitize everything. Then, let her go."

Vladimir's left eyebrow curled up.

"Yes, I don't want her killed. The minister is on my tail and the Danish are already asking questions. No more dead civilians."

Vladimir nodded.

"Once you're done with that, delete all files, communications, reports, any trace we had anything to do with the Arctic Wargame. Burn it all up."

"Sure thing, boss."

"Any questions?"

"Just one."

"Yes?"

"What did we do wrong?"

"We, you and I, we did nothing wrong. The people we selected for this operation, they failed us. They let us down. They were unprepared or performed miserably. I've learned the Canadians mounted a great resistance. Maybe we should have had a larger force carry out the attack." Smirnov paused and took a big breath. "In any case, this operation confirmed our initial suspicions. We can slip through their defenses with ease, but the Canadians are tougher than they seem. Next time, we'll just use a sledgehammer approach. We'll go in with professionals."

"Yes, boss."

"That's all." Smirnov nodded toward the door. "Get it done."

"Right away, boss."

EPILOGUE

Ottawa, Canada
May 28, 08:30 a.m.

The doctors had spent a lot of time to convince Carrie she was not ready to walk the five blocks from her apartment to the closest bus stop. They also prohibited her from driving her Nissan to work until the end of her six-week recovery period. Since her discharge from the Montfort Hospital two weeks ago, Justin had been taking Carrie to run errands, to the mall and grocery stores, to movies theatres and restaurants. On crutches, Carrie managed light chores around the house. Today, six weeks after the Arctic events, they were both on their way to the CIS headquarters on the outskirts of Ottawa.

"Tell me, how did your date go last night?" Carrie asked.

Justin, who was driving her blue Nissan, zoomed through an intersection, as the traffic light switched from amber to red. "What date?"

"The one with Anna, genius."

"Oh, that one. Why do you want to know?"

"I'm a curious girl, but save me the gross details, if there were any... were there any?"

Justin frowned but did not look at her.

"I'm kidding, relax. I just want to make sure things are going well between you two."

"Things are going well. Satisfied?"

"How well?"

"Obviously not satisfied." He sighed. "It's only our third date. She's sweet, and we have many common interests. I'm enjoying the time I'm spending with Anna."

"Is it like… like when we went out?"

"Oh, is this what you're fishing for, comparisons with the past?"

"Take it easy. That's not what I'm after."

"OK, tell me what *exactly* are you after?"

"I want to make sure she's getting the best of you, that part of you so often invested in work, research, or anything else but the girl. Anna deserves all your passion, your desires, your understanding. Even that part of you I never got."

Justin's frown melted, as Carrie's voice became softer. "Justin, you and Anna will make a great couple. Please, make sure you don't allow work to get in the way."

"Work is exactly what brought us together, and I will not let it pull us apart."

"If that starts to happen, I'll come and scream at you 'what the hell are you doing?'" Carrie said with a big smile.

"Yes, please do that."

"I will. I wish someone would have done it for us, but they didn't, and I can't change the past. But I can help you plan the wedding and name your babies."

"Whoa, whoa, hold on there. Aren't we rushing things here just a little bit? Wedding? Babies? We've gone out only three times!"

"Hey, it's never too early to plan who's going to be your kids' godmother. And now thanks to me, you've got one less thing to worry about. I'll let you and Anna take care of the rest."

"Gee, thanks. I'll let you know if I need more of this kind of help."

"Look, that's… isn't that Nick there?" Carrie pointed at a black sedan to their right. "No, I guess it's not."

"Nice change of subject, but thanks for changing it. Are you ready for today's meeting?"

"I've been ready two weeks ago. I told the surgeon at Montfort to give me a wheelchair. I could have rolled out in style through our office corridors. But he insisted I had to walk and regain control of my leg muscles."

"Do they hurt?"

"Is the sky blue? Of course they hurt. I have to sit down every fifteen minutes, otherwise they'll give in. But yeah, I'll think I'm ready to face the music."

* * *

No bagpipes were waiting for their arrival at the CIS headquarters, and no red carpet was rolled out for them. In fact, Carrie humbly submitted her aluminum crutches to the meticulous search of two heavyset guards at the entrance. A few acquaintances nodded quick hellos. No questions asked, no explanations sought. This was an intelligence agency and their missions were secret. Only the people who needed to know learned only what they needed to know.

The elevator ride to the sixth floor was fast and quiet. Carrie winced as she shifted her weight from one leg to the other a couple of times. They came out of the elevator and made their way to the office of Ms. Claire Johnson, Director General of Intelligence for the North Africa Division.

"Welcome back, Carrie," Johnson greeted them at the door, after Justin announced their arrival with a light knock.

She waited for Carrie to hobble inside and take a seat at the oval glass table.

"I'm glad to see both of you are doing well." She sat next to Carrie. "Much better than the last time I saw you at Montfort."

"You should have seen the Danes," Carrie replied, "the ones that made it alive, I mean."

Johnson grinned. Her gray eyes glowed. She turned to Justin. "Do you have the reports ready?"

"Yes. They're complete." He removed two manila folders from his briefcase. "This one," he said, pointing at the thick one, then sliding it toward his boss, "is the classified report. The only copy. The second file is for the public archives."

Johnson flipped through the classified report. "It's very detailed and comprehensive."

"I used the recollection of the events from my team members and the people on the ground. In addition, the intel provided by our foreign assets allowed us to recreate a clear picture of the Arctic Wargame."

Johnson opened the second folder. She smiled as she read the two-page document inside. "I like the words you've chosen to describe the Arctic Wargame operation for the public: 'The Arctic Wargame, executed through coordinated teamwork among various Canadian government departments, simulated hostile incursions in Canada's Arctic and the immediate defensive response by the local population and the Canadian Forces.' Bravo."

Justin nodded modestly.

Johnson set aside both folders. "Regarding your informants, they seem to have adapted quite well to the Witness Protection Program," she said with a smile. "And they gave us more intel about someone else other than the Danes pulling the strings of the Arctic Wargame."

"But we still have nothing concrete that the Russians organized this attack?" Justin asked.

"Yes, nothing concrete," Johnson replied, "but a lot of circumstantial evidence. And there was an interesting development in Denmark."

"The Danes are ready to apologize?" Carrie asked.

"Eh, far from it. They're still investigating. Canada's using all diplomatic channels to clear up this situation without making too many waves. We're talking to our counterparts in the Danish intelligence to clarify everything."

Carrie shook her head. Justin closed his eyes. "What's the interesting development?" he asked.

"Ms. Helma Madsen, the wife of Gunter Madsen, is claiming to have been kidnapped. According to her, she was released a couple of weeks ago and the kidnappers were Russians."

Carrie frowned. "She has some evidence for her claims?"

"No. She insists the men who took her spoke Russians. She says she can recognize their voices, but she never saw their faces."

"Is that it?" Justin asked.

"That's insufficient," Carrie said.

Johnson nodded. "Yes and no. Yes, we know the Russians organized the Arctic Wargame. No, we don't have evidence to prove it."

Justin sighed. Carrie frowned but said nothing.

"On the bright side of things," Johnson said, "the government has almost finished revising its Arctic Strategy, focusing on its enhancement and its expansion. The budget proposal will almost double the funding for the defense of our Northern borders over the next five years. We'll have more Rangers on the ground and they'll be better equipped with state-of-the-art technology. Two other deep-water ports are being proposed, one at Banks Island and the other at Baffin Island, at each end of the Northwest Passage, in addition to the one in Nanisivik. Canada will have five more vessels with year-round icebreaking capabilities in addition to the one in Nanisivik."

Johnson glanced at her watch. "Moving forward, there's one last thing to do before I let you go."

She retreated to her desk, reaching for a notepad and her phone handset. Justin glanced quickly at Carrie, who raised her index finger to her lips. A glimmer of mischief flickered in her eyes, as if she knew what scheme Johnson was plotting.

"It's exactly nine o'clock." Johnson began dialing a number. "We have to be absolutely punctual for this phone call, which is probably the most important in your entire life."

"Is this another job?" Justin asked.

Carrie hushed him with a headshake.

Johnson smiled. "You'll get your answer in a second… oh, yes, good evening madam, this is Claire Johnson, Director General of Intelligence for the North Africa Division with the CIS, the Canadian Intelligence Service. Yes, that's why I'm calling. Of course, I'll wait."

Justin began to wiggle in his chair.

"OK, let's tell him." Johnson nodded at Carrie. "Someone very important wants to give you Her recognition."

"Pardon—" Justin began, but Johnson's hand gesture stopped him.

"Your Majesty, this is Claire Johnson."

She's really talking to the Queen?

"Yes, of course, Your Majesty. Very well, thank you. As scheduled, I have Mr. Justin Hall and his partner, Ms. Carrie O'Connor, on line. They will be delighted to talk to you."

Justin had no time to get over the initial shock. Johnson offered him the phone handset. He cleared his throat and hesitated a moment, before walking to her desk.

"Come on, Justin," Johnson whispered, covering the receiver with her hand. "We can't make Her Majesty wait."

Justin picked up the phone and took a deep breath. "Your Majesty," he said finally. "Mr. Hall at Your service."

AUTHOR'S NOTE

Thank you for reading this story. I appreciate your feedback, and you can always reach me at fictionwriter78@yahoo.com. I promise to answer all e-mails.

If you noticed any typos, mistakes or other factual errors in this book, please let me know, so I can correct them.

Visit my blog at http://ethanjones.blog.com and my Facebook page at http://www.facebook.com/pages/Ethan-Jones/329693267050697 to learn about my new projects.

And if you like this story, please check out my other works and share the word about them.

BONUS CONTENT FROM
TRIPOLI'S TARGET

Please enjoy the prologue and Chapter 1 of Tripoli's Target, the second novel in the Justin Hall series, which will be released this fall.

Canadian Intelligence Service Agents Justin Hall and Carrie O'Connor are back. Instead of the frozen north, they find themselves in arid North Africa on the trail of an assassination plot against the US president during a G-20 summit. But the source of their information is the untrustworthy leader of one of the deadliest terrorist groups in the region. Ambushes and questionable loyalties turn an already difficult mission into a dark maze of betrayal and misdirection.

Justin and Carrie are forced return to Tripoli, Libya, a place they barely escaped alive not long ago, to assist the US Secret Service in thwarting the plot. New intelligence comes in, and they realize something is very, very wrong with their plan.

The summit is only forty-eight hours away and they still have an assassination to stop.

PROLOGUE

Tripoli, Libya
May 13, 6:15 p.m. local time

Satam, the driver of the fifth suicide truck bomb, turned onto Ar Rashid Street, merging with the warm evening traffic. He rubbed his sweaty palms against his short khaki pants, his gaze glued to the silver BMW Suburban in front of him. He heaved a wheezing sigh and tapped on the brake pedal. A red traffic light halted the five-vehicle convoy.

A stream of vehicles rushed through the intersection leading to the business district of downtown Tripoli. Tall skyscrapers rose over most of the city's old colonial-style buildings. The green and gold banner of Jacobs Properties—one of the major British real estate developers in Libya—beamed from atop the glass-and-steel façade of the newly finished Continental Hotel. The same logo had been painted hastily on the left side of the BMW packed with Semtex explosives. Walid, its driver and a Jacobs subcontractor, had exchanged his blue coveralls for a business suit and the promise of martyrdom.

A glance at the dashboard clock told Satam the synchronized explosion would take place in ten minutes. The thought of the coming carnage drained the last drop of courage from his heart. He rolled down the window, but the humid air—blended with the aroma of fried falafel, onions, and lamb donairs from a nearby street vendor—made him nauseated. He gasped for air, sticking his head out of the window. He coughed and struggled to catch his breath. The drivers in the other vehicles gave him curious glares. Behind the truck, the driver of an old Mercedes honked his horn twice. Satam swallowed hard and wiped the sweat off his narrow forehead. He waved at his audience to show them he was doing all right.

"Satam, what's the matter, brother?" the radio set on the dashboard crackled. He recognized Walid's gruff voice.

Satam looked at the BMW. His watery eyes met the reflection of the driver's face in the rear-view mirror of the Suburban. The driver's usual wicked smirk stretched his lips, revealing his large buckteeth. Walid waved his hands wildly. Satam could not see behind Walid's black aviator shades but assumed his eyes were ablaze with rage.

"Nothing's wrong. Just needed some air," Satam replied over the radio.

He rolled up the window before Walid could scold him with another howl.

"Great. Now that you've closed the window, open your eyes!" Walid barked. "You're not a coward like the infidels, are you?"

Satam shook his head.

A third voice came on air before he could say anything.

"Cousin, I pledged my honor so you could be a part of this mission. Don't you back down now!" Satam's cousin said. He was driving the Toyota at the head of the convoy.

Satam sighed and paused for a couple of seconds. "I'm not backing down. You can trust me. I will not disappoint you or the brotherhood."

"That's my flesh and blood who is soon to be a martyr," said the cousin in a relaxed tone. "Our families will be proud of us, and our reward will be glorious."

"It's easy for you to say, since tonight you'll be welcomed to paradise," Satam said.

He noticed the traffic lights changing and stepped cautiously on the gas pedal. The truck jerked forward a few inches before the ride turned smooth again.

"Won't take long before you join us there," Walid said.

"Yes, but not before being dragged through the secret police hellish cells…" Satam's voice trailed off.

"Allah will give you strength, cousin, and soon he'll take you home."

"He will, brother, he will." Walid revved the BMW's twelve-cylinder engine. "For sure, I'm going to miss this ride."

"There will be plenty of rides up there to keep you and everyone else busy," the cousin said with a quiet laugh. "Now may Allah be with us all. Over and out."

Walid nodded and turned left toward the Continental Hotel.

Satam's destination, the Gold Market, was to the right. He steered in that direction. He zigzagged through a few crooked streets and slowed down when reaching the Old City. The blacktop disappeared, and the uneven gravel crackled under the tires. Old cars, horse carts, and pedestrians came into view, along with whitewashed stores selling gold and jewelry. The streets narrowed into barely a single lane.

Satam rolled down the window for sideways glances to avoid brushing against planters, chairs, and vendors selling all kinds of junk. A stomach-churning stench from days-old fish, fried grease, and sweat overwhelmed him. Satam felt his head grow heavy, and he hit the brakes.

The street vendors lost no time peddling their wares. A crowd of young boys swarmed his truck. He yelled and shoved away a few of the bravest salesmen waving handfuls of souvenirs in his face. He kept brushing away the hagglers, when suddenly a pointed metal object was shoved against his forearm. Startled, Satam withdrew his arm inside the cabin. He glanced at one of the boys holding a string of scimitar replicas, the sword tribesmen in North Africa carried in ancient times. The curved blade was dull with a rounded point to prevent accidental stabs. Still, the swift jab at his forearm summoned awful visions of the future.

He saw himself hanging upside down in a dark, grim dungeon, tied to the ceiling beams, while three secret police agents "interrogated" him. They would use various methods to "jog" his memory and break his psyche. Sleep deprivation and intimidation by police dogs were just the welcome package. Other techniques included breaking fingers and simulated suffocation with plastic wraps and water boarding. *I will tell them everything right away before they even touch me.* He struggled to wipe the vivid images from his mind.

Satam slammed on the truck's horn to clear a path through the crowd. The blaring horn startled him more than the boys and the occasional onlookers. He glanced at the dashboard, realizing he had less than two minutes to reach the busy marketplace square five blocks away. *It will be impossible to make it on time.*

He blasted the horn again and stepped on the gas. The truck moved slowly, and Satam wrestled to make a left turn. The alley grew wider. The truck sped up, its wheels dipping and climbing in and out of the potholes. He rushed straight ahead, inches away from oncoming taxis, their honks protesting his unsafe speed. A few sidewalk vendors dove out of the way, their overflowing baskets of bananas and grapes spilling all over the place. Tires screeched as he turned right, jumping the curb and narrowly missing a large bronze planter outside a soap store.

The Mediterranean Sea was now visible to his right, through palm trees, coffee shops, and fruit vendor stands. Satam stared ahead at the wide square, one of the busiest markets in El Mina, the ancient city. The bazaar rumbled with vendors squabbling over a few dinars with tight-fisted tourists. *I made it. Yes, I made it.* He turned his gaze to the left, toward Tripoli's skyline, and slowed down before parking the truck in front of a small restaurant. He took a deep breath and dabbed at his forehead with the back of his hand, wiping off a sea of sweat.

The dashboard radio crackled and he picked up the receiver.

"Allahu Akbar! Allahu Akbar!" The loud voice echoed over the radio. Satam recognized Walid's shouts.

A second later, a loud explosion rocked the entire square. Satam's gaze spun toward the business district, where a cloud of grayish smoke billowed around the Continental Hotel. Chaos erupted among the street vendors who scattered and forgot about their produce and the evening's clients. The patrons of coffee shops rushed to the streets, staring in disbelief at the sight. Cries of hysteria overtook the growing crowd. Elderly women beat their heads and chests with clenched fists. Young men pointed and shouted, their bodies restless. The sharp siren of an ambulance sliced through the cacophony of terror.

With a quick movement of his wrist, Satam consulted his watch. Just as the digits registered 6:31, another explosion shocked the crowd. This time, the bomb hit closer, much closer, merely five blocks away. From inside his parked truck, Satam looked at the bright yellow glow of the blast. High flames leapt at a ten-story office building. A thick cloud of black smoke began to swallow up the tower. The crowd broke into smaller groups. People scurried in all directions. Some ran back to their shops and apartments. Others simply circled the area, perhaps unsure of the safe way out.

Satam knew his time had come. He revved the engine and stomped on the gas pedal. The truck arrowed toward the vendors' tables. The market was mostly empty, and the truck crashed into crates of fish, baskets of grapes, and barrels of olive oil. Produce scattered everywhere as the truck rampaged through plastic tables and chairs.

A police truck zipped toward him. Satam steered around, not to escape, but to meet the approaching vehicle. The two policemen in the truck ignored Satam. They were going to drive past him, but Satam swerved hard. The right fender of his truck smashed into the left side of the police truck. The police truck jerked to the other side. He pulled over and stopped less than thirty feet away. The other policeman rolled down the window. Satam stared at the muzzle of an AK-47 assault rifle.

"Don't shoot. Don't shoot," Satam shouted and opened his door.

A quick burst of bullets sent him ducking for cover in the front seat. A shower of glass shreds fell over his head.

They're going to kill me before I even have a chance to open my mouth. Or one of the bullets will blow up the truck. I can't let that happen.

He looked at the back of the truck. Thirty pounds of Semtex explosives wired into a homemade bomb were stored inside the seat compartments. He noticed the cellphone on the floor mat by his left hand. He reached for the phone. All it would take for him to set off the explosives—and pulverize himself and the policemen—was to tap three preset numbers. His fingers hovered over the phone, but he remembered his family's honor and the reward waiting for him in paradise. He dropped the phone to the floor, buried his head in the seat, and locked his fingers behind his head.

A minute or so passed before the shooting stopped, but the screaming continued. At some point, he heard the distinct thuds of combat boots marching up the street. The police were approaching his truck. He looked up slowly as a policeman pulled open the driver's door of his truck and aimed an AK-47 at his head.

"Don't move!" the policeman ordered.

Satam nodded.

Without a word, the policeman juggled the rifle in his hands and slammed its buttstock hard against Satam's head.

CHAPTER ONE

Cairo, Egypt
May 13, 6:25 p.m. local time

Justin Hall, Canadian Intelligence Service agent, did not want to fire his gun. Too many witnesses crowded the street.

I will kill those two men following me if I have to. Then, I'll clean up the mess.

His hand rested over the Browning 9mm riding inside the waistband holster at his thigh. He peered again at the reflections in the store window glass. He pretended to admire a black suit. In fact, he was checking every move of two young men behind him. Before he continued to his meeting, he wanted to make sure the pair, which had followed him for the last three blocks, were random strangers, rather than plain-clothes police doing a poor surveillance job.

Or worse. Assassins.

The two men did not stop by the store. They kept walking and, as they rounded the street corner, Justin followed. He tailed the men for a couple of minutes. They wandered along the north side of Nile City Towers Mall, stopping at times for quick window-shopping but never looking over their shoulders. Still, he found their actions suspicious. He used the same counter-surveillance tactic. Justin wondered if a second backup team had replaced the first, after he had made the two men. *If this is mukhabarat, there has to be more than one.*

The sun had begun to set, its last golden rays bouncing off the reflective glass of the nearby tall skyscrapers. A thin crowd was building up around the shopping district in downtown Cairo. Justin glanced around him on all sides. He tried to spot anyone who looked as if they belonged to a surveillance team. He scouted the area for operatives in dull or baggy clothing, wearing boring sunglasses, sporting earpieces, or simply standing out in the crowd. He listened for the slowing of footsteps, the shuffling of clothes, and any metallic click. No one fit the profile, but profiles were rarely helpful.

The men turned another corner and Justin continued to follow them. Twilight shadows and the flow of pedestrians out for the evening should have made it easier for him to track his prey, but the dry, sizzling air, scorched by a punishing sun for twelve hours, countered all his advantages. Drops of sweat formed on his broad forehead. The bulletproof vest underneath his loose-fitting polo shirt felt twice as heavy as when he put it on earlier in the morning.

His BlackBerry chirped from his pocket, the noise breaking his concentration. Without slowing down, he pulled it out and glanced at the screen.

"Where are you?" the short e-mail asked.

It was from Carrie O'Connor, his partner. He and Carrie should have checked in at the Fairmont Nile City Hotel an hour ago. They were scheduled to meet with Sheikh Yusuf Ayman, one of the masterminds of the terrorist organization Islamic Fighting Alliance, but the Sheikh had scrapped the meeting at a moment's notice. Carrie was still surveilling the Fairmont, while Justin was returning from following two of the Sheikh's associates to a previously unknown safe house.

I'll be there soon. He pocketed the BlackBerry. *A few more minutes.*

He followed the two men until they entered the Desert Rose, a hip bar favored by the young and rich. Justin kept a close eye on the main door, throwing casual glances at their table by the window. At the same time, he searched the streets for the elusive second surveillance team.

Ten minutes later, after the two men had finished their first drinks, Justin concluded they were not secret police and he was not being watched by them or anyone else. Still, this was Cairo, and one could never be too careful. In a country ruled by the General Intelligence Service, known simply as *mukhabarat,* one wrong turn could be the last, even for professionals like him. Controlled paranoia had saved his life more than once in the most dangerous back alleys of North Africa.

Justin headed toward The Castle, a small coffee shop, where Carrie waited for him. The Castle was to the left of the Fairmont, with an unobstructed view of the hotel's VIP entrance. Rahim, the owner of the joint, was on the CIS Cairo Station payroll. The coffee shop provided a casual yet safe place for CIS agents to run covert operations.

Before pushing open the carved wood door of The Castle, Justin stopped and glanced at the alley in front of the coffee shop. He noticed a white sedan, an old model Ford, parked halfway between the entrance to a three-story apartment complex across the alley and a grocery store. Justin squinted and noticed the silhouette of a small woman wearing a hijab crouched in the front passenger's seat. A tall man was talking to the shopkeeper by the fruit and vegetable stand in front of the grocery store. *Is that her husband? Her brother?* Justin scanned the windows of the apartments but noticed nothing suspicious. He threw another sweeping look at the other side of the street and stepped inside the coffee shop.

A thin cloud of tobacco smoke billowing from a handful of patrons smoking their water pipes engulfed him. Justin sneaked in, skirting around the tables, avoiding eye contact with anyone. He stood waiting with his elbows planted on the granite counter until Rahim, who was filling a couple of glasses with dark beer, took notice of his presence.

"Where have you been?" Rahim asked in a low voice. "You're late."

"Making sure I wasn't followed," Justin replied. "Is somebody waiting for a cab?" He gestured with his thumb back toward the door.

"I don't understand."

"There's an old Ford parked outside."

"That would be Leilah," Rahim said, his pot-like head bobbing with every word. "She's waiting for her husband, Farouk."

A few servings of *kofta*, minced lamb sprinkled with spices, sizzled on the grill behind Rahim.

"Did you send Nebibi for a closer look?" Justin asked.

"No. Why?"

A surveillance camera installed above the archway entrance to The Castle, hidden inside one of the lighting sconces, watched the building environs. It transmitted clear images to Rahim's computer screen, which doubled as a cash register. With a few clicks, he could keep a constant eye on what happened on the street. Justin preferred to be on scene, the difference between being an observer and actually understanding an evolving situation.

Justin pointed to his left, toward the kitchen separated from the bar by a reddish curtain. "Have him check things out."

Rahim nodded and disappeared inside the kitchen.

The CIS trusted Nebibi, the cook, like they trusted his uncle, Rahim. Justin, on the other hand, did not trust many people. He knew Rahim had great financial incentives to provide actionable intelligence to them, as the CIS paid him handsomely for his services. Justin worried about another buyer tempting Rahim. The man was willing to trade in nearly all secrets for the right price. The Egyptian was not bound by the same code of honor streaming through the veins of CIS agents. Justin realized the CIS had to rely on local sources to navigate the labyrinths of Cairo's streets and Egypt's foreign policies. Still, he kept his reliance on Rahim to the bare minimum.

Rahim returned.

"The driver was talking to some guy from the grocery store when I walked in," Justin said.

"Yeah, the store owner. They're good friends. Nebibi is going out the back. You hungry?"

"No, not really. Still two hours until supper."

"Yes, for Egyptians."

"I *am* half-Egyptian."

"You're half everything." Rahim turned around to attend to his grill.

Justin grinned, rubbing his dimpled chin. His Mediterranean complexion—dark olive skin, raven wavy hair, big black eyes, and a large thick nose—inherited from his Italian mother, allowed him to blend in naturally among the countless nationalities living in the bustling city of eighteen million. Youthful stamina, a natural talent for languages, and an overdose of stubbornness had allowed him to master spoken Arabic like a native Egyptian.

"Can I bring you some *mezze* at least?" Rahim asked, referring to appetizers.

"Sure." *He seems a little too eager to please today. Something's up.*

"Coffee?"

"Definitely."

Rahim turned around and poured coffee from a long-handled brewing pot into a porcelain cup. Justin savored the strong aroma of the thick, concentrated drink and clenched the cup in his left hand. He climbed the cement stairs, which took him to the second floor. A narrow hall led to two safe rooms, once part of Rahim's family apartment. Now they were reserved for the private use of CIS operatives. Justin knocked twice on the white door of the first room.

"Come in," a woman's soft voice called from inside.

"Hi," Justin greeted Carrie.

She sat cross-legged in a chair by one of the windows. A pair of powerful binoculars and two manila folders lay spread over a plastic table, next to a CIS-issued Browning 9mm and a tea mug. Poster-sized photographs of the Great Pyramid of Giza and the Sphinx covered the beige walls.

"Hey, you finally made it." Carrie tossed her reading glasses over one of the open folders. She tilted her head back, stretching her neck muscles. Her auburn shoulder-length hair, which she usually kept in a semi-ponytail, flowed down her slender neck. "What took you so long?"

"Trying to shake what I thought was a tail. A couple of guys who turned out to be nobody."

"Well, double-checking never hurt anyone."

"Sorry I'm late."

"Don't worry about it. Still hot out there, eh?" She pointed at the soggy shirt stuck to his chest. A trickle of sweat had made its way down his neck.

"Hell on Earth. Ninety degrees in the shade."

He placed his coffee cup on the table and stumbled onto an empty chair across from her. He took a deep breath, enjoying the cool breeze flowing down from the air conditioner mounted on the wall.

"Did you see a white Ford downstairs?" Justin asked.

"No. Nothing there when I came in."

"Rahim hadn't checked it out, but he's sending Nebibi now."

"OK, let's hope it's nothing."

Justin dabbed his face with a Kleenex. "Where did Team One lose Sheikh Ayman?"

"We didn't *lose* him. *Johnson* ordered us not to make contact, just track his movements, which we did. Sheikh Ayman arrived at Terminal 3 of Cairo International. Then he boarded a Sudan Airways flight bound for Khartoum."

Claire Johnson was the CIS Director General of Intelligence for the North Africa Division and their boss. Johnson's reputation within the CIS was that of a meticulously thorough individual. Terrified of committing a career-ending blunder, Johnson displayed a certain amount of sluggishness that crippled field agents. They joked that she was more efficient at witch hunting than terrorist hunting, as scapegoating often resulted from botched operations in her division.

Justin chewed on Carrie's words. The Sheikh's departure aboard a regular commercial flight meant he was not hiding from the Egyptian authorities.

"If mukhabarat is looking everywhere for the Sheikh and his brotherhood, how come he can sneak right under their noses?" Carrie asked, as if reading Justin's mind.

"I was thinking that too. The short answer: he's the Sheikh and this is Cairo. The Sheikh's men are everywhere, even inside mukhabarat. They may be looking for him, but that doesn't mean they're going to find him. And according to the Egyptians, the Sheikh is only *allegedly* linked to the Alliance."

"Allegedly? Allegedly? What more do they want? A written and signed confession saying *I am* the second-in-command of the Islamic Fighting Alliance?" Carrie clenched her fists.

Justin stood up. "It's more complicated than that. The new government is fragile, unable to defeat the militants by force, at least at this time. Maybe after the elections."

"Oh, that's six months away." Carrie sighed.

"That's why we usually don't accept *support* from the secret police. There's too much to lose by sharing intel with the mukhabarat."

Justin unfastened his holster and placed it on the table. Then, he unbuttoned his shirt and removed it, along with his bulletproof vest. He felt Carrie's admiring eyes. He thought he saw her cringe as he turned around, knowing she could never get used to the sight of three deep scars, almost eight inches long, carved along his shoulder blades. They were reminders of the time he was captured in Libya after a hostage rescue operation that went wrong.

Justin fetched a short-sleeve shirt from a white cabinet by the door. The shirt smelled of bleach. Rahim had forgotten to ask his wife, who often did their laundry, not to use chlorine. Justin sighed as he noticed a slight bleeding of his favorite navy blue shirt.

"Did any of the Sheikh's men come back to the Fairmont?" He returned to his seat and took a big gulp of coffee.

"Yes, one of his bodyguards. He retrieved the armored Mercedes from the valet parking."

"The Sheikh's abrupt, but not secret departure, is unusual. Why leave in such a hurry, and without giving a reason? What is so urgent? Is he afraid of something? In Egypt, he's protected. There's nothing to fear."

"Well, maybe there is something to fear."

"If so, it has to be something big. Something powerful for the Sheikh to abandon our long-planned meeting."

The meeting with Sheikh Ayman had been in the works for over a month. In late March, intermediaries of the Alliance contacted the CIS Cairo Station, seeking a meeting with them. Initially, Johnson chose another team of agents to handle this case, suspecting the militant was a common defector. Once the identity of the senior leader requesting the meeting became known, Johnson insisted Justin organize all aspects of the operation. His presence became even more essential when they learned Sheikh Ayman held information about an assassination plot against a Western head of state.

"So, what do you think spooked him?" Carrie asked.

"I don't know. Very few things would scare someone like Sheikh Ayman."

"Will he reschedule our meeting?"

"I hope so."

While the location and the time of their meeting were determined two weeks ago, they knew nothing about the specifics of the assassination or the intended target.

"I just don't want it to take place in Northern Sudan."

"Hey, why not? It's easier to bag him down there," Carrie replied with a wide grin.

Kidnapping or eliminating the Sheikh had crossed his mind too, albeit as a fleeting thought. Lawless Northern Sudan was the perfect place for such a hit. The zeal in Carrie's voice did not surprise him either. According to her, the most efficient solution to a problem was often also the most extreme. The one she always favored.

"That's not our mission," Justin said.

Carrie shook her head in resignation.

Justin walked to one of the windows that overlooked the Fairmont VIP entrance and the Nile. Glowing lights from towering buildings shown from Giza across the river. A constant stream of cars, their headlights flickering through the heavy smog, rushed through the top level of the Imbaba Bridge that connected the two parts of Cairo. Justin hated the Imbaba Bridge. In fact, he hated all bridges. It was a bridge that shattered his life when he was only eleven years old.

Justin took the last sip of his coffee. He stepped closer to the other window, facing the apartment complex across the alley. On a second floor apartment, two lights were on. They were almost in a clear line of sight to their room. Justin squinted but could not see anything more than the silhouette of a man wandering around the living room. A television set was flickering in one of the corners. A knock on the door startled him, and Justin turned around.

"It's me," Rahim said, "I brought the mezze."

"Come in," Justin said.

Rahim walked in, holding a round tray with pita and garlic bread, pickled olives, slices of cucumbers, and a few bread dips. Carrie began to make room on the table for their food when a bullet pierced the window glass and slammed into Rahim's chest. The man tumbled to his knees. The small plates of food flew across the table.

"Get down, get down," Justin shouted. Carrie had already hit the floor, her hand clenching her pistol.

A short burst of gunfire exploded, breaking the other window. Sharp slivers of glass rained over the agents' shoulders.

"Two shooters!" Carrie shouted.

Justin nodded, reaching for his Browning pistol. He cocked it and held it tightly in front of his face.

"You can handle them?" Justin asked, as he stared at Rahim. A dip dish still swirled next to Rahim's lifeless face.

"Yeah, I got them," Carrie replied.

"Cover me. And watch your head."

He crawled to the door and ran outside.

* * *

As soon as the gunfire paused for a brief second, Carrie took a quick peek over the shredded windowsill. A gun muzzle flash betrayed one of the shooters' locations. She squeezed her trigger, then she ducked as another hail of gunfire sailed past her head. The few long seconds dragged on. She lay low, her chest heaving with each quick breath. The gunfire stopped for a moment. She looked up just long enough to fire the rest of her magazine. Once she heard the dull clink of her empty gun, she slid in a fresh magazine. She leaned against the wall and listened. Chaotic screams and rushing footsteps came from the street, but no more gunshots.

Carrie looked out the window. Engines roared and tires screeched. Down in the street, Justin chased a white Ford, shooting even as he ran to keep up with the car. Despite his torrent of bullets that riddled the runaway target, the Ford rounded the corner and disappeared behind the grocery store. Justin, gun in hand, stood alone in the middle of the alley.

* * *

Carrie stepped cautiously around the dead body lying halfway through the entrance to the apartment complex. She noticed an AK-47 by the man's hand and her eyes rested on the wound in his neck. Justin had fired kill shots. Most of their targets wore bulletproof vests, so he never aimed at their chest. After a couple of clashes last year with mercenaries in Niger River Delta swamps, they both gave up shooting at the enemy's heads. Kevlar helmets were becoming increasingly resistant to small arms fire.

"There's another dead body upstairs in the hall," Justin said, drawing nearer to her.

Carrie nodded. "Is this the work of the Alliance?"

"If it is, it's lousy at best." Justin looked at the dead man.

"Did you get the men in the Ford?"

"Yes, I got the woman passenger on the shoulder."

"A woman?"

"Yeah."

Carrie raised her hand and touched Justin's bristly face. A reddish stain appeared on her fingers trailing over his chin.

"You're wounded?"

"Slivers. My favorite shirt is ruined, though." He ran his hand over his chest. "That's Rahim's blood."

"If Rahim had checked the Ford, *maybe* this would have not happened."

"If *I* would have checked it, this would *not* have happened."

"It wasn't your responsibility. It was his. You can't do everyone's job."

"Maybe Rahim didn't want to check the Ford."

Carrie's gray-blue eyes narrowed. "He wanted this to happen?"

"Well, not the part where he died."

She glanced back at The Castle. Some of its patrons had run away. A few curious souls peered from behind the windows. She scanned the apartment complex's windows and balconies. Residents' narrowed eyes glared in their direction. An old woman screamed at them in Arabic. A dog howl cut through the hot, heavy air.

Justin was staring at the dead man.

"What is it?" Carrie asked.

"I wonder if this is why the Sheikh disappeared."

"You mean, he lured us for a meeting and set up an ambush? That is, if Rahim gave us up."

"Yes, and before the ambush, the Sheikh disappears."

"Uh-uh, the Sheikh needs no alibi. It has to be something else."

Justin nodded and checked the magazine on his pistol. Four bullets left.

"You're right. But this was no coincidence either."

"Whatever it is, we'll find out."

"You're right about that too. Whoever it is, they made a grave mistake putting us in their crosshairs."

* * *

"Tell me what you see." The man passed his binoculars to the driver.

He took the Bushnell eyepiece and peered through it. The powerful magnification of the binoculars produced a sharp close-up image, even through the BMW's windshield. They had a clear view of the entrance to The Castle coffee shop from the Nile City Fairmont parking lot.

"He's standing outside the shop, talking to the woman," the driver said.

The man shook his gray-haired head.

"No, you see two brave soldiers ready for a fight."

The disappointment was clear in the man's voice. After so many years in the Islamic Fighting Alliance, Maksut failed to see beyond what was in front of his eyes.

"They still have their weapons drawn?"

"They do," Maksut replied.

"But for the driver, our people have become martyrs now." The man's voice held no regret. "Good thing they were our least talented shooters. Still, they served their purpose."

"You don't think we went too far?" Maksut raised the binoculars to his eyes. Justin and Carrie were now pacing in front of The Castle.

"No. We want to make this fight personal. Revenge is a powerful motivator. This way, they'll be more eager. More dedicated. That's exactly what we want."

Faint police sirens sounded in the distance.

"I've seen enough. Let's go," the man ordered Maksut, while scanning to his right for any police cars. "It's time to brief Sheikh Ayman and play our next card."

Made in the USA
Charleston, SC
27 May 2012